Blood Matters

Ian McFadyen

Copyright © 2024 Ian McFadyen
All rights are identified to the author of this work in accordance with the Copyright, Design and Patents Act 1988.

No part of this publication may be reproduced, transmitted, or stored in a retrieval system, in any form or by any means, without permission in writing from the author, nor be otherwise circulated in any form of binding or cover other than that in which it is published and without a similar condition being imposed on the subsequent purchaser.

All characters in this publication are fictitious and any resemblance to real people, alive or dead, is purely coincidental.

ISBN: 9798337922843

Book cover design by Big Red Illustration

This book is dedicated to my good friend

Steve Sydes

By the same author:

Little White Lies, first published 2008

Lillia's Diary, first published 2009

Frozen to Death, first published 2010

Deadly Secrets, first published 2012

Killing Time, first published 2015

Death in Winter, first published 2016

The Steampunk Murder, first published 2018

Blood on his Hands, first published 2019

The Murky World of Timothy Wall, first published 2021

Chapter 1

Wednesday 20th March

Miles Goodwyn felt a little uneasy as his ancient Yamaha moped noisily made its way down the unlit, narrow, winding road which joined the small hamlet of High Maudsey to the busy A59 to the west.
Had it not been for the slender beam of his headlights, the thin crescent-shaped moon that hovered just above the hedgerow and the occasional fleeting glimpse of a distant taillight, some way further down the lane, Jay Bank Lane would have been in complete darkness.
It was a journey the young man had taken many times on his way home from The Three Bells; the small country pub he'd made his local ever since he'd turned eighteen, six months earlier. If he was being honest, he didn't particularly like this part of the journey, Jay Bank Lane had no street lighting, but it was a short cut that took over three miles off his journey home, so, he always went that way.
Grasping tightly onto the handlebars and with his eyes concentrating hard on the numerous twists and turns in the road, Miles pushed on. His immediate goal was to reach the relative safety of the well-lit A59 as quickly as he could.
In his haste, and with his attention focused on the road ahead, he could have easily missed seeing the pair of feet jutting out from the drainage ditch by the side of the road. But he did notice them.

It may have been the brightly coloured socks, clearly visible between the brown suede shoes and the faded blue jeans that first caught Miles's eye. Whatever it was, he knew in an instant what he'd spied.

Jamming hard on the brakes, his bike skidded to a halt just a few yards ahead of the two protruding legs.

Breathing deeply and with his heart beating much faster than normally, Miles jumped down from the saddle. He carefully took out his mobile from the deep side pocket of his waxed jacket, turned on the torch feature and, with the area in front of him now illuminated brightly, tentatively walked back towards the lifeless limbs.

He'd only taken two or three paces before the light from his mobile revealed the torso, then, a few paces later, he saw the matted, crimson red, blood-stained hair on the back of the head; partially congealed but in the main still liquid. When he got up close to the body Miles looked down. He recognised the motionless figure immediately.

There was no doubt in his mind, it was the man he'd seen arguing in The Three Bells, less than thirty minutes earlier.

Chapter 2

It was ten fifty-five when DI Carmichael arrived at the crime scene, his black BMW pulling up just short of the blue and white tape which had been fastened tightly between two gnarled old tree trunks, standing like sentries on either side of Jay Bank Lane.
"What have we got here?" he asked DS Watson as he ducked under the cordon and walked briskly towards the white tent that shrouded the body.
"According to the credit cards in the wallet we found in his jacket pocket it's a man called Doug Pritchard," Watson replied.
Carmichael stopped walking at the entrance of the white tent. "Do we know anything about him?" he enquired.
Watson shook his head. "No," he replied. "Although the lad that found him reckons, he was in The Three Bells earlier tonight. That's a pub half a mile down the road."
"Is he still here?" Carmichael asked. "The lad that found him."
Watson pointed down the lane where a pale-faced, scruffy-looking youth in a fraying waxed jacket, stood quietly next to the newly promoted DS Dalton. "That's him with Rachel," Watson replied.

Carmichael nodded. "Don't let him go yet," was his instruction. "I'd like a word with him after I've taken a look at the body."
"Right you are, sir," replied Watson dutifully, as Carmichael disappeared into the tent.

*   *   *   *

Wade Freeman, the publican of The Three Bells, took a last drag of his cigarette, dropped it on the floor, squashed it under his right foot and wandered back towards the rear door of the pub.
He hadn't even had a chance to hang his coat up when his wife, Coral, arrived at his side, her eyes wide open.
"Where've you been?" she inquired, agitatedly.
Wade frowned and shook his head. "I just had a quick fag," he replied.
"They're saying they've shut Jay Bank," she continued, her voice hushed and earnest.
"Who have?" Wade enquired.
"The police," responded Coral. "Apparently there are loads of police cars down there, lights flashing and all that."
Her husband shrugged his shoulders.
"It's probably another car accident," continued Coral. "They drive far too fast down that road."
"If it is, I hope it's not anyone we know," he replied, before turning away and hanging his coat on the peg on the wall.

*   *   *   *

"Evening, Carmichael. Nice of you to join us," remarked Stock, sarcastically.
The portly head of the regional forensic team made eye contact for just a couple of seconds before turning back to the body, which had remained in precisely the same

position it was in when Miles Goodwyn found it just over an hour earlier.

Carmichael remained expressionless. "What are your initial thoughts?" he enquired, as he bent forward to take a better look at the deceased.

Stock sucked deeply through gritted teeth before rising from his crouched position and turning to face Carmichael. "I don't know for sure at the moment," he replied, "but I'd estimate the time of death as being within the last two hours and it wasn't a result of natural causes."

As there was a significant amount of blood clearly visible on the back of the dead man's head and on the soil, grass, and leaves where he had come to rest, Carmichael didn't feel any the wiser.

"I assume that he was killed here by a blow on the back of the head?" Carmichael suggested.

Stock shrugged his shoulders. "I'm not going to speculate until I've done a full post-mortem," he replied. "But that blow certainly happened before he expired, and with there being blood on the ground around the head, I'd say he definitely died here."

Carmichael nodded gently before turning away and making his exit out of the tent.

Once back in the cool night air Carmichael turned to face Watson. "Ok," he announced, "let's have a chat with the young man who found him."

Chapter 3

DS Dalton offered a kindly, welcoming smile at Carmichael as he and Watson approached where she and Miles Goodwyn were standing. "This is Inspector Carmichael, Miles," she told the young man.
Miles made eye contact with Carmichael for a few seconds before his head slumped down and his focus shifted to Carmichael's black brogues.
"Hello, Miles," Carmichael remarked in as friendly a manner as he could. "Can you tell me how you came across the dead man?"
"Was he murdered?" Miles enquired. His accent thick Lancastrian and his eyes transfixed on Carmichael's shoes.
"We are treating his death as suspicious," replied Carmichael.
Miles raised his head and looked directly at the two officers stood in front of him. "I was going home from The Three Bells," began Miles. "It must have been about nine forty-five when I saw him."
Miles paused for a second before continuing. "Well, his legs anyway."
Carmichael nodded. "And did you touch the body?" he asked.

Miles, his face pale with horror, shook his head. "No way," he replied. "I knew he must be dead, but I didn't check. I just called nine, nine, nine."

Before Carmichael had a chance to continue, DS Dalton gently took hold of Miles's wrist and cocked her head to one side so that their faces were a matter of inches away from each other. "Tell Inspector Carmichael what you told me before," she instructed him.

"What's that, Miles?" Carmichael enquired.

"He was in The Three Bells," announced Miles. "I don't know who he is, and I've never seen him in there before, but he was there tonight."

"Was he alone?" Watson asked.

Miles shook his head. "No, he was sat with another bloke," replied Miles. "A guy that's in there a fair bit. I don't know his name, but he's a regular."

"Can you describe him?" Carmichael asked.

"Oldish," responded Miles. "About fifty or sixty I'd say. Quite thin, always smartly dressed; a tie and that. And he has a small greyish beard."

"And did they leave together?" Carmichael asked.

Miles shook his head again, this time more vigorously. "No, they had a bit of a barney," he replied. "Then Wade had words and the dead guy stormed out."

"Wade!" remarked Carmichael. "Who's Wade?"

"He's the landlord," replied Miles. "Wade Freeman."

"What time was that?" Carmichael enquired.

Miles took a few seconds to reply. "I'd say it was about twenty past nine," he replied. "Maybe a few minutes earlier."

"So, you're saying you saw the dead man alive no more than half an hour before you found him in the ditch," remarked Carmichael.

Miles nodded. "Not just me," he replied. "Everyone that was in the pub, and there must have been a dozen or more in there when he left."

Carmichael looked across at Watson and then to Rachel Dalton. "What was the argument about?" Carmichael asked. "Between the dead man and the old man with the beard?"

Miles shook his head. "I've no idea," he replied. "But they did raise their voices and it was then that Wade had a word with him."

"Him?" repeated Carmichael with a degree of puzzlement in his voice. "Did the landlord just have words with the dead man? Not the man he was arguing with?"

Miles gently nodded his head. "As far as I remember it was just the dead man," he replied. "But I didn't take that much notice, I was talking to someone at the time."

"Who was that?" Watson asked.

Miles shrugged his shoulders. "It was Verity. She helps out in the kitchen some nights."

Carmichael nodded. "You've been extremely helpful," he said with a reassuring smile.

"Can I go home now?" Miles asked.

"You'll need to provide DS Dalton with a statement," Carmichael replied, "but after that you're free to go."

"Sir," interrupted Rachel. "The first officers on the scene breathalysed Miles and unfortunately he's just over the limit."

Carmichael looked a little surprised as the young man hadn't given him any indication that he was intoxicated during their discussion. He looked over at the Yamaha moped which was a matter of a few feet away.

"Is that yours?" he enquired.

Miles nodded. "Yes," he responded meekly.

"Well, I'm afraid it will now have to be impounded," remarked Carmichael. "And once DS Dalton has your statement, she'll arrange for you to be driven home. You'll have to come into the station in the morning to sort out the repossessing of your bike."

"Will I be charged?" Miles asked, a look of dread etched across his face.

Carmichael shrugged his shoulders. "That will be up to the officers who breathalysed you and the duty sergeant at the station," he replied, before turning away and walking back towards the crime scene; DS Watson a matter of just a few steps behind him.

They'd taken no more than five or six paces when Carmichael stopped and turned to face his sergeant.

"If Stock's correct and Doug Pritchard was killed here," he remarked in a hushed tone of voice. "What was he doing walking alone down this narrow, windy road in the dark?"

Watson thought for a few seconds. "Maybe he wasn't alone," he offered as his reply.

Carmichael thought for a few seconds. "Where does this road lead to?" he asked.

"It doesn't lead anywhere," replied Watson vaguely. "There's High Maudsey about half a mile or so that way, which is where he must have come from if he was in The Three Bells; but there's basically nothing down here until you reach the A59, which must be three or four miles away."

"Nothing!" exclaimed Carmichael. "That's a long way for someone to be walking at this time of night. With no pavement and no street lighting. I'd not fancy walking down here in the dark. Would you?"

Watson shook his head. "No way," he concurred.

The two men remained quiet for a couple of seconds before Watson spoke again. "Actually, I'm wrong," Watson said, his voice sounding like he'd remembered something important. "There's a farm a couple of hundred metres away. I don't come down here that often, but I think it's

called Hardcastle's Farm. It's a working dairy farm but I'm pretty sure it's also a B&B. Maybe he was staying there."
Carmichael gave a sage-like nod of his head. "That would stack-up," he remarked. "Once she's done with Miles Goodwyn," you and Rachel get on down there and see if they know anything about our dead man."
"Will do," replied Watson.
"And while you two are doing that, I'm going to ask a few questions at The Three Bells," continued Carmichael, who, even before he'd finished his sentence, had started to walk purposefully in the direction of his car.

Chapter 4

Wade and Coral Freeman were clearing away glasses and manoeuvring the pub furniture back into their usual positions when Carmichael knocked forcefully on the front door.
"We're closed," Wade bellowed.
Ignoring the landlord's words, Carmichael hammered even more vigorously on the door.
"Who the hell is that?" Wade Freeman shouted across at his wife before marching quickly towards the source of his frustration.
Carmichael had a broad, forced smile on his face and his identity card ready in his hand as the angry publican threw open the front door. "Sorry to disturb you," Carmichael said calmly. "My name's Inspector Carmichael. May I come in, please?"
"Can't this wait until the morning?" Wade enquired, his hand holding firmly onto the door as if to prevent Carmichael entering the pub.
"It won't take long," replied Carmichael, his expression now serious.
Wade opened the door wide and, grudgingly, ushered Carmichael inside.

* * * *

Watson waited until Miles Goodwyn had finished giving DS Dalton his statement and had clambered into the police car to be taken home before he approached his colleague. "Did he say anything else that you think might be relevant?" Watson asked.

DS Dalton shook her head. "Not really," she responded. "He maintains he didn't hear what the argument was about in the pub and didn't hear exactly what the landlord said to the dead man, either."

"What about afterwards?" Watson enquired. "Did he see anyone else on his way from the pub to here?"

DS Dalton shook her head again. "He says not," she replied. "He did say that he briefly saw the light from a vehicle disappearing way off down the road, but other than that he says he saw nobody. No pedestrians nor any other traffic on the road from the time he left the pub until he found the body."

Watson shrugged his shoulders. "Well, the boss wants us to get ourselves over to Hardcastle's Farm down the lane," he remarked. "We reckon our dead man may have been staying there. It's a B&B and the only place for miles, so we think he might have been walking back there when he was murdered."

DS Dalton nodded. "Makes sense, I suppose," she concurred before glancing at her watch. "I doubt whether they'll be that chuffed with us knocking on their door at this time of night, though."

Watson smiled. "I suspect not," he agreed.

* * * *

Carmichael leant against the bar, the landlord and his wife stood together on the other side. "I want to ask you about a couple of gentlemen who were in here tonight," he began. "Both in their fifties or early sixties."

"Do you have their names?" Coral enquired.

'We think one was a local man," continued Carmichael, "but probably not the other."

Wade shrugged his shoulders. "We were quite busy tonight, so they could have been any one of a number of people."

"I believe that these two had an argument," Carmichael added. "And I also understand that as a result you had a word with the one, we think wasn't from around here."

As soon as Carmichael mentioned the argument, it was clear that Wade knew exactly who Carmichael was talking about.

"Oh, that guy," Wade remarked in a tone suggesting he wasn't someone the publican was too enamoured with. "I don't know what his name is. Tonight, was the first time I'd clapped eyes on him as far as I can remember."

"What about the other man?" Carmichael enquired. "I take it he was someone you know."

Wade Freeman paused for a few seconds. He was clearly not sure whether he wanted to divulge the other man's identity. "What have they done?" he asked.

Carmichael looked sternly back at him. "We're investigating a serious crime, Mr Freeman," he replied firmly. "I need to know the man's name."

Reluctantly the publican answered Carmichael's question. "It's Ron Mason," he said. "He comes in here a lot."

Carmichael nodded. "And what was their dispute about?" continued Carmichael.

"I've honestly no idea," Wade replied. "And to be frank, I didn't hear much of what they were saying. But it was loud and there were lots of people here wanting to enjoy a quiet meal, so I told the fella to either tone it down or leave. And he left."

"What about Ron Mason?" Carmichael asked. "Did you not ask him to leave, too?"

Wade looked perplexed. "No," he replied. "Ron had stormed off to the gents, just before I started to have a word with the other guy; and when he came back his mate had gone, so there was no need. Anyway, I know Ron well and he's no bother. It was his friend that was the issue. And once he went everything was fine again."

Carmichael took a few seconds to consider what he'd just been told. "What time did the guy leave?" he asked.

Wade rubbed his chin then turned his head to face his wife. "What time do you think that was, Coral?" he asked her.

"It was just after nine fifteen, when they had the row," replied Coral without hesitation. "I remember as I'd checked the time and then just suggested to Verity that she could tidy up and get herself off, as all the covers had been served. So, I reckon it would have been about two or three minutes after that, when he stormed out."

"And you say that by the time Ron came back from the gents his companion had left?" Carmichael added.

"That's right," replied Wade. "I told Ron that I'd had a word with him, and Ron just apologised, and he got his pint and stood at the bar."

"And when he was at the bar did you ask him what the argument was about?" enquired Carmichael.

Wade shrugged his shoulders. "No," he replied. "I was busy, the drama was over, so I just carried on serving customers."

"And what time did Ron leave?" Carmichael asked.

Wade shrugged his shoulders. "He's actually not long left," he replied. "He was one of the last people to go. I'd say about ten forty-five."

Carmichael looked sideways at the publican's wife to try and see whether she was going to either challenge or corroborate the time her husband had given. She remained silent.

"And from nine fifteen, when they argued and ten forty-five, when he left the pub, did Ron go out at all?" Carmichael enquired.

Wade shook his head. "Not that I recall," he replied. "He just stood at the bar and drank. Another pint, then a few Jack Daniels, I think."

"What about other customers?" continued Carmichael. "Did anyone leave the pub at about the same time as Ron's friend?"

Wade shook his head gently. "I can't recall," he replied vaguely. "People are coming and going all the time."

"Miles left not that long afterwards," piped-up Coral. "He's a young lad that comes in here a few nights a week."

"What time did he leave?" Carmichael asked.

Coral looked across at her husband with a wry smile on her face. "It would have been shortly after nine thirty," she replied. "He's pretty predictable in that respect, and that's usually when he heads off on a Wednesday."

"But apart from Miles, you can't recall anyone else who left the pub between nine twenty and nine forty-five," Carmichael remarked.

Both Wade and Coral shook their heads.

"Can you tell me where Ron Mason lives?" Carmichael asked.

"I don't rightly know," replied Wade. "I think it's in one of those big houses at the other end of the village, but I can't be sure."

Carmichael forced a smile. You've been very helpful," he remarked. "I'm sorry to have disturbed you at such a late hour."

As he finished talking, Carmichael turned and walked slowly towards the exit.

"Are you able to tell us what all this is about?" Coral asked.

Carmichael turned back to face her. "You'll no doubt hear about this soon, anyway," he said, as if to justify what he

was about to tell them. "But there's been a serious incident tonight down Jay Bank Lane, which has led to a fatality. I can't tell you anymore, at the moment, but no doubt the local press and the bush telegraph will be swinging into action soon, if they have not done so already."
As he told them Coral Freeman put her hands over her mouth. Her husband, however, remained silent and expressionless.

*　　*　　*　　*

As soon as Carmichael had left the pub and the landlord had, for a second time that evening, bolted the door, Coral walked over and forcefully grabbed her husband's arm. "What the hell are you up to, Wade Freeman!" she exclaimed. "Lying to the police like that. What are you thinking?"
Wade pushed her hand away and pushed his face within inches of hers. "He's a mate," Wade replied through gritted teeth. "And mates look after each other."
Shocked and incensed, Coral glared back at her husband, who, seemingly impervious to her distain, strode off towards the kitchen, his mobile in his hand as if he was about to contact someone.

Chapter 5

It was eleven thirty-three when Carmichael clambered into his car in the empty, dimly lit car park of The Three Bells.
As he shut the door behind him, the heavens opened, and huge droplets of rain pounded down on the windscreen. The cloudburst was so heavy that, within seconds, only the blurriest of outlines were visible through the rivers of water that now cascaded from the roof and down onto Carmichael's car bonnet.
Relieved that he'd managed to escape the sudden deluge, Carmichael decided to sit tight for a few minutes and make a couple of calls.

* * *

Despite the late hour, Muriel Hardcastle was still up and about when DS Watson and DS Dalton rang her doorbell.
And, within the space of just a few minutes, the kindly, middle-aged farmer's wife had confirmed to the two officers that Mr Pritchard was indeed a resident, but that he'd only arrived late that afternoon and after depositing his bag in his room and leaving his car in one of the three tightly-packed car parking spaces, had been picked

up in a light coloured four by four, driven by a man who didn't get out and who Muriel hadn't recognised.

"So roughly what time did Mr Pritchard arrive?" DS Dalton asked, keen to get the details as accurate as possible.

"It was about seven," replied Muriel.

"And you said he left almost immediately," continued DS Dalton.

Muriel nodded. "Within half an hour he was off," she answered.

"And you've not seen him since?" Watson added.

"No," replied Muriel. "Is he in trouble?"

DS Dalton and DS Watson exchanged a quick glance at each other before DS Dalton answered.

"Sadly, there has been an incident, and we believe it involves Mr Pritchard," she said, trying not to give too much away.

Muriel Hardcastle looked shocked and on learning the news instinctively put her left hand to her mouth, before quickly returning her arm to her side. Despite looking like a woman who was curious to find out what sort of incident had taken place, Muriel, surprisingly, didn't ask anything.

"I expect you'll want to see his room," was all she offered.

DS Dalton nodded and smiled. "Yes, please," she replied.

In an instant, Muriel was off down the corridor and without stopping strode purposefully up the staircase towards the first floor.

* * * *

Having spoken to Dr Stock for an update from the crime scene, Carmichael decided to call DS Watson to see how he and DS Dalton were getting along.

His two sergeants had only just entered Doug Pritchard's room when his call came through on Watson's mobile. Seeing it was Carmichael, Watson turned his head, so he was facing Muriel Hardcastle.

"Can you leave DS Dalton and I for a few minutes," he remarked, a request that Muriel instantly obeyed.

Once the landlady had left the room and the door to the hallway was closed, Watson answered the call.

"Hi, sir," he said. "We're at the B&B."

"Are you free to talk?" Carmichael enquired.

"Yes," replied Watson. "We're alone. We've just entered Doug Pritchard's room."

"So, he was staying there," remarked Carmichael.

"Yes," responded Watson, "but according to the landlady he only got here at about seven, checked into his room, dumped his bag and was off about thirty minutes later."

"And does the state of his room support that?" Carmichael asked.

Watson glanced about the room before answering.

"It does," he replied. "If it wasn't for his bags on the floor and his mobile plugged in and being charged up on the bedside cabinet, the room looks like it's just been cleaned."

As he was talking, DS Dalton had opened the wardrobe, which was empty, and then taken a quick look in the bathroom. "No sign of him having been in there," she remarked to her colleague.

"Has the landlady mentioned anything else about him?" Carmichael asked.

"She said he was picked up by someone in a four by four," replied Watson. "But she didn't know who."

Carmichael thought for a few seconds. "So, is his car still there?" he enquired.

"Yes," replied Watson. "It's in the car park."

"What about the keys?" Carmichael asked. "Did he leave them in the room?"

"Not that I can see," replied Watson, who took another few seconds to think.

"Does the landlady have an address for him?" Carmichael enquired.

"We haven't asked her yet," Watson replied. "To be honest we've only just arrived."

"That's fine," Carmichael said, reassuringly. "Get as much as you can from her and have a look through his stuff. I want to know where he's from and what he was doing in Lancashire. Also, bag up his mobile and get someone from Stock's team to look at it and, if the car keys aren't in the room, see if he had them on him. Also, check to see who the car is registered to."

"Will do, sir," replied Watson. "Did you have any luck at the pub?"

"The landlord and his wife weren't terribly helpful," Carmichael replied, "and I'm not sure they told me the truth, but I do have a name for the man who Doug Pritchard was arguing with in the pub. It's a guy called Ron Mason."

"The record producer?" enquired Watson.

"Do you know him?" Carmichael enquired, with amazement.

Watson laughed. "I don't know him," he replied. "But I know of him, and I know he lives in a big house about a mile away from The Three Bells."

"How come you know of him?" Carmichael asked.

"He's quite famous around these parts," replied Watson. "He managed a few bands in the late eighties and nineties. I guess you could say he was the Simon Cowell of the time."

"Really," remarked Carmichael, who was still shocked that Watson was so knowledgeable about Ron Mason, someone Carmichael had never heard of. "Leave Rachel to sort out things there and get yourself over here to the car park at The Three Bells. If you know where Ron Mason lives let's strike while the iron's hot and get over and have a word with him."

"Will do," replied Watson, a split second before Carmichael abruptly ended the call.

Chapter 6

"It's that one on the right," announced Watson, as Carmichael's car drove slowly down Bentley Lane. Carmichael quickly indicated and then immediately steered his black BMW through the open gate and up towards a large, imposing, sandstone house.
"It's certainly a fine-looking property," he remarked as the car slowly crunched its way up the gravel drive to High Moor Grange, Ron Mason's eighteenth-century residence.
"Yes, you probably don't get many places as grand as this around here," announced Watson. "Got to be worth a couple of million, I'd say."
"Well let's see if our music impresario is still awake," announced Carmichael as he clambered out of the car and slammed the door behind him.
The two officers walked the short distance from Carmichael's car to the large house, then, using the bulky, shiny, brass knocker, Carmichael rapped hard on the oak door.
Within the space of ten seconds a smartly dressed, late middle-aged man, with a small greying beard opened the door wide.
"And what can I do for you gentlemen at such a late hour?" he enquired in a manner that suggested to

Carmichael the man before them was used to being in control.

"Are you Mr Mason?" enquired Carmichael.

"That's right," the man replied. "Ron Mason."

Carmichael smiled, glanced momentarily across at Watson, before brandishing his identity card in his outstretched right hand. "This is Sergeant Watson and I'm Inspector Carmichael," he announced. "We'd like to talk with you about your meeting with Doug Pritchard earlier this evening in The Three Bells."

"Why?" enquired Mason. "Has something happened?"

Carmichael nodded. "There has been an incident involving a man we believe to be Doug Pritchard," he replied, choosing his words carefully. "And we'd like to talk to everyone that was with him earlier this evening."

"You'd better come in, in that case," replied Mason who looked shocked at what he'd just been told.

Stepping back a couple of paces, Mason ushered them through with a theatrical sweeping movement of his right arm.

Carmichael and Watson walked into the grand, wide hallway, with its polished marble floor and stately-looking staircase ahead of them.

"You have a very impressive-looking house," remarked Carmichael.

Mason forced a small smile. "Yes, I like it," he replied. "It was built in seventeen ten. The land was a gift from Queen Anne to some baron who fought for her in the battle of Blenheim, I'm told. I bought it with the money I made from, 'The Full Package Tour', Chrissy's first outside UK."

"Chrissy?" enquired Carmichael.

"Chrissy Cream," replied Mason, as if it was inconceivable that Carmichael hadn't heard of her.

"Right, the popstar," Carmichael acknowledged.

"She was my first major signing," continued Mason. "And still the most lucrative one, too."
"But she died, didn't she?" interjected Watson.
"Yes," replied Mason, who walked his two guests into a large room just off the hallway. "She drowned in a tragic boating accident about twenty years ago. But her records are still played around the world and the royalties provide me and the surviving Vixens with a tidy little sum each year."
"The Vixens?" enquired Carmichael as he and then Watson sat themselves down on a large green sofa.
"Chrissy Cream and the Vixens," announced Mason again, as if Carmichael should have known. "The first British all-girl rock band to make it big in the US. You must have heard of them!"
"I do vaguely remember them," conceded Carmichael, "but I'd struggle to recall any of their songs."
Mason laughed before pouring himself a large Jack Daniels. "I assume you're both on duty," he remarked while at the same time raising the bottle as if to offer them a drink.
"Yes, we are," replied Carmichael, "but thanks anyway."
Mason took his half-filled tumbler of bourbon and plonked himself down in a large armchair.
Directly behind Mason, Carmichael spied a number of framed photographs on the wall. All seemed to have the owner of the house, golf club in hand and in colourful jumpers (that Carmichael wouldn't appear dead in), smiling broadly. Some depicted him with a trophy, others presumably with some well-known golfer – not that Carmichael would recognise one even if he was in the top ten.
"I see you admiring my photos," remarked Mason proudly. "Do you play golf, Inspector?"

Carmichael smiled and shook his head. "There's not a great deal of spare time in this job," he remarked. "Certainly not enough to allow me to take up golf."

"You must," insisted Mason. "It's a great way to get exercise and you meet a whole range of people. In fact, I've become very friendly with some very senior policemen and women through golf."

"Really," replied Carmichael, with no attempt to disguise his disdain at Mason's unsubtle attempt to communicate his connections. "That must be nice for you."

"Anyway, you're not here to talk about golf," added Mason with a smug grin. "What exactly is it you need from me?"

"As I said before, we'd like to ask you some questions about your meeting in The Three Bells earlier this evening with Doug Pritchard," Carmichael replied.

Mason took a large swig from his glass before answering.

"Fire away," he remarked.

"How long have you known Doug Pritchard?" Carmichael enquired.

Ron Mason puffed out his cheeks and shook his head gently from side to side. "About twenty-five years," he replied. "I don't know him well and he's certainly not a mate of mine, but I've known him for a long time."

"How come you were having dinner together this evening?" Carmichael asked.

"He called me out of the blue and said he'd like to talk with me about a project he was working on and asked if I'd have dinner with him," replied Mason. "I told him I was free tonight. Then he messaged me to say he'd booked himself into that B&B down the lane from The Three Bells, so I reserved us a table at the pub and told him I'd pick him up at seven thirty, which I did; then we had dinner."

"And what was this project?" enquired Carmichael.

Ron Mason exhaled deeply. "He told me that he was working on a story about Chrissy. He reckoned that he had indisputable evidence that she wasn't killed in the boating accident and that she was alive and well and living abroad."

"Where?" interjected Carmichael.

Mason shrugged his shoulders. "God knows," he replied. "To be honest we didn't get that far. I told him he was mad, that sadly, Chrissy was dead, and I wasn't interested in being involved in his crack pot project."

"Is that why you argued?" interjected Watson.

Mason nodded vigorously. "He had the cheek to accuse me of knowing where she was and being part of the cover-up and said I'd come out looking bad if I didn't cooperate. I told him to stuff it, or words to that effect. I then went to the gents and when I got back, he'd gone; leaving me to pick up the tab, too. To be honest, I should have known it wasn't going to be a straightforward story about Chrissy he was doing, when he contacted me. Doug Pritchard's been doing dodgy stories about people in the music business for decades, most of which are either total fiction or colossal exaggerations."

"So, you didn't drive him back to his B&B?" Carmichael added.

"No bloody way," replied Mason angrily. "I paid the bill for the meals and hung around talking with Wade until closing time, then I came home."

Mason took another slug of his bourbon before looking over at Watson.

"And before you ask, I did drive home but I wasn't over the limit. You can check if you want. Ah, but I might be now as I've had a few since getting home."

Carmichael smiled. "We're not interested in driving violations," he remarked. "We're investigating a much more serious crime."

"So, I take it he's dead," proclaimed Mason, who took another gulp of his drink.

"What time exactly did you leave The Three Bells?" Carmichael asked deliberately evading Mason's question.

"Not totally sure," Mason replied. "Wade would probably remember better than me, but I'd say it was about ten forty-five and home about ten minutes later.

Carmichael glanced across at Watson before rising to his feet.

"You've been a great help, Mr Mason," he remarked with a smile. "I'm sorry we troubled you so late in the evening. We'll leave you in peace."

Ron Mason looked a little surprised by the suddenness of Carmichael's ending of their discussion but seemed relieved that the ordeal was over. "I'll see you out," he said although he remained in his chair.

"No need," replied Carmichael. "I'm sure we can find the way."

"Excellent," remarked Mason, who, as he spoke, drained what was left of the contents of the glass.

As the two officers reached the door, Carmichael turned. "Actually, there are a couple of things you might be able to help me with," he announced.

"What's that?" replied Mason.

"Do you know where Mr Pritchard lives and whether he's married?" Carmichael asked.

"Brighton, I think," replied Mason. "He's gay, I know that, but I don't know whether he has a partner or is in a relationship."
Carmichael nodded. "And do you know anyone who'd want to harm Mr Pritchard?" he asked.
"So, he is dead then," replied Mason, before shrugging his shoulders. "Given his line of work I'd reckon there must be a fair few people who hated his guts. But around here there's probably only me and the last surviving Vixens who even knew of him."
"The last surviving Vixens," repeated Carmichael. "And who would they be?"
"Pam Hutton and Suzi Ashcroft," replied Mason. "They both still live locally, but I can't see either of them killing anyone. Suzi's totally against violence. She spends most of her time on peaceful demos and so-called good causes, as far as I know. At least that's where all her band royalties seem to end up. And Pam's only interests seem to be her menagerie of cats and dogs, followed closely behind by her love of anything alcoholic; a passion that she indulges in on a regular basis, if you get my drift. I don't see either of those two being up to murder."

* * * *

"I wouldn't trust him as far as I could throw him," Watson remarked as he and Carmichael made their way back to The Three Bells.
"I'm inclined to agree with you, Marc," replied Carmichael. "But his story ties in with the one Wade Freeman gave me, so I'm not sure we can charge him with anything. Not even drink driving, as he smugly reminded us."
"So, what's the plan?" Watson asked.

Carmichael thought for a few seconds before replying. "Stock's doing the post-mortem first thing in the morning," he replied. "So, I suggest we call it a night and the four of us get back together at the station in the morning. Shall we say eight?"

Watson initially looked perplexed. Then the penny dropped. "That's right, PC Twamley's joining us tomorrow, I forgot about that."

"DC Twamley," corrected Carmichael. "Rachel's replacement as our new detective constable." As he finished his sentence, Carmichael's car pulled up beside Watson's in The Three Bells car park.

"Before I head off, I'll check in with Rachel and see how she's getting on," Watson remarked. "I suspect she'll need a lift as we both came in my car."

Carmichael smiled. "Tell her to let me know if she's unearthed anything significant," he remarked. "Otherwise, I'll see you both bright and early in the morning."

Watson returned the smile before shutting the door and walking away towards his own car.

Chapter 7

Thursday 21st March

Having arrived at the office at just after seven o'clock, Carmichael had already made a few headings on the whiteboard before his team arrived, and once the clock on the wall indicated it was eight o'clock, he promptly started the meeting.
"Morning, everyone," he announced. "I guess the first thing I should do is to formally welcome Donna."
As he spoke Carmichael gazed across at DC Twamley, whose beaming smile signified just how delighted she was at being selected to join Carmichael's team.
"Following the departure of DS Martin, the confirmed retirement of DS Cooper, and, of course, the well-deserved promotion of Rachel to DS," continued Carmichael, who smiled across at the equally chuffed DS, "I'm pleased to announce that Donna has agreed to join the team."
As DS Dalton and DS Watson nodded their congratulations in Donna Twamley's direction, Carmichael turned his attention to the whiteboard.
"Just in time too," he remarked, "as I suspect we'll need all four of us on this case." Pointing up towards the notes he'd made earlier, Carmichael continued.
"What we know is that our dead man, who we believe to be a man called Doug Pritchard, left The Three Bells

pub in High Maudsey at around nine twenty last night. His body was discovered in a ditch down Jay Bank Lane less than half an hour later by a young man on his moped called Miles Goodwyn."

"The call we received from Miles has been documented at nine forty-seven," added DS Dalton, as if to support what Carmichael was saying.

Carmichael nodded. "And based upon the times we have for Doug Pritchard leaving the pub, the time the body was found, and the distance it was found from the pub," continued Carmichael, "it looks like, having left The Three Bells, Pritchard headed straight for the B&B he'd checked into that evening. And, if he walked at a pace of around three miles per hour, he'd have probably arrived at the place he was found, in about ten to fifteen minutes."

"Which means that he was killed between half nine and a quarter to ten," interjected Watson.

"That's right, Marc," responded Carmichael.

"Do we know exactly how he was killed?" DC Twamley enquired.

Carmichael shook his head. "Stock and his team have yet to confirm exactly what the cause of death is," he replied, "however he'd received a nasty blow to the back of his head, which may well prove to be how he died. As soon as we've finished here, I'm going to go down and talk with Stock about their findings, but I suspect that blow was what killed him."

DC Twamley nodded.

"So, what else do we know?" Carmichael asked, his question aimed at everyone in the room.

"We know that Pritchard arrived at Hardcastle's B&B at around seven that evening," remarked DS Dalton. "And according to Mrs Hardcastle, he simply dumped his bag before being picked up by someone in a four by four at seven thirty."

"That person we now know was Ron Mason," added Watson, his comments aimed at his two female colleagues. "He confirmed that to the boss and I last night."

"Ron Mason also confirmed that they'd had a meal together in The Three Bells," continued Carmichael, "and that they'd argued."

"According to Mason the quarrel was about a story Pritchard wanted Mason to help him with about a pop singer who Mason used to manage, called Chrissy Cream," added Watson, his comments again aimed at the two female officers. "According to Mason, Pritchard had said he had evidence that Chrissy wasn't killed in a boating accident, as had been reported at the time, and that she was alive and well and living abroad."

"And Mason took exception to that," remarked Carmichael, "hence the argument."

DC Twamley looked confused. She glanced quickly in DS Dalton's direction, however the exaggerated shrug of her shoulders indicated that her colleague wasn't much more the wiser than her. "Sorry to sound dumb," DC Twamley said, rather hesitantly, "but I've never heard of Chrissy Cream. Was she a big star?"

Carmichael smiled. "You're not dumb at all," he replied. "Until last night, I didn't know much about her either. Maybe you can answer that one, Marc, as you seem to be more familiar with her."

DS Watson shook his head gently, as if he was amazed at the lack of knowledge about someone who's songs he remembered so well from his youth. "Chrissy Cream and the Vixens were a massive group about twenty-five years ago," he remarked. "They had several top ten hits and toured all over. You must have heard of them."

DS Dalton and DC Twamley shook their heads.

"Well, they were a local rock band," continued Watson, "however, it all ended abruptly when Chrissy and one of the other band members were killed in a tragic boating accident. As I recall, the other one killed was Chrissy's sister, Jo."

"So, if this Chrissy Cream is still alive that would be big news," suggested DS Dalton.

"I'd say so," replied Watson.

"And something that Ron Mason may want to hide," she added.

"Maybe," Watson replied.

"The problem is," interjected Carmichael, "that according to Wade Freeman and his wife, Coral, who run The Three Bells, Ron Mason didn't leave the pub until ten forty-five. Which, if true, means he couldn't have killed Doug Pritchard."

"And do you believe them, sir?" DS Dalton enquired.

Carmichael considered the question before answering. "I'm not totally convinced the Freemans were telling me the truth," he replied. "But unless we can prove that they are wrong, Ron Mason has a cast iron alibi for the murder."

"I'm not sure about Ron Mason either," added Watson. "I got the feeling he knew something had happened to Pritchard before we told him."

Carmichael nodded. "Maybe Wade Freeman tipped him off," he replied.

"Yes, maybe he's covering for him, and Mason wasn't in the pub," suggested Watson. "That would be my guess."

"You may be right, Marc," remarked Carmichael, "but we'll need a lot more than your gut feel if we're going to find who's responsible."

Watson nodded. "I know," he muttered quietly.

"What did you find out at the B&B, Rachel?" Carmichael enquired; his eyes now focussed on DS Dalton.

DS Dalton shrugged her shoulders. "Not much," she replied. "As I said before, Muriel Hardcastle said he arrived at about seven, dumped his stuff in his room then went out in a four by four at seven thirty. He left his car, which the SOCO team are looking at, and he also left his mobile on charge in his room which they are looking at, too. Apart from that, I've not much else."

As she finished talking, DS Dalton suddenly remembered something. "Oh, Mrs Hardcastle was able to give me the details of his home address," she remarked, "or at least the address he gave when he made the booking with the on-line booking company."

"Is it a Brighton address?" Carmichael enquired. "That's where Ron Mason thought he came from."

"It was in Sussex," replied DS Dalton as she turned the pages of her notebook, "but not Brighton."

DS Dalton suddenly found her note. "13b, Berryduke House, Seafront, Hove," she announced. "Sounds like it may be an apartment."

Carmichael smiled, "Hove's right next door to Brighton," he explained. "And a very expensive place to live it is, too."

"So, what's the plan?" Watson enquired, hoping that with Carmichael going to the mortuary, he was going to get a more interesting task, for once.

Carmichael thought for a few moments.

"I'd like you, Donna, to do some digging into our dead man," he said looking directly at his new DC. "I want to know his age, if he has family, marital status, and anything that you can find about him. Mason reckoned he was gay, but don't take that as gospel. Also, check out what books or articles he's written recently and speak to the local police in Hove. We particularly need to root out the details of anyone who might have wanted to do him harm."

"Will do," replied DC Twamley, who was clearly pleased with her assignment.

"Also, we'll need to have his body formally identified," Carmichael added. "Find out who his next of kin are and, once they've been properly informed, try and get them up here."

"Got it, sir," DC Twamley remarked.

"As for you, Marc," continued Carmichael, who pointed up at the name Ron Mason written in large red pen on the whiteboard. "You focus on Ron Mason, Chrissy Cream, and the surviving members of her group. That's Suzi Ashcroft and Pam Hutton."

As he spoke, Carmichael moved his finger down the whiteboard to the names of the two Vixens that Mason had mentioned to them the night before.

"I want to know everything about Mason from the time he managed that band up to now," Carmichael instructed him. "Find out if he's any criminal record and see if he and Doug Pritchard have locked horns before; maybe due to some previous article Pritchard published. Also, see if you can find out if he's as wealthy as he claims, as I can't believe the royalties from a band that finished decades ago will be that much. It's not like they're the Beatles."

By the bemused expression on Watson's face, it was clear he didn't agree with his boss's assumption about the flow of royalties; but simply nodded and kept quiet.

"Will do, sir," he replied.

Carmichael then turned his attention to DS Dalton. "Rachel, I'd like you to double check Ron Mason's alibi," Carmichael announced. "Speak with Miles again and see if he can give you the names of anyone else who was in the pub last night. I want to know if anyone heard what those two argued about and I want some additional verification about the exact time Ron Mason left."

DS Dalton nodded. "Got it, sir," she replied.

"And get back to The Three Bells and try and talk with Coral on her own," Carmichael continued. "She didn't say much to me last night with her husband around. Maybe if you were to talk with her on her own, she may tell you more than she told me."

DS Dalton nodded again. "I'll try," she replied.

With all their assignments now communicated, Carmichael grabbed his jacket.

"Right," he remarked loudly as he walked briskly towards the exit. "I'll go and see what the good Dr Stock can tell me."

As he spoke, Carmichael looked up at the clock. "Let's meet back here again this afternoon at two for a quick update but call me if you turn up anything you think I need to know."

Carmichael neither expected nor waited for an answer, making his exit from the office just seconds after he'd finished talking.

"Welcome to the madhouse, Donna," remarked Watson with a wry smile, before turning his attention to his computer screen.

Chapter 8

At precisely eight thirty, as she'd done every weekday morning for the last nineteen years, Lydia Brook-Smith pulled back the three large bolts on the door of The Muffin Maid and turned the sign to open.
As was invariably the case for her well renowned bakery, a group of loyal customers had gathered outside eagerly waiting to come in to buy from Lydia's small village shop.
As her customers filed into the shop, Lydia took a few seconds to breath in the bright spring morning; the air filled with its invigorating sense of renewal and anticipation. Lydia loved mornings, especially in springtime; a good job, too, given the early starts her occupation dictated.
With the help of Mrs McMullen, the white-haired assistant who'd been a faithful employee ever since Lydia had first taken the plunge and opened the bakery, they quickly cleared their initial rush, at which point Lydia smiled, a relieved satisfying grin, which indicated it was time for her first mug of tea of the day.
"Ready for a brew, Margaret?" she asked, albeit she knew full well that Margaret McMullen wasn't going to decline, having never done so in all the time she'd worked there.
"Go on then," replied Mrs McMullen, as if she'd had her arm twisted. "I might try one of those lovely Eccles cakes too, if that's alright with you."

Lydia smiled and headed into the back, and the gleaming stainless steel work tops where all the early-morning action had taken place from the moment she'd come down at four that morning.

"Hello darling," she bellowed as she spotted her daughter, Verity, who'd just emerged from the living space above the shop. "How did the pie night go at The Three Bells last night?"

"It was brilliant," replied Verity with a smile, grabbing a large croissant off the tray as she spoke. "We sold out by about nine," Verity continued. "Coral was well chuffed."

"Really!" Lydia exclaimed. "All forty pies?"

Verity took a bite out of the croissant, tipping her head down and holding her left hand under her chin, to catch the falling flakes of pastry. "All forty," she confirmed. "And if we'd taken more, they'd have sold most of them too, I suspect."

"Wow," remarked Lydia, as she started to fill up the kettle in one of her large gleaming silver sinks. "Do you want a brew?"

With her mouth and cheeks bulging with croissant, Verity nodded.

"So, what time did you get home?" Lydia enquired.

"It was quite early," responded Verity. "Coral let me start clearing up not long after nine, and I was away by half nine."

"Really," replied her mother. "We will have to send more pies next time."

Verity stopped chewing her croissant for a moment. "Anyway, where were you last night?" she enquired, a cheeky grin on her face. "I didn't know you were going out."

"I had to go and see someone about a cake they want us to make for them," replied her mother. "I must have got back not long after you got home."

Verity nodded and started munching away again. "I was shattered so had a quick wash and went to bed."

Lydia didn't doubt what she was saying, seeing the smudged mascara on her daughter's face. She smiled and shook her head gently. "It must have been rammed in there for them to sell so many pies," she suggested, getting back to last night's sales in the pub.

"It was," replied Verity. "Mainly the local crowd, but there were a fair few other people in there who I'd not seen before. It must be the reputation of those famous Muffin Maid pies."

Lydia laughed. "I wish," she said, although deep down she thought it may well have been a contributing factor. "Did Ellis come in?" Lydia asked.

Verity shook her head. "No, he had an assignment to do for his college course, which he must hand in this morning. And, in true Ellis fashion, he hadn't started when I spoke with him at six. He's coming round tonight, and we're going to have a *Domino's* and start to watch that new crime series with that Irish woman from that pottery show you like."

"Siobhán McSweeney," Lydia said, knowing exactly who her daughter was referring to.

"That's the one," replied Verity, before grabbing her second croissant.

"Hey," shouted her mother. "I'll have none left to sell if you carry on eating all the stock."

Verity smiled, rolled her eyes skyward and sunk her sparkling white teeth into the soft, flaky pastry.

"You shouldn't make them so well," she replied glibly, crumbs flying all over the kitchen floor as she spoke.

"And was Miles there last night?" Lydia asked, a mischievous expression now on her face.

Verity put the croissant down on the worktop, closed her eyes and shook her head gently. "Sadly, yes," Verity replied. "I couldn't get rid of him. Every time I turned around, he was there staring at me like some love-struck pup. And, of course, when he found out that Ellis wasn't coming, he seemed to take that as his chance. If I've told him once I've told him a million times that I'm with Ellis, and I'm absolutely not interested in his clapped-out motor bike, those stupid computer games he plays, or anything else about him."

Lydia shrugged her shoulders. "I know he's a bit wet, but he's harmless though."

"Harmless but annoying as hell," replied Verity, who resumed eating the second croissant.

"Well, I suspect he'll give up once he sees you starting to show," suggested Lydia, just as the kettle started to boil. "In my experience, a woman loses her attraction to the opposite sex once they know they're expecting another man's child. I suspect it's a primal thing."

"Well, the sooner that happens the better," replied Verity as she stuffed the last morsel of the croissant into her mouth. "As long as Ellis still loves me that's all that matters."

"And your old mum, too," added Lydia, before giving her daughter a squeeze. "Don't think I'm going to be frozen out when baby comes."

Verity smiled. "Don't worry, there's no chance of that, Mum," she assured her. "Ellis and I will need you to babysit once this thing's born and we start clubbing again."

"Dream on, young lady," replied Lydia. "Once the baby comes, I'm playing a supporting role. It's yours and Ellis's responsibility. So, I don't want you two to start getting the wrong idea. I'm going to be a proud, loving grandma, not an unpaid nanny."

Chapter 9

Pam Hutton was bent over, placing the last of the newly filled bowls of cat food onto the lino next to the back door, when she spied Ellis, her adopted son and the apple of her eye, walking slowly down the hallway.
"Morning darling," she remarked with a broad wide smile, while at the same time carefully unfolding herself to the vertical. "Did you get your assignment finished?"
Looking worn out, from what Pam assumed must have been a late night burning the midnight oils, Ellis nodded.
"All done and emailed over to Mr McCready," he replied, as he arrived at the fridge and extracted an already-opened carton of milk. "If I don't get an A for that I'll be really pissed."
On finishing his sentence, Ellis put the carton to his mouth and started to knock back its contents in large gulps.
"I wish you wouldn't do that," announced Pam, her sharp indignant voice matched only by the look of disgust on her face.
"Apart from the cats it's just me that drinks cow's milk," replied Ellis. "And I'm sure the cats don't mind."
"I may have guests for tea, you know," replied Pam, before walking over to him, standing on tiptoe and giving him a friendly kiss on the cheek.
"When do you ever get guests?" responded Ellis rudely.

"And did I hear you go out last night?" Pam added, with an air of mild disapproval. "I assume it was to see the lovely what's her name."

"It's Verity, Mum," replied Ellis, his reply delivered with a prickliness forged from Pam's constant, not so subtle, reminders that the young woman, who in less than four months' time was going to produce a baby, was not the choice she'd have made for her adored son. "We've been seeing each other for ten months now," he added. "And we will be getting married once baby comes, so you need to start getting used to the idea and her name."

"She's trapped you," remarked Pam. "At your age you should be out there, having fun and sowing ……"

"That's how the baby happened," Ellis reminded his adoptive mother. "And I know you don't like it, but Verity is my choice and we're very happy."

Pam's expression softened and her shoulders slumped. "I know you are," she said before putting her arms around him. "It's just that you are both so young."

Ellis pulled Pam close to him, even though her head didn't come much above his chest. "I know you are just worried about me," he remarked. "But there's no need. I'm twenty-three. By that age my birth mum had already had me."

Although he'd always known the details of his adoption, and that his adoptive mum and his birth mum had not just been friends but in the same band, Ellis was forever on his guard when he mentioned his birth mum. He knew he owed everything to Pam, and he loved her as much as anyone could love a mother.

"She had," conceded Pam. "And she was headstrong like you, too."

As she spoke there was a noise from the cat flap, and a jet-black cat with long hair and emerald-green eyes emerged from outside.

"Hello Lucy," exclaimed Pam in a voice that resembled someone talking to a new-born child.

The angry-looking cat ignored her, preferring to sidle over to the food bowl, where she started to pick out bits of food she didn't want and drop them on the floor, before wolfing down the remaining items; those that she clearly preferred.

"You're worse than Ellis," remarked Pam, again in her baby voice, before releasing her grip on Ellis and walking over towards the cat.

Ellis put the carton back to his lips and, in a matter of seconds, made short work of draining what milk had remained. "The answer to your question is no," he replied. "I did go out for an hour or so in the car to clear my head, but I didn't see Verity. She was working last night in The Three Bells. I'm seeing her tonight."

*   *   *   *

As far as Carmichael was concerned, his timing couldn't have been better, as when he entered through the doors of Dr Stock's scrupulously clean forensic lab, the renowned head of central Lancashire's forensic team had just completed his autopsy on the man they believed was Doug Pritchard.

"You've missed all the fun," remarked Stock sarcastically, knowing full well that Carmichael, in keeping with most policemen he knew, wasn't keen on viewing post-mortems as they took place.

"Tell me then, Stock, what's the verdict?" Carmichael enquired.

"I'd put the age of the deceased at about sixty," replied Stock who, as he spoke, pulled down the shroud that had covered the body to reveal the dead man's head and upper torso. "He was in reasonable health for a man of his age, despite being a smoker and clearly liking the odd drink, now and then."

"And can you confirm exactly how and when he died?" Carmichael asked.

"I'd say time of death was no more than an hour before we arrived at the scene," replied Stock.

"About nine thirty," suggested Carmichael.

"Give or take fifteen minutes either side, yes," replied Stock, as he lifted the dead man's head off the small support which had been placed behind his neck.

"But as for the how, that's not so clear," added Stock.

"And why's that?" Carmichael enquired.

"Because he was struck twice," replied Stock. "Here on the back of his head and here on his temple. Either blow would have been enough to kill him, but it's not easy to say which one did the job."

Carmichael looked closely at the heavy bruising on the front and rear of the corpse's head. "Were the blows from the same weapon?" he asked.

"Now that I am sure about," replied Stock. "It was almost certainly the same weapon; a smooth rounded object with a circumference of about fifteen centimetres. Maybe a baseball bat or a fence post."

"But you don't know which blow came first," Carmichael remarked.

Stock took a few seconds to consider the question. "The one to the front of the head was a heavy glancing blow that connected at an angle of about forty-five degrees," he explained. "I'd say it was made by a right-handed person who was stood next to him. The likelihood is that it was made by someone who was a little shorter than our victim."

"And the one to the back of the head?" Carmichael pressed.

"That was the interesting one," Stock replied. "It was delivered with similar force as the other, but the contact was in a horizontal line right behind his ears. Which suggests that either our victim was bent over, or the person who delivered the blow was standing on something or was significantly taller than the dead man."

It was Carmichael's turn to think for a few seconds. "And how tall was our victim?" he asked.

"One metre seventy centimetres," replied Stock. "That's just five foot seven inches, in old money."

Carmichael smiled. Despite having been from the era when kids had been taught both metric and imperial measures at school, he still struggled with anything other than feet and inches when it came to measuring height.

"Could the blows have been made by two different people?" Carmichael enquired.

Stock shrugged his shoulders. "They might have been," he replied, "but I'm certain they were either inflicted with the same weapon or, if not, with two identical weapons."

"What about that bruise above his right eye?" Carmichael asked pointing at a small crescent shaped graze about two centimetres long.

"That would have happened at about the time of death, but is certainly not the blow that killed him," replied Stock. "It may have been caused when he hit the ground, but I couldn't be sure."

Carmichael nodded sagely. "Ok," he remarked. "What else have your team uncovered?"

"They're still looking at the car," Stock replied, "but they found a fuel receipt from a garage at Norton Canes services from yesterday, timed at five fifteen, which implies he travelled north on the M6 and M6 toll road yesterday."

"That ties in with what we know," announced Carmichael. "Anything else?"

Stock shook his head. "Not yet," he replied, "but I'll get you our full report later today."

"What about the mobile?" Carmichael asked. "Anything on that?"

Stock smiled. "It would appear that our victim was a bit old school, like me," Stock replied. "No stored photos, no Facebook page, no twitter account, and he sent few messages. In fact, he pretty much used his mobile as a phone."

Carmichael nodded. "And do we know who his last calls were with?" he asked.

Stock walked over to his desk and handed over a single sheet of A4 paper to Carmichael.

"It's all on there," Stock replied, a smug look of satisfaction on his face. "An entire record of the mobile's activity in the last three months."

Carmichael took the sheet of paper from Stock and looked at it for a few seconds before placing it in his pocket.

"Can you email this over to DC Twamley back at the station?" Carmichael asked.

Stock nodded. "I heard she'd joined your team," he remarked. "No doubt, she's thrilled to be the latest disciple in the great detective's band of sleuths."

Carmichael tried to ignore the portly forensic scientist's facetious remark but couldn't help smiling.

"I look forward to receiving your full report later today," he said, before heading away to the exit.

Chapter 10

As soon as he'd clambered into his car, Carmichael removed the record of Doug Pritchard's mobile phone activity from his jacket pocket and rested the single A4 sheet of paper between his lap and the steering wheel. As he studied its details, Carmichael dialled DC Twamley's number and placed his phone in its cradle, so he'd be hands free when she picked up.
"DC Twamley," she announced, her voice bright and enthusiastic, exuding the very eagerness Stock had been alluding to just minutes earlier.
"Donna," announced Carmichael, "you'll be getting an email from Dr Stock with the details of Doug Pritchard's mobile phone activity. I'd like you to check out who the various calls and messages he had were with. I particularly want you to concentrate on the incoming and outgoing calls and messages in the last ten days."
"Do you want me to focus on that before completing the other duties you assigned to me at this morning's briefing?" DC Twamley enquired.
"Yes," replied Carmichael firmly. "It shouldn't take you that long as I've got a copy of the activity in front of me and he only made nine outgoing calls in the last ten days, four of them to the same number and the others to three other numbers. And of his incoming calls there appears to be only one number that wasn't one of the

numbers he'd called. His text messages were to two of those numbers too, so you only have five people to trace."

"I'll get on to it as soon as it comes through," remarked DC Twamley.

"I'll be back at the station in about an hour," added Carmichael. "You can bring me up to speed then."

DC Twamley was just about to say something along the lines of 'right you are, sir' when the line went dead.

Chapter 11

Suzi Ashcroft gently pushed open her son's bedroom door to find him sound asleep, the clothes he'd had on the night before strewn across the floor.
She gently rested the tray she'd been carrying on the bedside cabinet beside him and looked down on her sleeping boy.
"It's half past ten," she whispered. "I thought you were going to see Ron at ten about releasing some cash for that car you want."
"I'll go round later," mumbled Tom from below the duvet.
Suzi remained calm, her facial expression unmoved by her son's apparent indifference.
"I've left some tea for you, Tom," she announced. "And some crumpets with that jam you like from Waitrose."
Emanating from deep beneath the duvet Suzi could just about pick up an approving, acknowledging grunt, which brought a loving smile to her face; an expression which remained in place as she departed Tom's bedroom.

* * * *

To see her now, it would be almost unimaginable to believe that, at the height of the Vixens' fame, Suzi Ashcroft had been the wild one in the band. Back then the group's lead guitarist was forever on the front pages of not only the music magazines, but also the national red tops. Her circle of friends included famous actors (from both sides of the pond), TV personalities, leading lights in the fashion industry and, it was rumoured, even minor royals. Seen on the arm of a string of Premier League footballers and global pop megastars, Suzi was, for sure, right at the top of the A listers back in the day. When, famously during one interview, she'd been asked what her motto should be, she'd simply smiled, downed the glass of champagne in her hand, passionately kissed the unsuspecting interviewer and replied, 'live for the day and let tomorrow care for itself'. It was certainly a mantra she'd observed with fastidious dedication some twenty-five years earlier.

However, Suzi Ashcroft's life had changed dramatically. Although her looks and figure hadn't totally deserted her, she no longer did celebrity parties, she largely shunned the limelight and rarely drank alcohol.

In fact, to those still close to her, she now only appeared to have two passions. The first was to fight tooth and nail against anything she felt was unjust. And secondly, Tom, her dear friend Chrissy's son, who Suzi took in at the age of two, when Chrissy had tragically died; and who she had subsequently adopted.

Way back then, of course, it was with the support of her on-off partner and the bands manager, Ron Mason, who amongst others, she'd been dating when the boat sank. In fact, it had been Ron who had suggested they should take care of Tom. However, for the last eighteen years Suzi had mainly managed alone. Ron, to give him some credit, was still a fleeting influence in Tom's life,

allowing him some access to the significant trust fund set up by his late mother, when prompted by Suzi, or some fatherly advice, again when pushed and prodded by Suzi. But it would be fair to say that, in the main, since Ron and Suzi's romantic relationship had finally ended, it was mainly Suzi who'd been there for Tom, which was exactly how Suzi liked it.
"It's just the two of us against the world" was the phrase Tom had heard her say for just about as long as he could remember.

*   *   *   *

As soon as his adoptive mum had shut the door behind her, Tom hauled himself out from beneath the duvet and, without a stitch on, ambled across the bedroom carpet, scratching his head and his private parts at the same time. He headed for the small set of drawers where he'd deposited his mobile in the early hours of the morning, when he'd finally arrived home.
Tom checked his messages and the one he'd been expecting flashed up.

It's sorted. I'll be round at six for my money.

Tom smiled before rapidly tapping out a reply; his thumb and fingers moving at lightning speed.
Once sent, Tom deleted the conversation, put his mobile back on the chest of drawers and went back to bed.

Chapter 12

Donna Twamley had long dreamt of shedding her police uniform and becoming a plain clothed detective. So, when Carmichael had approached her, she'd said yes immediately. There was no hesitation, no "*Can I have a little time to think about it*". It was an unqualified, instantaneous "*Yes, sir. Thank you, sir. You won't regret it, sir*", response; coupled with the widest grin that Carmichael had seen in some time.
With her instructions clear, DC Twamley, motivated and eager to show what she was made of, set about tracking down names for the numbers she'd been sent by Dr Stock's team.
Similarly focused on the task in hand, but maybe not quite as enthusiastic as her new colleague, DS Dalton stood at the door of The Three Bells preparing herself for the impending conversation with Coral Freeman.
As for DS Watson, the most experienced of the three members of Carmichael's team, he simply leaned back in his chair and stared aimlessly at yet more information he'd found online about Chrissy Cream, the Vixens and their (back in the day) young Svengali, Ron Mason.
In truth, Watson hated doing desk research; that wasn't why he'd joined the police force. However, on this occasion he didn't mind too much, consoling himself with the fact that there was a huge amount of information, not just about the band, but the Cream

sisters, the circumstances of their untimely deaths and their careers. Watson knew that by the time the team next had an update he'd be more than able to provide Carmichael with a wealth of information about Ron Mason, Suzi Ashcroft and Pam Hutton, the surviving members of the group, and as such felt under no pressure at all.

*   *   *   *

As Carmichael had hoped, Coral Freemen was alone at The Three Bells when DS Dalton called; her husband doing another of his trademark nips out somewhere to do something or other (he'd said it was to the supermarket to get some milk and toilet rolls on this occasion).

Having brandished her warrant card and with her best friendly smile on show, DS Dalton introduced herself to Coral and was ushered into the snug, just to the side of the main bar, where she made herself comfortable on one of the pub's upholstered benches.

"I know you've already spoken to DI Carmichael," she began, 'but I'd like to go through the events of yesterday evening again, in a bit more detail, if that's ok with you, Mrs Freeman?"

"It's Coral," the landlady replied, with a faint smile. "What exactly would you like to ask?"

Pleased that Coral appeared to want to cooperate, DS Dalton opened up her notebook.

"I want to ask you specifically about the two men who were arguing in here last night," she began. "Ron Mason and his companion. Did you hear them arguing?"

Coral shook her head. "To be honest, I heard raised voices, but I can't recall what was said. I was busy serving drinks and food. It was pie night last night and the place was packed out."

DS Dalton smiled and nodded gently. "You told DI Carmichael that the argument occurred just after nine fifteen," she continued. "Is that correct?"

Coral nodded.

"Your husband, Wade, spoke with the other man, telling him to calm down and the man then left the pub."

Coral nodded again. "That's right," she remarked.

"Then I understand that Mr Mason remained in the pub right up until…" DS Dalton checked her notes, "until about ten forty-five. Is that correct?"

DS Dalton could see in Coral's eyes that she wasn't sure how to answer.

"It was probably about that time," Coral replied vaguely. "I was really busy, so I wasn't keeping track on the movements of anyone."

DS Dalton smiled and nodded reassuringly. "Are you saying it might have been earlier?" she asked.

"It may have been," replied Coral awkwardly. "I'd not want to swear to a specific time."

DS Dalton nodded again. "Could it have been as early as nine twenty or nine twenty-five?" she enquired.

"I'm not sure," Coral replied. "I know I'm not being that helpful, but I was really busy last night. I wasn't paying much attention to the times people arrived and left."

DS Dalton could sense quite clearly that Coral wasn't feeling at all comfortable; nervousness was etched across her face and in her voice. However, she didn't feel there was much more to be gained from continuing to push Coral on the time, so moved on.

"You say the pub was packed," DS Dalton continued.

"Very busy," replied Coral, who seemed relieved that questions about Ron Mason's departure time appeared to have stopped. "We were fully booked from about seven until half nine."

DS Dalton smiled. "Do people have to book a table on a Wednesday night?" she enquired.

Coral nodded. "We strongly suggest people do, but if we aren't fully booked people can just get a table on arrival."

"But last night you were fully booked?" DS Dalton asked.

"That's right," replied Coral. "We had no available tables until up to nine thirty, which is normally when we finish serving food for the evening."

"In that case, I take it, Ron Mason or his friend must have booked a table?" observed DS Dalton.

Coral nodded. "Ron booked it for seven thirty," she replied. "Table four, his usual table."

"Can you show me table four, please?" DS Dalton asked.

Without any hesitation whatsoever, Coral stood up and walked briskly out of the snug, followed closely by DS Dalton.

"Here you go," she remarked as they reached the table next to the wall that was unmistakably table four; the giveaway being the shiny, circular, brass plate screwed onto the table with the number four clearly visible.

DS Dalton looked at the three tables that were directly adjacent to table four.

"Can you provide me with the names and contact details of the people who were occupying these three tables when the argument broke out last night, please?" continued DS Dalton, her right hand then pointing to the three nearest tables. "That's tables one, five and nine".

"Certainly," replied Coral, who then scooted off in the direction of the bar to retrieve the details DS Dalton required.

As Coral was making her way across the floor, DS Dalton allowed herself a small smile of satisfaction. Although there was at least half a metre between tables, she felt reasonably sure that, even in a noisy pub, at least one of the diners close to Ron Mason and Doug Pritchard would have heard what the men were arguing about. With that as a distinct possibility and with Coral's nervous demeanour earlier suggesting the time Wade Freeman had given Carmichael for when Ron Mason had left the pub may have been fabricated, DS Dalton felt certain that her trip to The Three Bells had been worthwhile.

Chapter 13

When Carmichael entered the incident room, he could only see DS Watson, who was slumped back in his chair intently reading something on his computer screen. It took a few seconds before he realised that DC Twamley was also there, her head initially obscured from sight, it being a matter of just a few inches from her large vertical monitor.
"Any joy?" Carmichael enquired randomly, to neither of his officers in particular.
It was DC Twamley who responded first.
"I've got the names of all five of the people that Doug Pritchard had contact with in the last ten days," she announced, with an element of triumph palpable in her voice.
"Excellent, Donna," replied Carmichael. "Tell me more."

*   *   *   *

Pam Hutton had just drained the contents of her favourite mug when her mobile rang.
She gazed down at the name on her screen before pressing the green button and putting the phone to her ear. "Hello Ron," she said, cheerily.
"We need to talk," Ron responded, in his customary authoritative tone. "Are ou free this afternoon?"

"I have the animals to feed," replied Pam, "but if you come around between two and five, I'll be free."

Pam could almost hear Ron's brain ticking away as the line went quiet for a few seconds.

"Let me talk with Suzi and see when she's free," he announced. "I'll call you back."

"I assume it's either band business or to talk about the boys' trust money," Pam suggested.

"Neither," replied Ron briskly, "But it's important. All will be clear this afternoon. I'll speak with Suzi and one of us will call you back."

The phone line went dead.

Pam placed the mobile on the kitchen table in front of her, refilled her mug with gin from the now almost-empty, green bottle and took a long swig. Then, placing the mug on the kitchen worktop, she allowed herself a small, smug grin. For some sadistic reason she always enjoyed it when Ron was in one of his flaps; and as she savoured the thought of Ron being stressed out, one of her cats jumped up onto the table and started to purr loudly and rub herself against her arm.

"Hello, lovely girl," said Pam in kindly infantile way, as though she was speaking to a young child. "Sounds like Uncle Ronnie is getting himself in a bit of a tizzy."

*   *   *   *

Buoyed by the discussion she'd had with Coral and armed with the contact details of the diners at tables one, five and nine at The Three Bells, DS Dalton decided to focus on those people first before reinterviewing Miles Goodwyn. Two of the three names on her list had local addresses, so DS Dalton decided to head over to talk with them.

* * * *

"Two at Pam's is fine for me," confirmed Suzi upon learning that Ron wanted an urgent meeting at Pam's house that afternoon. "But what is it that's so important?"

As he had with Pam, Ron avoided giving any more information. "You'll find out at two," he replied vaguely and unhelpfully. "Just don't be late!"

Without waiting for her response Ron ended the call, put his mobile in his pocket and slowly sat himself down in his favourite chair.

For the next ten minutes he sat quietly, contemplating his situation and how he was going to manage the meeting he'd organised that afternoon. He'd have remained even longer in his chair had the front doorbell not rung.

Chapter 14

The team briefing started at exactly two o'clock.
"Who's going to kick off?" Carmichael enquired.
When nobody volunteered, Carmichael grabbed a blue marker and walked over to the large whiteboard.
"Why don't I take the lead, in that case," he continued. "As we established this morning, although he's still to be formally identified, our murdered man is believed to be Doug Pritchard, who we think drove up from Brighton late yesterday afternoon and was picked up at about seven thirty from Hardcastle's B&B. A story that ties in with a fuel receipt from Norton Canes service station that Stock's team found in Pritchard's car, which had a time of five fifteen."
"Do we have Stock's report?" Watson enquired.
Carmichael shook his head. "Not yet, Marc," he replied, "but he was able to give me that piece of information along with the fact that our victim was struck twice, once across the back of his head and once across his forehead. Stock's not able to say for sure which blow killed him but he thinks both blows were made by a similar or the same weapon, which was rounded like a baseball bat or a fence post."
Carmichael looked around the room for a few seconds before continuing. "We need to try and find that weapon. So, Marc, after we've finished here get some PCs down that road and in the adjoining fields to do a

thorough sweep of the ditches and hedges to see if it was discarded by our killer as they made off."

Watson nodded. "Will do, sir," he replied.

Carmichael then wrote the words murder weapon on the whiteboard, followed by a large question mark.

"Where was I?" Carmichael asked.

"Doug Pritchard leaving the B&B at about seven thirty," confirmed DC Twamley.

Carmichael smiled over in DC Twamley's direction. "Yes, that's right," he said. "We know it was Ron Mason who picked up Doug Pritchard and they went together to The Three Bells as they'd arranged. We also know that during the meeting, at around nine to nine-fifteen, they argued, that Mason stormed off to the gents and, while he was away, Wade Freeman, the landlord of the pub, had a word with Pritchard and shortly afterwards he left the pub alone and was subsequently found dead by Miles Goodwyn, around thirty minutes later, down Jay Bank Lane; presumably as he walked towards his bed for the night at Hardcastle's B&B."

Carmichael paused for a few seconds to see if there would be any comments from his team. When there wasn't, he continued. "Hopefully, you can shed more light on this, Rachel, but we've been led to believe that Ron Mason didn't leave the pub until almost closing time, after Doug Pritchard's body had been found. As such, he would appear to have a cast iron alibi."

DS Dalton shook her head gently. "After speaking with Coral Freeman earlier, I thought her husband's account was highly suspicious," she stated. "Coral didn't say it in so many words, but she wasn't anywhere near as certain about the time Ron Mason left the pub as he was. And having now spoken to some of the people who were at the tables adjacent to Ron Mason and Doug Pritchard, they have a very different story about when Ron left the pub."

"Looks like we have a prime suspect," suggested DS Watson.

"Maybe," replied Carmichael, "but let's not get too far ahead of ourselves. What did the diners say, Rachel?"

DS Dalton smiled; her notebook was already open at the page where she'd taken down the notes from her first call. "I spoke to a Mr McNamara, who was at table one last night," she began. "He was there with his wife celebrating her seventy-third birthday. He said it was very noisy in the pub and although he did admit that, in his words, his hearing isn't as good as it used to be, he said he was sure it was Ron Mason doing all the shouting and he is absolutely adamant that Mason left the pub no more than five minutes after Pritchard."

"Really," Carmichael exclaimed. "That is interesting."

DS Dalton smiled before continuing. "I also spoke to two work colleagues from a small metal fabrication company around the corner, who were having dinner with their partners at table nine. Their table wasn't as close as Mr McNamara's but they both confirmed that Ron Mason left shortly after Doug Pritchard, and that Doug Pritchard seemed very calm during the argument. In fact, one of the men, a guy called Harry Barlow, who was looking directly at Doug Pritchard when the altercation took place, reckoned Pritchard had a 'sadistic, smug grin on his face' as if he was enjoying seeing Ron Mason in such a state."

"And could either of them recall anything that was said?" Carmichael asked.

"Not much, I'm afraid," DS Dalton replied. "Ed Cantwell, the other bloke on the table, said he heard one of the men saying '*Who told you that? Was it bloody ...*'"

DS Dalton paused for a few seconds. "He couldn't recall the exact name the man said," she continued, "but he thought it was either Mia, Tia or Leah."

"I think that might have been Leah Barnes he was referring to," DC Twamley remarked.

"Why do you say that?" Watson asked.

"Because that's one of the names that came up on Doug Pritchard's mobile activity report," replied DC Twamley.

"We can get on to that shortly," interrupted Carmichael, keen to keep the conversation focused on what DS Dalton had uncovered. "And did he say which man it was that he heard?"

DS Dalton shook her head. "He had his back to them." she replied. "So, he didn't see. But he assumed it was Mason as he appeared to be doing all the shouting."

Carmichael nodded gently as he digested what DS Dalton had told him.

"Great work, Rachel," he announced once he'd had a chance to think. "What about their partners and the people on the other table? What do they have to say?"

DS Dalton shrugged her shoulders. "I've still to speak with them and I also didn't have a chance to talk any further with Miles Goodwyn," she replied.

Carmichael nodded again, but more vigorously this time. "Make that your focus for this afternoon," he remarked. "Get formal statements from all the people on the surrounding tables and push Miles for more information on what he saw. He should have calmed down by now and may have remembered something he didn't mention last night."

"Will do, sir," acknowledged DS Dalton, before closing her notebook.

* * * *

Suzi looked at her watch; it was two fifteen. "It's not like Ron to be late," she suggested to Pam, who was cuddling one of her cats on the sofa.
"Probably caught up in traffic somewhere. Either that or off on the golf course," replied Pam, who didn't appear to be in any way concerned that the man who'd summoned them to a meeting was late.
"He only lives ten minutes away if that! And he made a point of saying that the meeting had to be at two as he was teeing off at three thirty," proclaimed Suzi.
"And as we all know, Ron can't be late for his bloody golf," remarked Pam sardonically. "That would never do."
Suzi got out of her chair and walked over to the window. "Some of us have stuff to do," she announced, her mood even more angry than it was before.
 "Give him a ring if you're worried," suggested Pam, calmly.
Suzi considered Pam's advice for a few seconds. "Let's give him a few more minutes," she replied, once more glancing down at her wristwatch.

Chapter 15

With DS Dalton's update completed, Carmichael turned his attention to the newest recruit to his team.
"Ok, Donna, why don't you share what you've uncovered this morning?" he said. "You can start with the activity reports on Pritchard's mobile phone."
It was now DC Twamley's turn to gaze down at her notebook. "I've spent most of my time so far looking at Doug Pritchard's recent mobile phone activity," she announced. "I've not yet had the chance to do much research into Doug Pritchard. I'll get onto that this afternoon."
"That's fine, Donna," remarked Carmichael. "Share with the team what you told me earlier."
DC Twamley smiled back in Carmichael's direction and continued. "In the last ten days he made nine outgoing calls, four of them to the same number and the others to three other numbers. As for his incoming calls, he received just one, which was seven days ago, from a number belonging to a lady who lives in Kirkwood, Leah Barnes."
After a few seconds pause, DC Twamley resumed her update. "Doug Pritchard also sent out and received text messages from Ron Mason," reported DS Twamley. "Nothing earth shattering, just confirmation of his expected arrival time, sent at lunchtime yesterday, and a

short 'fine will see you between seven and seven thirty' reply from Mason."

"No other texts?" Watson enquired.

"Just one," replied DS Twamley, "that was to someone called Ted Heslegrave. It was sent ten minutes after Pritchard received the call from Leah Barnes."

"What did it say?" DS Dalton asked.

DS Twamley looked down at the print-out on her desk. "It said *'GIVE ME A CALL TED. I'VE GOT THE SCOOP OF THE YEAR'*" replied DS Twamley.

"But there was no reply?" DS Dalton enquired; her question raised with incredulity in her voice.

DC Twamley shook her head. "Nothing by text and no incoming return call either," she said, "despite the fact that in the next twenty-four hours Doug Pritchard called him on three separate occasions and then again on Tuesday of this week."

"And does the duration of those calls suggest Ted Heslegrave answered any of them?" DS Dalton added. A question that impressed Carmichael, who'd asked the very same question earlier.

DC Twamley nodded. "The last one, received two days ago, does," she replied. "That one lasted fifteen minutes."

"Who else did Doug Pritchard talk to in the last ten days?" Watson asked.

"He spoke with three other people," DC Twamley replied. "Two calls were made to Hardcastle's B&B, the last one about two hours before he arrived yesterday."

"What about the other calls?" DS Dalton enquired.

"One call was made a week ago to Eckersall and Stanley, a dental practice in Hove," replied DC Twamley.

DS Watson grinned. "Well at least we now know where we can get the dead man's dental records for formal identification if we can't find anyone to do that for us."

"Indeed," remarked Carmichael.

"The other two calls were made to the same person," continued DC Twamley. "The first which was only ten seconds long, so mustn't have been answered, was within an hour of Leah Barnes calling him. The second was an hour later and lasted about six minutes."

"Who were those to?" Watson asked.

"They were to a guy called Liam Thomas," replied DC Twamley.

"Liam Thomas the rock star?" DS Dalton exclaimed. "My mum adores his music. I used to have to put up with that in the car when I was still at home."

DC Twamley shrugged her shoulders. "To be honest I'm not sure," she replied, her expression one of amazement. "I've never heard of Liam Thomas. My mum likes Take That!"

Chapter 16

Suzi looked at her watch for the umpteenth time: it was two forty. "I'm going to call him again," she announced, her angry comment aimed towards Pam, who was still cuddling one of her cats and remained indifferent to their ex-manager being late.
"I told you," Pam remarked calmly. "He's probably caught up in traffic somewhere."
"Still no answer!" proclaimed Suzi in frustration as Ron's mobile, once more, went into answer machine mode. "I'm going round. Are you coming?"
Pam gently put down her cat onto the floor and raised herself up from the sofa. "Ok, if we must," she sighed, somewhat indignantly.

* * * *

"So, to summarise," remarked Carmichael, a marker pen in his hand, having scribbled additional notes onto the incident room whiteboard. "In the ten days prior to his death, Doug Pritchard gets a call from this person Leah Barnes, he then sends Ted Heslegrave, who is presumably an editor, a text saying he has a major scoop, he subsequently speaks with this guy Heslegrave and also Liam Thomas…"
"An old pin-up of Rachel's mum," added Watson with a smile.

Ignoring DS Watson's comment, Carmichael set his gaze on DC Twamley. "And you said the call that got through to Ted Heslegrave happened after Pritchard had spoken with Liam Thomas," he said, his eyes fixed firmly on the young DC.

DC Twamley checked her notes, to ensure her response would be accurate. "After, definitely after" she said.

Carmichael paused for a few moments, while he absorbed what DC Twamley had just told them.

"Ok," he said as soon as he'd decided what needed to be done. "I want you, Donna, to do the background checks on Doug Pritchard as we talked about at this morning's briefing, but before you do that, track down this Ted Heslegrave. I want to know who he is and what it was that Doug Pritchard was so excited about telling him."

"Will do, sir," DC Twamley replied enthusiastically.

"As for Leah Barnes and Liam Thomas, I'd …." Carmichael was stopped mid-sentence.

"It might be a good idea if I share what I've uncovered this morning," announced DS Watson. "It may have a bearing on the Liam Thomas and Leah Barnes connection."

Carmichael, his eyes wide open and his attention now focussed on DS Watson, nodded. "Absolutely, Marc," he said, almost apologetically. "By all means share what you've got."

* * * *

Suzi Ashcroft's rather battered and rusting white van stuttered to a standstill on Ron Mason's well-kept, white-stoned, gravel drive; the exhaust letting out a small bang as it did, supplemented by a not-so-insignificant plume of toxic-smelling, dark gas.

"Well, he's not stuck in any traffic jam," Suzi announced, her I-told-you-so stare fixed on her still-unperturbed friend.

Pam remained calm and said nothing.

"His car's still here!" Suzi continued, her head nodding in the direction of Ron's gleaming maroon Jaguar some twenty metres away, parked-up in front of his opulent-looking, double-fronted, oak-beamed cart lodge. "I bet the sod's forgotten. Or, more likely, been side-tracked by some bit of skirt."

Not wishing to feed her friend's fury, Pam clambered out of the car and headed off towards Ron Mason's front door, Suzi a matter of only two or three paces behind her.

* * * *

Having scoured the substantial amount of data available online regarding Chrissy Cream, her band, her manager, and her tragic death some twenty years earlier, DS Watson felt confident that he had as much background as was possible to gather in the hours that had elapsed since their last debrief that morning. "Firstly," he remarked, in an assured almost condescending fashion, "let me give a brief summary of Chrissy Cream and her band."

Carmichael took a few steps towards DC Twamley and handed her the marker. "Can you do the honours, Donna, and make a note of Marc's key findings."

"No problem, sir" replied DC Twamley, who eagerly took the marker from her boss.

* * * *

When the doorbell had been rung three times, without any reply, Suzi decided to go around the back of the house and see if there was any sign of Ron there; leaving Pam at the front peering through the sitting room window to try and spy any sign of their ex-manager. As Suzi walked past Ron's maroon Jaguar, she suddenly spotted him lying face down behind the car in a pool of blood, a bloodstained golf club abandoned beside his lifeless body.

Chapter 17

With DS Watson hardly stopping for breath, DC Twamley did a remarkable job documenting her senior colleague's words onto the whiteboard.
"Let's just pause there for a moment, Marc," Carmichael announced. "I want to just absorb what you've said so far before we continue.
Watson nodded positively; he'd pretty much finished so a short break for the rest of the team to read through the eleven points that DC Twamley had recorded seemed a reasonable suggestion.
The room fell silent as the four officers looked up at the summary of what Watson had just shared with the team.

1. *Chrissy and Jo Cream were sisters from High Maudsey (Chrissy being 3 years older than Jo).*
2. *The Vixens were originally Jo's band, but after their original lead singer left, Chrissy joined with her best friend Suzi Ashcroft and they get another school friend, Ron Mason (also from High Maudsey) to be the band's manager.*
3. *Within a year, they'd replaced all the original band members, apart from Jo, with Pam Hutton the last to be added. The band's drummer. The band then becomes known as Chrissy Cream and the Vixens.*

4. *They have 6 top 20 hits in the next 3 years and are the first all-girl rock band to have a number 1 hit in the USA.*
5. *Shortly after each other Chrissy and Jo have a baby, Chrissy's (Tom) rumoured to be the child of another rock star, Liam Thomas, (a rumour denied by both Chrissy and Liam). Jo's child (also a boy, called Ellis) is thought to have been the son of a Premier League footballer. Tom and Ellis are now in their early twenties and were adopted by Suzi and Pam respectively when their mums died.*
6. *Chrissy and Jo were both killed twenty years ago in a tragic boating accident in the North Sea. This was just before they were due to fly out to the US for their first American tour. The skipper of the boat was also killed, so no survivors.*
7. *The band broke up after their deaths and didn't release any more records.*
8. *Ron Mason remains in control of all royalties that the band still earns and is also the sole trustee of the trust funds set up for the two boys, which is rumoured to be a significant amount of money. The boys won't get control of their inheritances until they are 25 years old.*
9. *Ron Mason is now 53, he's only managed one other major artist other than The Vixens, a singer called Ferne Cramley, who had 3 minor hits 10 years ago, but has now retired from the music business and lives with her husband and family in rural Herefordshire.*
10. *Pam and Suzi, the only 2 surviving band members live in the area still. Pam has a brother who is a farmer in one of the villages. She appears to be quite reclusive spending her time looking after Ellis and a host of cats and other animals. Suzi, who was the*

> *wild child of the band now appears to spend the majority of her time and energy fighting for a variety of causes, including saving the planet, women's rights and third world poverty. She is devoted to Tom and, like Pam, has never married.*
>
> ***11. Doug Pritchard lived in Hove and has been a music journalist for over 30 years. He specialised in uncovering salacious stories about the rich and famous in the music industry. Although he'd had a number of big stories published over the years, his credibility and methods of obtaining information are viewed with great suspicion.***

"That's quite a comprehensive job you've done," remarked Carmichael after spending a good amount of time reading through the notes. "Well done, Marc."
Watson smiled broadly. It wasn't often the boss paid him a compliment, so he was going to savour it.
Carmichael was still considering what tasks he'd assign to DS Watson for the remainder of the afternoon, when the incident room door opened, and a timid looking young officer entered.
"I'm sorry to interrupt, sir," she said apologetically, "but another body has been found in High Maudsey."
The four officers, in unison, looked over in the young officer's direction waiting to hear what she was going to tell them.
"PC Dyer and PC Richardson, who called it in," she continued, "say they think the dead man's called Ron Mason."

Chapter 18

Keen to get to the crime scene, Carmichael turned on his blues and drove at speed down the A59. The satnav indicated eight miles to go before they arrived at their destination; a journey it suggested would take twelve minutes. Carmichael didn't believe his satnav; he was sure they'd get there much quicker than that.

"If it is Ron Mason, who's been murdered," remarked Watson, his right hand holding tightly to his seat belt, his left grasping the handle above the door with equal intensity, "that throws a spanner in the works. In my mind, he had to be our main suspect for Pritchard's death."

Carmichael nodded. "He was certainly right up there," he conceded, "but let's not get ahead of ourselves. Just because PC Dyer and PC Richardson say it's him, it doesn't mean it is. We need to keep an open mind."

Watson nodded. "I guess you're right," he acknowledged. "Come to think of it, we're not certain our first body is Doug Pritchard. That's still got to be verified."

"Exactly," exclaimed Carmichael, as he swung the car left off the A59 and headed down Jay Bank Lane. "We may well have to check his dental records, as you suggested."

DS Watson nodded gently but didn't continue the conversation, knowing that if he did, he may well get that as an additional assignment.
Less than five minutes later Carmichael's black BMW sped past the spot where, the evening before, the body of the man they assumed was Doug Pritchard had been found. "Glad to see they're still out there looking for the murder weapon," Carmichael remarked as they shot past a group of white-clad members of Stock's team who were conscientiously scouring the hedgerows and fields to either side of the murder scene.
Watson smiled. "He may be a total pain in the backside at times," he said, "but Stock's team are very efficient." Carmichael looked across at his colleague, smiled and nodded gently before turning his attention back to the road ahead. "He's the best SOCO I've ever worked with," he replied. "But don't ever tell him I said so, as he's also the most insufferable person I've ever met, too. He needs no positive reinforcement about his capabilities from us."
Watson sniggered. "I'll not argue with that," he concurred.

* * * *

"Are you ok with the assignments the boss has given you, Donna?" DS Dalton asked, knowing DC Twamley's list of things to do was going to keep her very busy.
"I think so," DC Twamley confirmed, her response suggesting she was a little overwhelmed. "It's knowing what to focus on first."
DS Dalton smiled. "I'd talk with Ted Heslegrave first and then speak to Liam Thomas," she suggested. "After that try to locate Leah Barnes. I'm sure if you can

achieve all that before Carmichael gets back, he'll be …"

DS Dalton was about to say happy, but then corrected herself.

"… reasonably satisfied."

Glad of the steer, DC Twamley's apprehensive expression dissolved, as if a weight had been marginally lifted off her shoulders. "Will do," she replied cheerily.

"And I'd better get off and try to get those statements the boss wants," continued DS Dalton, who grabbed her jacket and headed for the door.

"See you," remarked DC Twamley from behind her computer screen. "Good luck."

DS Dalton smiled as she exited the incident room. It was only a few years since she was the rookie on the team, so she was all too aware of how Donna Twamley was feeling.

*　　*　　*　　*

When Carmichael's car pulled up on Ron Mason's gravel drive, there were already three SOCOs on the scene, including Stock and his nephew, Matthew. Before they clambered out of the car, Carmichael looked across at Watson "Are Rachel and him still a couple?" he asked.

Watson nodded positively. "Yes, it's still very much on, as far as I'm aware," he responded. "They've not moved in together, yet, but that's only a matter of time, as far as I can make out."

Carmichael nodded and without saying anything more, climbed out of the car and walked swiftly towards PC Dyer who, having spotted Carmichael's distinctive BMW as it arrived, had already made his way over.

"What have we got, constable?" Carmichael enquired as the two men met.

"The dead man is Ron Mason, who lives here," replied PC Dyer. "He's been positively identified by those two ladies over there."

As he spoke, PC Dyer half turned and gestured towards a small brick wall which edged part of the driveway.

"And they are?" Carmichael responded.

"Pam Hutton and Suzi Ashcroft," DC Dyer confirmed.

"Ah, the Foxes," remarked Carmichael, turning to face Watson, his eyes widening as he spoke.

"Vixens, sir," corrected Watson in a hushed, half-embarrassed tone.

"Isn't that what I said?" retorted Carmichael gruffly. "You start taking their statements, Marc, I want to talk with Stock and take a look at our victim. I'll join you shortly."

Without waiting for a response, Carmichael marched purposefully across the gravel to where Ron Mason's body lay.

Chapter 19

DC Twamley's surprise and delight was etched across her face when she got through to Ted Heslegrave within minutes of DS Dalton leaving the incident room.
"Good afternoon, Mr Heslegrave, my name's DC Twamley and I'm calling from Mid Lancashire Police," she announced.
 "Oh yes," replied Ted Heslegrave. "And to what do I owe this pleasure?"
"I'd like to talk to you about your relationship with Doug Pritchard," responded DC Twamley.
"I know him," Heslegrave confirmed, "but there's no relationship. I've printed some of his stuff over the years, but not for ages. Why, what has he done?"
DC Twamley was a little surprised that Heslegrave had to ask the question. She'd assumed a newspaper editor would have known that a man believed to be Doug Pritchard was dead. True, it had only happened the evening before, but it had already been reported online by Norfolk George, the local newspaper proprietor, so she'd expected he'd have at least picked up the story of a well-known reporter being murdered in Lancashire, by now.
"Have you not heard?" she continued. "A body was found last night in one of our villages. We're treating the

death as suspicious and although we have yet to formally identify the individual, we are reasonably certain that the deceased is Doug Pritchard."

There was a brief pause from the other end of the line before Ted Heslegrave spoke again.

"Well, I'll be blown," he remarked, his words delivered slowly and in a tone that suggested he was, indeed, shocked to hear this news.

* * * *

When Carmichael reached the body, Matthew Stock was crouching down taking a photograph of the back of Ron Mason's head, his portly uncle standing just behind him with his gloved hands firmly on his white-suited hips.

"Is that your Toby Jug impression?" quipped Carmichael; a comment that was met with surly silence from Dr Stock, although Carmichael was fairly sure he heard a snigger from the young man behind the camera.

"Similar modus," confirmed Stock senior. "Severe blow to the head, but this time just one blow. As far as I can ascertain and without jumping the gun, I'd say we've got a better idea of the murder weapon this time."

As he finished his sentence, Stock turned and pointed down at the golf club a few metres away from Ron Mason's body; a wooden driver with clear signs of blood on the club's head.

"Any indication of the time of death?" Carmichael enquired.

"Not precisely at the moment," replied Stock. "However, certainly within the last few hours."

Carmichael nodded slowly before moving away from the body and walking towards where Watson and the Vixens were located.

* * * *

Pleased with how the call had gone with Ted Heslegrave, DC Twamley leaned back in her chair and, with her hands clasped behind her head, allowed herself a self-satisfied smile.
"Now for Liam Thomas," she muttered before dialling the number she'd extracted from Doug Pritchard's mobile.

* * * *

"This is Inspector Carmichael," Watson announced as his boss arrived at where they were sitting. "This is Pam Hutton and Suzi Ashcroft. They found Mr Mason."
"Good afternoon, ladies," said Carmichael with a faint nod of his head. "I'll be in charge of this investigation."
When neither of the two ladies responded, Carmichael continued. "I realise this must be a very harrowing experience for you both, but can you tell me exactly what you saw when you arrived here today."
Clearly shocked by what they'd stumbled across, the two women exchanged a quick glance before Pam Hutton spoke. "We arrived together at about three o'clock," she began, "and we just found him here like that."
As soon as she finished speaking, Pam raised her hand and put it over her mouth.
"You arrived together?" Carmichael enquired.
Pam and Suzi both nodded in unison.
"We drove over from Pam's house in my van," responded Suzi, pointing as she spoke to her rusting van on the drive.
"And did you see anyone else when you arrived or as you approached?" Carmichael asked.

The two women exchanged another look before shaking their heads.

"Nobody," replied Suzi.

"And why did you come over to see Mr Mason?" Carmichael enquired.

"He'd asked to meet us both at Pam's house," continued Suzi. "At two. But he never showed up, so we came over here to find out what was going on."

"And what did he want to meet with you for?" Carmichael asked.

"No idea," replied Suzi. "But it seemed important to him."

Carmichael thought for a few seconds before continuing. "Did he mention the name Doug Pritchard?" he enquired.

At the mention of Doug Pritchard, Suzi rolled her eyes. "That creep," she announced. "Do you reckon he's got something to do with this?"

"You know him, then?" Carmichael remarked.

"Haven't seen or spoke to him in donkeys' years," replied Suzi, "but we know him alright. The finest example of the gutter press you could ever come across. Well at least he was, back in the day."

Carmichael nodded gently before turning his gaze upon Pam Hutton. "And what about you?" he asked.

Looking a little flustered, Pam shook her head vigorously.

"Ron never mentioned Pritchard to me either," she remarked, "and it's probably over twenty years since I last saw or spoke with him."

Carmichael smiled. "You've been very helpful," he remarked. "I'll leave you with DS Watson, who'll need you to make statements. I'm sorry about your friend."

Carmichael had only taken a few steps away from the Vixens when he stopped in his tracks and turned to face them again.

"Does the name Leah Barnes mean anything to either of you?" he enquired.

A look of shock came over the two women who glanced once more at each other before staring back at Carmichael.

"What do you want with Leah?" Suzi asked, her tone clearly indicating that she knew her.

"It's just a name that's come up that I wanted to bounce off you," he replied as vaguely as he could.

"What do you mean come up?" asked Suzi firmly. "You've only just arrived here, and we found Ron's body less than an hour ago. How can my little sister's name have already come up?"

It was now Carmichael and Watson's turn to exchange a glance of surprise.

"Sister," repeated Watson. "Leah Barnes is your sister?"

"Yes," replied Suzi. "I've twin younger sisters, Leah and Coral."

"Coral," announced Carmichael with even greater surprise in his voice. "That wouldn't be Coral Freeman by any chance, would it?"

Looking totally bemused and concerned by what she was hearing, Suzi gently nodded her head.

"How come you know Coral?" she asked.

Chapter 20

Having managed to speak with Joan McNamara, who was on table one when Pritchard and Mason had their argument, and with Sophie Cantwell, who was on table five with her husband, DS Dalton didn't feel she'd learned anything new about Pritchard and Mason's altercation in The Three Bells.

On a positive note, though, they'd both confirmed two things. Firstly, that it was Ron Mason who had been doing all the shouting and, more importantly in DS Dalton's eyes, that Mason had left the pub no more than five minutes after Pritchard. This meant that her suspicions were justified. Wade Freeman had lied to Carmichael about him having remained in the pub all evening; something DS Dalton was eager to follow up as soon as possible.

With voice messages to call her left on the respective mobiles of Ellie Johnson, the only person she hadn't spoken to from table five, and with Michael and Sue Quigley from table nine, DS Dalton decided to get herself over to see Miles Goodwyn, to conduct the 'more vigorous' interview that Carmichael had insisted upon.

When they were talking at the murder scene the evening before, Miles had told her that he worked in the warehouse at Coopers Hardware store in Kirkwood, so with the time still only four fifteen, DS Dalton figured she'd be able to catch up with him before his shift ended.

*　　*　　*　　*

As soon as he heard that Leah Barnes and Coral Freeman were Suzi Ashcroft's sisters, Carmichael decided he needed to join DS Watson in grilling the Vixens, which had suddenly taken priority over going back to talk with Stock. Having relocated themselves to a rather luxurious summer house in Ron Mason's back garden, Carmichael began the conversation.
"You asked a couple of very reasonable questions earlier," he said, his remark aimed at Suzi. "So, before we continue the discussion, let me tell you what I can."
The two Vixens remained silent, waiting to hear what information Inspector Carmichael was going to share with them.
"Following your discovery of Mr Mason's body," began Carmichael, his eyes transfixed on the two Vixens, "my officers are now investigating two suspicious deaths in High Maudsey."
If Suzi Ashcroft or Pam Hutton were aware of Doug Pritchard's murder, they hid it well.
"Who's the other one?" Pam asked, her voice trembling as she spoke.
"We've yet to formally identify the man's body," replied Carmichael, "but it's someone who we know had a heated argument with Ron Mason last night in The Three Bells."
"The Three Bells," exclaimed Suzi. "That's my sister's pub. Is Coral aware of this?"

Carmichael nodded. "Your sister has been helping us," he replied. "Did she not mention the incident to you?"
"I've not spoken or messaged her for days," replied Suzi, "so, no she hasn't."
Carmichael nodded and smiled. "It's just a procedural matter," he continued, "but I need you both to tell me where you were yesterday evening, between the hours of nine and ten."
Suzi and Pam exchanged a startled gaze before they answered.
"I was at home," responded Suzi, her tone mildly indignant at being asked.
"Me too," added Pam.
"Were you both alone last night, and can anyone vouch for you?" Watson added.
"My son was at home with me," announced Pam.
"Mine was too, until about nine," added Suzi. "He went out about then with some friends, which is about the time I went to bed."
"You're not a night owl then," Carmichael alluded.
Suzi shook her head. "Those days are long gone, Inspector. An early night with a good book is about as exciting as it gets for me nowadays."
Carmichael paused for a few seconds before continuing his questioning.
"I understand that you were both members of Chrissy Cream's group," he remarked. "That must have been an exciting time for you all."
"It was a mad three or four years," replied Suzi, with little sign of any desire to expand much more. "But it was a long time ago and we're not involved in the industry anymore."
Carmichael smiled and nodded. "But I guess you're still getting royalties from those hits as they must still be played frequently on radio and TV?"

Suzi shook her head. "We get an income," she admitted, "but it's peanuts. We didn't write any of the songs, that was mainly Chrissy, although Jo co-wrote a few."

"But with them now dead," interjected Watson, "where do the royalties go?"

Suzi and Pam exchanged another look, this time one of clear irritation.

"It goes mainly into trust funds that Chrissy and Jo set up for their boys," Pam confirmed. "Although a fair bit goes to Ron."

"Or it did," added Suzi.

"As always, Ron made sure he'd be alright if anything happened to Chrissy or Jo," continued Pam. "We just get a small income, which Ron was forever at pains to tell us was a gift from him rather than a legal entitlement."

"But the bulk goes into a trust fund for Chrissy and Jo's sons?" Carmichael confirmed.

Suzi and Pam nodded.

"And when are they eligible to gain access to the funds?" Carmichael enquired.

"When they are twenty-five," replied Suzi. "So, in a couple of years, as they're now twenty-three and twenty-two."

As she spoke, Suzi again looked over at Pam, who nodded in agreement.

"And I understand that you each adopted one of the boys after Chrissy and Jo died," Carmichael continued.

"Yes, Tom's my son," confirmed Suzi.

"And Ellis is mine," added Pam.

Once again Carmichael took a few seconds before looking directly at Suzi and continuing his questioning.

"You mentioned that you hadn't communicated with your sister, Coral, recently," he remarked. "But what about Leah?"

"I saw Leah on Sunday afternoon," announced Suzi. "But I haven't spoken to her since.

Carmichael nodded. "So, your sister lives locally?" he enquired.

Pam put her hand uneasily to her mouth and gazed away from the two officers, which gave Carmichael the instant impression that all wasn't well.

"Leah's quite poorly," Suzi said, quietly. "She's in St Jude's, a nursing home in Douglas Bridge, a small hamlet between Kirkwood and Southport."

"I've driven through Douglas Bridge," Carmichael confirmed with another nod of his head.

"Cancer," continued Suzi. "It's quite advanced now I'm afraid, so we're anticipating the worst any day now."

"I'm very sorry to hear that," Carmichael said, with genuine sympathy, before standing up and forcing a smile. "I'll leave you with Sergeant Watson, who'll need to take formal statements from you both."

Neither Pam Hutton nor Suzi Ashcroft said anything as Carmichael turned and took a few steps towards where Ron Mason's body lay.

"Oh, by the way," Carmichael said, having stopped abruptly and half turned to face the two ladies, "who are the trust fund executors?"

Suzi looked over in Carmichael's direction. "Well, until he was murdered, it was Ron," she responded. "But I've no idea who it will be now."

"There must have been a solicitor involved, too," remarked Watson. "Any idea who that would have been?"

"It will be Attwoods in Kirkwood announced Pam. "Chrissy and Ron always used them for legal stuff. Angus Frazer was the person they used to deal with. Well, it was twenty years ago. I guess he might have retired by now."

Carmichael smiled. "No, he hasn't," he replied. "I've had dealings with Mr Frazer quite recently."

Chapter 21

As DS Dalton had expected, Miles Goodwyn was still in the warehouse at Coopers Hardware store when she arrived.
Red-faced and clearly embarrassed by the sudden appearance of DS Dalton and the interest the police officer seemed to have generated with his colleagues, Miles quickly marshalled his visitor into the far corner of the large dusty stockroom, where he hoped they'd not be overheard. "Why do you need to talk to me again?" he enquired, his voice muted but showing undoubted signs of frustration. "I've told you everything I know."
DS Dalton smiled to try and reassure him.
"Just a few additional questions," she replied casually. "It won't take long."
This didn't do much to alter Miles's troubled demeanour; despite realising there was no way he could avoid further scrutiny from DS Dalton.
"I'd like to ask you a little bit more about the argument at the pub last night," DS Dalton began. "You say you couldn't remember what was said exactly, but surely you must have heard something."
"I wasn't paying much attention," replied Miles. "I was at the bar."

DS Dalton glanced down at her notebook. "That's right, with the barmaid, Verity," she remarked, repeating something Miles had mentioned the night before.

"Yes, Verity and Mrs Freeman," confirmed Miles. "But Verity's not a barmaid, she just helps with the food on some days."

"I see," responded DS Dalton.

"They were both busy, Mrs Freeman and Verity," continued Miles, "taking out food, and Verity was also tidying tables. But when they weren't too busy, we'd chat."

"So, when the argument broke out, the three of you were at the bar chatting?" DS Dalton asked.

"As I recall, yes," replied Miles vaguely. "The pub was heaving, and they were on their feet quite a lot, but I think we were all together when the argument happened. Anyway, I didn't hear anything."

DS Dalton's facial expression and slight shake of her head suggested she wasn't convinced. A message that came across loud and clear to Miles.

"You may want to talk with Mrs Freeman or Verity. They may have heard something," Miles remarked in a hushed tone. "But I didn't."

DS Dalton didn't think she'd get much more about what Miles heard, so decided to move her questioning to another subject. "You were very helpful in identifying the time when you last saw the dead man in the pub," she continued, "you said he stormed out at about nine twenty-five. But what about the other man?" Again, DS Dalton referred to her notes. "The oldish man in his fifties or sixties, thin, smartly dressed, wearing a tie and with a small, greyish beard," she regurgitated from Miles's description during their discussion on the previous evening. "When did he leave?"

Miles shrugged his shoulders. "I didn't see him leave. To be honest, he may have still been in the pub when I left, I don't know."

"But surely, you'd have been interested in what happened with him after such a huge row?" DS Dalton suggested, her tone much more assertive.

"No," replied Miles. "I was chatting with Verity. I'd no interest in him."

"If you know something more, you can tell me," DS Dalton remarked, frustratedly. "You're not in any trouble."

Miles shrugged his shoulders again. "There's nothing more to tell," he replied.

DS Dalton couldn't help feeling that Miles was withholding something from her but didn't know what or why he would feel he needed to do that. However, she was fairly certain he wasn't going to tell her much more.

"Ok, if you say so," DS Dalton said, indicating that she was going to move on, "tell me about Verity. Is she your girlfriend?"

The question clearly unsettled Miles, whose expression looked a mixture of shock and embarrassment.

"No, we're just friends," he replied, his eyeline suddenly dropping down to the floor. "She's got a boyfriend."

DS Dalton, realising she may have hit a bit of a nerve, pushed ahead with her questions. "But I sense you'd like her to be more than just a pal," she remarked in a friendly tone and with a faint smile.

"It's not a crime to fancy a girl," he replied, his voice still muted to avoid being overheard.

"Absolutely not," replied DS Dalton. "But not ideal when the person you're fond of is already taken."

Miles's eyeline rose to meet DS Dalton's.

"Maybe she is at the moment," he remarked firmly, "but there's no reason why that can't change."

"Absolutely," remarked DS Dalton for a second time. "Tell me, who is your rival?"

Miles pulled a face that indicated his feelings towards the person in question.

"He's called Ellis Hutton," Miles spat out. "Although he's adopted. He's the son of one of those pop singer sisters that died twenty-odd years ago."

"The Creams?" DS Dalton enquired.

"Yes, they're the ones," replied Miles, "and Verity says he's going to get access to a big chunk of cash in a few years off the back of his birth mother's royalties."

DS Dalton shrugged her shoulders.

"In that case, for your sake, I only hope Verity's affections aren't swayed by the trappings of wealth," she remarked.

Chapter 22

It took Watson less than thirty minutes to take statements from Pam Hutton and Suzi Ashcroft, neither of whom added anything new to what they'd mentioned already. Carmichael used that time to try and get a status report from Stock, but as often was the case, Mid Lancashire's Head of Forensic Services was very reluctant to make any further comments about his findings. "Not until I do a full post-mortem, and we get the exhibits back to the lab," he commented firmly when pushed by Carmichael to share any thoughts he may have on the murder scene.

However, Carmichael didn't draw a complete blank with the forensics team as Matthew Stock, who was infinitely more amenable than his uncle, informed Carmichael that he'd found a text message sent on Ron Mason's mobile at one forty, to someone called Charles Gray.

Carmichael read the message.

Hi Charlie – Just to let you know that Thomas will be coming round with a note from me confirming that he can draw out £2000 from his trust fund. Can you give him the cash, please?
Cheers Ron

Carmichael nodded gently as he read the note. "I assume this guy, Charles Gray, is a bank manager," he observed. "That's what I think," replied Matthew, "but I've only just seen it myself and haven't had time to check the number".

"No need," announced Carmichael. "I'll get one of my officers to check that out."

"Ok," replied Matthew. "Do you want me to send the details over to Rachel?"

Carmichael thought for a moment before nodding his head.

"Yes," he remarked. "Send it to Rachel."

"No problem," replied Matthew, before walking away, his own mobile already in his hand.

Carmichael turned on his heels and quickly made his way to the car to call DS Dalton and DC Twamley, while he waited for Watson to conclude his discussions with the Vixens.

* * * *

"Nothing earth shattering in their statements," Watson despondently confirmed as he clambered into Carmichael's car. "Anything more forthcoming from Stock?"

Carmichael didn't reply, his attention focused on Suzi Ashcroft's dirty, beaten-up, white van as it made its exit from Ron Mason's driveway, its exhaust spluttering as it disappeared from view.

"I bet that's totally unroadworthy," Carmichael remarked with a wry smile. "What did you make of them, Marc?"

Watson smiled. "A bit like the van," he replied, "I think both have seen better days."

Watson's comment made Carmichael laugh out loud. "I mean as suspects?"

"No chance," replied Watson without hesitation. "There's no way either of them did it. They're far too…" He paused as he tried to find the appropriate adjective.

"Compassionate?" offered Carmichael.

"No," replied Watson. "I think timid is the word I was looking for."

Carmichael smiled but at the same time shook his head slightly. "Never judge a book, Marc," he remarked, before starting his engine. "And to answer your question," Carmichael continued, "we do have something new from our forensic team. There's a text on Ron Mason's mobile to someone called Charles Gray. It's sanctioning a payment of two thousand pounds to Thomas from his trust fund. It was sent at one forty, so just before Ron Mason was killed."

"Really," exclaimed Watson, with genuine interest.

Carmichael nodded. "I've just spoken with Rachel, and she's going to try and get hold of Charles Gray."

Watson nodded his approval. "I've also just put the phone down to Donna," Carmichael continued as his car glided out of the driveway and onto the narrow road. "I told her to take a uniformed officer with her and pay a visit to Thomas Ashcroft and bring him into the station. I want to talk with him to find out what time he was at Mason's house as he's possibly the last person to see him before he died."

"Or maybe he's his killer," added Watson.

"Possibly," remarked Carmichael, "but if Mason agreed to let him take some money out of the trust fund, I'm not sure why he'd kill him. That doesn't sound logical at all."

Watson shrugged his shoulders but didn't say anything more.

"I also told them to be back at the station for seven thirty," Carmichael continued, "for a final debrief today."

"And what are you planning for us to do in the next couple of hours?" Watson enquired.

"It's a trip over to see Leah Barnes for me and you," replied Carmichael. "From the timings of the calls and texts to Doug Pritchard, I think her discussion with our first victim may prove to be central in all this. I want to know what that call was about."

Chapter 23

Suzi Ashcroft arrived back home at five forty, having dropped off Pam Hutton some ten minutes earlier. Exhausted and still totally confused by what she and her fellow Vixen had witnessed at Ron's house, Suzi's first thought was to make herself a strong cup of coffee, and, for one of only a handful of occasions since she'd given up the booze, over a decade before, the idea of a couple of vodka shots had fleetingly entered her head. Although it seemed an attractive notion, for a split second, she dismissed the thought almost immediately.
It was then she saw his van, a huge gleaming white monstrosity with a roof rack laden with lengths of cylindrical poles of all sorts of sizes and the words, **Wood & Son Award Winning Roofers** emblazoned on the side. Suzi had always loathed Spencer. Even when he was a small boy in Tom and Ellis's class, she disliked the snotty-nosed kid who, even back then, always appeared to be up to no good.
As her van came to rest, Suzi could see Tom and Spencer in deep conversation and, although she couldn't be one hundred percent certain, she was pretty sure she saw her boy hand over an envelope to Spencer. A wrinkled buff envelope, which Spencer swiftly crammed into his jacket pocket.

Suzi was sure her son didn't do drugs, but in that instant, whether it was based upon her experiences in the music business where drugs were so commonplace or just a primal fear that all mothers have, Suzi's first thought was that she'd stumbled upon a payment for illicit substances of some form or other.

Her fears were only heightened when the boys, as she still called them, realised that she had arrived home. The guilty look on Tom's face and the speed at which Spencer turned his back on her as she clambered out of the car only served to enhance her already heightened levels of anxiety.

"Hi, Mum," Tom shouted over, his smile wide but forced and in no way masking the nervousness which shone from his eyes.

Suzi's immediate urge was to confront them, there and then, about what they were doing, but she knew she shouldn't. Tom wasn't a child anymore and if her suspicions were wrong, she knew she'd regret it. Anyway, there was no way they were ever going to admit to anything shady going on between them, even if they were up to no good.

"Hi, boys," was all she said, as casually as she could, as she brushed passed them and walked briskly down the hallway.

"I'll be off then," muttered Spencer, before turning on his heels and dashing over to his van, leaving Tom to close the door and walk down the hallway after his mum.

* * * *

Douglas Bridge, was a small village between Kirkwood and Southport, consisting of no more than a couple of dozen ancient-looking sandstone houses, a general store, a car bodywork repair shop, a tiny village primary school and St Jude's nursing home; an impressive double-fronted building surrounded by beautifully maintained gardens.

"I bet it costs a pretty penny to live here," DS Watson announced as Carmichael's car came to rest in a free parking space right outside the imposing front door.

Carmichael nodded. He remembered all too well the cost of his own father's care, some fifteen years earlier, when he'd been moved to an end-of-life home. Costs that within under a year, had totally wiped-out the old man's savings and in the end, had to be subsidised by Carmichael and the rest of the family. It had been about six hundred pounds a week back then, and his father's care home was quite modest, so God only knew how much it would cost to stay at St Jude's.

"No doubt about that," Carmichael concurred, as the two officers simultaneously opened their doors and clambered out of the car.

* * * *

"What was he doing here?" enquired Suzi brusquely as soon as Tom joined her in the kitchen.

"Spencer?" replied her son, as if there was the possibility Suzi was talking about someone else.

"Of course, I mean Spencer," Suzi snapped back. "I hope you're not hanging around with him again. He's nothing but trouble, Tom. And he's the sort of lad that will drag you into things, too."

Tom smiled and gently shook his head. "He's not that bad, Mum," he replied. "He's grown up a lot since he's taken over his dad's business, and he's now a dad himself."

"Leopard and spots, that's all I'm saying, Tom," Suzi replied.

Tom took a few paces forward and grabbed hold of his mother by the shoulders, pulling her close. "Just chill, Mum," he said gently before kissing her on the forehead. "I'm not hanging around with Spencer, he just came over to discuss something with me. It's all cool, I'm not going to get involved in anything you need to worry about."

Although she wasn't completely convinced that he was telling her the whole story, Suzi couldn't find the energy to press him any further. Tom had always been able to melt her heart, no matter what the circumstances were. It had been an awful day so far, and the last thing she wanted was to argue with the boy she adored more than anything in the world.

As he held her tightly, Tom could see she was crying. His mum almost never cried, so this worried Tom. "Are you that worried about Spencer leading me astray?" he enquired, his tone suggesting it was the stupidest thing he'd heard in ages.

Suzi gazed up into his eyes, hers moist and already turning red. "No, silly," she replied, "it's Ron. Something terrible has happened."

Chapter 24

To Carmichael's surprise, Leah Barnes was sitting up when he and Watson entered her room. However, as he approached, it was clear that without the two enormous pillows supporting her, she'd almost certainly be flat out on her back.

She forced the tiniest of smiles and nodded as they approached. "I understand you want to talk to me," she said in a faint voice, her lips hardly moving.

"We won't keep you long," replied Carmichael as he reached her side. "We'd just like to ask you a few questions."

As Leah Barnes nodded, Carmichael couldn't help staring at the tiny frail-looking figure in front of him. However, his visual examination and the look of surprise on his face was not due to Leah's pale yellowish skin which clung tightly to her diminutive head, nor the pair of tubes protruding from her nostrils emitting a regular sucking noise as the air was forced into her nose from the large air cylinder by her bed. It was the extent of Leah's tattoos that took Carmichael by surprise.

Carmichael wasn't a fan of tattoos, especially when they'd been applied on the owner's hands, neck, or head. He'd come across hundreds of people in the course of his work who clearly didn't share his view, so the sight of someone with multiple tattoos wasn't uncommon to him. However, he'd rarely come across a woman of Leah's age, which he'd estimated at around forty-five, with as much art as she had adorning her arms, neck and face.

"Do you want me to stay?" enquired Mrs Wright, the proprietor of St Jude's, who'd escorted Carmichael and Watson from reception.

Leah glanced across and nodded. Even in her condition she'd noticed the look of shock on Carmichael's face; a look she'd seen from other people and, as with them, she instantly took a dislike to Carmichael. "If that's ok with you," she replied, a signal for Mrs Wright to take a gentle hold of Leah's hand and sit herself down on the chair next to the bed. "Is it them tubes or my tats that are bothering you?" Leah then asked, her small dark eyes fixed on Carmichael.

"No," replied Carmichael, with a forced smile, his spur-of-the-moment attempt to reassure the fragile-looking woman in the bed. "There's nothing bothering me."

"Then fire away," continued Leah in her croaky voice, her eyes still focused on Carmichael's face, and her face showing no desire whatsoever to return his smile.

"I'd like to talk with you about your relationship with Doug Pritchard," began Carmichael. "Have you known him long?"

Leah didn't answer immediately. Her air unit sucked and blew for three or four times before she responded.

"I've known of him for over twenty years," she replied. "But there's no relationship as such and I only know him through Ron."

"So, when did you last talk with Mr Pritchard?" continued Carmichael.

Again, Leah took her time to respond. "Why are you so keen to know?" she enquired.

"We're investigating his sudden death," replied Carmichael, "and your name's come up as someone who spoke with him in the days leading up to his death."

"Dead," exclaimed Leah, who was clearly taken aback by the news. "When did he die?"

Under normal circumstances, Carmichael would have refused to answer a question like that, coming from 'a person of interest'. However, this wasn't normal. Doug Pritchard had been bludgeoned to death, and with her looking like she was so close to the end herself, Carmichael decided he'd answer Leah's question more fully.

"He died near High Maudsey, yesterday evening," replied Carmichael.

"And I assume he was murdered," suggested Leah, "otherwise it would just be uniformed officers at my bedside."

Carmichael forced a smile and nodded. "We are treating his death as suspicious," he confirmed. "So, anything you can tell us would be very helpful."

Leah sighed deeply and looked anxiously over at Mrs Wright before turning her gaze once more upon Carmichael. "My suggestion is that you talk with Ron," she remarked, her voice now sounding very weak and tired. "He'll be at the bottom of this."

"Ron Mason," Watson said, to verify exactly who Leah meant.

"Yes," replied Leah, "Ron Mason."

"And why do you say that?" enquired Carmichael.

Leah sighed again, this time even more acutely. "Because he's at the centre of everything," she responded curtly. "I was his PA for over twenty years, so I know just about everything there is to know about

Ron Mason. And although he's not all bad, he's always been the puppet master around here, so when anything happens you can be sure he'll have something to do with it."

Carmichael looked across at Watson before continuing. "Like what?" he enquired.

Leah's oxygen machine pumped away as she considered what to say next. "I probably shouldn't say anything else as Ron can be pretty cruel if he thinks you're being disloyal," she added.

Carmichael decided to bring the discussion back to Doug Pritchard. "We know you had a telephone call with Doug Pritchard on Saturday," he said. "What was that all about?"

Again, Leah paused, then glanced over at Mrs Wright. "I'm feeling rather tired," she remarked, slowly shutting her eyes as if to emphasise her point. "Can we maybe resume our discussion another day."

Again, Carmichael looked across at Watson.

"Ron Mason is also dead, Leah," Carmichael announced. "He was found dead at his home earlier today."

Leah's eyes shot open, and a look of horror appeared on her face.

"So, if you could tell us the details of your call with Doug Pritchard, that would be much appreciated," remarked Carmichael.

Leah again closed her eyes, but this time tight shut. "I'm feeling really worn-out," she replied. "So, send someone back here tomorrow, Inspector. Maybe someone who's not revolted by my tats, and I'll tell them about that call then."

Carmichael was desperate to find out why Leah had called Doug Pritchard but had no desire to put any undue pressure on a person who was clearly very poorly, particularly with Mrs Wright sat at her side. So, reluctantly, he concluded that he'd no choice other than to leave.

Carmichael made a motion with his head, indicating to Watson that it was time to depart. "I'll organise for one of my team to come back in the morning," he said as compassionately as he could.

Mrs Wright stood up as if to walk them off the premises. "It's fine," Carmichael remarked, holding up his left hand, "we'll be able to find our own way out."

Mrs Wright smiled and sat down again.

* * * *

As soon as the sound of Carmichael and Watson's footsteps could no longer be heard down the corridor, Leah's eyes opened wide. "Can you ask my sister to come and see me urgently?" she asked Mrs Wright.

"Of course," replied Mrs Wright with a kindly smile. "Which sister do you mean?"

* * * *

Once the pair were back in the reception area, Carmichael suddenly stopped walking and looked across at Watson. "I wonder why Leah wasn't keen to talk with us," he remarked.

Watson shrugged his shoulders. "She certainly seemed to take an instant dislike to you, sir," he replied.

Carmichael nodded. "She did, didn't she," he said, before forcing another smile. "I guess even I can't be popular with everyone."

Watson said nothing.

Before leaving St Jude's, Carmichael checked the names in the visitors' register. He discovered that, as she'd told them earlier in the day, Suzi had visited Leah on Sunday, arriving at one twenty-five and leaving at four forty. Carmichael also established that the only other visitors Leah had had in the last seven days were Coral, who'd last dropped in to see her on Friday afternoon; a visit of just over two hours from two twenty-five to four thirty-three, and Ron Mason, who'd arrived at four thirty and left at four forty-five on the same day.

"Interesting," remarked Carmichael, ostensibly to himself, as he made a careful note of the dates and times in his pocketbook.

Chapter 25

As instructed, DC Twamley, accompanied by two uniformed officers, collected Tom Ashcroft and brought him to Kirkwood station.
Despite the strong protestation by Suzi, Tom didn't seem overly anxious and came freely and without any fuss. "No, I don't need a solicitor," he assured his mum as he was led to the police car. "I've done nothing wrong so don't get yourself all stressed out about it."
But Suzi was very worried. She knew her son couldn't hurt a fly. However, he'd never liked Ron and although she was sure he'd never inflict any physical harm on the band's old manager, she couldn't say the same thing about Spencer Wood, the boy she'd seen her son acting furtively with only an hour or so earlier.

* * * *

When DS Dalton arrived at the bank, she was greeted by Charles Gray, a short man in his early sixties, with a jolly, round face, eyes as big as saucers and an engaging smile.
That grin however, evaporated completely when she broke the news of Ron Mason's death, something he assured her he hadn't known about until she'd told him.

From that point on, Charles Gray's demeanour remained sombre, almost crestfallen, as if Ron Mason had been a family member rather than one of the bank's clients. Despite his solemnity, Mr Gray was fully cooperative and after spending over thirty minutes in conversation with the bank manager, DC Dalton stepped back out into the evening sunshine feeling very pleased with herself. She had a considerable amount of information to share with Carmichael and the others at seven thirty; something that was always a plus at one of Carmichael's debriefs.

* * * *

By the time Carmichael and Watson arrived back at Kirkwood police station, Tom Ashcroft was sitting calmly alone in interview room one, coffee mug in front of him.
With DS Dalton not yet back and there still being forty minutes until the time allotted for their evening debrief, Carmichael decided to talk to Tom straight away.
"Many thanks for coming in to talk to us, Thomas," Carmichael began, the us referring to him and DC Twamley, who was sat to his right, ready to take notes.
"I hate Thomas so please call me Tom," the young man sat opposite Carmichael responded with a warm, friendly smile, which he appeared to direct mainly towards the officer sat to Carmichael's right rather than the man who was about to ask the questions. "Only Ron and Suzi, when she's mad, call me Thomas," he continued, his eyes still fixed upon DC Twamley.
Carmichael smiled. "Thank you, Tom," he said. "I'll do that."
Sat upright and with his arms folded in front of him, Tom now turned his gaze towards Carmichael.

"What can I help you with?" he asked, as if the death of Ron Mason meant little to him.

"Well, Tom," continued Carmichael, "we understand that you may have been one of the last people to see Ron Mason alive, so we'd like to find out more about your meeting with him earlier today."

"Of course," replied Tom, who suddenly moved his chair, so his whole body lined up with and focussed directly upon Carmichael; presumably, Carmichael thought, to give the impression he was taking the situation seriously. "What would you like to know?"

"Why did you go round to see Ron Mason today?" Carmichael asked.

"He manages a trust fund that my birth mother set up for me," Tom replied. "I needed some money, so I went to see if he'd allow me to withdraw from it."

"Your birth mother being Chrissy Cream?" interjected Carmichael.

Tom nodded gently. "Yes," he replied, "Chrissy Cream."

"And how much were you asking for?" Carmichael enquired, although he knew full well it was two thousand pounds based on the text message he'd seen earlier.

"Two grand," confirmed Tom.

"And did Mr Mason approve that withdrawal?" DS Twamley asked. Tom smiled.

"To my surprise, he did," he replied. "He's normally really tight when it comes to me having advances, but today he was fine. He didn't even give me the third degree on why I wanted it."

"Does he normally do that?" Carmichael asked.

"Always," replied Tom. "I don't want to speak ill of the dead, but Ron was a real control freak, and he loved the power he had over me and that money."

"But now he's dead he no longer has that power, does he," remarked Carmichael.

"Hold on," Tom bellowed loudly. "I didn't kill him. I went over and asked him for the cash. He agreed. He told me to get over to see Mr Gray and that was that. I left within ten or fifteen minutes and that's the last I saw of him. But when I left, he was perfectly fine."

Carmichael paused for a few seconds during which time he glanced across at DS Twamley, before returning his gaze upon Tom. "Nobody's suggesting you killed Ron Mason, Tom," he said in a slow but calm voice. "But as he almost certainly died very soon after you met with him, we're very keen to know what happened and what you saw. So, tell us what time you arrived at Ron's today?"

Tom considered the question for a few seconds before replying. "It was about one twenty, maybe one thirty," he replied. "And I was only there for five or ten minutes, max. As I said, he agreed to the advance without any fuss, so I headed off."

"And did you go alone?" Carmichael enquired.

Tom nodded. "Yes, it was just me."

"And when you arrived and left, did you see anyone else hanging around?" continued Carmichael.

Tom took a longer pause as he cast his mind back. After about fifteen seconds of silence, he responded. "Nobody that I can recall," he replied. "It was really quiet down his road, as I remember."

Carmichael nodded gently. "And how was Ron when you met him?" he asked. "You said you were surprised he didn't ask you more about why you wanted two thousand pounds. So, was anything else different about him?"

Again, Tom took his time while he considered the question. "Yes, he was totally disinterested in me," Tom replied, "as if he was thinking about something else completely."

"Any idea what that might have been?" enquired DS Twamley.

"No idea," responded Tom, without any hesitation. "He just scribbled a note down on a scrap of paper, put it in an envelope and handed it to me like he usually did. He then said I could get the money from Mr Gray and that was it."

"And that's what you did, was it?" Carmichael enquired.

"Yes," replied Tom. "I went straight over to see Mr Gray and got the cash."

"And what time did you arrive at the bank?" Carmichael asked.

"About two, I guess," said Tom. "But I can't be totally sure."

"And when you got there, was there any issue with Mr Gray handing you over such a large amount of cash?" Carmichael asked.

Tom shook his head. "No, he said he knew I was coming, so I assume Ron called him or sent him a text message. When I got there, he had the two grand, in twenties, ready for me."

Carmichael paused for a few seconds before continuing with his questioning. "I understand you went out last night," he remarked.

Tom looked puzzled. "Who told you that?" he asked.

"Your mother mentioned it earlier when I spoke with her," replied Carmichael. "She said that you were with her until about nine, then you went out."

Tom shrugged his shoulders. "It was probably about that time," he replied vaguely, "I didn't check the exact time."

"And where did you go?" Carmichael enquired.

"Just out with some mates," responded Tom, his answer deliberately brief and lacking in detail.

Carmichael smiled then rose to his feet. "You've been very helpful, Tom," he said. "I'll leave you to give DC Twamley a full written statement of your movements last night and also of this afternoon's meeting with Ron, then you can go."

"That's it?" exclaimed Tom, who was clearly expecting a longer session with Carmichael.

"For now, yes, that's it," confirmed Carmichael who started to make his way out of the interview room. He was just a few paces short of the door when Carmichael stopped and turned back to face Tom Ashcroft. "Do you still have the money?" he asked.

Tom's face reddened. "Most of it," he replied. "I owed a friend some cash, so I had to give him some, but the rest I still have back at the house."

Carmichael smiled, turned away again, and left the room.

Chapter 26

It was exactly seven thirty when the four officers assembled at Kirkwood police station for their evening debrief.
Only minutes before, Carmichael received a copy of Dr Stock's autopsy report on Ron Mason; a document he'd glanced at quickly to see if there were any unexpected findings. As far as he could see there weren't any.
"Evening, everyone," he announced, to ensure he had their full attention. "We've got a hell of a lot to get through so let's try and keep this on point."
Neither of his three colleagues wanted to spend a large chunk of their evening in a long and convoluted debrief, so nobody protested.
Looking around the team, Carmichael tossed over the red marker pen to DS Dalton, which she caught, expertly, in one hand. "Will you do the honours, please, Rachel?" he asked.
Rachel Dalton rose from her seat and walked briskly over to the whiteboard and immediately wrote *Background on Chrissy Cream and the Vixens*, above the eleven points DC Twamley had written earlier in the day. Once she'd done that, she made three new headings in a line at the top of the board. *Facts, Unknowns* and *Suspects.*
Carmichael allowed himself the teeniest hint of a smile as he watched her write those headings. After working

on countless cases with him, Rachel Dalton clearly knew the drill.

"So, in summary," continued Carmichael, "we have two murders, committed within twenty-four hours of each other and within a couple of miles."

"More like sixteen hours," interjected Watson, who'd picked up Stock's autopsy report and was looking at the likely time he'd put down for Ron Mason's death.

"Precisely," remarked Carmichael, as if Watson's comment only emphasised the point he was about to make. "And," Carmichael continued, "we know that Doug Pritchard and Ron Mason, our two dearly departed, had a somewhat boisterous climax to the meeting they had in The Three Bells, just minutes before Pritchard was killed."

DS Dalton scribbled down a summary of the key elements from what Carmichael had said in the facts list.

"What else do we know?" Carmichael asked, his question aimed at all three officers present.

"Both were killed by heavy blows to the head," DS Dalton remarked, while writing down her comments onto the whiteboard.

"Yes, Mason with one of his own golf clubs," confirmed Carmichael, "but as far as I'm aware, we've yet to identify the weapon used in the first killing."

As he spoke, he looked around to see if anyone in the room could offer an update on that.

"That's true, sir," DC Twamley confirmed. "The searches around the murder scene and in the adjoining fields haven't come up with anything."

"But Stock's report suggests that the blow was from a rounded weapon, about two inches in diameter," added DS Dalton.

"Like a fence post," suggested Watson.

DS Dalton shrugged her shoulders. "A fairly light-weight one if it was. It sounds more like a metal pole." Carmichael thought for a moment. "Well, whatever it was it looks like our killer took it away with him," he remarked.

"Or her," added DS Dalton.

"Yes, you're right, Rachel," conceded Carmichael. "It may well be a her." After a brief moment of silence Carmichael continued. "What other facts do we have?" he asked.

"We know from his mobile records," Watson announced, "that Leah Barnes, sister of Suzi Ashcroft and twin of Coral Freeman, made a call to Doug Pritchard on Saturday the sixteenth of March, which appears to have got him excited and prompted him to call Ron Mason, then the newspaper editor, Ted Heslegrave and also make contact with Liam Thomas, the pop star."

"Not to forget his text to Heslegrave," added DC Twamley. "The one saying he had the scoop of the year."

"And, as we know, this all culminated in him travelling up here to meet with Ron Mason," added Carmichael, "and being murdered within hours of arriving."

"What did Leah Barnes say about her call?" DS Dalton enquired.

Carmichael and Watson exchanged a brief glance before Carmichael answered. "Leah's a very poorly lady," he remarked. "She told us precious little, but prior to us informing her that Ron Mason was also a murder victim, she was all for saying he'd killed Pritchard, but then when she learned that Mason was dead, too, she clammed up."

"She maintained she was tired," added Watson, "and with her being so ill we had no option other than to leave her."

"She'll need visiting again first thing in the morning," announced Carmichael. "Maybe one for you two."

As he spoke, he directed his piercing blue eyes firstly at DS Watson then at DS Dalton.

"I guess the floors yours, Donna," Carmichael then said, looking directly at DC Twamley. "Tell us all that you've found out about those other calls and messages on Doug Pritchard's mobile."

DC Twamley opened her pocketbook, where she'd made a detailed record of what she'd discovered since the last team meeting earlier in the day. "I'll start with Ted Heslegrave," announced DC Twamley. "He's the sub-news editor at *The Mail,* based in London. He confirmed that he'd received the text message from Doug Pritchard on Saturday, but said he decided not to make contact with Pritchard because, in his words, 'Doug was a small-time chancer', who'd proved to be 'a waste of time' on many occasions over the last twenty years."

Watson laughed out loud on hearing this damning reference, which, from the look Carmichael gave him, clearly hadn't gone down well with his boss.

"Carry on, Donna," Carmichael said firmly.

"Heslegrave said that he couldn't remember the last time they'd printed anything that Doug Pritchard had sent them," added DC Twamley.

"So, what about the call they had on Tuesday?" Carmichael enquired. "That was a fairly long one, as I recall."

"Yes, fifteen minutes," confirmed DC Twamley.

"Did Heslegrave tell you what they talked about?" Carmichael asked.

DC Twamley shrugged her shoulders and looked a bit hesitant to answer. "Yes, sort of," she replied.

"What do you mean, sort of?" Carmichael enquired; his brow furrowed as if he now fully expected to hear something that he wasn't going to like.

"Heslegrave said that Pritchard told him he had a massive scoop on Chrissy Cream and the Vixens," continued DC Twamley. "He said it was a front-page story and that he'd be wanting a six-figure sum for it. However, he wasn't prepared to share any of the scoop with Heslegrave unless Heslegrave gave a personal assurance that *The Mail* would pay Pritchard that sort of sum."

"And I bet Heslegrave said he couldn't," remarked DS Dalton.

"Not quite," replied DC Twamley. "Heslegrave said he'd need something more concrete before he'd even think of talking to the money men at *The Mail,* upon which Pritchard told him he'd get something to him within a couple of days. Apparently, Pritchard said he wanted to talk with a few people first, but he'd send him some details within the next forty-eight hours, which of course he didn't."

"Given he was dead," added Watson.

Carmichael considered what DC Twamley had just told the team before continuing. "And what was Heslegrave's opinion about the likelihood of Doug Pritchard having a proper story, after having spoken with him?" Carmichael enquired.

DC Twamley smiled broadly, as she'd asked Heslegrave that very question. "He said he wasn't sure," she replied. "In his view, he was convinced that Doug Pritchard thought he had a scoop, and he said that in his day, Pritchard had been a very successful investigative reporter. However, Heslegrave wasn't convinced at all

that Pritchard would have anything that he could print. In short, and again in his own words, Heslegrave thought Doug Pritchard was *'well past his sell by date'."*
Carmichael again paused for a few seconds, which DS Dalton appreciated as it allowed her to complete the sixth bullet point in her Facts list.

"And have you spoken with Liam Thomas, the other person Doug Pritchard appears to have been desperate to talk to, following his call with Leah Barnes?" Carmichael enquired.

"Yes, but it wasn't the longest of calls," replied DC Twamley. "At first Liam wouldn't come to the phone, and he wasn't overly helpful when I asked him to tell me what was discussed. To be honest, it was almost like he couldn't fully remember."

"Sounds like another one past their sell by date," added Watson, with a wry smile. "Or maybe the cocaine and wacky baccy has finally caught up with him."

Although she tried not to, DS Dalton couldn't supress a grin at her colleague's comment, much to the annoyance of Carmichael.

"Come on, guys," Carmichael said in exasperation. "We've a lot to get through."

"However," added DC Twamley, who, having more to divulge, wanted to share her information, "he did eventually confirm that he'd spoken with Doug Pritchard."

"And what did he say they talked about?" Carmichael asked, an element of frustration still in his voice.

"He said it was a brief call," continued DC Twamley, "that Doug Pritchard asked if they could meet and he told him, in his own words to 'F off back into his gutter'."

"Did he ask Pritchard why he wanted a meeting?" Carmichael enquired.

"Yes," replied DC Twamley, "he says it was to discuss Chrissy Cream and the rumours that he was Thomas's father. Which is when he told Pritchard to …"

"F off," repeated Carmichael.

"That's right, sir," replied DC Twamley, with a faint shrug of her shoulders.

*   *   *   *

Tom Ashcroft spent an uncomfortable twenty-minute journey back to his house in the passenger seat of Suzi's rickety old van.

They hardly spoke during the journey, although he found himself having to reassure his clearly worried mum that he was fine, on more than one occasion.

As soon as they arrived back at the house, Tom quickly got out of the van and headed up the drive. Once inside, he made his way to his bedroom where, door firmly closed, he speed-dialled one of the many numbers stored on his mobile.

Chapter 27

After filling in the team on his discussions with Leah Barnes and Tom Ashcroft, Carmichael turned his attention once more towards DC Twamley. "Did Tom's statement add anything more than he told us in the interview?" DC Twamley shook her head. "Not much," she confirmed. "He gave me the names and contact details of the people he went out with last night. I'll check with them tomorrow to see if they corroborate his story."

"Anyone we know, Donna?" enquired DS Dalton.

DC Twamley shook her head again. "No, the names he gave me are Spencer Wood and Robin McEvoy."

DS Watson's eyes lit up at the mention of Tom's companions. "We've had dealings with those two before," he remarked. "Nothing too serious, but when they were teenagers, they were always getting arrested for minor incidents."

"Like what?" enquired Carmichael.

Watson shrugged his shoulders. "Drunk and disorderly, that sort of thing."

Carmichael nodded. "If he wasn't telling us the truth, I'd imagine that by now Tom Ashcroft will have spoken with them to make sure all their stories match, but you should certainly see what Spencer and Robin have to say. Do it tonight before you go home rather than in the morning."

"Will do, sir," responded DC Twamley.

"How did you get on with the rest of the diners at The Three Bells last night, Rachel?" Carmichael enquired; his piercing blue eyes now focussed on her. "And what about Miles? Did you talk with him again?"

DS Dalton nodded. "I've now spoken with everyone seated close to Mason's and Pritchard's table when they argued, but to be honest, they've been a bit of a disappointment. Although they all confirm they witnessed the quarrel, nobody seems to have heard that much about the details of what was said or the reason they argued."

"That doesn't make any sense to me, Rachel," remarked Carmichael, whose pained facial expression made no attempt to hide the fact that he was mystified at what he was being told. "Between them, they must have heard or witnessed something."

DS Dalton shrugged her shoulders.

"About all I've got is a unanimous confirmation that the argument happened, that it was over very quickly, with Ron Mason storming off to the toilets," DS Dalton replied. "They also said that it was Ron who was shouting."

"But they said nothing relating to what the bust up was about?" Carmichael added, his tone of voice incredulous.

"Well, from what they told me," continued DS Dalton, "it does sound like whatever they were arguing about involved Chrissy and Jo Cream, as a few of the people I spoke to remembered Ron shouting their names. But there was nothing that any of them said that was specific."

Carmichael shook his head. "And what about Miles Goodwyn?" he enquired.

"Did he tell you anything new?"

DS Dalton shook her head. "Nothing new," she confirmed. "Although it's clear he's got a thing for the young girl, Verity, who helps at the pub on a Wednesday evening serving pies from her mum's bakery, The Muffin Maid. To be honest, I think that's the only reason he goes to the pub."

"And have you spoken to her?" Carmichael asked. "Maybe she heard something."

DS Dalton shook her head. "I've not had time. I'd got that down on my list of things to do tomorrow."

Carmichael nodded. "Yes, get onto that after you and Marc have spoken with Leah Barnes."

"Will do, sir," DS Dalton replied.

"And I'd like you, Marc," continued Carmichael, "after you and Rachel are through with Leah, to pay a visit to Ron Mason's solicitor, Angus Frazer, at Attwoods. I want to know who benefits from Ron's will."

DS Watson nodded, to show he'd be on to it.

Carmichael then turned his head to face DS Dalton again.

"Is that everything from you, Rachel?" he enquired.

"Not quite," DS Dalton replied. "I had a very interesting meeting with Mr Gray, the manager at the bank where Tom's and Ellis's trust funds are located. He was very upset when I told him about Ron being murdered, but he told me a lot of information about the trust funds."

"Really?" remarked Carmichael. "Tell us more."

* * * *

Tom Ashcroft remained in his room long after his call had ended. He wanted to believe what he'd been told, but there was something inside of him that suggested the story he'd been given wasn't totally correct.

He desperately wanted to believe it and it was certainly plausible, but he wasn't sure. With the implications, if he'd been lied to, being almost unimaginable, Tom decided to take the evening to think about it and if need be, sleep on it, too.
Then, once he'd thought it through, decide what to do in the morning.

* * * *

"Ok, Rachel," announced Carmichael. "What did Mr Gray tell you that was so intriguing?"
"First of all," replied DS Dalton, "he told me that the income that's still coming into the bank account of Chrissy Cream and the Vixens from their records being played and other royalties, even after all these years, is in the hundreds of thousands each year."
"Really?" exclaimed DS Watson.
DS Dalton nodded her head.
"And, when Tom and Ellis reach the age of twenty-five, they will both be very wealthy men. Tom, being Chrissy's son, has the bigger pot according to Mr Gray, but they'll both be multi-millionaires."
"Blimey," DC Twamley remarked.
"And does all the income go to their trust funds?" Carmichael enquired.
DS Dalton shook her head. "No, it doesn't," she replied. "I've written it down as it's quite involved."
As she spoke DS Dalton opened her notebook.
"According to Mr Gray, until the boys reach the age of twenty-five, Pam and Suzi get an index linked annual payment, which currently stands at around forty-five thousand, nine hundred pounds each. But once the boys get access to their trust funds that will be reduced by fifty percent."

"I guess that's in recognition of them looking after the boys," Carmichael remarked.

"That's what Mr Gray said," confirmed DS Dalton.

"And what about the rest?" Carmichael asked.

DS Dalton checked her notes carefully before responding.

"After Pam's and Suzi's payments, taxes and any expenses that Ron Mason claimed as the estate and trust funds executor, which Mr Gray has to approve," she replied, "it's split three ways. Forty-five per cent goes straight into Tom's trust fund, thirty per cent into Ellis's trust fund and twenty-five goes to Ron Mason."

"So, what happens to Ron's twenty-five per cent now he's dead?" Carmichael enquired.

"That's the really interesting thing about it all," replied DS Dalton. "Chrissy and Jo Cream, who basically set this all up, stipulated that should Ron die, his share would be split between Suzi and Pam."

"Really!" exclaimed DS Watson. "Now if that's not a reason to kill someone, I don't know what is."

"That's exactly what I thought," concurred DS Dalton.

"Maybe," remarked Carmichael, "but that wouldn't explain why Doug Pritchard was murdered, and it can't have any relevance to the fracas between the pair last night."

"But worth investigation, I'd say," suggested DS Watson.

"Yes," concurred Carmichael. "I think that's a job for me and you in the morning, Donna."

DC Twamley was ecstatic at the news that she was going to spend the morning with the boss, but she tried her best not to let it show.

"Absolutely, sir," she replied.

Chapter 28

Carmichael sat quietly, alone in the incident room, gazing up at the items recorded, initially by DC Twamley, and updated at the debrief by DS Dalton. He'd let the team go home just before nine, each taking with them a printed copy of the bullet points that had been recorded on the whiteboard.

However, Carmichael had stayed put. He wanted time to think and to study each and every point they'd documented.

Despite his customary listings being incomplete, there being nothing recorded under either the suspects or unknown headings, there was more than enough up there for him to scrutinize, an analysis he always preferred to do alone.

Slowly and methodically, he read each point line by line.

Background on Chrissy Cream and the Vixens

1. *Chrissy and Jo Cream were sisters from High Maudsey (Chrissy being 3 years older than Jo).*
2. *The Vixens were originally Jo's band, but after their lead singer left, Chrissy joined with her best friend Suzi Ashcroft and they get another school friend, Ron Mason (also from High Maudsey) to be the band's manager.*

3. *Within a year, they'd replaced all the original band members, apart from Jo, with Pam Hutton the last to be added. The band's drummer. The band then becomes known as Chrissy Cream and the Vixens.*
4. *They have 6 top 20 hits in the next 3 years and are the first all-girl rock band to have a number 1 hit in the USA.*
5. *Shortly after each other Chrissy and Jo have a baby, Chrissy's (Tom) rumoured to be the child of another rock star, Liam Thomas, (a rumour denied by both Chrissy and Liam). Jo's child (also a boy called Ellis) is thought to have been the son of a Premier League footballer. Tom and Ellis are now in their early twenties and were adopted by Suzi and Pam respectively when their mums died.*
6. *Chrissy and Jo were both killed twenty years ago in a tragic boating accident in the North Sea. This was just before they were due to fly out to the US for their first American tour. The skipper of the boat was also killed, so no survivors.*
7. *The band broke up after their deaths and didn't release any more records.*
8. *Ron Mason remains in control of all royalties that the band still earns and is also the sole trustee of the trust funds set up for the two boys, which is known to be a significant amount of money. The boys won't get control of their inheritances until they are 25 years old.*
9. *Ron Mason is now 53, he's only managed one major artist other than The Vixens, a singer called Ferne Cramley, who had 3 minor hits 10 years ago, but she has now retired from the music business and lives with her husband and family in rural Herefordshire.*

10. Pam and Suzi, the only 2 surviving band members live in the area still. Pam has a brother who is a farmer in one of the villages. She appears to be quite reclusive spending her time looking after Ellis and a host of cats and other animals. Suzi, who was the wild child of the band, now appears to spend the majority of her time and energy fighting for a variety of causes, including saving the planet, women's rights and third world poverty. She is devoted to Tom and, like Pam, has never married.

11. Doug Pritchard lived in Hove and had been a music journalist for over thirty years. He specialised in uncovering salacious stories about the rich and famous in the music industry. Although he'd had a number of big stories published over the years, his credibility and methods of obtaining information are viewed with great suspicion.

Facts

1. *Doug Pritchard was murdered at approx. 9:35pm in Jay Bank Lane, High Maudsey on Wed 20th March.*
2. *Ron Mason was murdered between 1:40pm and 3pm on his drive in High Maudsey on Thursday 21st March.*
3. *Pritchard and Mason had argued at The Three Bells pub about 20-30 minutes before Doug Pritchard was killed – subject unknown.*
4. *Both men were killed by blows to the head. Ron Mason by a single blow with one of his own golf clubs; Doug Pritchard was struck twice by a cylindrical weapon – identity unknown.*

5. *Pritchard received a call from Leah Barnes on Sat 16th March.*
6. *Leah was Mason's PA for years and is the younger sister of Suzi Ashcroft and twin sister of Coral Freeman (the landlady of The Three Bells where Ron Mason and Doug Pritchard argued on the night of Doug's murder.)*
7. *Pritchard tried to make contact with National Sub-Editor, Ted Heslegrave, and pop star, Liam Thomas, almost immediately after Leah called him.*
8. *Thomas Ashcroft met with Ron Mason at Ron's house shortly before he was murdered.*

Realising the background notes written by DS Twamley were made when they thought Ron Mason was still alive, Carmichael made his last task before leaving the station, to change the text where Ron Mason was concerned into the past tense.

With that completed, and the time on the wall clock indicating it was nine twenty-five, Carmichael decided to call it a day and head home.

Chapter 29

Verity, with her head tilted and resting on Ellis's shoulder and her right hand slowly rubbing her bump, suddenly opened her eyes wide. "He's really moving about a lot this evening," she exclaimed excitedly, before grabbing Ellis's hand and placing it firmly on her tummy. "Can you feel that?" Ellis couldn't but didn't want to burst Verity's bubble of euphoria. "Wow, yes," he replied, with as much enthusiasm as he could muster. As always, his acting didn't work with Verity. "What's the matter?" she enquired. "You've been quiet all evening."

Ellis shrugged his shoulders. "It's just the news about Ron," he replied. "It's thrown me completely."

Verity leaned forward and kissed Ellis tenderly on the lips. "I know," she replied. "It's awful."

"Everyone knows I was never a great fan of Ron's," continued Ellis, "but nobody deserves to be killed like that."

Verity looked deep into Ellis's eyes and nodded. "I know my love," she replied. "You and Tom both had your issues with Ron, him being so mean with your inheritances. And I dare say there were probably dozens of other people out there who he'd upset along the way, but Ron wasn't so bad that you'd think someone would want to kill him."

Ellis nodded slowly. "But someone did," he responded, his eyes staring into space. "And it may well be someone we know."

* * * *

When he was deep into a case, Carmichael could arrive home at all hours of the evening and often well into the night; so, Penny was pleasantly surprised when she heard her husband's car pulling up on the drive at ten past ten. She expected he wouldn't have even thought to eat, and she knew the first thing he'd want when he stepped inside was a large glass of Pinotage, his favourite red wine.

By the time Carmichael made it through to the kitchen, the casserole pot Penny had kept warming in the oven for the last three hours had been removed and placed on a heat-resistant silicone trivet; a purchase she'd made online a few days earlier for this very eventuality. Next to the casserole pot Penny had rested a large glass of the deep-burgundy-coloured wine, which Carmichael took hold of before he'd even said a word.

After a long gulp, Carmichael smiled over at his wife and sat himself down.

"They said on the news that there's been a second murder in High Maudsey," Penny remarked, as she removed the lid from the casserole dish, allowing a delicious smelling plume of steam to rise from the extremely well-cooked lamb casserole.

Carmichael took another drink from his glass, albeit this time a much smaller amount. "There has," he replied. "And the annoying thing is that the second murder victim was my main suspect for the first. So, to be honest, I'm a bit perplexed by this one."

Penny leaned over and dumped two huge ladles of casserole onto Carmichael's plate. Before she had a chance to make the portion size even bigger, Carmichael held up his hand. "That's plenty," he remarked. "I'm starving but any more than that and I'll have trouble sleeping tonight."

Penny smiled and shook her head. "Will you be so restrained with the wine?" she asked; a question her husband didn't answer. "Have you any leads as to why these men were killed and any idea at all who might have killed them?" Penny enquired.

Carmichael put a forkful of the casserole into his mouth and immediately opened it wide and started to draw in air as quick as he could.

"Well, it's going to be hot," remarked Penny, with no sign of sympathy, "it's been in the oven for hours."

After drawing in lots of air and then taking a very large glug of wine, Carmichael managed to reduce the temperature in his mouth. "The only real lead we have is

Ron Mason's ex-PA," he replied. "A lady called Leah Barnes. As far as we can see, everything started after she called our first victim, a well-known, albeit not well-respected, aging hack. Our guess is that something she said in the call will provide a big part of this jigsaw."

"And have you not managed to track her down yet?" Penny enquired.

Carmichael blew hard on his second forkful of dinner before placing it carefully in his mouth. "We have," he replied, "but she's terminally ill and in a hospice. She maintained she was too tired to talk with us, so Marc and I backed off. I've asked Rachel and Marc to go back and talk to her in the morning."

"Not you and Rachel, then?" enquired Penny. "When the suspects are so important, you normally don't delegate."

Carmichael shrugged his shoulders "I'm not sure why," he replied, "but I got the impression she wasn't that keen to talk with me."

Penny shrugged her shoulders and tried hard to conceal a smile. "I can't believe that," she remarked cynically, before turning away and walking down the hallway, with a broad grin across her face.

Chapter 30

Friday 22nd March

It was instantly apparent to both DS Watson and DS Dalton that something wasn't right. The blank look on the face of the young eastern European assistant who met them at the reception desk at St Jude's, and who ordered them to wait before scurrying away to find Mrs Wright, could only mean one thing.
"She's passed away, hasn't she?" suggested DS Watson, who at the same time spun the visitors' book around and studied who'd arrived and left since he and Carmichael were there.
"That would be my guess," whispered DS Dalton.
"Interesting," remarked Watson. "She had another visitor last night."
"Who?" enquired DS Dalton just as the ashen-faced Mrs Wright emerged from a door at the rear of the reception area.
"DS Watson, I regret that Leah's brave battle ended a short while ago," remarked the proprietor of St Jude's. "I was about to call Inspector Carmichael to inform him."
Watson looked across at DS Dalton and nodded gently.
"I'm sure you have much to do, Mrs Wright," he said sympathetically, "so we'll get out of your hair."

Mrs Wright smiled, put her head to one side and nodded back.

"I've just called the next of kin, which is obviously our main priority," replied Mrs Wright. "They said they'd get here as soon as they could."

"Of course," interjected DS Dalton.

"I see one of them was here last night after Inspector Carmichael and I left," added Watson, his finger pointing down at the name Coral Freeman, which had been written in the visitors' book.

"Yes," replied Mrs Wright sheepishly, "Leah asked for her just after you'd left. She was here for about an hour."

Watson smiled. "As I said, we'll get out of your hair." Mrs Wright remained at her post as the two officers walked towards the door, almost as if she was making doubly sure that they departed.

However, as they reached the exit, DS Dalton turned back to face her.

"So, which doctor attended Leah to confirm her death?" she enquired.

"Er, it was Doctor Enright," replied Mrs Wright. "He's only just this minute left."

DS Dalton smiled. "Thank you," she said, before turning back and making her exit.

* * * *

With DC Twamley in the passenger seat, Carmichael's black BMW headed out in the direction of Suzi Ashcroft's house, which was the nearest of the two Vixens' homes.

"So, did Tom's pals verify his story for Wednesday evening?" Carmichael enquired.

DC Twamley smiled and nodded. "It was exactly as you'd suggested," she replied. "Their accounts were almost word perfect and match what Tom told us regarding his movements at the time Doug Pritchard was killed."

Carmichael glanced briefly across at his young DC and smiled. "What did they say?" he asked.

"They confirmed that he was the driver and that he picked them up from the Farmers Arms pub, in the village of Rainham Moss, at about nine fifteen and they then drove to Southport where they went to a club called Josephine's until it shut at two the next morning, when they drove back; getting home at about two forty-five."

"How far do you reckon it is from Rainham Moss to High Maudsey?" Carmichael enquired.

DC Twamley thought for a few seconds.

"About seven or eight miles," she replied.

"Would you say that High Maudsey is on the way from Rainham Moss to Southport," Carmichael enquired.

DS Twamley shrugged her shoulders. "It's not the way I'd go, but I suppose it's not that far out of their way."

"But the point I'm making is that they could have been in the area at the time Doug Pritchard was killed," announced Carmichael.

"They could I suppose," concurred DC Twamley. "It's certainly feasible."

"Get on to the station and ask them to check the CCTV footage from the Farmers in Rainham Moss to Southport on Wednesday evening between the hours of nine and two the following morning, to see if they have any footage of Tom's car," Carmichael said. "And see if they can find any footage from inside or outside Josephine's, too."

"Will do, sir," replied DC Twamley as she extracted her mobile from her jacket pocket.

* * * *

"The boss isn't going to be happy, Rachel," remarked Watson as he and DS Dalton clambered into his car.
"No, he won't," she concurred, "but I'm impressed with how you spotted that Coral had visited Leah last night." Watson smiled. "Just something I always try and do," he remarked, smugly. "It's amazing what visitors' books can tell you in these sorts of places."
"Well, it came up trumps this time, that's for sure," added DS Dalton.
Watson smiled broadly. "And thanks to you we now know who the doctor was that certified Leah as dead, so I guess we need to check that out."
"I'll toss you for it," remarked DS Dalton, taking a pound coin out of her pocket.
"Heads I talk to Dr Enright, and you tell the boss about Leah. Tails I tell the boss and you talk to the doctor."
Watson nodded. "It's a deal," he replied, hoping the coin toss landed on tails.

Chapter 31

"Sorry to be the bearer of such bad news," announced DS Dalton, "but Leah died this morning."
Listening in disbelief as his car glided down the windy country lane, Carmichael remained silent.
"Marc's going to speak with the doctor who pronounced her dead, but at this stage there's nothing to suggest it's suspicious," added DS Dalton.
"And with her has gone any chance we had of knowing why she called Pritchard," Carmichael eventually replied, the exasperation evident in his voice.
"Not necessarily," replied DS Dalton. "Marc took a peek at the visitors' book, and last night Coral Freeman came to visit Leah. Apparently, Leah asked Mrs Wright to call her as soon as you and Marc had left yesterday evening."
"Really," exclaimed Carmichael.
"I'm on my way to see Verity, do you want me to change my plans and do that later and head over to The Three Bells?" DS Dalton asked.
"No," replied Carmichael, firmly. "You carry on and talk to Verity. Donna and I will go and talk to Coral Freeman. We're close to the pub so we can be there in five minutes."
"She may be on her way ......" began DS Dalton, but Carmichael had already ended their call.

Despite this not being the first time her boss had ended their calls so curtly, this habit always exasperated DS Dalton, who'd never dream of doing anything like that herself.

Irately, she turned off her mobile, put it on the passenger seat and started her car's engine.

"Well, Verity Brook-Smith, let's see what you have to say for yourself," she muttered out loud, before heading off in the direction of The Muffin Maid some twenty minutes' drive away.

* * * *

Coral Freeman and Suzi Ashcroft sat quietly alone in the lounge of The Three Bells.

Pallid-faced and still in shock from not just the news of the death of her sister, but also the potential implication of the information Coral had just shared with her, Suzi tried to work out what to do.

As she reflected on everything, Suzi spied Carmichael's car pulling into the car park.

"It's that bloody Inspector," she announced through gritted teeth. "Say nothing about this to him."

"I'm not sure about that," replied Coral. "I think I should."

"No," responded Suzi firmly. "We keep this between you and I until we decide what's best to do."

Coral nodded. "Whatever you say, Suzi," she replied, meekly.

Suzi stood up. "Now, let's get rid of the annoying Inspector," she said, "and then we can get over to St Jude's and make sure everything's done properly for poor Leah."

Teary-eyed, Coral rose from her seat and followed her big sister towards the front door.

* * * *

The welcoming aroma of freshly baked bread, cream cakes and homemade pies filled DS Dalton's nostrils as soon as she entered The Muffin Maid; and reminded her that she'd only had an apple and a rushed mug of coffee so far that morning.

After allowing the only customer in the shop to complete their purchase and depart, DS Dalton held up her identity card so Mrs McMullen could see who she was before asking if Verity Brook-Smith was at home. Mrs McMullen studied the identity card closely before asking DS Dalton to wait a moment and disappearing into the back office.

Normally DS Dalton would use a wait like this to think about how she was going to approach the person to be interviewed, however, this morning her thoughts were on what to buy before she left; or more accurately, what would provide the best option balancing taste and practicality.

She'd ruled out filled rolls and pies, which were far too messy to eat and had also decided against a croissant, which would inevitably drop loads of crumbs all over her car.

It was just as an anxious looking young woman, who DS Dalton took to be Verity, appeared from the back office, that she decided upon a cheese and ham balm cake. Easy to eat and reasonably filling, she'd concluded.

"You want to talk with me?" remarked Verity, nervously.

DS Dalton smiled. "I'm DS Rachel Dalton, she replied as warmly as she could. "I'd just like to ask you a few questions about Wednesday evening when you were at

The Three Bells. Is there anywhere we can go that's a bit more private?"

Appearing suitably reassured, Verity smiled back before pointing to the open doorway she'd just come through. "We can go into the back," she announced.

*   *   *   *

"I was so very sorry to hear the sad news of the passing of your sister," Carmichael began as soon as Coral opened the door of the pub to him and DC Twamley. "I know you must have much on your mind at this difficult time, however, I need to understand what it was that Leah wanted to discuss with you when she asked you to visit her yesterday evening."

Even before he'd finished talking, Suzi emerged from the side room and, stony-faced, glared at Carmichael. "Now's not a good time, Inspector," Suzi spat out, with unmasked anger. "Our sister is dead, and we need to be allowed to grieve in peace. Can't these questions wait a few days?"

"I totally understand," replied Carmichael calmly. "But we believe that Leah may well have shared some information with Coral that will prove to be crucial in our investigations into the deaths of Doug Pritchard and Ron Mason."

Coral shook her head. "Leah didn't tell me anything," she insisted. "She didn't mention Ron at all and nothing whatsoever about her call with Doug Pritchard."

"So, if you can leave now, Inspector," added Suzi angrily. "We have arrangements to start making regarding Leah's funeral."

Carmichael nodded and took a step backwards. "I fully understand," he remarked. "And once again, please accept my condolences for the loss of your sister."

The door slammed shut on Carmichael and DS Twamley, leaving him frustrated that the details of the conversation between Leah and Doug Pritchard were still a mystery.

"That's annoying," remarked DC Twamley.

"Yes and no," replied Carmichael. "We may not know what Leah and Pritchard talked about on that call, but I'm satisfied that the details of that conversation were shared with Coral. I didn't mention anything about there being a telephone conversation between Leah and Doug Pritchard, but by denying she knew the details of the call Coral has admitted she did know about it. Something only Leah could have told her."

Chapter 32

It was only when Verity tentatively sat down in the small kitchen at the back of the shop, that DS Dalton realised she was pregnant.
"When's baby due?" she enquired.
Verity smiled. "He's due at the start of July."
"So, you know it's a boy," added DS Dalton.
Verity rubbed her stomach and smiled. "No," she replied. "Ellis and I decided we'd wait until it comes, but we're referring to it as he."
DS Dalton smiled broadly. "It must be very exciting for you."
Verity nodded enthusiastically. "We're both thrilled," she replied.
DS Dalton waited a few seconds before starting her interview.
"I understand that you were in The Three Bells on Wednesday when Ron Mason and his friend had their argument," she began. "Did you hear what it was about?"
Verity shook her head. "Not all of it," she replied. "It was very busy on Wednesday. Coral and I were run off our feet. But I did pick up a little of their argument."
"And what did you hear?" DS Dalton asked.
"It was mainly Ron Mason doing the shouting," remarked Verity, her face now looking very serious. "He

was proper angry. He was calling the other guy a liar and threatening to take him to court if he printed any bullshit."

"Really," remarked DS Dalton. "Did you hear what else he said?"

Verity thought for a few seconds before shaking her head. "Not really," she replied, "but there were other people around. I expect they will have heard more than me."

DS Dalton shook her head. "That's the thing," she added, "nobody heard the detail, just the shouting."

"Really," said Verity, who looked astonished to be told that there hadn't been more details from other people in the pub.

DS Dalton nodded. "Yes, so if you can think hard about what you heard it would be really helpful."

Verity nodded enthusiastically. "I will," she replied.

DS Dalton smiled again. "And what time did you leave the pub?" she enquired.

Verity pondered the question before answering.

"It was at about nine thirty, maybe a little bit earlier," she replied. "We'd sold the last of Mum's pies and Coral said I could shoot off. So, I tidied up and headed home."

"That would be about the time we believe the man that Ron Mason was arguing with left the pub," said DS Dalton. "Did you see him after he left?"

Verity nodded. "Yes, he stormed off in a huff and walked away down the road opposite."

"Jay Bank Lane," remarked DS Dalton.

"Yes," replied Verity. "That's the one."

"And was he alone?" enquired DS Dalton.

Verify nodded. "I didn't take that much notice, to be honest as I was chatting to a guy I know, but I think he was alone."

"And did you see anyone go down Jay Bank Lane shortly after the man went down there, or did any cars follow him down?" DS Dalton asked.

Verity shrugged her shoulders. "Not that I recall."

DS Dalton paused for a second.

"I've not been much help," Verity confessed. "I'm sorry about that."

DS Dalton shook her head. "No, you've been really helpful."

"Actually," remarked Verity, her eyes lighting up as she spoke, "there is something he said which I've just remembered."

"What's that?" enquired DS Dalton eagerly.

"Ron said, she's dead you pillock," announced Verity, "she died in that bloody accident years ago."

"Who was he talking about?" DS Dalton asked.

"I assumed it was Chrissy Cream, Tom's real mum," replied Verity. "But I'm not sure."

DS Dalton noted down Verity's words in her notebook. "Anything else?"

Verity shook her head. "No, sorry," she replied.

DS Dalton smiled, put her hand in her pocket, pulled out her card and handed it to Verity.

"If you remember anything else give me a call," she said. "Even if it seems insignificant."

Verity took the card and nodded. "I will," she promised.

"Anyway, thanks for your time, Verity," remarked DS Dalton as she rose to her feet. "I'll get off now."

Verity smiled once more and got up as well. "I'll show you out," she remarked.

"No need," replied DS Dalton. "I'm going to buy something to eat before I go. The smell in here is driving me nuts and I've hardly eaten anything so far today."

Verity smiled. "Mum's stuff is the best you'll find in the whole of this part of Lancashire, so I'm not surprised," she remarked. "I'd recommend her Eccles cakes, they're to die for."

"I was going to buy a cheese and ham balm cake," said DS Dalton, "but I may try some Eccles cakes too."

Verity watched as the DS took a few steps away back towards the shop, before stopping and turning to face her again.

"The young man you were talking to outside the pub," she said, "what's his name?"

Verity looked surprised.

"It was Spencer Wood," replied Verity. "He's a mate of Ellis and Tom."

DS Dalton nodded, instantly remembering the name Spencer Wood as one of the mates that Tom Ashcroft had given as being with him on Wednesday evening.

"And what time was that, again?" DS Dalton enquired.

"About nine twenty or maybe nine thirty," replied Verity, her response quite hazy.

"And do you drive down Jay Bank Lane to get home?" DS Dalton asked.

Verity shook her head. "No that takes me miles out of my way and it's a narrow unlit lane, so it's awful to drive down at night. I go down the main road."

DS Dalton smiled. "And what about Spencer," she enquired, "would he go down that road to get home?"

"He may do," replied Verity vaguely, "but he was talking about going to a club in Southport, so I'd think he'd go the other way out of the village."

DS Dalton smiled and nodded. "Thanks, Verity, I'll get out of your hair. I'm looking forward to trying one of those Eccles cakes. And, whatever you do, look after yourself and good luck with the new arrival."

Verity smiled and rubbed her stomach again.

"Thanks," she replied.

Chapter 33

Carmichael and DS Twamley were about halfway to Pam Hutton's house when DS Dalton's call came through.

"I've just had an interesting discussion with Verity," she announced, her excitement to share the information abundantly clear in her voice.

"Really," responded Carmichael. "What did she tell you?"

"Well, she's saying that on Wednesday evening she heard Ron Mason shout at Doug Pritchard. Verity's certain she heard him say something along the lines of, she's dead you pillock, she died in that bloody accident years ago. And when I asked Verity who she thought Ron was referring to, she said she thought it was Chrissy Cream."

"That would suggest Doug Pritchard believed that Chrissy isn't dead," Carmichael remarked, his words delivered more rhetorically than as a question to DS Dalton.

"Exactly," continued DS Dalton enthusiastically. "And Verity also claims she was with Spencer Wood between nine twenty and nine thirty outside The Three Bells, just before she headed home."

"That's interesting," remarked Carmichael, "as he told Donna that he met Tom at the Farmers Arms pub in the village of Rainham Moss at about nine fifteen. So, one of them must be lying,"

"Do you need me to check the Farmers Arms CCTV?" DS Dalton asked.

"No, that won't be necessary," replied Carmichael. "We've got that in hand already. No, you locate and interview Spencer Wood. I want to know whether he lied to Donna, or Verity is lying to you."

DS Dalton smiled. "I'm on to it, sir," she replied. "I'll call you once I've spoken with him."

"That's great, Rachel," uttered Carmichael, before speedily ending the call.

Carmichael turned his head to face DC Twamley. "Well Donna, let's get ourselves over and talk with Pam Hutton," he said enthusiastically. "It will be interesting to find out what she knows about her royalty windfall now Ron Mason's died."

He then turned his head back to the road ahead and put his foot down on the accelerator.

*   *   *   *

As soon as he'd parked his car in one of only two visitors' spaces at Attwood's Solicitors, DS Watson called Doctor Enright, who confirmed that in his opinion, there was nothing suspicious about Leah Barnes's death and, unless the police specifically requested a post-mortem, having seen her less than twenty-four hours before, he was happy to sign the death certificate stating that she'd died of natural causes. Watson wasn't sure whether Carmichael would make such a request but concluded the call by telling the doctor to hold fire until he'd checked with his boss. Watson thought about making that call, straight away, but after considering the matter for a few seconds, decided to talk with Angus Frazer first. Afterall, he'd only have to call the boss with an update on how that meeting had gone, so he decided to do both in one go after he'd met with Ron Mason's solicitor.

* * * *

Pam Hutton, not unsurprisingly, was fussing over one of her cats when the doorbell rang.
"Who's that?" she enquired of the spiteful looking Bengal cat that had been rubbing itself up against her leg seconds before. The cat didn't answer, although by the vindictive look on its handsome face, he was equally as perturbed by the unwanted visitors at the door.
Pam Hutton strode purposefully to the front door and opened it wide.
"Oh, it's you, Inspector," she announced, with undisguised exasperation. "Did I not cover everything with you and that other officer yesterday?"
Carmichael smiled. "I've just a few more questions to ask you if that's ok?"
By the expression on Pam's face, it certainly wasn't ok, but she let the two of them in anyway.

* * * *

Over the years there had been several occasions when DS Watson had met Angus Frazer; an undeniably capable solicitor albeit prone to venture into the realms of pomposity and he could be an awkward man, depending upon his mood.
Fortunately for Watson, Frazer's disposition was favourable on this particular morning; in fact, he couldn't have been more helpful. Within less than twenty minutes, Angus Frazer had furnished Watson

with a copy of Ron Mason's last will and testament; a document that Mason had only updated three days earlier, and a handwritten letter, dated the nineteenth of March, outlining in detail why he'd left no provision for his long-serving personal assistant. He also had recounted, in some detail, the conversation Ron and he had had on Tuesday when the will had been updated.
As he read through the will for the second time, Watson took out his pocketbook and made a note of the rough value of the legacies against an ever-growing list of beneficiaries of Ron Mason's will.
If Ron's murder was for personal gain, he thought, there were many who should be on the list of suspects; a list he knew Carmichael would be compiling before too long.

* * * *

Having made themselves as comfortable as they could on the threadbare sofa, Carmichael began his interview.
"I'd like to talk about the royalties from the band," he began.
"I don't get any of them," replied Pam, with an air of resentment in her voice.
"But you do get an income," he interjected. "A sum of forty-five thousand nine hundred pounds a year, I understand."
"Yes, that's correct," conceded Pam. "But that's to help raise Ellis. When he reaches the age of twenty-five, he gets access to his trust fund, and I then get just half that amount."
Carmichael nodded. "And with Ron now dead, are you aware of how his twenty-five per cent share of the band's royalties will be divided?"

Pam shrugged her shoulders. "I assume it gets split between Tom and Ellis," she replied.

"No," continued Carmichael, his gaze fixed on Pam's face as he spoke. "That is now shared between you and Suzi."

If Pam did know about her windfall, she hid it well. "Really," she exclaimed, a small cheery smile on her lips and a twinkle appearing in her eyes. "I didn't know that."

Carmichael maintained direct eye contact with Pam. "Yes, it would appear that Chrissy and Jo Cream, who set this all up, stipulated clearly that should Ron die his share would be split between you and Suzi."

"Well, thank you, girls," Pam exclaimed, her smile now even broader. "That should keep me going well into my declining years."

"And you never know," added DC Twamley, "Ron may have left you something in his will."

"Fat chance," replied Pam, without hesitating. "That mean sod won't have left anything to me. Suzi, Leah, and a couple of hundred other women around the country, maybe, but not me."

"Why do you say that?" Carmichael asked.

"Because," she announced at the top of her voice, "there's no history between me and Ron, if you get my drift."

"But there was with Suzi and Leah?" Carmichael enquired.

Pam suddenly looked uneasy, as if she may have said too much.

"Of course, I can't say for certain," she replied. "All I can say is that Ron, in his younger days, put it about a lot. If you know what I mean."

Carmichael nodded. "Yes, I think we get your drift."

157

Chapter 34

As soon as the two officers were out of Pam Hutton's house, DC Twamley turned up the volume on her mobile and checked her messages. She'd felt the vibration of their arrival when they were inside but didn't want to interrupt the flow of Carmichael's questioning.
"Two results," she announced with enthusiasm. "Forensics have confirmed that our first victim is Doug Pritchard, and the station have checked the CCTV footage from outside the Farmers Arms on Wednesday evening and it was ten fifteen when Spencer Wood's van arrived."
"Who identified Doug Pritchard?" Carmichael enquired. "I thought you were having issues finding someone."
DC Twamley nodded. "I was," she admitted, "and I didn't want to waste too much time finding someone suitable, so in the end I followed DS Watson's suggestion and got Eckersall and Stanley to forward over his dental records."
Carmichael smiled. "Good call. We'll make a detective of you yet," he remarked, much to DC Twamley's delight.
"What do we do with Spencer Wood now we know he wasn't telling us the truth?" DC Twamley enquired.

Carmichael nodded once again. "You better call Rachel and let her know, before she interviews him," he said. "It'll be interesting to see how Spencer reacts when he knows we know he's been lying to us."
"Will do sir," replied DC Twamley.
"And tell her I'm having our next team briefing at two this afternoon," Carmichael added. "So, she needs to be back at Kirkwood by then."
DC Twamley smiled and nodded, before pressing speed dial on her phone.

* * * *

Watson's initial thought, when he was out of the building, was to call Carmichael. However, he knew how his boss worked and figured the information he'd gleaned from the uncharacteristically helpful Angus Frazer would be better received if delivered by him in person at the next debrief, which he knew from working for so long with Carmichael, would be within hours. So, instead of making the call, Watson pointed his car back in the direction of Kirkwood police station, where he intended to write up his list of beneficiaries following the demise of Ron Mason.

* * * *

It wasn't difficult for DS Dalton to locate Spencer Wood. The vague response from his mother when DS Dalton called the number purporting to be the office contact for Wood and Son, that he was on a job on the old council building in Kirkwood, guided her right to him. He and another man were erecting what appeared to be a very precarious-looking structure, some twenty foot long and about as high, taking up the whole end of the old building.

Having parked just around the corner, DS Dalton walked to the bottom of the ancient wooden ladder.

"Spencer, it's DS Dalton," she hollered. "I need to talk with you again."

"She's fit," announced his mate as he peered down over the rail.

"Fit but a pain in the arse," replied Spencer, before smiling down and acknowledging he'd heard her.

* * * *

"Tell me, Donna, what would be your next step if you were in charge of the case?" Carmichael enquired as he and DC Twamley sped back towards Kirkwood.

The young DC thought for a few seconds before replying. "It looks like everything started from that call Leah Barnes made to Doug Pritchard," she said. "So, I'd say we need to know what was said in that call. But from the way she was this morning, I think it will be tricky to get Coral Freeman to even admit that her sister told her anything about the conversation."

"I agree," Carmichael replied. "But I think she may be more willing to talk if we can get her alone. I think she's told Suzi, and her big sister is the one who's preventing her from talking."

"Why would she be so worried about us knowing what Leah told Pritchard?" DC Twamley asked.

"I don't know," replied Carmichael, "but I suspect it's something rooted over twenty years ago and involves Chrissy Cream and the Vixens."

* * * *

Spencer Wood wasn't in the slightest bit phased when DS Dalton told him she'd learnt that he was outside The Three Bells on Wednesday evening, when he'd said he'd been at the Farmers Arms, and that CCTV footage had shown him arriving at the Farmers Arms about an hour later than he'd previously told her.

"I don't pay that much notice to time," he responded, offering up his wrists to DS Dalton, showing he wasn't wearing a watch.

"But you seemed quite specific when I asked you before," she remarked. "Or was that a time that Tom told you to tell us?"

Spencer shrugged his shoulders. "I've no idea what you're talking about," he replied, his arms now folded tightly across his chest.

"Come on, Spencer," she exclaimed, "do you think I was born yesterday?"

Spencer just shrugged his shoulders again.

"So, what were you doing at The Three Bells on Wednesday evening?" DS Dalton asked.

"I had a bit of business with Coral and Wade," he replied vaguely.

"What sort of business?" DS Dalton enquired.

"It's private," Spencer replied, "nothing to do with your murders."

"I think that's for us to decide, don't you?" DS Dalton said, her tone now much more annoyed than before.

"I just wanted to see if they were able to host a party," Spencer remarked.

"And were they?" DS Dalton asked.

"They said they were too busy to check the diary, so I went back the next day and got it sorted," Spencer replied.

"So, when I speak with Coral, she'll corroborate your story, will she?" DS Dalton added.

"Well, it's the truth, so I'd expect her to," responded Spencer.

DS Dalton nodded. "Did you go down Jay Bank Lane at all on Wednesday?" she asked.

Spencer shook his head.

"So, what way did you go to get to the Farmers Arms once you'd left The Three Bells?" she enquired.

"Down the High Street then I picked up the main road," replied Spencer. "It's the quickest route."

"But it took you almost an hour to get there," DS Dalton remarked. "Surely that's a twenty-five-to-thirty-minute journey, at most."

Spencer shrugged his shoulders.

"I stopped off on the way for a smoke," he replied. "Don't smoke in the van so I pulled up in a layby for fifteen minutes."

"Was that a cigarette or something a bit stronger?" DS Dalton enquired.

"I don't do weed anymore," replied Spencer, indignantly.

DS Dalton smiled. "And what about yesterday afternoon?" she asked. "Where were you between one thirty and three?"

Spencer looked horrified.

"You don't think I killed Ron Mason, do you?" he replied angrily.

"I have to ask," she said in a deliberately calm voice. "We're asking everyone."

Spencer shook his head. "I was in Kirkwood in the morning taking down a scaffold outside the old bank in Market Street. Then I went over to see Wade and Coral at The Three Bells, to sort out about the party, then I went home."

"And what time did you see Coral and Wade?" DS Dalton enquired.

"Wade wasn't about," replied Spencer, "but I'd say I got there at about one forty-five and left at about two thirty. Coral will probably be able to be more specific, as I say, I'm not big on times."

DS Dalton nodded. "I've just one last question," she announced. "Did you see anyone go down Jay Bank Lane on Wednesday evening, either on foot or in a vehicle?"

Spencer shook his head. "Nobody," he replied, "but I wasn't taking much notice."

DS Dalton looked up at the metal poles Spencer and his mate were erecting.

"They could do some real damage if you were hit by one of those," she remarked.

Again, Spencer shrugged his shoulders. "I suspect so," he replied. "But I've never been hit by one, so I wouldn't know for sure."

Chapter 35

True to form, Carmichael started the debrief at exactly two o'clock. DS Watson had been in the incident room for forty minutes before his three colleagues arrived, which gave him plenty of time to write up the list of beneficiaries he'd started to compile after speaking with Angus Frazer.

"Someone's been busy," announced DS Dalton, with a wry smile, when she spied the details on the whiteboard.

"And surprisingly legible, too," added Carmichael, mockingly.

DS Watson chose not to rise to the bait but remained standing by the whiteboard as if to say, "I want to start". Carmichael didn't disappoint his sergeant. "You better tell us what this all means," he remarked.

"Well, as you know, I talked with Ron Mason's brief this morning. He gave me a copy of his will and a codicil letter that he'd added to the will," began DS Watson who, as he spoke, handed around copies of both documents.

"This is dated Tuesday of this week," commented DS Dalton.

Watson smiled. "Yes," he replied. "According to Frazer, Ron called him on Monday and went in on Tuesday to amend his will and add the codicil."

"Presumably," continued DS Dalton, "as a result of him knowing something even before he'd met Pritchard."

"Remember, he went to see Leah on Sunday," Carmichael reminded the team. "I suspect that meeting prompted him to change his will."

"That's basically how I saw it too, sir," added DS Watson. "And, having talked to Frazer about Ron's old will, it looks like the only change he made was to remove Leah completely. According to Frazer, Leah previously was to inherit the house."

"Which is now to be made into a museum dedicated to Chrissy Cream and the Vixens, managed by Pam Hutton and Suzi Ashcroft," added DC Twamley, who had been reading the codicil while the others were talking.

"You're clearly a step ahead of us, Donna," suggested Carmichael, "so, why don't we all take a few moments to read the will and the codicil before we continue."

DS Watson nodded. "I think that's a good idea," he concurred.

* * * *

Ellis Hutton read his cousin's message for a second time, before responding.

ALL SOUNDS VERY SERIOUS MATE. ANY CLUES ABOUT WHAT THE MEET'S ABOUT AND WHY SO URGENT? ... EL's

He pressed send and waited for a reply. He didn't have to wait long.

JUST MEET ME THERE IN 30 MINUTES .... T

* * * *

As soon as Carmichael had finished reading his copy of Ron Mason's will and the attached codicil, he looked across at DS Watson. "You'd better fill us in on what else Angus Frazer told you and then go through those notes you've written up on the board."

"Of course," DS Watson replied with glee. "As I said before, Frazer told me that Ron called him on Monday wanting to change his will. They met up the next day, which is when he made this will and added the codicil."

"A will telling us that he, for some reason, owned substantial shares in three local businesses," Carmichael remarked, "which he's giving back to the owners. Did Frazer give you any background on this?"

DS Watson nodded his head. "He reckons these go back years and were basically secured loans that he'd made to each of them, when they needed a financial injection."

"And I assume he took a proportion of each of the company's profits?" added Carmichael.

"That's the thing," DS Watson replied, "according to Frazer, he never took a penny out of any of them."

"That's not what I'd expect from a hard-nosed businessman, like Mason," remarked Carmichael.

"I agree," concurred DS Watson. "But that's what Frazer told me."

"Interesting," Carmichael muttered.

"But the only change that Ron Mason appears to have made to his will, as was mentioned before," continued DS Watson, "was to turn High Moor Grange over to become a museum dedicated to Chrissy Cream and the Vixens."

"Which is to be managed by Suzi and Pam," added DS Dalton.

"Correct," confirmed DS Watson.

"And in his codicil," continued Carmichael, "he's made a few specific conditions that the new trust administering the museum have to adhere to."

"Exactly," replied DS Watson.

"He sounds like a control freak right to the end," DS Dalton remarked.

"You're probably not wrong there, Rachel," concurred Carmichael with a faintest of smiles, "but it's his house to do with as he wishes, so he's entitled to make certain conditions, I suppose."

By the look on her face, DS Dalton didn't seem to agree but said nothing.

"So," continued DS Watson, keen to move along to his beneficiaries list, "I thought it might be wise to list all those people who we now know benefit financially from Ron's death. Which is the list I've put up on the whiteboard."

As DS Watson spoke, everyone's eyes turned to focus on his list of the six beneficiaries.

"And you've added values against them," observed Carmichael. "Which you say are estimates, but how did you make those estimates?"

DS Watson shrugged his shoulders. "Just my best guesses," he responded.

Carmichael's expression indicated that he wasn't particularly impressed.

"I think the list is a great idea, Marc," he announced. "And it's clear all six of these people will have major financial windfalls because of Mason's death. However, can you delete those assumptions until we know for sure the sort of sums we are talking about."

DS Watson didn't argue and, taking the marker in his hand put a line through his financial estimates.

The room went silent for about a minute while Carmichael, DS Dalton and DC Twamley read through the six people who appeared to benefit most from Ron Mason's demise.

<u>Beneficiaries of change to royalty payments and from Ron Mason's will</u>

1. Suzi Ashcroft receives 12.5% of future band royalties .... ~~est £50K - £100K per annum~~

2. Pam Hutton receives 12.5% of future band royalties .... ~~est £50K - £100K per annum~~

3. Coral and Wade Freeman given Ron's 35% stake in The Three Bells Pub.... ~~est £300K - £500K.~~

4. Martin and Spencer Wood given Ron's 50% stake in Wood and Son's scaffolding business .... ~~est £50K.~~

5. Lydia Brook-Smith given Ron's 25% stake in The Muffin Maid... ~~est £100K.~~

6. Rose Commerford (Ron's cousin) receives the remaining assets after funeral costs and inheritance dues .... ~~est £500K to £1M.~~

"Thanks, Marc," said Carmichael. "We don't need to cover the first two, but let's go through the other four on your list. I'm particularly interested in those three names that haven't come up so far in our enquiries."

Chapter 36

"Where are you off to?" Pam enquired, as her son brushed passed her and out through the front door.
"Won't be long," Ellis shouted back. "Just meeting Tom."
Pam watched until the apple of her eye disappeared round the corner and out of her sight. Then, after giving out a huge sigh, she closed the front door and walked down the hallway into the kitchen. Ever since he'd hooked up with Verity, Pam had felt as if she'd been demoted a step in her son's affections; something she was finding ever so hard to come to terms with. Momentarily ignoring the friendly pooch, who'd brushed affectionately up against her leg, Pam reached up to one of her kitchen cabinets and pulled down a dark-green bottle; a close friend and source of solace in trying times.

* * * *

"Who do you want to talk about first?" DS Watson asked his boss.
"Why don't you start with Ron's cousin, Rose Commerford," Carmichael replied.
"I don't know too much about her," admitted DS Watson. "According to Frazer, she's married and lives on a farm somewhere in Minnesota."

Carmichael nodded gently. "Well, someone needs to get hold of her and find out when she was last in contact with her cousin."

"I'll do that, if you want," volunteered DC Twamley.

"Thanks, Donna," Carmichael replied. "And when you talk to her, find out if she had any idea she was in Mason's will."

"Will do, sir," replied DC Twamley.

Carmichael turned again to face DS Watson. "So, you have no idea what the stories are behind Ron Mason owning stakes in The Three Bells, this scaffolding company and a bakery?" he enquired, his expression one of bewilderment.

DS Watson shrugged his shoulders. "All I know is what I said before," he replied. "Frazer reckons they all go back years, they were secured loans that he'd made to each of them, at various times, when they needed a financial injection."

Carmichael thought for a few seconds before speaking. "Let's take one each," he said, his eyes focussed on his two sergeants. "Marc, you take the scaffolders. Rachel, you talk with Lydia Brook-Smith, and I'll try to speak to Coral, preferably without her husband or her sister looking over her shoulder."

Without waiting for either officer to respond, Carmichael continued. "Now let's talk a bit about the changes to Ron's will and that codicil," he remarked, waving his copy in the air.

* * * *

Although Ellis was almost a year older than his cousin, there had never been any doubt as to the pecking order in their relationship. Almost as soon as they could talk, it was Tom who called the shots; a trait that both Suzi and Pam, who'd discussed it at some length over the years, likened to the bond between their late mothers, with Tom's birth mum, Chrissy, always being the dominant force in that sibling relationship.

As he'd been ordered, Ellis arrived at the cricket pavilion at two thirty on the dot, where he found his cousin impatiently pacing up and down, Tom's face looking intense, verging on angry.

"What's all the drama about?" Ellis enquired in his normal affable way.

Tom turned and glared at his cousin. "You need to be straight with me," he said.

"Aren't I always?" replied Ellis, in a jovial mood. "And you need to chill out, bro, you look like you're about to have a coronary."

* * * *

"So, Leah's removed from the will," began Carmichael, "and High Moor Grange is put into trust and becomes some sort of shrine to Chrissy Cream and the Vixens."

"Managed by Pam and Suzi," DC Twamley stated.

"And he leaves strict and very specific instructions in the codicil about how the trust should be managed," added DS Watson.

"In keeping with someone who's a control freak," remarked DS Dalton, who despite never having met Ron Mason had already painted a picture of what sort of man he was, in her mind.

"I'm not sure I totally agree with that," Carmichael replied, his eyes gazing once more on the short codicil. "Although he is very particular about a few things, it's certainly not all encompassing. He makes it clear that Pam and Suzi are to manage the trust, he indicates that all profits are to be ploughed back into it, and he mentions some very specific things that he won't allow, mainly building alterations. But apart from that, it's quite open."

The team, almost in unison, took a minute to re-read the codicil once more.

DS Dalton was the first to look up from the document. "True enough," she concurred, "but he is very particular about where modifications can and can't be made to the house and gardens."

"To the front entrance and the east side," remarked DC Twamley, reading it as it was written down.

"And the walled garden is to be left as it is and made into a memorial garden to Chrissy and Jo," added DS Dalton.

Carmichael nodded his head and took a few seconds to think. "It's all very laudable," he remarked, "but what I want to know is why he did it now?"

"I'd say his will change was almost certainly a result of his conversation with Leah, on Sunday," suggested DS Watson.

"On that point I'm sure we all agree," concurred Carmichael. "And that's why it's crucial that I speak again with Coral. I'm as certain as I can be that she's got some, if not all, of the answers to what's been going on in the last three days."

* * * *

Ellis emerged from behind the pavilion, his shirt torn and stained with grass, mud and blood.

Exhausted, with his knuckles smarting from the blows he'd inflicted on his cousin, and with blood oozing slowly from his nose and dripping out of several small cuts to his face, he took out his mobile and pressed speed dial.

"Can you come to the cricket pavilion?" he asked. "I think I may have hurt Tom."

Chapter 37

Carmichael ended the team briefing at two forty-five and, within seconds, his three officers had dispersed leaving him alone with his thoughts in the incident room.
Between them, they'd now created four lists: the background on Chrissy Cream and the Vixens, a facts list, a list of suspects and a series of questions needing answers.
Carmichael took a few moments to carry out some additional updates, as he'd remembered further items that he wanted documenting, which he slotted in where there was space. Once he felt that they were complete, he carefully read through the forty-three noted items from the four lists and then, once more, he studied the codicil that Ron Mason had made to his will, just two days earlier.

Background on Chrissy Cream and the Vixens

1. *Chrissy and Jo Cream were sisters from High Maudsey (Chrissy being 3 years older than Jo).*
2. *The Vixens were originally Jo's band, but after their original lead singer left, Chrissy joined with her best friend Suzi Ashcroft and they get another school friend,*

Ron Mason (also from High Maudsey) to be the band's manager.

3. *Within a year, they'd replaced all the original band members, apart from Jo, with Pam Hutton the last to be added. The band's drummer. The band then becomes known as Chrissy Cream and the Vixens.*
4. *They have 6 top 20 hits in the next 3 years and are the first all-girl rock band to have a number 1 hit in the USA.*
5. *Shortly after each other Chrissy and Jo have a baby, Chrissy's (Tom) rumoured to be the child of another rock star, Liam Thomas, (a rumour denied by both Chrissy and Liam). Jo's child (also a boy called Ellis) is thought to have been the son of a Premier League footballer. Tom and Ellis are now in their early twenties and were adopted by Suzi and Pam respectively when their mums died.*
6. *Chrissy and Jo were both killed twenty years ago in a tragic boating accident in the North Sea. This was just before they were due to fly out to the US for their first American tour. The skipper of the boat was also killed, so no survivors.*
7. *The band broke up after their deaths and didn't release any more records.*
8. *Ron Mason remained in control of all royalties that the band earnt and was also the sole trustee of the trust funds set up for the two boys, which is rumoured to be a significant amount of money. The boys won't get control of their inheritances until they are 25 years old.*
9. *Ron Mason was 53, he'd only managed one major artist other than The Vixens, a singer called Ferne Cramley, who had 3 minor hits 10 years ago, but has now retired from the music business and lives with her husband and family in rural Herefordshire.*

10. *Pam and Suzi, the only 2 surviving band members live in the area still. Pam has a brother who is a farmer in one of the villages. She appears to be quite reclusive spending her time looking after Ellis and a host of cats and other animals. Suzi, who was the wild child of the band now appears to spend the majority of her time and energy fighting for a variety of causes, including saving the planet, women's rights and third world poverty. She is devoted to Tom and, like Pam, has never married.*
11. *Doug Pritchard lived in Hove and had been a music journalist for over thirty years. He specialised in uncovering salacious stories about the rich and famous in the music industry. Although he'd had a number of big stories published over the years, his credibility and methods of obtaining information are viewed with great suspicion.*

Facts

1. *Doug Pritchard was murdered at approx. 9:35pm in Jay Bank Lane, High Maudsey on Wed 20th March.*
2. *Ron Mason was murdered between 1:40pm and 3pm on his drive in High Maudsey on Thursday 21st March.*
3. *Pritchard and Mason had argued at The Three Bells pub about 20-30 minutes before Doug Pritchard was killed – subject unknown.*
4. *Both men were killed by blows to the head. Ron Mason by a single blow with one of his own golf clubs; Doug Pritchard was struck twice by a cylindrical weapon – identity unknown.*
5. *Pritchard received a call from Leah Barnes on Sat 16th March.*

6. *Leah was Mason's PA for years and is the younger sister of Suzi Ashcroft and twin sister of Coral Freeman (the landlady of The Three Bells) where Ron Mason and Doug Pritchard argued on the night of Doug's murder.*
7. *Pritchard tried to make contact with National Sub-Editor (Ted Heslegrave) and pop star, Liam Thomas, almost immediately after Leah called him.*
8. *Thomas Ashcroft met with Ron Mason at Ron's house shortly before he was murdered.*
9. *Verity Brook-Smith claims that during their argument, in The Three Bells, Ron Mason got angry when Doug Pritchard had suggested that Chrissy Cream was still alive.*
10. *Spencer Wood lied about being at the Farmers Arms pub in the village of Rainham Moss with Ellis when Doug Pritchard was murdered, which means that neither have an alibi for the time of Pritchard's murder.*
11. *Wade Freeman lied about when Ron Mason left the pub on Wed 20th March, the night Doug Pritchard was killed. Ron appears to have left very soon after Doug Pritchard, not just before closing time, as Wade had claimed.*
12. *Ron Mason amended his will, adding a codicil, just two days after he'd met with Leah at the care home. Leah was removed from his will and his home (High Moor Grange) was now to become a memorial to the band.*
13. *There are numerous people who benefit financially from Ron Mason's death (all listed in the suspects list).*
14. *Leah asked for Coral to visit her at St Jude's on the evening she died.*

Questions needing answers.

1. *What did Leah and Doug Pritchard talk about on the phone?*
2. *Why did Doug want to talk to Ron and what caused them to argue?*
3. *Why did Wade lie about the time Ron left the pub on the evening Doug Pritchard died?*
4. *Why did Ron change his will?*
5. *Why did Ron want to meet with Suzi and Pam?*
6. *Why did Spencer Wood lie about his whereabouts when the murder happened?*
7. *Why had Ron become involved in a cake shop, a scaffolding company, and a pub? And why wasn't he taking any income from his significant shares in those businesses?*

Suspects

1. *Suzi Ashcroft (Motive Financial gain)*
2. *Pam Hutton (Motive Financial gain)*
3. *Tom Ashcroft*
4. *Ellis Hutton*
5. *Coral Freeman (Motive Financial gain)*
6. *Wade Freeman (Motive Financial gain)*
7. *Martin Wood (Motive Financial gain)*
8. *Spencer Wood (Motive Financial gain)*
9. *Lydia Brook-Smith (Motive Financial gain)*
10. *Leah Barnes*
11. *Rose Commerford (Motive Financial gain)*

Codicil

I, Ronald Adam Mason, upon my death direct the trustees of High Moor Grange to ensure that the entire house and all its land remains forever a venue honouring the lives and legacy of the group known as Chrissy Cream and the Vixens. Under no circumstances should any of the property placed within the trust be sold or devoted to any other activity other than to provide members of the public the opportunity to be better acquainted with the band, its members and, most importantly, its music.

I gladly place the day-to-day decision making regarding the running of the trust in the hands of Suzi Ashcroft and Pamela Hutton on the understanding that they, and their successors, adhere to the above and with the following additional provisions:

1. *That all profits generated from the trust are invested back into the trust.*
2. *That any additional building, should it be required, is confined to the front entrance and east side of the house, only. No additional building is permitted to the west or rear of the property and save pathways, rest room facilities and refreshment stalls, no building is permitted within the grounds of the property.*
3. *That the walled garden is to be left as it is at present, a rose garden. This should be used exclusively as a place of contemplation dedicated in the memory of Chrissy and Jo Cream.*
4. *Should she survive me, I give specific instructions that Leah Barnes shall be expressly forbidden to have any involvement with the trust in any capacity.*

Carmichael looked at his watch. It was now exactly three o'clock. He printed off copies of everything on the whiteboard, which he folded and placed in his jacket pocket.

"That's fifteen minutes well spent," he muttered to himself as he made his way out of the door.

Chapter 38

As soon as she'd finished talking on the phone with Ellis, Suzi Ashcroft was on her feet and had raced out of The Three Bells, leaving Coral bemused as to what could possibly be so important.
It had taken her just fifteen minutes to get to the village cricket pavilion, where she found Tom perched alone on the large concrete roller, conscious but clearly still dazed and bruised after his altercation with Ellis.
"What happened?" Suzi asked, her voice shrill and clearly expressing her concern for her son.
Tom looked up. "What are you doing here?" he enquired.
"Ellis called me," replied Suzi, "he said he thought he'd badly hurt you. What on earth happened?"
"I'm fine," said Tom, shrugging off his mother's attempt to engulf him in her soothing embrace. "We just had a minor disagreement. It's all sorted now."
"It doesn't look like a minor disagreement," replied Suzi. "And from the sound of his voice when he called me, Ellis didn't think so either. Anyway, where is Ellis?"
"Probably with Verity, or that lush who calls herself his mother," said Tom scathingly.
"Don't talk about Pam like that," replied Suzi, angrily. "She's been good to you over the years, she doesn't

deserve that. And she is Ellis's Mum, just like I'm yours."

Tom couldn't deny what Suzi was saying, and felt bad about it, too, so didn't argue.

"Has this got anything to do with Spencer Wood?" Suzi enquired.

Tom frowned and shook his head. "No, Mum," he replied. "I can assure you that Spencer has absolutely nothing to do with our argument."

"I saw you giving him an envelope yesterday when he was on our doorstep," remarked Suzi. "What was that all about?"

"That's none of your business," snapped Tom. "But it's got nothing to do with my argument with Ellis."

Suzi wasn't totally sure she believed him but decided not to probe any more.

"Let's get you home," she said, putting an arm around her son's shoulders, "and get you cleaned up."

Tom was hurting just about everywhere, so, despite wanting to be alone in his moment of defeat, he reluctantly decided it was in his best interest to do as Suzi suggested.

"Not a word about this to anyone," he said to Suzi as they slowly walked towards her van. "It's bad enough being beaten senseless by that wimp without it becoming common knowledge, too."

"If that's what you want," replied Suzi. "But I will be having harsh words with Ellis the next time I see him."

Tom gently shook his head and forced a faint smile.

"Mum, I'm twenty-two," he replied. "I think those days are long gone, don't you? Anyway, I started it. It wasn't Ellis's fault."

This perplexed Suzi even more, but she said nothing.

*   *   *   *

DC Twamley was checking the time difference between the UK and Thief River Falls, the small town in Minnesota where Rose Commerford lived, when Carmichael's call came through.
"Hi sir," she said, just as Google informed her, they were six hours behind.
"How are you getting on tracking down Mason's cousin?" Carmichael enquired.
"I've got her address and was just trying to work out what time it is there," DC Twamley replied. "I thought I'd give the local police a call to see if they had her telephone number."
"They'll be no more than six hours behind us," remarked Carmichael. "Penny has some relatives in Minneapolis, which is why I know."
"Thanks, sir," replied DC Twamley, who decided not to tell him she'd just managed to find that out for herself. "I'll make that call straight after we've finished."
"And when you've done with that," continued Carmichael, "I'd like you to get hold of the coroner's report for the accident that killed, Chrissy Cream and Jo Cream. Get the details of anyone who was called upon at the inquest and, if they're still alive, track down their contact details."
"Do you think their deaths have something to do with our murders?" DC Twamley asked.
"Like everything else to do with this case at the moment, I can't be certain," replied Carmichael honestly, "but it's almost a sure thing that whatever Leah told Pritchard was the catalyst. And I think there's more than a fair chance it involves Chrissy Cream in some way."
Before DC Twamley could say anything more, the phone line suddenly went dead, catching her completely

on the hop. Guessing her boss had intentionally ended the call, DC Twamley started to dial the number she'd written down for the police station at Thief River Falls. Carmichael, who had deliberately rung off, put his foot down on the accelerator of his black BMW and turned his mind to his strategy for the meeting he was shortly going to have with Coral and Wade Freeman, at The Three Bells.

Chapter 39

Wood and Son's yard was located to the side of the large house that Martin Wood had built himself when he was more able. Set in the middle of a large plot of land, the Wood residence, which he'd mischievously called Large Hampton, was a square-shaped, red-bricked dwelling with two white columns standing proud on either side of the front door and enough space in the front for several vehicles. Had it not been for the fact that the drive was strewn with a variety of seemingly discarded items, ranging from a pile of bricks to what appeared to be the shell of a washing machine, anyone approaching could have taken this to be a house belonging to someone with a bit of money. But that wasn't the impact it made on DS Watson. Showy and large it may have been, but the overriding, first impression he had, when his car came to a halt on the gravel drive, was of a pretentious monstrosity of a dwelling, typical of a handyman who had some skill when it came to building, but that was almost certainly going to be riddled with the sort of shoddy issues that would drive Susan, his other half, into a tailspin. Added to the obvious lack of any maintenance over many years, it appeared to be, as Watson's grandmother would have said, a case of 'fur coat and no drawers'. His suspicions only heightened when, after trying to ring the doorbell, the button he'd pressed remained inside its housing. However, in fairness to the owner, the bell must have worked, as within a few seconds the door was opened by an exhausted-looking, middle-aged woman, whose expression suggested she wasn't keen to talk with visitors. After looking him up and down the woman asked what he wanted.

DS Watson smiled and held up his identity card. "I'm DS Watson from Mid-Lancashire Police. May I speak with Mr Martin Wood, please?"

* * * *

DS Dalton's reception at The Muffin Maid couldn't have been more different to that which, unbeknown to her, had greeted DS Watson. With her work pretty much done for the day, Lydia Brook-Smith was just about to go into the backroom and put her feet up when DS Dalton introduced herself at the counter.

"Come through," Lydia said with a genuine warm smile. "Do you want a brew? I'm just doing myself one."

"That would be wonderful," replied DS Dalton, who followed the shop's proprietor towards the room behind the counter.

As Lydia passed by the end of the counter, she picked up a tray of cream cakes that had been perched at the far end.

"Let's bring these in too," she remarked with another broad smile. "They're fresh cream, so they won't keep."

* * * *

Although Martin Wood was a man in his mid-fifties, he'd clearly had some health issues; so much so that he looked at least ten years older.

"What is it you want from me?" enquired Wood, as he slowly eased himself down into a threadbare red armchair.

"What happened to your leg?" Watson asked, the pain and difficulty Wood had with every move he made, quite evident.

"Fell off a ladder eight years ago," replied Wood. "Broke both legs and damaged my back. The doctors said I'm lucky to be able to walk at all. But I don't feel that bloody lucky."

DS Watson smiled, although judging from the scowl that remained on Wood's face, he instantly realised that perhaps it wasn't the correct response.

"Lucky you have Spencer to help out," Watson remarked.

Wood shrugged his shoulders. "At first it was a real problem. We had no income of any note and, of course, Spencer was still a kid. But in the last three or four years it's picked up and Spencer's stepped up. Good job really, as I'll not be going up ladders again, not in this state."

"I'd like to talk to you about Ron Mason," announced DS Watson. "Did you know him well?"

Wood considered the question for a while. "We've hardly spoken in the last dozen years or so," Wood replied. "But we've known each other since we were at school together, so for fifty years."

"And what sort of man was he?" DS Watson asked.

For the first time since they'd met, Wood permitted a small grin to appear on his pursed lip, albeit a fleeting signal. "A flash git would be my summary of him," replied Wood. "Always looking for an angle on something, always looking to make a quick buck. A ducker and a diver who hit the mother lode with Chrissy's band."

"Is that how you see it?" DS Watson enquired.

"Well, he's made their manager and within weeks they get their first number one hit," replied Wood. "Nothing to do with him, but of course he's suddenly rolling in it."

"I see," said DS Watson. "So, you weren't what you'd call friends?"

Wood shook his head. "We tolerated each other, but that was about it."

"But Ron invested money into your business and, as far as I'm aware, never received any dividends or interest on his investment. How did that come about?"

Wood looked a little surprised that his inquisitor knew about this. "It was a gesture he made after the band split up," replied Wood. "A pay off."

DS Watson frowned. "What do you mean?"

Pleased that the officer sat in front of him evidently didn't know everything, Wood smirked again. This time a fuller smile. "I was in charge of the lighting and organising the logistics at the band's concerts," he replied. "Didn't you know that?"

DS Watson shook his head. "No, I didn't," he replied.

"So, even though he didn't have to," continued Wood, "Ron gave me some cash to help start the scaffolding business. As I say, he didn't need to, so I guess some would say it was a kind act by him. But he stood to make millions even after Chrissy and Jo died, so it was a drop in the ocean to him and, to be honest, it made him feel superior. He loved to portray himself as the great benefactor."

"I see," replied DS Watson.

"And you're right, he took nothing out of the business, but apart from the cash he invested, he put nothing in. And, of course, he still owned fifty per cent of Wood and Son," added Wood with more than a hint of annoyance in his voice.

"Well up until he was killed," remarked DS Watson, staring directly into Wood's eyes to see how he reacted.

But Martin Wood gave nothing away. "True enough," was all he said.

"Do you know the terms of Ron Mason's will when it comes to your business?" DS Watson asked.

Wood suddenly looked interested but at the same time anxious. "I don't," he replied, a response that looked totally genuine to DS Watson.

"He's left it all to you and your son," DS Watson informed him.

Wood's posture immediately changed. He sat upright, straight backed with his eyes wide open and a broad beam of a smile etched across his face. "Really?" he exclaimed jubilantly. "Now I didn't expect that. That's a real result. Maybe there is a god after all."

Chapter 40

"There's nothing better than a cup of tea and a cream cake in the afternoon, in my view," remarked Lydia Brook-Smith as she bit deeply into a chocolate eclair, the cream instantly oozing out of the opposite end and falling upon the china plate, which she'd carefully placed no more than an inch below her chin.

Much as she'd have loved to have a large cream cake, too, DS Dalton didn't trust herself to be able to manage questioning Lydia while still retaining some semblance of professionalism, so she'd opted for the cake on the tray with the least cream inside, an iced cream slice.

"Can you tell me why Ron Mason invested money into The Muffin Maid?" DS Dalton asked, not wishing to dilly-dally with small talk.

Lydia didn't seem at all unsettled by the question. "He was just a really kind guy," she responded. "He was a fair bit older than me, but we both grew up around here and when he heard I needed a largish deposit to buy The Muffin Maid, he just offered to give me the money. I refused to take it as a gift, so he said he'd take a twenty five percent share in the business for his thirty thousand pounds."

"Thirty thousand!" exclaimed DS Dalton. "And when was that?"

Lydia thought for a few moments before responding. "Would have been almost twenty years ago now."

"That's a massive gift," DS Dalton remarked. "And you didn't have to do anything for it?"

Lydia still looked unfazed. "No," she replied, shaking her head. "He was a nice guy, he knew I needed cash and, let's face it, he was loaded. It was probably nothing to him, but a massive help for me. If it wasn't for that I'd never have been able to buy this business."

DS Dalton found it hard to get her head around what Lydia was saying, but she did sound credible, despite the story seeming outlandish.

"What about Ron's will," continued DS Dalton. "Do you know his instructions regarding his twenty-five per cent stake in the business?"

For the first time since they'd sat down, Lydia looked a little disconcerted.

"I hadn't thought about that," she replied, her expression one of alarm. "I suppose someone else will now own that won't they."

DS Dalton shrugged her shoulders ever so slightly. "Well kind of," she replied. "He's bequeathed that to you."

If Lydia did know this already, she did a wonderful job in hiding the fact. "Goodness me," she remarked, her eyes wide open in astonishment. "Wait until I tell Verity."

DS Dalton smiled. "He was clearly keen to help you and Verity," she announced.

"Yes," replied Lydia. "He's always been good to us."

DS Dalton wasn't sure where to take the conversation from there, and found herself saying, "I met Verity the other day. How long has she got before the baby comes?"

Lydia smiled broadly. "Sixteen weeks," she replied definitively.
"I must be getting old," remarked DS Dalton, "but Verity looks so young to be becoming a mum."
Lydia nodded. "She is," she agreed. "She's only nineteen, but as she keeps telling me, I was very young when she was born."
DS Dalton nodded. "And can I ask about Verity's dad?" DS Dalton continued. "Is he on the scene?"
Lydia shook her head. "He was a very brief encounter," she replied. "Moved on before she was born, and he doesn't even know he's a dad. Which is how we both want to keep it."
"I see," said DS Dalton, who wanted to know more, but didn't feel further questions on that subject were within the remit of their investigation, or a discussion that would be welcomed by Lydia. DS Dalton did, however, have one more question that she felt she needed to ask. "Tell me, when Ron Mason gave you the funding for the shop, was Chrissy Cream still alive?" DS Dalton enquired.
Lydia shook her head. "No, it would have been one or two years afterwards," she replied.

*   *   *   *

Wade Freeman was looking out of the window of the pub's lounge, talking on his mobile, when he spied Carmichael's car pulling up.
"Talk of the devil, he's here now," he said. "Thanks for the heads-up, Woody."
Wade then ended the call and put his mobile onto the table beside him.

"It's that bloody copper again," he shouted through to his wife, who was standing behind the bar; the two of them now the only people left inside the pub.

Carmichael was just about to clamber out of his car when his mobile rang. It was DS Watson.

"Hi Marc," he said, remaining inside his BMW. "I take it you've finished talking with Martin Wood?"

"I have," replied DS Watson and I'm as sure as can be that he didn't know anything about Ron Mason's will. He seemed shocked and, well, almost joyous when he learned that he and Spencer now own all their scaffolding company."

"Did he tell you anything else?" Carmichael enquired.

"He did," said Watson, keen to share his findings. "He told me that when the band was at its height, he was the lighting and logistics organiser at their concerts. It sounds like the investment Mason made into the business was a payoff of sorts when the band broke up."

"Really," remarked Carmichael. "Now that is interesting."

Carmichael thought for a few seconds before continuing. "And what sort of guy is Martin Wood?"

DS Watson also took a couple of seconds before replying. "A very bitter man, in my view," he replied. "I don't think life's been that kind to him, well I don't think he thinks it has at any rate."

"Could he be our murderer?" Carmichael asked.

"I'd say not," replied DS Watson. "I think he'd struggle to overpower anyone, given his mobility issues, but I guess if he surprised them maybe he could have done it."

"Ok," Carmichael said. "And what are your plans now?"

"I was intending to head back to the station," DS Watson replied.

"Good," added Carmichael. "And when you do, can you help Donna? I've asked her to get the coroner's report on Chrissy and Jo's accident, and to locate any living witnesses. I think we need to know more about what happened that evening and in the days, before."

"Will do, sir," Watson confirmed. "I take it you've not spoken to the Freemans yet?"

"I'm just about to go in now," Carmichael advised him. "It will be interesting to hear what they have to say for themselves this time. Will see you later."

"Will …"

The phone went dead before DS Watson could say "do".

Chapter 41

"Good afternoon, Mrs Freeman," remarked Carmichael as soon as the large wooden door of the pub opened, and he saw the landlady standing in front of him. "May I come in for a few minutes? I've a few more questions I'd like to ask you."

Coral Freeman forced a smile and took a step sideways, pulling open the door to allow Carmichael to enter. As he crossed the threshold, Carmichael spotted Wade Freeman, who was leaning against the bar, his expression suggesting he wasn't in the best of moods. Ignoring Wade's surly demeanour, Carmichael strode into the centre of the room and nodded over at the landlord. "I was hoping you'd be here, Mr Freeman," he remarked. "There are a few questions I have for you as well."

"I hope they're quick ones," replied Wade curtly. "There's a bereavement in the family and I've got a cash and carry run to do this afternoon, so we're not exactly flush with time at the moment."

"Of course," responded Carmichael sensitively. "Once again, I'm so sorry about your loss, Mrs Freeman," he said, his attention now focussed on Coral. "I'll be as quick as I can. In fact, if you must be away, Mr Freeman, maybe I'll start with the questions I have for you, then you can get about your business while I talk more with your wife."

"In that case," interrupted Coral, "I'll go out back until you're ready for me."

"That sounds ideal," replied Carmichael, who waited until Coral was out of sight before turning his attention back to Wade Freeman. "So, why did you lie to me, Mr Freeman?" Carmichael enquired. His expression now stern and serious.

"About what?" replied Wade, with an air of surprise in his voice.

"About Ron Mason being here in the pub on Wednesday until almost closing time," announced Carmichael. "We know that's not true. In fact, we know he left quite soon after Doug Pritchard. Why did you try to mislead us?"

Wade Freeman looked nervous. He rubbed his chin with his right hand as he tried to think of what to say. Carmichael fixed his stare directly on the publican but said nothing. "Look, he's an old mate," commented Wade after a pause of a few more seconds. "It was stupid, I know, but I thought I was just helping out a friend."

"So, I take it you thought he was involved in Doug Pritchard's death?" Carmichael enquired.

Wade paused for a few seconds before answering. "Well, they'd been quarrelling like crazy that evening, so I just thought ..." Wade didn't finish his sentence. "But with Ron being murdered, too, that puts him in the clear, doesn't it?" he added, as if his initial lie was of no consequence.

Carmichael shook his head. He was having none of it. "No," he replied firmly. "And what you did was deliberately mislead the police in a murder enquiry at a critical time in our investigation. This is a serious issue, Mr Freeman."

Carmichael's words clearly had an immediate impact on the previously self-assured publican. Standing well over six foot tall and ordinarily having the bearing of a man who looked even taller, Wade Freeman was normally an imposing figure. However, his posture seemed to change in front of Carmichael's eyes. Although still standing, the publican appeared to shrink by several inches and the lean he'd adopted against the bar now appeared to be the only thing holding him upright.

"But surely, Ron's in the clear for that journalist's death," he protested again. "It can't have hampered your investigation that much?"

Carmichael elected not to respond directly to Freeman's plea. "Unless you want to make matters even worse for yourself," he remarked, "I'd start by telling me exactly what happened on Wednesday evening."

Wade Freeman's eyeline fell to a point somewhere close to Carmichael's shoelaces. "What do you want to know?" he asked meekly.

* * * *

It was four thirty-five when DS Dalton left The Muffin Maid. As she walked over to her car, the pink, brightly painted company van pulled up beside her, and as she was opening her door, Verity and Ellis clambered out of their respective sides of the vehicle.

Verity spied DS Dalton almost straight away and although she gave her a smile, she looked a little concerned. "Is everything ok?" Verity enquired.

"Everything's fine," DS Dalton replied, before looking across at the figure of the young man in his early twenties. "I just had a few questions for your mum."

As she spoke, DS Dalton noticed that the young man accompanying Verity had scratches on his cheek, a shiner of a black eye and some nasty-looking grazes on his knuckles.

"You look like you've been in the wars," she remarked to him, her light tone matched by the broad smile on her face.

"This is my boyfriend, Ellis," Verity quickly announced, as if to buy him a few seconds to think of a reply.

"Pleased to meet you, Ellis. Have you been in some sort of altercation?"

Ellis shrugged his shoulders. "I just fell over last night when I was out," he replied. "A little too much drink, I'm ashamed to say."

DS Dalton didn't believe a word of it, but just nodded and clambered into her car.

* * * *

"So, let's start with what you heard inside the pub on Wednesday," announced Carmichael. "What, exactly, were they arguing about?"

His usual bravado having evaporated completely, Wade Freeman nodded gently.

"I didn't hear anything that Pritchard said," he replied. "He seemed very calm throughout. In fact, by the expression on his face, I think he was enjoying seeing Ron getting so irate."

"So, what did you hear Ron say?" probed Carmichael.

"He shouted *that's a lie*," he replied. "Then he got really angry, which is just before he stormed off to the toilets, and he shouted *if you print that I'll sue you for every penny you've got you effing lowlife.*"

"And did you have any idea what he was talking about?" Carmichael enquired.

Wade Freeman raised his head and looked quizzically into Carmichael's eyes. "Chrissy Cream, I'd suspect, wouldn't you?" he replied.

Carmichael thought for a few seconds before continuing. "And why did you have a word with Pritchard when it was Ron who was making all the kerfuffle?" he enquired.

Wade shrugged his shoulders. "As I say, Ron was a mate," he replied.

"And he also owned thirty-five per cent of the pub," added Carmichael. "I suspect that may have had something to do with it, too."

"He was a sleeping partner," responded Wade as quick as a shot. "He never got involved in the business."

"But you wouldn't want to get on the wrong side of him, I assume," remarked Carmichael.

By the look on Wade Freeman's face, Carmichael could see his observation was correct.

"How did Ron's involvement in the pub come about?" Carmichael asked.

"It was a weird thing really," replied the publican. "He knew I was looking for a pub to buy and being an old pal from school, who'd done alright for himself, he just offered to help out with the deposit."

"Just like that, with no strings attached?" enquired Carmichael, with a look of bewilderment on his face.

Wade Freeman nodded. "Yes, that's pretty much how it was," he replied.

"And when was that?" Carmichael asked.

"About twenty years ago now," replied Wade.

"Was that before or after Chrissy and her sister died?" Carmichael asked.

Wade Freeman once again looked uncomfortable. "It was after," he replied, not needing to think too hard about the question.

Chapter 42

Having finally had confirmation from Wade Freeman that Ron Mason actually left the pub on Wednesday evening within a matter of minutes of Doug Pritchard, and with Wade maintaining he had no knowledge of Ron leaving his thirty-five percent of the pub to him and Coral, Carmichael let the pub landlord go on his way.

"Remember, I'll need you to go down to the station in the next twenty-four hours to give us a new, detailed and totally accurate statement of what you saw and heard on Wednesday evening," Carmichael had shouted over to him just before he exited the pub.

"Now for Coral," Carmichael muttered to himself as he walked over to the other side of the bar.

* * * *

Donna Twamley's afternoon was progressing well. Having had a positive conversation with the ever-so-helpful officer at Thief River Falls police station, who'd given her Rose Commerford's telephone number, DC Twamley had managed to have a lengthy conversation with Ron's cousin and main heir.

She'd discovered that Rose was fifteen years Ron's senior and had last seen him when she was still a teenager, just before her father, an American air force engineer, and her mother, Ron's father's sister, had emigrated to the wilds of Minnesota; a location where Rose had remained ever since. Although Rose remembered the child she used to babysit with fondness, she'd confessed that she'd not seen him since they'd emigrated and had no idea what he'd been up to in the forty-plus intervening years. The news of her inheritance was greeted with surprise but tinged with a deep regret that she'd allowed time to pass without making any effort to contact her English cousin.

Once her conversation with Rose ended, DC Twamley had thrown herself headlong into Carmichael's latest directive, namely getting hold of the coroner's report for the accident that killed Chrissy Cream and Jo Cream and trying to identify anyone who was called upon to give evidence to the enquiry. To her surprise and delight, with minimal effort, she found plenty to report back on.

* * * *

Carmichael sat directly opposite Coral Freeman at a small table in the middle of the pub's main lounge.

"I think it's time you came clean with me and started to share what you know about what's been going on," Carmichael announced, his piercing blue eyes fixed on the forlorn-looking landlady. "I appreciate you must have so much running through your head at the moment, and I'm so terribly sorry about your loss, but it's time you started telling me the whole truth."

Coral gazed down at the tabletop between them and didn't offer any resistance.

"What is it you'd like to know?" she simply enquired.

Carmichael maintained his penetrating glare. "You could tell me first why it was that you misled us about when Ron Mason left the pub on Wednesday?"

"I didn't," replied Coral, her denial rather sheepishly delivered. "You never asked me, as I recall."

"But you knew it wasn't as late as your husband was saying," continued Carmichael. "You knew it was much closer to the time Doug Pritchard left than last orders."

Coral shrugged her shoulders. "I'm not certain when he left."

Carmichael shook his head gently from side to side. "I don't believe you, Mrs Freeman," he remarked. "I think you're just choosing not to tell us. Your husband has just admitted he lied, so I'd think hard about what you put in the new statement I need you to give us."

Although Coral didn't respond, Carmichael was confident that his words had hit home. "I'd now like you to tell me exactly what it was that Leah told you last night," he continued.

Coral thought for a few seconds before responding.

"She told me that, in her view, it was because of her that Ron and that reporter had been killed," Coral announced. "She wasn't sure who had killed them, but she was sure that they died as a result of something she'd told Pritchard."

"And what was that?" Carmichael enquired, his pulse now starting to race.

"Leah refused to tell me all the details as she said she didn't want me to come to any harm," replied Coral in a calm, clear voice.

"And that's all she said?" remarked Carmichael, who was now feeling deflated at being told so little.

Coral nodded. "Pretty much," she added.

"What do you mean, pretty much?" Carmichael enquired. "Did she tell you something else?"

Coral shrugged her shoulders. "She told me there were skeletons in the cupboard, that I shouldn't get involved and that I should trust no one."

"And what do you think she meant by that?" Carmichael asked.

Coral shrugged her shoulders.

"Leah wasn't one to get melodramatic about anything," Coral continued. "She was a very down to earth, practical person who didn't get overexcited about stuff. So, her telling me not to get involved is significant. She must have thought I'd be in danger if I started to meddle."

Carmichael thought for a few seconds.

"What about Suzi?" he enquired. "Did Leah want her to be careful, too?"

Coral nodded. "She did. Leah told me to speak with Suzi. Which I did this morning."

"And was Suzi shocked?" Carmichael asked.

Coral nodded. "She was, of course," Coral replied, as if the question was stupid. "She told me not to tell anyone. In fact, when I tell Suzi I've told you she'll probably go mental."

Carmichael nodded. "But Leah didn't say anything else that gave you a clue about what it was she told Doug Pritchard?"

"No," replied Coral. "Not a hint of it."

Believing he'd got about as much as he could from Coral Freeman, Carmichael stood up.

"In that case, I'll leave you, Mrs Freeman," he remarked in a gentle tone of voice. "I realise you'll have a lot to be doing over the next few days, with Leah passing away."

Then after giving Coral as warm a smile as he could muster, Carmichael turned away and started to walk towards the exit.

"There was one thing she told me," announced Coral, her voice a touch excited that she'd remembered something.

Carmichael half turned to face her. "What was that?"

"I asked her why she'd called Pritchard," Coral replied. "And she said it was because Ron was going back on his promise."

"What did she mean by that?" Carmichael enquired.

"Search me," responded Coral, unhelpfully. "It was at that point that Leah fell asleep, and I left her.

Carmichael nodded sagely before giving Coral a forced smile and heading out of The Three Bells pub.

Chapter 43

DC Twamley's afternoon had been a series of exciting revelations surrounding the circumstances leading up to the tragedy of the Workington Jenny; driven largely by the coroner's report, which was very detailed and had given the young DC a variety of avenues to pursue.

With so much information coming to light and knowing how much Carmichael liked these sorts of things being recorded in list form, she'd spent the last thirty-five minutes documenting her findings, which had resulted in eleven bullet points for her to share with Carmichael and the team upon their return to the station.

Feeling well chuffed with herself, DC Twamley took a moment to sit back and admire her handiwork and take a sip of her coffee, the only drink she'd had time to make in the last three hours.

It was at that point that the rest of the team started to arrive back; and within twenty minutes all four of them were together and the last case review meeting of the day started.

*   *   *   *

"With such a comprehensive list of discoveries on the whiteboard, I suggest you start the meeting off with an update on what you've uncovered this afternoon," announced Carmichael, his words directed at the junior member of the group.

Thrilled to be asked to kick-off the meeting, DC Twamley stood up and turned to face the rest of the team. "I've spoken to Rose Commerford, Ron Mason's cousin and main beneficiary," DC Twamley announced. "She's now sixty-eight and has been living for years in a very remote, small town in Minnesota. She had no idea about being in Ron's will and maintains that, although as a teenager she used to be his babysitter now and then, since emigrating to America, almost fifty years ago, she hasn't seen or spoken to him. They exchanged Christmas cards for many years, but she said even that had stopped over ten years ago."

"So, she's off our list of suspects," DS Watson suggested.

DC Twamley nodded. "I'd say so."

"What about the boat accident?" enquired Carmichael, who'd been studying DC Twamley's list while she'd been talking. "Why don't you run through the various items you've documented up there."

DC Twamley quickly passed out copies of the coroner's report to each of her three colleagues: a hefty document some thirty pages long.

"The report's very thorough and contains lots of interesting details that I think could help us," she remarked, before turning to face the whiteboard and her eleven bullet points. "But these are the key things I took from it."

Impressed with the DC's approach, Carmichael nodded slowly and waited for her to start running through the points in turn.

Keen to share her findings, DC Twamley started, her voice full of enthusiasm. "The accident took place in late September," she announced. "The Chief Maritime Investigator, a man called Adam Aitken, wasn't able to put an exact time to when the boat got into trouble, but he thought it would have been between the twenty-fourth and twenty-sixth of September, a period that the pathologist at the time fully supported."

Carmichael, having already quickly scanned all the items listed on the board, interrupted. "So, it left from Whitehaven," he remarked.

DC Twamley nodded, "Yes, the Workington Jenny was a forty-foot craft with a keel and adequate accommodation for up to six passengers and crew," she said confidently. "It left the harbour at Whitehaven at two thirty-five on Friday afternoon, the twenty-second of September, heading for an island west of the Outer Hebrides called Allen's Island. It had three people on board. The skipper, a man called Mitch McCauley, who was described at the hearing as experienced and competent. Also on board were Chrissy Cream and Jo Cream."

"Just the three of them," remarked DS Dalton. "No other crew?"

DC Twamley nodded her head. "Just the three of them."

"Wouldn't that be a bit shorthanded when it came to operating the boat?" DS Watson asked.

DS Dalton shook her head. "My uncle has a boat of a similar size, and he can sail it single handed. I doubt there would have been an issue for the skipper having just two people with him, even if they knew nothing about sailing."

"Unless they got seasick like I'd have been," interjected DS Watson, with a broad grin on his face.

"Do we know why they were going there?" Carmichael enquired.

"One of the witnesses at the hearing stated that they were going there to spend a few days birdwatching and, hopefully, writing for their next album," replied DC Twamley.

"In late September!" remarked Carmichael, with more than a hint of astonishment in his voice. "I'd have thought the Outer Hebrides in late September would be a pretty unhospitable place."

DC Twamley shrugged her shoulders. "That's what was claimed at the hearing."

"What was the conclusion of the hearing?" Carmichael enquired, keen to keep the discussion moving.

"Well," replied DC Twamley, "Mr Aitken believed that the accident had been caused by the keel being sheared off the vessel, leaving it unstable. He thought that with the currents being so strong, the boat would have capsized almost immediately, which is how he explained the skipper being unable to send out a distress message."

"And where did the ship capsize?" Carmichael enquired.

"Not that far from its destination," replied DC Twamley. "It was about ten miles west of the southern tip of South Uist."

"And I see from your bullet points that only two bodies were ever recovered," continued Carmichael.

"That's right," replied DC Twamley. "Jo Cream's body, was in one of the cabins and the skipper was found dead in the water about five miles away from his boat, a day later."

"But they never recovered Chrissy's body," DS Dalton remarked.

DC Twamley shook her head. "No, that was never found," she replied, "but the local coastguard at the hearing commented that the tides are so strong and so variable in direction at that point, and at that time of the year, he was surprised they found McCauley."

"And what was the verdict of the hearing?" Carmichael asked.

"That the Workington Jenny probably hit an object just under the waterline, between the twenty-fourth and twenty-sixth of September, which caused her to capsize and led to the drowning of the three people on board," DC Twamley confirmed.

"No suspicious circumstances and no doubt about there being three passengers on board?" DS Dalton enquired.

"Although Chrissy's body was never recovered," replied DC Twamley, "the hearing didn't seem to question that fact as there were three witnesses who'd testified that she had been on the boat."

"And who were they?" Carmichael enquired.

DC Twamley's eyes rolled briefly to the ceiling.

"Ron Mason, who said he'd spoken to Chrissy on the phone just before she'd boarded, imploring her and Jo not to be so foolhardy and to return to Lancashire," replied DC Twamley. "Leah Ashcroft, who was the band's PR Officer back then, who claims she saw Chrissy and Jo get into their limousine at about eight on the twenty-second, to be driven up to Whitehaven. And there was the car's driver, too."

"Who was?" Carmichael asked, a rhetorical remark given that DC Twamley had written his name clearly on the whiteboard.

"Wade Freeman," replied DC Twamley, confirming what they had all read for themselves. "It would appear he was employed by the band back then as their head roadie."

Chapter 44

"What exactly did you tell Carmichael?" Suzi enquired, her tone on the end of the line distinctly irate.

"I told him the truth," replied Coral. "That Leah wasn't sure who had killed them, but she was sure that they died as a result of something she'd told Pritchard."

"What else?" Suzi asked.

"He asked if it had anything to do with Chrissy," responded Coral. "And I told him that I didn't know. Which is true. I also told him that Leah had refused to tell me all the details as she said she didn't want me to come to any harm."

"And did he believe you?" Suzi asked.

"I think so," replied Coral. "Why wouldn't he?"

"And that was it?" continued Suzi, ignoring her sister's question.

The silence at the end of the line suggested it wasn't.

"So, what else did you tell him?" Suzi asked, her voice even more incensed than before.

"I told him that she'd called Pritchard because Ron had gone back on his promise," replied Coral.

"You didn't tell me that," retorted Suzi. "What promise was that?"

"I honestly don't know," responded Coral, "which is what I told Carmichael."

* * * *

Carmichael took a few seconds to consider what DC Twamley had just told them. "Wade never mentioned that he'd worked for the band," he remarked. "I wonder why he'd want to conceal that from us?"

"I reckon he's got to be our main suspect," suggested DS Watson, an announcement that was met with supportive nods from DS Dalton and DC Twamley. Carmichael also nodded, but his was nowhere near as enthusiastic. "Wade's certainly got to be a person of significant interest and on our suspect list, but I don't want us to jump ahead of ourselves. Let's take this step by step, for now."

DS Watson gave a quick shrug of his shoulders, as if he wasn't in total agreement with his boss but said nothing.

"Getting back to the accident," continued Carmichael, "is there not some sort of protocol for boats when they leave the harbour?" he enquired. "Don't they have to let the harbour master, or someone know where they are going and who they have on board?"

DS Watson and DS Dalton looked back at their boss with vacant expressions on their faces, but DC Twamley was quick to reply. "I wondered that, too," she said, "so I checked. It would appear that at the time, there was nothing compulsory. As the boat was remaining in British waters it could sail wherever it wanted without having to declare where it was going, who was on board or what else it was carrying."

"I see," replied Carmichael, despondently. "That's a shame."

"Do you have doubts about Chrissy Cream being on board?" DS Watson enquired.

Carmichael took a few seconds before he replied. "With no body ever being found, I'd say it's got to be an avenue we examine," he eventually announced.

DS Dalton shook her head. "That will be difficult to establish, it being so long ago and with two of the people who testified that she was on board no longer here for us to challenge."

"But Wade Freeman is still about," remarked Carmichael.

* * * *

As soon as her conversation ended with her sister, Coral took a deep breath and headed into the kitchen to find Wade.

When he saw the intense, determined look on her face Wade guessed she hadn't arrived to help him prep the vegetables. "What's with that mardy face?" he remarked, his feeble attempt to mollify his wife.

Coral was having none of it. "I need to know the truth, Wade," she announced, her eyes focused on her husband. "Are you involved with these murders?"

Wade stared back at Coral, clearly stunned by her question.

"You think I killed Ron?" he enquired. "You're as barking mad as your sisters. I thought you were the sane one, but clearly, I was wrong."

"Don't you dare say that about Leah," replied Coral, her voice angry but controlled. "She's not been dead a day yet, so don't you dare say anything like that about her."

Realising he'd overstepped the mark, Wade took a few paces toward his wife and held his arms out as if he was about to hug her.

"And I want none of that either," remarked Coral, who took a step back. "I want the truth, Wade, about those murders and I also want to know if what Leah told me was true."

Wade's face changed upon hearing his wife's words.

"And what did Leah tell you?" he enquired; his words delivered slowly but through gritted teeth.

Coral knew in an instant that there must be something to her hunch.

"Let's start with what you were doing on Wednesday evening when Pritchard left the pub," she replied calmly but with equal intensity. "You were gone for ages. And don't just tell me you had a fag break. Even your epic fag breaks don't take that long."

Chapter 45

"What about you, Rachel?" Carmichael enquired. "What have you turned up since we last spoke?"

DS Dalton smiled. "As you know, I talked with Lydia at The Muffin Maid, and I also bumped into Verity and Ellis as I was leaving. I asked Lydia how Ron came to invest in her business."

"And what did she say?" Carmichael asked.

"I don't know if I fully believe her," she replied, "but she just said he was a kind man, that they'd grown up together and he just offered to help. She said she'd refused to take it as a gift, so he said he'd take a twenty-five percent share in the business for his thirty thousand pounds."

"Thirty thousand pounds is a massive gift," DS Watson remarked. "Especially twenty-odd years ago."

"That's what I said," replied DS Dalton. "But it's what she told me."

"But do you believe her?" Carmichael enquired.

DS Dalton thought for a few seconds before replying. "I know it does sound crazy, but on balance I think I do."

"What about Ron's will?" Carmichael asked. "Did she know about that?"

"She maintains she didn't," DS Dalton replied. "And again, she sounded genuine to me."

"And did she tell you anything else?" DS Watson asked.

"Just that the loan was made a few years after Chrissy Cream died and that Verity's dad was a one-night stand. Other than that, nothing of any worth, not that I can recall."

"And what about your meeting with Verity and Ellis," Carmichael enquired, "how did that go?"

"It was just a short chat," replied DS Dalton, "but what was noticeable were scratches on Ellis's face, a belter of a black eye and some grazes on his knuckles; all of them looked recent."

"So, he'd been in a fight," Carmichael suggested.

"He reckoned he'd fallen over when he was drunk last night when he was out," she replied, "but I don't think they happened last night, they looked like they'd happened today if you ask me."

"Interesting," remarked Carmichael. "I wonder who he'd be fighting with and why."

DS Dalton shrugged her shoulders.

Carmichael nodded gently before turning to face DS Watson. "How about you, Marc," he enquired. "What have you discovered?"

DS Watson took a few seconds before replying. "The first thing I'd say is that Martin Wood is a miserable sod," he remarked. "Mind you, I think he's got a pretty good reason as he's not in great shape."

"How do you mean?" Carmichael enquired.

"He had a bad accident years ago and can't work anymore," replied DS Watson. "His son, Spencer, appears to do all the work now."

"That's as a scaffolder?" Carmichael interrupted.

"That's right, sir," confirmed DS Watson.

"Why don't you share with the team what Martin Wood had to say for himself?" Carmichael suggested.

"He was quite guarded," replied DS Watson, "but he said that he and Ron Mason had hardly spoken in the last dozen years or so, although they'd known each other since they were at school together, so about fifty years. He described Mason as a flash git, always looking for an angle on something and always looking to make a quick buck. In his words a ducker and a diver. He also said that Mason had hit the mother lode with Chrissy's band. I sensed he was very envious of Mason."

"They weren't best buddies then," interjected DS Dalton.

DS Watson smiled and shook his head. "According to Wood, they tolerated each other, but that was about as far as it went."

"Why then would Ron Mason invest in his business?" DS Dalton asked.

"Martin Wood reckoned it was a gesture Mason had made after the band split up. A pay off he called it."

"A pay off for what?" DC Twamley enquired; her curiosity having been heightened.

"Well, that's the interesting thing," replied DS Watson, "it would appear that Martin Wood was in charge of the lighting and organising the logistics at the band's concerts."

"Really," exclaimed DC Twamley. "That's both him and Wade Freeman being involved with the band."

"It is, isn't it," concurred Carmichael. "And both get business loans from Ron Mason."

"What about the will?" DS Dalton asked. "Did you get the sense that Martin Wood knew anything about it?"

Watson shook his head. "I'm certain he didn't," he replied definitively. "But had his condition not stopped him, he'd have been doing cartwheels when I gave him the good news."

* * * *

Despite never having been that close to Leah and knowing for some time that her little sister was going to die imminently, the realisation that Leah had now gone forever had hit Suzi harder than she'd expected.

Nevertheless, her love for Tom, as always, overshadowed anything else that was going on around her, as it had done for the last twenty years. She had tried tirelessly to find out why he and Ellis had been fighting, but Tom wouldn't tell her. In fact, it seemed to make him angry at her, as if was her fault.

Suzi was therefore pleased when, as early evening was upon them, her son brushed past her in the hall, with his shorts, tee shirt and trainers on.

"I'm off for a run," he shouted at her, without bothering to make eye contact. "I'm going to try and do at least 10k. See you in about fifty minutes."

Tom was an excellent distance runner and meticulous with his times, so Suzi knew if he said fifty minutes he'd be back within a minute or two of the time he told her.

"See you later then," replied Suzi, although Tom never heard her as he'd already slammed the front door behind him and turned up his favourite running tracks which were belting at him through his tiny yellow earplugs.

Chapter 46

With the team now having shared their findings, Carmichael wanted to start documenting what they knew and set everyone new targets. But before he did, he felt it only fair to share the details of his conversations with the Freemans.

"I spoke with Wade first," Carmichael told them. "He's such a shifty guy and although I'm not sure he's our killer, he's certainly someone who's hiding something. He, at last, admitted that he lied about Ron Mason being in the pub until almost closing time on Wednesday, as he was a mate. Mind you, he didn't tell me that he used to work with him. He also said he didn't hear anything Pritchard was saying to Mason, which I find a bit hard to believe. And the only thing he could remember hearing Mason say was that Pritchard was a liar, and apparently, he also said that Mason shouted if you print that I'll sue you for every penny you've got you effing lowlife."

"You sound like you don't believe him," remarked DS Dalton.

"I'm not sure," replied Carmichael honestly. "He was undoubtedly rattled this time as he knew what sort of trouble he'd be in if he lied to me again, but I'm still not sure he was being totally honest with me. He may be our killer, but even if he's not, I think he's still hiding stuff from us."

"Did he say how Ron's financial involvement in the pub came about?" DC Twamley enquired.

"That's something else I didn't buy," Carmichael replied. "He maintained that Ron Mason got to know he was looking for a pub to buy and, being an old pal from school, just offered to help out with the deposit. With no strings attached."

"The thing is," interrupted DS Dalton, "although that sounds so ridiculous that it can't be true, it's almost exactly the story Lydia told me about how Ron Mason came to invest in The Muffin Maid."

"And not a million miles from what Martin Wood told me, too, about his scaffolding company," added Watson. "Maybe the three of them are in on this together. Stock's team said that Pritchard was struck twice. Maybe there was more than one person down Jay Bank Lane on Wednesday evening."

"Or maybe they're actually telling us the truth," suggested DC Twamley pragmatically.

*　　*　　*　　*

Tom Ashcroft was almost at the halfway mark of his run when he saw the headlights of the oncoming vehicle as it approached. Although it was a winding country road, with no pavements, Bentley Lane was wide enough for two cars to pass without any major issues, so Tom thought nothing of it as he, head down, maintained the steady pace of seven and a half miles an hour that he'd adopted since leaving home. With his running music blaring into his ears and his eyes on the ground just in front of his feet, Tom didn't appreciate that the vehicle had gained speed and by the time he did realise what was about to happen, the vehicle, which had now veered over onto his side of the road, was only a few feet away from him. At the very last moment, Tom tried to push himself off his right leg towards the ditch to his left, but his last gasp attempt to avoid a collision simply wasn't early enough. The impact propelled Tom headfirst over the wing of the vehicle. As his feet left the floor, Tom's body twisted sideways in the air, and he landed on his neck in the ditch. The vehicle didn't stop. It just corrected its position, back to its rightful side of the road and sped on and out of sight.

* * * *

"What about Coral?" DS Dalton enquired. "Did she tell you what Leah had said to her?"

Carmichael's expression told the team all they needed to know. "She told me nothing of any great value, I'm afraid," he confessed. "Coral said Leah told her that, in her view, Mason and Pritchard had been killed because of something she'd told Pritchard. According to Coral, Leah wasn't sure who had killed them, but she was sure that they died as a result of something she'd said."

"And what was it she'd said?" DS Dalton asked.

Carmichael shrugged his shoulders. "Coral said Leah had refused to tell her anything more as she said she didn't want her to come to any harm. But she did tell Coral that there were skeletons in the cupboard and that she shouldn't get involved or trust anyone."

"That's bloody helpful," remarked DS Watson sardonically.

"Exactly," concurred DS Dalton.

"Apparently, Coral had asked why she'd called Pritchard," Carmichael continued. "And Leah had said it was because Ron was going back on his promise. But of course, Coral couldn't say what promise that related to."

"So, we're not a great deal further with Leah," remarked DS Watson.

"Not really, Marc," Carmichael confessed. "Although I think it's fair to assume that it may well be connected with Chrissy Cream's death all those years ago. But, unless any of you have any bright ideas as to what that link is, it's still a mystery, I'm annoyed to have to admit."

*　　*　　*　　*

When Tom hadn't arrived back after an hour, Suzi started to become concerned. When that hour turned into ninety minutes, she really started to worry. And, once two hours had elapsed, she decided she needed to drive out and find him. Suzi knew the route Tom took, he always took the same course when he did a 10K, so she was confident she'd be able to come across him relatively easily.

Suzi was about four kilometres into the journey when she saw the blue lights flashing ahead of her. She knew immediately it would be an ambulance attending to Tom. She put her foot down hard on the accelerator and sped on, hoping, and praying that she was wrong.

Chapter 47

Carmichael looked up at the whiteboard, then turned his gaze on his three colleagues. "What do you think, team?" he enquired.

After a few seconds pause, DS Dalton spoke. "I think we've got to keep the Freemans, the Woods and Lydia Brook-Smith on our list," she remarked. "They all benefit significantly from Ron Mason's death, so although my gut feel after getting to know Lydia is that she's not our killer, I can't prove that."

Carmichael nodded, "I agree," he responded.

"What about the boys, Ellis and Tom?" Watson asked. "Ron Mason seemed to control their trust funds. Maybe they wanted to get easier access."

Carmichael shrugged his shoulders. "I'm not sure that's a strong reason, as they'll be old enough to get control of their funds in a few years' time, but we probably do have to leave them on the suspects list for now."

"We surely have to keep Suzi and Pam, too," remarked DC Twamley. "I know they found Mason's body, but that doesn't mean one or both of them didn't kill him."

Carmichael sighed deeply. "So, we think it could be just about anyone," he announced despairingly, "either working alone or working with someone else."

Grudgingly the three other officers in the room gently nodded, demonstrating they all reluctantly agreed with their boss.

Once again Carmichael took a few seconds to consider how to proceed. "These all may be potential suspects for Ron Mason's murder," he said, "but what about Doug Pritchard? To our knowledge, the Woods didn't know he was around. Spencer Wood probably had never heard of him, and you could say that about Lydia Brook-Smith, Ellis and Tom as well."

"Unless Pritchard made contact with them before he came up," suggested DS Watson.

"I'd say our main suspects have to be Coral and Wade Freeman," announced DS Dalton, "maybe working together, maybe working alone.

"I'd be willing to believe that Wade could have carried out these murders alone," concurred Carmichael, "but I can't see Coral being the murderer unless she's in it with Wade or someone else."

"Martin Wood couldn't have done these murders by himself," remarked DS Watson, "but Spencer could. And if the murders are linked to the sinking of that boat twenty years ago, it's highly likely, in my view, that Pritchard would have contacted Wade Freeman and Martin Wood before he travelled up here."

"There's no evidence of that on Pritchard's mobile phone activity report," DS Twamley reminded the team.

"That may well be true," Carmichael replied, "but it certainly makes sense for them to be on the list. Now, does anyone else want to add anything at this stage?"

When nothing more was forthcoming from the group, Carmichael looked across at DS Dalton.

"Highlight the Freemans and the Woods," he instructed her. "We'll focus on them first."

After pausing again for a few seconds, Carmichael faced his team.
"Ok, let's put together our plan of action."

*　　*　　*　　*

Suzi's worst fears were proved correct. She arrived just as the stretcher bearing Tom was being hoisted up into the ambulance.
"I'm his mother," she shouted, when she saw one of the paramedics looking concerned as she headed rapidly in their direction. "Is he going to be ok?"
The paramedic looked worried. "He's had a nasty accident," she replied. "His leg's badly broken and he has multiple rib fractures. We need to get him to hospital quickly to see if there's any internal damage, but I must warn you, it's a serious accident he's been in."

Suzi looked at her son's even more grazed and swollen face, well what she could see of it, given the breathing apparatus around his mouth and nose, and the heavy, red cushioned supports all around his head.
"Has he been conscious?" she enquired.
The paramedic looked worryingly at Suzi. "No," she replied with a sense of foreboding in her voice.
Suzi stood in silence as the ambulance doors closed and the vehicle sped off, its blue lights flashing and siren sounding.

Chapter 48

After updating the whiteboard, Carmichael asked DS Dalton to print everyone a fresh copy of all four lists, which they pored over in silence for the next ten minutes.

<u>Summary of Coroner's report into the Workington Jenny tragedy:</u>

1. *The Chief Maritime Investigator, Adam Aitken, wasn't able to put an exact time when the accident happened, but he thought it would have been between 24th and 26th September, an estimate which was supported by the pathologist.*
2. *Vessel was a forty-foot Freedom 40 with a keel and adequate accommodation for up to six passengers.*
3. *It left Whitehaven harbour at 2:35pm on Friday 22nd September, heading for an island west of the Outer Hebrides called Allen's Island.*
4. *It had three people on board; the skipper, a man called Mitch McCauley, who was described at the hearing as an experienced and competent skipper. Also on board was Chrissy Cream and Jo Cream*

5. *Mr Aitken believed that the accident had been caused by the keel being sheared off the vessel leaving it unstable.*
6. *It was about ten miles west of the southern tip of South Uist when the accident occurred.*
7. *Only two bodies were recovered, Jo Cream's body in one of the cabins and Mitch McCauley about five miles away from his boat, a day later. They never found Chrissy's body.*
8. *Ron Mason, at the hearing, stated that Chrissy and Jo were going there to spend a few days birdwatching and hopefully do some writing for their next album.*
9. *The verdict was that the vessel probably hit an object just under the waterline between 24th and 26th September, which caused her to capsize and led to the drowning of the three people on board.*
10. *There were no suspicious circumstances, and no doubt about there being three passengers on board.*
11. *Even though Chrissy's body was never recovered, the claim that there were three people on board was never questioned as there were three witnesses who testified that Chrissy had been on the boat: Ron Mason, Leah Ashcroft and Wade Freeman.*

Background on Chrissy Cream and the Vixens

1. *Chrissy and Jo cream were sisters from High Maudsey (Chrissy being 3 years older than Jo).*
2. *The Vixens were originally Jo's band, but after their original lead singer left, Chrissy joined with her best friend Suzi Ashcroft and they get another school friend, Ron Mason (also from High Maudsey) to be the band's manager.*
3. *Within a year, they'd replaced all the original band members, apart from Jo, with Pam Hutton the last to be*

added. The band's drummer. The band then becomes known as Chrissy Cream and the Vixens.

4. *They have 6 top 20 hits in the next 3 years and are the first all-girl rock band to have a number 1 hit in the USA.*
5. *Shortly after each other Chrissy and Jo have a baby, Chrissy's (Tom) rumoured to be the child of another rock star, Liam Thomas, (a rumour denied by both Chrissy and Liam). Jo's child (also a boy called Ellis) is thought to have been the son of a Premier League footballer. Tom and Ellis are now in their early twenties and were adopted by Suzi and Pam respectively when their mums died.*
6. *Chrissy and Jo were both killed twenty years ago in a tragic boating accident in the North Sea. This was just before they were due to fly out to the US for their first American tour. The skipper of the boat was also killed, so no survivors.*
7. *The band broke up after their deaths and didn't release any more records.*
8. *Ron Mason remained in control of all royalties that the band earnt and was also the sole trustee of the trust funds set up for the two boys, which is rumoured to be a significant amount of money. The boys won't get control of their inheritances until they are 25 years old.*
9. *Ron Mason was 53, he'd only managed one major artist other than The Vixens, a singer called Ferne Cramley, who had 3 minor hits 10 years ago, but has now retired from the music business and lives with her husband and family in rural Herefordshire.*
10. *Pam and Suzi, the only 2 surviving band members, live in the area still. Pam has a brother who is a farmer in one of the villages. She appears to be quite reclusive, spending her time looking after Ellis and a host of cats and other animals. Suzi, who was the wild child of the*

band, now appears to spend the majority of her time and energy fighting for a variety of causes, including saving the planet, women's rights and third world poverty. She is devoted to Tom and, like Pam, has never married.

11. *Doug Pritchard lived in Hove and had been a music journalist for over thirty years. He specialised in uncovering salacious stories about the rich and famous in the music industry. Although he'd had a number of big stories published over the years, his credibility and methods of obtaining information are viewed with great suspicion.*

12. *Wade Freeman (roadie) and Martin Wood (rigging and lighting) were both employed by the band.*

Facts

1. *Doug Pritchard was murdered at approx. 9:35pm in Jay Bank Lane, High Maudsey on Wed 20th March.*
2. *Ron Mason was murdered between 1:40pm and 3pm on his drive in High Maudsey on Thursday 21st March.*
3. *Pritchard and Mason had argued at The Three Bells pub about 20-30 minutes before Doug Pritchard was killed – subject unknown.*
4. *Both men were killed by blows to the head. Ron Mason by a single blow with one of his own golf clubs; Doug Pritchard was struck twice by a cylindrical weapon – its identity unknown.*
5. *Pritchard received a call from Leah Barnes on Sat 16th March.*
6. *Leah was Mason's PA for years and is the younger sister of Suzi Ashcroft and twin sister of Coral Freeman, (the landlady of The Three Bells where Ron Mason and Doug Pritchard argued on the night of Doug's murder).*

7. *Pritchard tried to make contact with National Sub-Editor (Ted Heslegrave) and pop star, Liam Thomas, almost immediately after Leah called him.*
8. *Thomas Ashcroft met with Ron Mason at Ron's house shortly before he was murdered.*
9. *Verity Brook-Smith claims that during their argument, in The Three Bells, Ron Mason got angry when Doug Pritchard had suggested that Chrissy Cream was still alive.*
10. *Spencer Wood lied about being at the Farmers Arms pub in the village of Rainham Moss with Ellis when Doug Pritchard was murdered, which means that neither have an alibi for the time of Pritchard's murder.*
11. *Wade Freeman lied about when Ron Mason left the pub on Wed 20th March, the night Doug Pritchard was killed. Ron appears to have left very soon after Doug Pritchard, not just before closing time, as Wade had claimed.*
12. *Ron Mason amended his will, adding a codicil, just two days after he'd met Leah at the care home. Leah was removed from his will and his home (High Moor Grange) was now to become a memorial to the band.*
13. *Ron Mason invested in Wade & Coral Freeman's pub, Martin Wood's scaffolding company and Lydia Brook-Smith's bakery business; without seemingly requiring any involvement or significant financial reward.*
14. *Leah asked for Coral to visit her at St Jude's on the evening she died.*

Suspects list:

1. *Suzi Ashcroft*
2. *Pam Hutton*
3. *Tom Ashcroft*
4. *Ellis Hutton*

5. *Coral Freeman*
6. *Wade Freeman*
7. *Martin Wood*
8. *Spencer Wood*
9. *Lydia Brook-Smith*

Carmichael looked up at the clock on the wall; it was six forty-five.

"I don't think we're going to get much more done tonight," he remarked. "But let's bring Wade Freeman and Spencer Wood in, under caution, first thing and see how they stand up to some proper questioning."

Pleased that Carmichael was prepared to call it a day, his three colleagues nodded their approval.

"Before you go tonight, Marc," he continued, "can you arrange support with uniform to help you get them both here for nine?"

DS Watson nodded vigorously. "Will do, sir," he replied.

"I suggest you bring in Spencer Wood," continued Carmichael, "and Rachel and Donna, you bring in Wade Freeman."

DS Dalton and DC Twamley acknowledged that they were both happy with the plan and after their brief farewells, the room emptied leaving Carmichael alone with his thoughts and the four lists spread out on the desk in front of him.

Chapter 49

Carmichael spent thirty minutes alone reading and re-reading the various bullet points on the four lists, before starting a new list of questions he felt needed answering. Before he called it a night and headed for the door, he'd written down nine questions, randomly scribed, in no particular order other than the way they'd entered into his head:

- Why did Mason want to see Suzi and Pam on the afternoon he died?
- Why did Mason change his will?
- Why was Pritchard killed?
- What weapon was used to kill Pritchard?
- What happened to Chrissy?
- Why did Mason lend 3 people so much money for no financial return? (Not in keeping with his character.)
- Why was Mason killed?
- Is there one killer or are more than one person involved?
- If more than one did different people murder Pritchard and Mason?

He was sure that if he found answers to just a few of these questions he'd be able to make great strides in the case, but even after looking at them for some considerable period of time, the solutions to these nine unanswered dilemmas weren't at all obvious.
Reluctantly Carmichael folded up his lists (there now being five in total), placed them all in his jacket pocket, grabbed his mobile and car keys and headed for the exit. As he entered the reception area at the front of the police station, the desk sergeant shouted over to him.
"I was told you'd already left, sir," he remarked.
Carmichael shook his head. "No," he replied, "but I am now, though," his way of indicating he didn't want to be bothered by anything the desk sergeant may want to tell him.
"I did try DS Dalton and DS Watson," continued the desk sergeant, "but they didn't respond to my call."
Carmichael stopped in his tracks and turned to face the nervous-looking man behind the desk.
"What is it?" he enquired, his tone making it perfectly clear that he didn't really want to get involved.
"We've had a report from PC Dyer and PC Richardson who are at the scene of a hit and run," remarked the desk sergeant.
Carmichael looked blankly back at the officer as if to say, *so what*.
"PC Dyer thought CID needed to be aware," continued the sergeant, "as the victim is a man that might be connected with those murders."
"Who is that?" Carmichael enquired.
"It's a young man called Tom Ashcroft," replied the desk sergeant. "He's been taken to Southport General, but they say he's in a bad way."
Carmichael's eyes widened. "Keep trying to get hold of DS Watson, DS Dalton and also call DC Twamley," he

commanded. "I want two of them at the crash scene immediately and the other needs to meet me at Southport General."

The desk sergeant nodded vigorously. "Will do, sir," he replied, before grabbing his phone.

*　　*　　*　　*

Coral Freeman slowly removed her mobile from her ear but remained planted firmly to the spot.

"What's up?" enquired Wade, seeing the anguish on her face.

"That was our Suzi," replied Coral, "Tom's been in an accident, they're at Southport General. He's in intensive care."

"What," exclaimed Wade. "What happened?"

"Suzi wasn't that clear, but it sounds like he's been involved in a hit and run while he was out jogging," Coral replied. "I said I'd get over there."

"I'll drive you," announced Wade, quickly grabbing his car keys from the bar. "It's almost empty in here tonight, so Janet and Debbie will have to cope."

Coral heard but didn't answer at first, but once they started walking towards the exit, she grabbed her husband by the arm.

"What on earth is happening around here?" she said anxiously. "Who'd want to hurt Tom?"

"It's probably not related to Ron or that journalist," remarked Wade. "No doubt it's just an awful coincidence."

Within a couple of minutes Wade and Coral had clambered into their white Volvo V60, a battered workhorse of a car that had seen better days, but, as Wade continually reminded Coral, it was totally reliable.

"I may be ages in there," Coral said as they exited the pub car park. "You just drop me off and I'll call you if I need picking up."

Wade Freeman looked across at his wife with a concerned frown on his face.

Coral put her hand on his thigh. "I'll be fine," she assured him. "You can't do anything by being there and Tom probably won't be expecting to see you. Anyway, Janet and Debbie don't know how to lock up. You get off back once we're there, and I'll call you."

Wade knew his wife was talking sense so didn't argue. "Will have you there in twenty minutes," he announced as he put his foot down.

"Thirty in one piece will be fine," replied Coral with a look that confirmed she wasn't happy with her husband speeding.

A small smirk appeared on Wade's face as he eased the pressure of his right foot on the accelerator.

Chapter 50

As Carmichael's car sped down the A570 towards Southport, he tried to stop his mind from connecting the hit and run on Tom Ashcroft with the murders of Doug Pritchard and Ron Mason. Deep down he suspected there was a link, but too often he'd seen colleagues, particularly when he was at the Met, putting two and two together then blindly following a bogus path until it was abundantly clear they'd made a big mistake and wasted days, weeks, or in some cases, months as a result. He didn't want to do that and had made a conscious decision during his time as inspector to always try and establish the facts; although even he'd admit that occasionally he, too, had fallen way short of this noble ideal. He was about halfway into the thirty-minute journey when his mobile rang. "I'm just about ten minutes away from the hospital," remarked DS Dalton, much to Carmichael's surprise.

"How did you manage to get there so quickly?" enquired Carmichael, who'd left Kirkwood police station as soon as he'd spoken to the desk sergeant.

DS Dalton sighed. "I was due to meet some friends for dinner in Southport tonight, so I was on my way in that direction when Sergeant Hunt called me."

So that's his name, thought Carmichael, who'd seen the new sergeant on the desk and around the station for a few weeks, and was probably even introduced to him when he arrived, but his name had eluded him when they were talking.

"You'll be there before me," Carmichael replied, so find out which ward he's been admitted to and let me know once you know."

"Will do," replied DS Dalton, as she sped through the village of Scarisbrick.

* * * *

DC Twamley was the first of the two CID officers to arrive at the collision spot, which had been cordoned off and was already being inspected by a couple of Dr Stock's team from forensics. "Found anything?" DC Twamley asked.

The two men shook their heads. "Not yet," one replied, "but we've only been here fifteen minutes ourselves. We're still at the gathering information stage."

"So, no initial theories?" DC Twamley enquired.

The second investigator, an older man who looked like he was in his mid-to-late forties, glared back at the young DC and shook his head as if to emphasise his displeasure at her line of questioning.

"Young lady," he remarked condescendingly, "we gather the information, analyse our findings, and then start to share our conclusions. Not the other way around."

DC Twamley couldn't help thinking that the response of the arrogant man addressing her would, almost certainly, have been different had Inspector Carmichael been there asking the question rather than her, but she decided to back off and let the two investigators get on with their work.

* * * *

DS Dalton had just arrived at the hospital when she spotted Coral Freeman quickly jumping out of her husband's Volvo. "Wow, that old thing looks like it's been in a fare few scrapes in its life," she said out loud as she watched Wade Freeman make his way past her, through a row of parked cars and towards the gate.

Her mind then turned to finding a parking space, something that at first sight looked as though it was going to be no mean challenge.

* * * *

 With just about ten minutes to go before he'd be arriving at the hospital, Carmichael tried again to think of logical answers to the nine questions he'd written down earlier, but specifically two of them:

What happened to Chrissy and why did Mason lend 3 people so much money for no financial return?

The only logical answers he could come up with were that Chrissy was almost certainly dead. Whether she died in the boat accident or in some other way, Carmichael found it impossible to believe she'd have just disappeared without trace. Although he knew very little about Chrissy Cream, he couldn't imagine she'd have left her young son; few mothers would be capable of doing that, in his view. And, if she had just simply absconded, with her being so recognisable, how would it be possible for her to create a new life anywhere? Even in disguise and under a pseudonym, she'd be recognised, surely? With regards to the three loans, Carmichael's only workable theory was that these were payoffs. Maybe they all had something on Mason? Maybe it was the same thing or maybe different things, but in Carmichael's mind, keeping the three of them quiet was the most logical solution for such an out-of-character act of generosity by Ron Mason. And if that was the reason, was that secret something to do with Chrissy Cream's apparent death on the boat? Although these theories seemed to hold water, and maybe knowing about this could be the reason Doug Pritchard had been killed, try as hard as he could, Carmichael couldn't then link his train of thought to Ron Mason's death. And as for the hit and run on Tom, that was even more difficult to connect. So, despite them both dying within twenty-four hours of each other and even though the way they died suggested that the same person was responsible for both deaths, Carmichael started to seriously consider the possibility that, maybe, they needed to be looking for not one but two different murderers.

Chapter 51

DC Twamley had been at the scene of the hit and run for almost twenty minutes before she was joined by DS Watson. "What's the score here, Donna?" DS Watson asked.

"They don't want to share anything with us yet," replied DC Twamley. "I asked but was given short shrift."

Watson sniggered. "Oh, that's just MacAllister," responded Watson offhandedly. "He's old school. Can't bring himself to answer to a woman. Leave him to me, I'll find out what they think."

Before he'd even finished talking, Watson started to walk over to where the two men from forensics were stood. "How's it going Mac?" enquired Watson, as if he was talking to an old buddy. "What's your first impressions?"

MacAllister looked up at Watson and then briefly across at DC Twamley, before producing a small smirk of a smile. "Oh hi, Marc," he responded warmly. "So, it's you who's the senior officer that's been sent over for this one."

"That's correct," he replied, "but, as you well know, there's no hierarchy in Carmichael's team. He's the boss and then the rest of us are foot soldiers instructed to do his bidding. A bit like you guys with Stock."

MacAllister laughed. "You're not wrong there."

"What do you think happened here?" continued Watson.

MacAllister looked over at his colleague before answering. "I'd say it was probably deliberate," he replied. "There's no sign of the car braking at all, it was on the wrong side of the road and, with it being a fairly straight stretch of road, in daylight, I don't think he could have missed seeing the runner…"

"Maybe he wasn't looking at the road," interjected DC Twamley. "He could have been on his mobile or fiddling with the sound system."

MacAllister shrugged his shoulders. "Possibly," he replied, "but we measured it and the last bend he'd have taken is almost exactly two hundred metres away." As he spoke MacAllister half turned and pointed down the road in the direction the vehicle had been travelling from. "If he came around the bend at thirty miles per hour and then accelerated, it would have taken him between twelve and fifteen seconds to reach the runner. That's a hell of a long time to have your eyes off the road. But I'd agree it's possible."

DC Twamley was still unhappy about the patronising way she'd been spoken to by MacAllister, but reluctantly she had to admit that what he was now saying did make sense.

"Anything else?" enquired DS Watson.

MacAllister rolled his eyes. "Give us a chance, Marc," he replied. "We've only been here about thirty minutes."

DS Watson grinned. "Point taken, mate," he said. "We should let you get on, in that case."

MacAllister and his colleague exchanged a quick look before turning away and continuing to carefully part the tall, dry grass at the side of the road with a couple of long, white poles.

"It's all high-tech apparatus with those guys isn't it, Donna?" Watson muttered to his colleague, just loud enough for the forensics team to hear; a huge grin spread wide across his face.

* * * *

Carmichael didn't manage to find a space in the carpark at Southport General, so he was forced to abandon his BMW in one of the side roads that wasn't already full of cars and didn't have double yellow lines. This unwelcome inconvenience meant he now had a good quarter of a mile to walk before he reached the hospital entrance.

Feeling less than happy, Carmichael checked his mobile to confirm the name of the ward DS Dalton had texted him about ten minutes earlier.

"Stanley Ward," he muttered out loud as he looked at the blue signage in the hospital's main foyer.

Third floor, north wing, the sign informed him, which prompted an audible, frustrated sigh from the already exasperated inspector, given that the entrance was in the south wing.

Fortuitously, the lift at the north wing was working, there were only two other people waiting to use it and, with a capacity of two thousand, five hundred kilos, according to the notice inside, there was plenty of room and leeway even if several people got in on either the first or second floors.

When the lift passed both floors and opened at floor three, Carmichael at last breathed a sigh of relief.

"Hi, Rachel," he said as DS Dalton met him halfway down the corridor. "What news is there about Tom's condition?"

DS Dalton shrugged her shoulders. "It's still unclear," she replied. "He's stable but having a brain scan at the moment. Apparently, he was conscious briefly in the ambulance but didn't say much."

"So, he's not critical," Carmichael remarked.

"He's got a broken right fibula and tibia," replied DS Dalton, "they reckon his right knee will need operating on and he's broken several ribs, but I didn't get the sense from the specialist I spoke to that he was in imminent danger."

Carmichael nodded gently. "I guess the brain scan may tell them more," he said.

DS Dalton then pointed down the corridor at Suzi Ashcroft and Coral Freeman, who were sat together opposite what Carmichael assumed was where Tom was having his scan. "I was just trying to get some background from Suzi, when you arrived," she said.

"What has she told you so far?" Carmichael enquired.

"Only that Tom went out for a run at about five-thirty, saying he'd be back in fifty minutes," announced DS Dalton, "but when he wasn't back some two hours later Suzi was worried and drove along his normal route to find him."

"And was it her who found him?" enquired Carmichael.

DS Dalton shook her head. "No, apparently it was a man walking his dog," she replied. "He phoned the emergency services but by the time Suzi arrived he'd gone. I suspect the officers who were first at the scene must have a statement from him."

"I'll call Marc and get him to check into that," Carmichael remarked. "Is there anything else?"

DS Dalton nodded her head. "It may be nothing," she said. "But when I arrived, Wade Freeman was dropping off Coral. They were in a white Volvo."

"And?" enquired Carmichael, trying hard to get DS Dalton to get to the point.

"Well, as I say, it may be nothing," she continued, "but it did have a few dents on it. One was on the corner of the front driver's wing. May be worth getting forensics to check to see if it was caused by the hit and run."

"We should certainly do that," Carmichael replied reflectively. "Good spot, Rachel."

Chapter 52

Saturday 23rd March

For Carmichael's team there was no such thing as a day off when they were working on a murder case, and this day proved to be no exception. At exactly nine o'clock, with the melodious harmony of robins, sparrows and blackbirds chirping cheerfully as their audible springtime backdrop, DS Watson and two uniformed officers arrived at Spencer Wood's house. At about the same time DS Dalton and DC Twamley, also accompanied by two uniformed officers, knocked loudly on the heavy, wooden front door of The Three Bells in High Maudsey. Knowing it would take at least an hour, probably more like two or three, before the two cautioned men would be at Kirkwood police station with their legal representation briefed and in place, Carmichael was in no great hurry to leave the house that Saturday morning. Showered, dressed, and sitting at the breakfast table, the first thing he did was grab the two letters for him that were on the front doormat when he'd come downstairs. He slit open the first one, which he realised was just one of those personalised junk mails, trying to lure the recipient into a purchase. This time it was for an electric mobility scooter, with a picture of a smiling, white-haired gentleman. How on earth he was on their mailing list, God only knows, he thought, shaking his head as he pushed it away from him. The second he recognised immediately, even before he'd opened it: his credit card statement. Slicing open the envelope, Carmichael started to gaze over his purchases from the last twenty-eight days. Bewilderingly, none seemed to register. "Tint and Swirl, sixty-six quid!" he muttered. "What the…"

Having realised what, he'd done Carmichael checked the name at the top of the page. It was Penny's.

Feeling guilty, but also astounded at just how much his wife was paying for her monthly hairdo, he quickly put the statement back in its envelope and pushed it across to the place Penny normally sat for breakfast. He then started to look at the nine questions he'd written the evening before, although his attention wasn't totally on those questions at first, as he was also busily trying to calculate how many haircuts, he'd be able to have from Paul Greenbank, the barber in the village, for sixty-six pounds.

When Penny finally sat herself next to him, Carmichael was fully engrossed in his nine questions.

"What's this?" she enquired as she peered down, firstly at her opened letter and then at the list. "Is that one of the famous Carmichael lists I see before me?"

"It is," replied Carmichael with a wry smile. "And don't mock. These help me focus my thoughts."

Penny decided not to mention the opened statement as she could guess what he'd done. Instead, she kissed him on the forehead. "I know," she conceded. "It's one of your endearing foibles."

"Is it," replied Carmichael, refusing to rise to the bait.

Taking a bite of her toast, Penny leaned over her husband's arm so she could see the list more closely. "So, have you any answers to these crucial questions?" she enquired.

"Maybe," Carmichael replied, deliberately trying to be mysterious.

Penny took her eyes off the list for a second and peered into her husband's blue eyes. "Go on then," she remarked, "tell me where your head is?"

Carmichael pointed his finger at the first question. "Why did Ron want to see Suzi and Pam," he said aloud. "Either to tell them about him changing his will, or to let them know that a secret the three of them shared was known by Doug Pritchard."

"I thought he was already dead then," announced Penny.

"He was," responded Carmichael, "but maybe Ron Mason was worried someone else knew about it."

"The killer, you mean?" said Penny.

"Possibly," replied Carmichael, with deliberate elusiveness.

Penny shrugged her shoulders. "And what about this next question?" she asked. "Why did he change his will?"

"To cut out Leah Barnes," replied her husband. "I'm certain of that."

"Because of something she'd told Pritchard?" enquired Penny.

"Undoubtedly, I'd say," Carmichael responded, with absolute certainty in his voice.

"What about the next questions?" Penny continued.

Carmichael sighed deeply. "Why Pritchard was killed, what weapon was used to kill him and whether there's one or multiple people involved are still questions I've no answers to," he reluctantly had to admit.

Penny nodded, took another bite of toast then pointed down to another one on her husband's list. "What happened to Chrissy?" she said, her mouth still full of toast.

Carmichael, stared blankly towards the garden through the large window in their kitchen. "That's another one that's still eluding me," he confessed. "But I don't think she's alive. She either died on that boat or …"

"Or what?" enquired Penny, keen to hear Carmichael complete his sentence.

"Or somewhere else," muttered Carmichael, who suddenly went quiet as if a thought had just come into his head.

"Do I sense a revelation?" Penny enquired.

"Possibly," Carmichael replied as he quickly sprang to his feet, grabbed his jacket and mobile phone, and headed for the front door. "I'll have to be off and get to the station."

Surprised by her husband's sudden surge of energy, Penny followed him down the hallway, giving him an affectionate kiss on the lips as he reached the door. "And what about the last question on your list?" she enquired as the front door opened and Carmichael started to exit the house. "Why did Ron Mason lend three people lots of money for no financial return?"

Carmichael smiled. "That's an easy one," he replied. "To buy their silence."

Penny watched as her husband's car made its way down the road with absolutely zero idea of when he'd be back. "Have a nice day, dear?" she muttered out loud with a mixture of weariness and sarcasm, as his car disappeared into the distance. Then, as she had done thousands of times before, Penny turned, re-entered the house on her own and closed the door behind her.

Chapter 53

Carmichael had left Southport General at seven minutes past nine, the night before; he'd checked the time on his mobile as he departed the building.
Before leaving, he'd waited to find out the latest prognosis on Tom Ashcroft; and when the news was reasonably positive, he'd instructed DS Dalton to wait until the PC (the night watchman as he'd called him) arrived before she headed home, and to instruct whoever had been assigned to that unglamourous task to call one of them immediately should Tom regain consciousness.
With there being no contact at all from the PC on duty during the night, Carmichael assumed that Tom Ashcroft was still unconscious, but decided to give DS Dalton a call just to check. He was just about to make the call when his mobile rang.
Carmichael didn't answer straight away as he needed to negotiate a tight bend and wanted to make sure he had his eyes on the road and both hands on the wheel. However, once he'd completed the manoeuvre, he pressed the answer button on his steering wheel and the loud, unmistakeable voice of Dr Stock emanated forth from the car speakers.
"Is it a convenient moment?" enquired Mid-Lancashire's head of forensics.

"Of course, it is," replied Carmichael cheerily. "What have you got for me?"

"My team have completed their assessment of last evening's hit and run," Stock replied, "and there isn't a great deal for you to go on, I'm afraid."

"I see," remarked Carmichael. "Not even an idea of the type of car that hit Tom Ashcroft?"

Carmichael could hear Stock sucking in air on the other end of the phone before he replied.

"No idea of the make at present," continued Stock, "but it was probably a white vehicle, as when it left the road it looks as though it brushed passed a sapling in the verge and deposited a fragment of paint."

"Can you not identify the make of the vehicle from the paint?" Carmichael enquired.

Stock sucked in air once more, before responding. "We cannot be totally sure it was the same car," he replied, "but we're hopeful we should be able to narrow the car down to at least the manufacturer after we've done a little more work."

"Try Volvo, first," Carmichael said. "We think it may have been a Volvo car that's owned by a local publican."

"In that case, I'll ask them to start with the paint used on Volvos," replied Stock. "Any other manufacturers in the frame that I need to know about?"

Carmichael tried to remember the make of Suzi Ashcroft's white van, although he was pretty sure she wouldn't have deliberately tried to kill her son.

"No," he said. "Just do Volvo first, then the others."

"Will do," replied Stock before ending the call.

* * * *

The two police cars transporting Wade Freeman and the four police officers who'd called on him that morning, had just arrived at Kirkwood Police Station when DS Dalton took the call from Carmichael.
"Morning, sir," she said with as much cheerfulness as Carmichael had earlier afforded Stock. "We've got Freeman and are just about to take him into the station."
"Excellent," replied Carmichael. "I'm about ten minutes away."
"He's very jumpy this morning," continued DS Dalton.
"Really," remarked Carmichael. "That may not be a bad thing. Now he's under caution we might, at long last, start getting the full truth from him. Anyway, I was wondering whether you'd heard anything from the hospital?"
"No," replied DS Dalton. "I'll call Richie to get an update by the time you arrive, as I've heard nothing from him at all."
"Richie?" enquired Carmichael, his voice sounding unimpressed and puzzled at the same time.
"PC Richardson," replied DS Dalton. "He's the officer that was on duty there last night."
Carmichael thought for a few seconds before continuing. "It sounds like Tom must still be unconscious," he observed. "That's a blow, as I was hoping by now, he'd have come round and might be able to tell us who hit him last night. Or, at the very least, tell us the make of the vehicle involved."
DS Dalton nodded in agreement, not that Carmichael could see. "If it was a Volvo, that will put Wade Freeman well into the frame," she stated.
"I've just spoken to Stock and he's not sure but thinks the car might have been white," Carmichael informed his sergeant.

DS Dalton paused for a short while before replying. "That's interesting. And it would also put Spencer Wood into the equation," she said. "His van is white."
"And Suzi Ashcroft," Carmichael added. "I'm sure it won't be her, but she drives a battered white van." Carmichael exhaled deeply before continuing. "It looks like nearly everyone linked to this case has a white vehicle," he proclaimed.
"Apart from Lydia Brook-Smith," DS Dalton said with an air of positivity in her voice. "The Muffin Maid's van is pink and adorned with illustrations of cakes and pies."
Her words seemed to fall on stoney ground. "Let's just hope for our sakes the manufacturers don't all use the same paint suppliers," Carmichael responded gruffly. DS Dalton had no idea if they would or not, so said nothing.
"Anyway, call PC Richardson," continued Carmichael, "and get that update from him."
"Will do," replied DS Dalton just as the line went dead.

Chapter 54

Wade Freeman and his brief, Mr Fairfax, sat silently across the table from Carmichael, who for this interview was flanked by DS Dalton to his left and DC Twamley on his right.

"Morning, Wade," said Carmichael, with a welcoming smile. "For the purpose of the recording, I'm confirming that you have been cautioned and you have a duty solicitor in attendance."

Wade Freeman gave a small shrug of his shoulders but said nothing.

"We'd like you to help us with a number of matters, Wade," continued Carmichael. "And I'd like to reiterate to you that if you're not truthful with us it may well result in serious consequences."

Mr Fairfax cleared his throat. "My client will cooperate fully with you, Inspector," he replied. "But he also reserves his right to make no comment, should he choose which in no way should be interpreted by you or anyone else as anything other than he has no comment to make to that particular question."

As he spoke, Mr Fairfax looked across at Wade, as if to emphasise the instruction that he'd undoubtably given his client prior to the interview commencing.

Wade Freemen nodded once back at his brief but, again, said nothing.

Carmichael smiled once more. "I'd first of all like to ask you a question about your sister-in-law," Carmichael remarked.

"Suzi!" replied Wade, mystified as to what Carmichael would possibly want to know about her.

"No," responded Carmichael. "Leah Barnes."

Wade Freeman's expression remained perplexed. "What do you want to know?" he enquired.

"With her being a Barnes rather than an Ashcroft, I assume she was or is married," Carmichael remarked.

Wade's bearing changed as soon as he heard Carmichael's question. He even afforded himself a wry smile.

"She was, and may even have still been, married," replied Wade, "but that side of her life is something of an enigma to the rest of the family."

"And why's that?" Carmichael enquired.

Wade shrugged his shoulders. "When she was in her early twenties she decided to head off to Asia," he explained. "Totally out of character and a massive shock to her mother, and her sisters."

"And how long was she in Asia?" DS Dalton asked.

"I don't remember exactly," replied Wade with a genuine sense of vagueness in his voice. "I'd say roughly three years. But it was long enough to come back with a body full of tattoos and the claim that she'd married some Australian guy when she was out there. Neither of which went down well at all with the rest of the family."

"So, before she went, no tattoos and afterwards …" Carmichael began to say, before being interrupted.

"Tons of them," interjected Wade. "Arms, legs, neck and I don't know from seeing them myself, but Coral says they are pretty much everywhere else on her body, too."

"I see," Carmichael remarked. "And where is this Mr Barnes now?"

Wade shook his head. "God knows," he replied. "We've never seen him, heard from him, or even seen a photo of him. In fact, I reckon she just decided to call herself Barnes and made up the whole tale."

Carmichael nodded slowly. "So, was Leah prone to flights of fancy?" he asked, choosing his words carefully.

Wade shrugged his shoulders. "Before she headed to Asia, Leah Ashcroft was a quiet, sweet, mouse-like girl who'd never say boo to a goose," he remarked. "But when she came back, she was changed."

"Just in her appearance?" enquired DS Dalton.

"In appearance but also in her personality," replied Wade. "Leah Barnes, the woman that came back, was totally changed. Cocky, pushy, and often aggressive if she didn't get what she wanted. And it seemed to get even worse when she became Ron's PA."

"So, she wasn't involved in the band before she left?" DC Twamley enquired.

"She was," replied Wade, "as a junior PR girl, doing leafleting and stuff like that. But she was hardly a major cog in the machinery when the band were active. It was only afterwards she got involved."

"That's very helpful," remarked Carmichael. "Thanks for giving us that background."

"Happy to oblige," responded Wade, with a self-assured smile.

"Now," continued Carmichael, "I'd like to know a little more about your movements on Wednesday evening in the minutes after you'd had a strong word with the man you now know to be Doug Pritchard at The Three Bells?"

Wade took a deep intake of air before replying.

"I spoke with Pritchard, he then left the pub and that was the last I saw of him," Wade said, clearly wishing to be as succinct as possible in his response.

"But what did you do once Mr Pritchard had left the pub?" Carmichael enquired.

Wade shrugged his shoulders again and took another large breath.

"I stayed inside the pub for about three or four minutes then went out for a fag," he responded.

"And when you got outside, was Doug Pritchard visible to you, either in the carpark or maybe walking away from the pub?" Carmichael asked.

Wade shook his head. "No, as I said, I didn't see him after that."

"Was there anybody else in the carpark when you went out?" DS Dalton interjected.

"A couple of people," replied Wade, still being as cagey as he could.

"Can you name who these people were?" continued DS Dalton.

"Spencer Wood was there when I went out," replied Wade. "Then a few minutes later Verity came out, to pack up her stuff into her van."

"And how long were they there?" DS Dalton enquired.

Wade shook his head. "I've no idea," he replied vaguely. "I walked around the side to light-up and when I came back, they were both gone."

"And how long had elapsed between you coming out and coming back?" Carmichael enquired.

Wade shrugged his shoulders. "No idea," he replied.

"All I know is when I got back into the pub it was really busy, so I cracked on serving."

"So, five minutes or twenty minutes?" asked Carmichael. "You must have an idea how long you were outside."

Wade smiled and shook his head. "I've no idea," he replied, "I don't time my fag breaks."

"And when you were returning," interjected DC Twamley, "you say Spencer and Verity had both gone, but did you see anyone else leaving the pub?"

Wade puffed out his cheeks while he considered the question.

"There were a few people leaving," he confirmed, "but they were customers I'd not seen before, so I have no idea who they were."

"Men or women?" continued DC Twamley.

"Both," responded Wade. "Mostly couples who'd been dining with us I'd imagine."

It was now Carmichael's turn to inflate his cheeks.

"Anything else you'd like to add?" he enquired, assuming Wade would take this as an opportunity to say nothing more.

"Actually, there was, as I recall," Wade announced as if he'd just remembered something. "I heard Miles's whining moped heading off down the road. I didn't see it or him, but it was certainly his bike. You can't mistake that noise once you've heard it."

Wade then grinned widely.

* * * *

The first indication that Tom was gaining consciousness was when his eyes momentarily fluttered. Suzi, who was the only other person in the room, instantly spied this sudden sign of life returning to her son.

She clutched his hand even tighter, a broad relieved smile emerging on her face.

"Tom," she whispered slowly but with enthusiastic joy. "You're back."

Tom opened his eyes even more but shut them again as the bright light made them smart.

"What's going on?" he asked.

"You've been in an accident," his mother replied gently. "You're in hospital."

At first Tom plainly couldn't comprehend what his mother was telling him, but within a few seconds, he was clearly starting to remember things.

"It was Ellis," he announced in a surprisingly loud clear voice."

"What was?" enquired Suzi.

"It was him that killed Ron and it was him that ran into me," responded Tom, with absolute clarity.

Suzi frowned as she tried to take in what her son had just told her, which is when Tom drifted back into the deep slumber he'd evidently only temporarily emerged from.

* * * *

"What about Thursday afternoon, between one thirty and three?" enquired Carmichael. "Can you account for your movements between those times?"

"When Ron was killed?" announced Wade.

"Yes," replied Carmichael. "When Ron was murdered."

"Apart from the odd fag break, I was in the pub," replied Wade with confidence. "Well, up until about two thirty," he added. "I had to go to Fishers so I would have been in the car from two thirty, getting to Fishers at about three."

"Fishers?" enquired Carmichael.

"The cash and carry the other side of Kirkwood," Wade confirmed, as if Carmichael was a bit dim not knowing.

"So, you'd have driven almost right past Ron's house to get there," added DS Dalton, who unlike her boss, knew of Fishers and where it was located.

"I suppose I would have," replied Wade matter-of-factly. "But I didn't see anything, and I didn't kill him."

Carmichael retained his glare on Wade but said nothing for a few seconds.

"And what about yesterday evening between five thirty and six thirty?" he enquired.

"You've got to be joking," Wade announced indignantly. "You can't believe for one second that I tried to run down Tom. He's my bloody nephew for Christ's sake."

"That's not technically true," Carmichael replied. "He's not yours or Coral's flesh and blood."

"As good as," responded Wade indignantly. "He's called me uncle since he was two. That's good enough for me."

Carmichael remained impassive. "You didn't answer my question," he calmly remarked.

"I'd have been in the pub," Wade replied, his voice indicating he was still angry. "Probably, some of the time, down the cellar making sure all the barrels were ready for a busy Friday night, but I'd say I was mainly in the bar with a few regulars."

"And Coral?" added DS Dalton.

Wade shrugged his shoulders. "Some of the time," he replied. "Coral was out shopping in Kirkwood with a friend on Friday afternoon, but she was back by around six fifteen."

"Really," remarked Carmichael, in a tone that instantly made Wade feel he may have shared too much information.

"But you can scrub her off your suspects list, too," Wade added. "Lydia will vouch for her."

"Lydia Brook-Smith?" enquired DS Dalton.

Wade nodded. "Yes," he replied. "They've been mates for ages."

Carmichael and DS Dalton exchanged a quick glance before Carmichael resumed his questioning.

"I've been told that, back in the day, you were one of the roadies for Chrissy Cream and the Vixens." Carmichael stated. "In fact, head roadie I was told. Is that true?"

On hearing Carmichael's words, Wade Freeman's demeanour changed.

"That's a period of my life that still holds lots of bad memories," he announced. "I'm not prepared to go back there."

Carmichael frowned. "But surely, you can at least confirm that it's true you were a roadie for the Vixens," he remarked.

"We'd heard you were in charge of the whole roadie crew," added DS Dalton.

Wade sat back in his chair and folded his arms.

"No comment," he remarked resolutely.

Chapter 55

Suzi and the nurse she'd eagerly alerted to Tom's brief awakening had waited by his side for almost fifteen minutes, hoping he'd once more gain consciousness. However, when they realised that, although he seemed perfectly stable, he was unlikely to wake up again any time soon, the nurse rushed away to speak with the doctor on duty.

Suzi, who had thought of nothing else other than the accusation Tom had made against Ellis, decided to call Pam.

Uncharacteristically, Pam picked up almost immediately.

"Any news on Tom?" she enquired as soon as she realised it was Suzi.

By the slight slurring in her voice, Suzi figured that her friend may well have already had a few gin liveners, as Pam often called them, which, at that early hour was good going even by Pam's standards.

Suzi ignored the question. "Is Ellis there?" she enquired in a brusque, business-like fashion.

"No," replied Pam. "He and Verity have gone out somewhere. I think they said Southport."

Suzi sighed deeply. "When he gets back, tell him I need to talk to him," she announced. "And it's urgent."

"Will do," replied Pam, just before the line went dead.

Pam gently placed the mobile onto the worktop and wandered into the lounge; an entrance which prompted her son and soon-to-be mother of his child to swiftly disengage from the tight clinch they were in on the sofa.
"What the hell have you been up to, Ellis?" she enquired firmly. "Suzi has just called me. She wants to talk with you urgently. And she didn't sound like she wanted to bid you a good morning."
Ellis and Verity exchanged a puzzled look. "I've no idea, Mum" he replied frustratedly. "I'll call her."
Ellis jumped to his feet and marched out of the room, pulling out his mobile from his back pocket as he did. Pam waited until her son had departed before turning her enraged eyes in Verity's direction. "I hope you've not been stirring things up between those two," Pam announced. "They were good mates, those boys, until you appeared on the scene."
Verity frowned and stared back at Pam. "I have no idea what you're incinerating, Pam," she announced. "I've nothing to do with whatever they've been rowing about."
"Dating both of the boys, one after the other, is what's behind all this," Pam snapped back. "What sort of girl does that? And it's insinuating not incinerating. Although, creating fires is probably a good way to describe what you're all about, young lady."

* * * *

"Well, what did you make of that?" enquired Carmichael as soon as he and the rest of the team were safely behind the two-way mirror adjacent to interview room one.
"I've never seen anyone clam up so quickly as Wade did just now," remarked DS Watson, who'd been watching

and listening to the interview from behind the glass partition.

"Me neither," concurred Carmichael, standing inches away from the glass, staring at Wade Freeman, who had remained in the room and was chatting to his brief, his back turned away from the mirror.

"Very telling," DS Dalton observed. "He's happy to talk around where he was when Tom Ashcroft was hit and when Pritchard and Mason were killed but isn't prepared to talk about anything to do with Chrissy Cream's death."

"Although he did look a bit shaken when he mentioned about Coral being out when Tom was hit," added DC Twamley.

Carmichael nodded gently but said nothing for a few seconds.

"It's a good job I asked him about Leah at the start of the interview. Had I left that until later, no doubt he'd have clammed up about that, too."

"Yes," interjected DS Dalton. "What did you make of that?"

Carmichael nodded gently. "The change from a mouse-like, unassuming young woman to a confident, globetrotting, tattoo-festooned, aggressive individual does seem to be a massive transformation. It certainly creates even more questions for us to ask ourselves, although, to be frank, they may not be relevant to solving our murders. But I'd say her getting a position as Ron Mason's PA upon her return, strongly supports the theory that Leah knew something important."

"And she was using it as leverage with Ron," added DS Dalton.

Carmichael's eyes widened. "I'd say so," he remarked.

"Remember," interjected DC Twamley. "Pam Hutton suggested that Leah had been in a relationship with Ron. Maybe, that's more likely to be the reason she got the PA role."

"Maybe," responded Carmichael. "Assuming what Pam Hutton told us was true."

"And of course," added DC Twamley, "if Leah got the PA position when she came back from Asia, it may well be that the dalliance, if there was one, happened after she was made PA."

Carmichael remained silent for a few seconds. "It all needs checking out though," he remarked. "One for you, Rachel, I'd say. See what you can dig up on the timeline of Leah going to Asia and becoming Ron's PA on her return. Talk with Suzi, she may know more. And put it to her that we've heard she had a fling with Ron. See what she has to say about that."

"On it, sir," replied DS Dalton.

After another brief pause Carmichael spoke again. "Let's let Wade stew for a while and concentrate on Spencer Wood," he remarked, before starting to walk towards the exit.

Knowing this was his turn to accompany the boss, DS Watson nodded his agreement and started to follow.

"By the way," said Carmichael, his progress suddenly stopping, and his head now turned again in DS Dalton's direction, "any news from the hospital?"

DS Dalton shook her head. "Before he went off duty, PC Richardson said it had been quiet all night, and that Tom was stable, but he'd remained unconscious. But I'll check with whoever it was took over from him to get an update."

"And while you're chasing people up," Carmichael added, "find out how Stock's team are doing with that paint."

"Will do, sir," replied DS Dalton.

Carmichael then gazed over in DC Twamley's direction. "Donna," he announced, "did the dogwalker who found Tom have anything interesting to tell us?"

"DC Twamley shook her head, "He said he didn't see anything abnormal in or around the accident. He'd been walking across the fields and only came onto
the road about ten yards from where Tom was hit, so he hadn't seen or heard any vehicles prior to finding Tom in the ditch."

Carmichael screwed up his face, indicating the news wasn't what he was hoping to hear.

"Ok," he said, his thoughts now having moved on. "I need you to check with Coral to see if she was out shopping yesterday, as her husband told us."

"Will do," replied DC Twamley, much more enthusiastically than her more senior colleague had been, which brought a wry smile to Rachel Dalton's lips.

"And ask her about Leah's apparent personality change," he continued. "And whether she knows anything about this mysterious husband, whether Leah had had an affair with Ron and see if she can help with the timeline. Between you and Rachel, we may be able to get a better picture of what's been going on between Ron and Leah."

"Also, can you ask Coral if she knows anything about Suzi and Ron, too," added DS Dalton.

DC Twamley smiled. "Absolutely," she responded, her eagerness undiminished.

* * * *

"Look, Aunty Suzi," whispered Ellis, his voice hushed but resolute, "I'm really pleased that Tom is alright, but he's completely deluded. I didn't kill Ron and I certainly didn't try and run him down. I promise you."

"Well, I'm going to have to inform the police about what Tom said," continued Suzi, seemingly unconvinced by her nephew's denials.

"You do whatever you think is right," snapped back Ellis, still whispering, but a little less than before. "If anyone killed Ron it was Tom. I have no idea who tried to run him down and I know you must be out of your mind with worry, but don't pin any of this on me." Ellis didn't wait for his aunty to say anything more. He simply ended the call and irately thrust his mobile into the pocket of his jeans.

Chapter 56

Despite being given the opportunity to have a duty solicitor with him, when Carmichael and Watson entered the interview room, Spencer Wood sat alone behind the desk, with just the PC standing at the door. "Morning, Spencer," said Carmichael as he sat himself down. "You already met DS Watson earlier."

Spencer Wood nodded in Watson's direction and seemed quite relaxed.

"For the recording," continued Carmichael, "can you confirm that you have been offered, but have declined, legal representation here this morning?"

"I have and I have," replied Spencer. "I've done nothing wrong, so I don't need any help."

Carmichael smiled. "Can you tell me again, please, where you were on Wednesday evening at around nine-thirty?" he enquired.

Spencer thought for a few seconds before responding. "I was at The Three Bells, like I told the other officer."

Carmichael smiled and put a hard copy of Spencer's reply, when initially asked about that evening, in front of him. "So, why," enquired Carmichael, "when you first spoke with DS Dalton, did you tell her that on Wednesday evening you were with Tom and Robin McEvoy, at the Farmers Arms pub in Rainham Moss, at nine-fifteen?

Spencer shrugged his shoulders. "Like I said to that other officer," he replied calmly, "I forgot."

"Or, maybe, you were trying to give your mate, Tom, an alibi," remarked Watson.

Spencer smiled and gently shook his head. "I just forgot," he restated.

"Well now you've remembered," continued Carmichael, "and again, for the benefit of the recording, maybe you can tell us what you were doing at The Three Bells on Wednesday evening?"

Spencer shrugged his shoulders. "I've told DS Dalton all of this already," he replied, frustratedly. "It was just a bit of business with Wade and Coral."

Carmichael sucked in air between his clenched teeth before continuing. "Spencer," he said abruptly, his tone suddenly becoming slightly less friendly, "you are a suspect in a murder enquiry. Being deliberately vague and evasive about simple questions like this isn't going to help you."

Carmichael's mild reprimand seemed to do the trick.

"I was there to book their events room for a function a mate wants to organise in a couple of months," announced Spencer. "But Wade said they were too busy to take the details and the deposit so asked me to come back the next day. I was there about ten or fifteen minutes and went back the following morning and made the booking."

"With Wade?" DS Watson enquired.

"It was with Coral, as it happens," replied Spencer, "as Wade was out when I got there."

Relieved that Spencer was now giving them some answers, Carmichael reverted to his preferred, more calm approach to his questioning. "What time did you arrive at The Three Bells on Wednesday evening?" he asked.

"About nine twenty, maybe a tad later," replied Spencer.

"And what time did you leave to head over to meet Tom Ashcroft and Robin McEvoy at Rainham Moss?" Carmichael enquired.

"Like I told DS Dalton, it was between nine thirty and nine forty-five," Spencer replied.

"You also told DS Dalton that you stopped off on the way for a smoke," continued Carmichael. "Where exactly was that?"

Spencer shrugged his shoulders. "I don't know exactly," he proclaimed. "It was about halfway between The Three Bells and the Farmers."

"When you spoke with DS Dalton yesterday you also claimed that you were with Coral at The Three Bells between one forty-five and two thirty?" continued Carmichael.

"What do you mean, claimed?" responded Spencer angrily. "Did she not check with Coral?"

Carmichael ignored Spencer's outburst. "Which puts you in the vicinity of where Ron Mason was killed at around the time he died," he said calmly.

Spencer shook his head vigorously. "I've killed nobody," he announced. "Why would I kill either of them? I hardly knew Ron Mason and I didn't know the other bloke at all."

"But your dad knew Ron really well," added Watson, "and Ron had a big stake in your scaffolding business."

Spencer threw his head back and laughed. "So, you reckon my dad told me to kill them, do you?" he shouted. "You're really plucking at straws, aren't you?"

"What about last night?" enquired Carmichael. "Where were you between five thirty and six thirty?"

"Coming home from a job in Kirkwood, I suspect," replied Spencer. "I may have even been home by then. Can't be certain."

Carmichael looked briefly in Watson's direction before continuing. "Going back to Wednesday evening," he said, "you arrived at about nine twenty and left between nine thirty and nine forty-five. Is that correct?"

"That's roughly correct," confirmed Spencer.

"And you spoke briefly with Wade, who told you to come back tomorrow," continued Carmichael.

"That's right," replied Spencer.

"Well, that could have only taken a minute or two," observed Carmichael. "What were you doing for the rest of the time?"

Spencer shrugged his shoulders. "I had to wait a few minutes to speak with Wade," he replied. "Coral and Wade were both busy, so that took a little while. Then after I spoke with him, I went to leave and got chatting outside with Verity Brook-Smith for a few minutes. She was putting her stuff into her van. Then Wade storms out the pub, in a foul mood, lights-up and wanders off around the corner. I then talk some more with Verity, then I headed off."

"It sounds like most of the time you were outside the pub," Carmichael remarked.

Spencer nodded. "That's right, I was," he confirmed.

"And what did you and Verity talk about?" Watson asked.

Spencer shrugged his shoulders. "As the murdered bloke came out of the pub and walked away, Verity told me that Wade had had a real go at him," replied Spencer.

"You saw Doug Pritchard leave the pub?" announced Carmichael with surprise in his voice.

"Well, yes, but I didn't know who he was then," replied Spencer.

"So, why didn't you tell DS Dalton about seeing him when she spoke to you?" Carmichael asked, his voice slightly raised.

"She never asked me," replied Spencer, seemingly bemused at why Carmichael was so animated. "He came out of the pub and just walked away towards Jay Bank Lane."

"And Verity saw him leave, too?" Carmichael stated.

"Yes, of course," replied Spencer. "When he was out of earshot, she then told me about Wade shouting at him. She said Wade was really angry with him, which she reckoned was a bit unfair as Verity said it was Ron Mason who'd been the one making the most noise, not the guy Wade had a go at. She also asked what I was up to, but when I mentioned I was meeting Tom she said she'd have to crack on. We only talked for about five minutes then she went back inside the pub. It was then I got in my van and headed off."

"So, why did Verity clam up when you mentioned Tom?" Carmichael enquired.

Spencer considered the question for a few seconds before responding. "Because she was Tom's girlfriend first," he replied. "They went out for about a year, then she ditched him and started going out with Ellis. It's caused a massive issue between the lads and, of course, now she's pregnant … well, put it this way, I don't think that's helped mend the feud between Tom and Ellis."

"I see," remarked Carmichael.

"I'm mates with both of them," continued Spencer, "so I've tried to keep out of it. But it's not a great situation."

"I can imagine," remarked Carmichael, who once again exchanged a glance with Watson to his right. "Is there anything else you noticed that evening that we should know about?"

Spencer shook his head gently as if he was about to say not. Then his expression changed, as if something had just come to him. "I think I saw Ron Mason coming out of the pub as I was driving out of the car park," Spencer announced.

"Are you sure it was him?" Watson asked.

"I'm pretty sure," replied Spencer. "It was in my wing mirror I saw him, and it was as I was about to turn onto the road, but I'm as certain as I can be it was him."

"And was he alone?" Carmichael enquired.

Spencer nodded. "Yes," he replied. "He was definitely on his own."

"Which direction was he heading?" Carmichael asked.

Spencer shrugged his shoulders. "I only saw him for a second or so. I didn't see which way he went, but I'd guess he'd be making his way to the car park."

Carmichael turned his head and made eye contact with Watson, whose expression indicated that he was also intrigued by what Spencer had just told them.

Chapter 57

Back in the safety of the small viewing office, situated between interview rooms one and two, with its two-way mirrors, Carmichael looked over in DS Watson's direction. "What did you make of Spencer?" he enquired.

DS Watson stroked his stubble-laden chin with his left hand for a few seconds before replying. "He's a cocky little sod," he remarked bluntly, "but I think, in the main, he was telling us the truth. I don't really see him being our killer."

Carmichael nodded. "I agree," he concurred. "But I'm glad we brought him in as he told us a few things that we didn't know."

"Like seeing Ron leave the pub, you mean?" suggested Watson.

Carmichael nodded. "And just how angry Wade was," added Carmichael. "I think our Mr Freeman has a bit of a short fuse."

"Sounds very much like that, doesn't it?" Watson acknowledged.

"And young Verity Brook-Smith keeps coming up," continued Carmichael. "I'm not saying she's our killer either, but she's in the pub when there's the argument, she's outside with Spencer, she leaves to go home not long after Pritchard heads off into the night, and her mum's bakery is one of the businesses Ron helped out."

"If what Spencer said is true, she's also dated both Tom and now Ellis, continued DS Watson, "and she's having Ellis's baby, too."

Carmichael thought for a few seconds more before speaking again.

"But having dated the two lads doesn't make her a murderer and being so young she wouldn't have known Doug Pritchard, so I can't see why she'd kill him," he announced. "And I can't think of many pregnant ladies who'd so viciously attack a grown man in the dark, as she'd have had to do down Jay Bank Lane on Wednesday evening."

DS Watson couldn't help but agree but didn't say anything.

"Maybe we should get Rachel's opinion on her", Carmichael said, just as DS Dalton entered the room.

"My opinion on who?" DS Dalton enquired, having caught what Carmichael had said.

"Verity," replied Carmichael. "Her name keeps coming up, so we were wondering what sort of impression you got after talking with her."

"She seems nice enough," DS Dalton began vaguely. "A bit immature, and probably a bit spoilt by her mum, being the only child, but as nineteen-year-olds go, I'd say she's a decent sort of girl. Mind you, I think she'll have a rude awakening when baby comes. Not that I'd know what it's like having a baby to look after."

"But could she be involved in these murders, in your view?" Carmichael enquired directly.

DS Dalton looked a bit surprised at the question. "I guess she could," she replied. "It's possible, I suppose. But she's a tiny thing. Can't be more than five foot three tall and even with her little bump, she can't weigh more than fifty kilos. She'd have had to really surprise Pritchard and Mason to be able to kill them both single handed. If they'd fought back, they'd have overpowered her in seconds."

"But as far as we can tell, neither did fight back," remarked DS Watson.

Carmichael nodded. "That's true. And maybe if she was involved, she didn't act alone."

"So, do we add her to our list of suspects?" DS Watson enquired.

Carmichael considered Watson's question for a second or two. "I may go over and talk with her, later today," he replied. "But let's keep her off the list for the moment."

DS Dalton and DS Watson both nodded in agreement, as neither really thought Verity was a serious contender.

"Did Spencer tell you anything new?" DS Dalton asked.

"He reckons he saw Pritchard coming out of the pub," replied DS Watson.

"Interesting," remarked DS Dalton. "So, that would put the time Spencer left the pub at about nine thirty."

Carmichael nodded. "Which ties in with the story he gave us, that he drove over to the Farmers, stopping for a fag in a layby."

DS Watson shook his head. "I don't buy this stopping over for a fag in a layby story. Spencer strikes me as someone who'd smoke in his van while driving."

DS Dalton smiled, amused by her colleague's opinion. "Maybe we should check his van for traces of ash," she suggested.

"Whether he smokes in his van or not," interjected Carmichael, "we've got nothing substantial to link Spencer with the murders or the hit and run, so he needs to be released. Can you sort that out, Marc?"

DS Watson nodded. "Will do," he replied.

"Anyway," announced Carmichael, his piercing blue eyes fixed on DS Dalton. "Any news about the paint or from the hospital?"

DS Dalton pulled a face suggesting what she was about to say may not be what Carmichael wanted to hear. "I've an update on both," she said gingerly. "What do you want first, the good news or the not-so-good news?"

Carmichael rolled his eyes skyward. "Bad first," he responded. "You may as well get that out of the way."

"I spoke with Matt Stock, and he told me that they are certain the paint flecks they found at the scene of Tom's hit and run isn't paint used by any major car manufacturer," DS Dalton announced. "They think it's more likely to have been used by an enthusiast, who does up cars. And they are now saying that it might have been there up to a month prior to the accident. So, may even be nothing to do with Tom's hit and run."

Carmichael nodded gently. "I don't think Wade, Spencer or Suzi are what you'd call car buffs," he remarked gloomily.

"Not at all, considering the state of the vehicles they drive," Watson added.

"And now the good news?" enquired Carmichael, his attention once more returning to DS Dalton.

"Apparently, Tom Ashcroft opened his eyes and spoke to Suzi for a few seconds, before drifting off again," she announced, with a confident smile. "Only Suzi was there and according to PC Tyler, who was just outside in the corridor at the time, Suzi said he didn't make much sense. But he definitely spoke to her."

"That's great news," remarked Carmichael. "You need to talk to Suzi, so get yourself down there and, if he comes round, try and find out from Tom if he has any recollection of the incident last night."

DS Dalton frowned. "That's the issue," she said, "according to PC Tyler, as soon as she came out of Tom's room, Suzi just shot off."

"That's strange," remarked Carmichael. "Now he's coming round, you'd expect her to want to be there with him."

"That's exactly what I thought," replied DS Dalton.

Chapter 58

The one sure fire thing that confirmed it was the weekend at Kirkwood police station was the lack of hot food in the canteen. It's true the sandwich machine was always reasonably well stocked, and the hot drink machine served passable coffee, however, if you wanted a bacon roll or something more substantial, Saturdays and Sundays were not the time to find yourself stuck in the office.

With DS Dalton having been despatched to find Suzi Ashcroft, DC Twamley with Coral Freeman, and DS Watson sorting out Spencer Wood's release, Carmichael found himself alone at a large table in Kirkwood police station canteen, with a steaming coffee in front of him, along with a discarded half-eaten ham sandwich and the handwritten list of nine questions he'd penned the evening before.

He took a sip of coffee before taking out a pen and scribbling notes against four of them, which he then underlined so his latest observations were crystal clear.

- *Why did Mason want to see Suzi and Pam on the afternoon he died?*
- *Why did Mason change his will?*
- *Why was Pritchard killed? <u>He knew something about Chrissy's disappearance.</u>*

- What weapon was used to kill Pritchard?
- What happened to Chrissy? <u>*She didn't die on the boat*</u>
- Why did Mason lend 3 people so much money for no financial return (not in keeping with his character)?
- Why was Mason killed?
- Is there one killer or are more than one person involved? <u>*Yes*</u>
- If more than one did different people murder Pritchard and Mason? <u>*No*</u>

As he read the results of his handiwork, he was suddenly joined by DS Watson.

"What have you got there, sir?" he enquired, clearly intrigued by the scribbled note in front of the boss.

Carmichael hadn't seen Watson until he was at his side but having had the best part of a day to go over the nine questions, he was only too pleased to talk them through with one of the team.

"They're questions I think may get us to the bottom of all this," Carmichael replied. "I'm not sure I know the answers to any of them yet, but I've a few ideas."

"Do you want to run them by me?" asked DS Watson enthusiastically, as he perched himself on the corner of Carmichael's table.

Carmichael nodded. "Ok," he replied, "here's what I'm thinking."

Before he could utter another word, Carmichael's mobile rang.

"Not just us working this weekend," Carmichael announced with a wry smile. "It's the good Dr Stock."

With his left hand, Carmichael pushed and simultaneously rotated the note so that it was near DS Watson and the right way up for him to read. "You take a look while I talk with Stock," he told his sergeant, before turning away from Watson and taking Stock's call.

"I thought you'd be at the golf club today," Carmichael irreverently remarked.

"I would have been, Carmichael, if it wasn't for you finding my team dead bodies all over the shop and hordes of crime scenes that need analysing," the head pathologist countered.

Carmichael smiled. "What have you got for me?" he asked.

"I suppose DS Dalton has told you about the paint," Stock began. "We're still working on that, but I've not got a match for any of your suspects' vehicles, unless they've been repainted or touched up."

"Rachel did tell me," confirmed Carmichael. "But you must have something, otherwise you wouldn't have called."

"As it happens, I do," replied Stock. "I sent details of the head injuries to a colleague of mine in London, who specialises in brain traumas."

"Right," noted Carmichael, wishing the pathologist would hurry along to the meat of news. "Well, he confirmed what I had thought was the likely sequence of events leading up to Mr Pritchard's death."

"Which are?" Carmichael enquired.

"That the first blow was the horizontal blow to the back of the dead man's head," announced Stock. "A massive blow that probably would have killed the poor man eventually.

"Eventually," repeated Carmichael. "So, it was the second blow that actually killed him?"

"Yes," replied Stock. "The angled blow to the front of the head was the one that would have killed him. And instantly, too."

Carmichael thought for a few seconds. "And how soon after the first blow did the second one come?" he asked. Carmichael could hear Stock sucking in air before he answered.

"I'd say within a matter of a few seconds," Stock replied.

It was now Carmichael's turn to take a little time. "Any more thoughts on whether it was one or two people who administered the blows?" Carmichael enquired.

"No," replied Stock firmly. "It could have been one person or two. But if it was two, they either used the same weapon or weapons that were very similar."

"Anything else you and your colleague have managed to uncover?" Carmichael asked.

"As it happens there is," responded Stock, his voice sounding full of glee.

"Well please do tell," continued Carmichael, now very keen to find out what nugget Stock was about to share with him.

"The person who administered the first blow to Mr Pritchard could have been left or right-handed," remarked Stock, "however the assailant who delivered the second blow to Mr Pritchard and the blow that killed Mr Mason, was definitely right-handed."

"So, ninety per cent of the population," remarked Carmichael, sounding less than impressed by this revelation from Stock.

"True," replied Stock. "But that puts any lefties you may have on your suspect list out of contention. Well, at least for Mr Mason's untimely demise."

"Any other clues about these killers?" Carmichael asked.

"So, you think there were two, do you?" Stock responded.

"I have no idea, to be honest," Carmichael replied. "But I'm keeping that option open for now."

"There is one observation I can share with you," continued Stock.

"What's that?" enquired Carmichael.

"Due to the fact that the second blow to Pritchard and the single blow to Mason were both angled, I have no idea how tall the person who caused those blows would be," Stock explained. "It would depend on the length of the weapon used."

"But you can make a reasonably good estimation for the other blow to Pritchard?" interjected Carmichael.

"Yes," proclaimed Stock. "Assuming the person who administered the first blow wasn't standing on anything to increase his height, and with that blow being a horizontal one across Pritchard's head, I can make a fairly good estimation of that assailant's height." proclaimed Stock.

"How tall, is he?" Carmichael enquired.

"Well Pritchard was one hundred and seventy centimetres tall," announced Stock, "so, I'd say his attacker would have to be in the region of one hundred and ninety centimetres. Maybe a little taller."

"What's that in feet and inches?" Carmichael asked.

"You really must enter into the twenty-first century, Inspector Carmichael," replied Stock contemptuously. "It translates to about five foot seven inches for Mr Pritchard and six foot three inches for his attacker." When the line went quiet, Stock filled the void. "Do you have a six-foot three- inch man on your suspects list?" he enquired.

"I think I just might," replied Carmichael.

Chapter 59

"Good news?" enquired DS Watson when Carmichael ended the call with Stock and turned back to face his sergeant.

"Could be," replied Carmichael, "but tell me first what you made of my hurriedly scribbled list."

DS Watson shrugged his shoulders before responding. "I'd like to hear what you think," he said cautiously, "but I'd agree with there being two people involved in Pritchard's murder and I'd agree also with this all being linked to the boat accident."

Carmichael nodded, as if to signify he concurred with his sergeant so far. "Anything else?" he asked.

"Well, going through them one by one," continued Watson, "I think Ron Mason probably wanted to see Suzi and Pam to either advise them about the change to the will or maybe, more likely, to alert them to some dark secret about Chrissy potentially coming out."

When Carmichael nodded, Watson continued. "I think Mason changed his will to make sure Leah got nothing and I think Pritchard was killed because Leah had told him something that someone didn't want to be made public. Almost certainly involving Chrissy Cream."

"I can't fault your logic so far," said Carmichael.

Encouraged by his boss's apparent approval, DS Watson ploughed on. "As I said already, I fully agree with your note indicating that Pritchard was killed because of something he knew about Chrissy's alleged accident, I have no idea what weapon was used to kill him, and I also think it's unlikely that Chrissy died on that boat."

"We're pretty much in sync," announced Carmichael. "So, what about those last four questions?"

DS Watson paused and ran his hand over his chin before responding. "These are more difficult," he acknowledged. "But if pushed, I'd say that the loans were pay offs to keep people quiet. Again, as I just said, I'd agree with your note that there were two killers responsible for Pritchard's death, but I think just one for Mason's murder."

"And why do you think Ron Mason was killed?" Carmichael asked.

DS Watson took a deep breath. "I'd say it was Ron Mason and Wade Freeman who killed Pritchard," he proposed. "I think it was clear Pritchard had been told something by Leah Barnes that they didn't want to come out, so they had to silence him."

"And what about Mason?" Carmichael enquired.

"To be frank, I'm not sure why he was murdered," Watson conceded, "but my guess is that Ron Mason must have double crossed Wade somehow, and Wade decided he had to be disposed of, too."

Carmichael nodded. "You're not a million miles from my train of thought, Marc," he acknowledged. "And Stock just told me he thinks one of the blows which killed Doug Pritchard was probably made by someone over six foot tall. How tall do you reckon Wade is?"

Watson smiled; his eyes suddenly becoming wide open. "I'd say about six foot three or six foot four," he replied.

* * * *

Following her husband's arrest that morning, Coral Freeman had decided not to open The Three Bells at lunchtime. She'd figured the half dozen or so usuals could find an alternative watering hole for once. They'd moan no doubt, she expected, but they'd have no say in the matter, as Coral wanted to be alone rather than put on a brave face. So, when, with a broad smile, DC Twamley appeared at her door, holding up her identity card, it was the last thing Coral expected or wanted. Coral closed her eyes, shook her head and, without bothering to apply any filters, loudly blurted out, "What the hell do you want now?"

DC Twamley retained her professional smile. "I've just a few questions I need to ask you," she replied.

"Well, you can ask them from there," countered Coral angrily. "Unless you've a warrant, you're not coming in."

"That's perfectly fine," responded DC Twamley, with not a hint of this being an inconvenience.

"Go on then," Coral urged her.

"Can you confirm where you were yesterday afternoon?" DC Twamley asked.

"Why do you want to know that?" replied Coral.

"If you could just answer the question, please?" returned DC Twamley, firmly.

Coral rolled her eyes and shook her head. "I was with Lydia, in Southport, shopping until the shops started to close and then we came home," said Coral.

"What time did you go out and when did you get back home?" DC Twamley asked.

Coral thought for a few seconds before replying. "I left here at about twelve thirty, picked up Lydia and then went on to Southport," Coral announced. "We'd have got there about one fifteen, I'd guess. Then we left at about five thirty and I dropped Lydia home and would have got back here at about six fifteen."

DC Twamley smiled. "And you drove?" she asked.

"Yes," replied Coral, "in Wade's heap, over there."

As she replied, Coral pointed across to her husband's battered white Volvo.

"That's great," remarked DC Twamley, who was starting to feel edgy about how she'd be able to tackle her next few questions. She decided to stick to the plan she'd formed in her head on the drive over; talk about Ron first, then Leah and avoid spending any time flowering things up. Basically, to just go for it.

"I'd like to ask you a few questions about Ron Mason if I may," she began.

"Ok?" replied Coral, "but I didn't know him that well."

"I'm told he was a bit of a ladies' man," announced DC Twamley, who regretted her turn of phrase as soon as it came out of her mouth.

Coral at last allowed her face the slightest of smiles, a major break from its, up to then, incensed persona. "I'm told that may have been the case," she replied, "but that's just what people said. I've no first-hand experience of Ron the lothario."

"But did he ever have a relationship with either of your sisters?" enquired DC Twamley.

Coral nodded. "There was something going on between Leah and Ron," she conceded, "but that was years ago. In fact, decades ago."

"So, how long were they together?" DC Twamley asked.

Coral shrugged her shoulders. "About a year, maybe eighteen months," she replied. "It was so long ago I couldn't be certain."

"Was that before or after Leah went travelling?" DC Twamley enquired.

Coral looked a little shocked that DC Twamley knew so much already about Leah, so took her time before answering. "I think it was before," she eventually replied. "But it was so long ago I might have that wrong."

DC Twamley maintained her smile. "How long did your sister stay abroad?" she continued.

"Best part of two years," replied Coral.

"And I'm told when she returned, she was a changed woman," added DC Twamley. "Full of confidence, heavily tattooed and a married woman."

Coral raised her eyebrows. "You've been doing your homework," she remarked with genuine admiration in her voice.

"And Ron makes her his PA," continued DC Twamley.

"All correct," confirmed Coral, who DC Twamley could see was starting to try and keep her replies as brief as she could.

"What do you know of Mr Barnes?" DC Twamley asked.

Coral threw her head back and laughed loudly. "I'm not sure there even was a Mr Barnes," she replied. "We never saw a photo of him, she never talked about him and as far as I know, if he does exist, he never tried to contact her. I'd not be surprised if she made the whole thing up."

"Was Leah like that?" DC Twamley asked. "A bit of a fantasist?"

Coral resumed her more solemn face. "DC Twamley," she said firmly, "with Leah only just passing, it's not right for you to make insulting comments about her. She was a free spirt, is all I'll say, but she was a good person, too."

"Of course," responded DC Twamley. "I fully understand."

"Are we finished?" Coral asked, as she started to slowly close the door.

"You didn't answer when I asked about Suzi and Ron," DC Twamley reminded her. "Were they ever romantically involved?"

Coral continued to close the door slowly. "Suzi's still alive," replied Coral, "so I'd ask her yourself, if I were you."

Upon finishing her sentence, the door closed, leaving DC Twamley abandoned on the threshold.

Chapter 60

As soon as Coral was safely back inside the pub and the door firmly closed, Suzi emerged from the back room and joined her younger sibling.
They watched in silence as DC Twamley clambered into her car and drove away.
"Now that she's gone," announced Suzi, resolutely, "maybe you can tell me exactly what Leah said to you?"
Coral looked indignantly back at her sister. "Leah didn't give me any details about what she'd told Pritchard. And she certainly never mentioned Ellis," she replied with equal firmness."
By the cynical look on Suzi's face, it was crystal clear to Coral that her sister didn't believe she was telling her everything that Leah had said at that last meeting.
"Did you have a fling with Ron?" Coral asked, trying her best to change the subject.
"Back then I had flings with anything that moved in trousers," Suzi replied with shameless nonchalance.
"Ron probably included. But that was years ago."
Coral shook her head before staring straight into her sister's eyes.
"So, you really think it was Ellis that killed Ron?" she remarked, incredulously.

Suzi shrugged her shoulders. "I don't want to believe it, Coral, but Tom says it was Ellis and that's good enough for me."

Coral shook her head again. This time more vigorously. "That's part of the problem with you, and with Pam, too," she announced. "Your precious little boys can't ever do any wrong in your eyes. The rest of us sometimes see them in a slightly different light."

Under normal circumstances, Suzi wouldn't have allowed anyone to say such a thing about her Tom; but on this occasion she bit her lip and let it pass.

* * * *

DS Dalton knocked again on Suzi Ashcroft's front door, this time with greater purpose. There was still no answer.

With her van not on the drive and having unsuccessfully tried Suzi's mobile on three occasions, DS Dalton decided her best course of action would be to head over to the hospital. Armed with the knowledge that Tom had woken at least once already, DS Dalton figured it would only be a matter of time before Suzi returned to his bedside. And even if she didn't, there was a chance of speaking to Tom to see if he had any idea who it was behind the wheel of the vehicle that had almost killed him.

* * * *

DS Watson turned on the recording equipment.

"The time is twelve fifty-seven," he announced. "Interview with Wade Freeman at Kirkwood police station, conducted by Inspector Carmichael and Sergeant Watson, with Mr Fairfax in attendance."

Carmichael smiled in Wade's direction.

"I'd like to resume our discussions from this morning, Wade," he began. "I'd specifically like to hear from you details of what really happened on the day that the Workington Jenny left harbour at Whitehaven for the last time."

Carmichael paused for a moment, but kept his eyes firmly fixed on Wade Freeman.

"You told the coroner at the inquest that you'd driven Chrissy Cream up there that morning and she'd boarded just before it set off," continued Carmichael.

"That wasn't true was it, Wade?"

Wade Freeman stared straight ahead of him.

"No comment," he replied calmly.

"You lied, didn't you, Wade," suggested Carmichael. "Just like Leah lied. Why was that?"

Wade remained impassive. "No comment," he announced for a second time.

Carmichael glanced momentarily towards DS Watson before continuing.

"Shall I tell you what I think?" continued Carmichael. "I don't think Chrissy went anywhere near that boat. I think she was either killed by you, Leah, or by Ron Mason; or she may have simply absconded. But my bet is that you, Leah, or Ron killed her and together you tried to cover it up by making up a story about her being on the Workington Jenny. The timing of that tragedy must have been so convenient for you three. Isn't that how it was?"

Wade shook his head. "No comment," he uttered again.

"On balance I think it was probably Ron who actually did the deed," continued Carmichael. "You and Leah were just accomplices. Paid off after the event to keep schtum. You got that loan to finance the pub, and Leah, I'd guess, got some cash to go travelling and then the role of Ron's PA when she got back. Don't you think that makes sense, DS Watson?".

As he finished speaking, Carmichael turned his head to face his sergeant.

"Makes perfect sense, sir," replied Watson.

"You're just fishing about, Carmichael," proclaimed Wade. "You've no proof of any of this."

"Why don't you tell us how it was, then, if this isn't what happened, Wade?" interjected Watson.

"Yes, if I've got any of this wrong, now's your chance to put the record straight," added Carmichael. "As I'm sure Mr Fairfax can confirm, perverting the course of justice by lying to the coroner is a serious crime, but it's not in the same league as murder."

It was clear by the look on his face that Wade Freeman was thinking about what they had said, but he didn't respond.

After allowing Wade a few seconds, Carmichael smiled and continued. "And then Pritchard comes along, shooting his mouth off in your pub about what Leah had told him," he stated. "To have the nerve to do that in your pub, well that must have really riled you."

Wade Freeman's face remained impassive, and he stayed silent.

"So, you throw him out," continued Carmichael. "Then you and Ron follow him down Jay Bank Lane and you kill him. You caved his head in then just went back to the pub as if nothing had happened. You even try to give Ron a false alibi. One you now admit was a lie."

"That's not as it was," responded Wade.

"Then, on Thursday, you go over to see Ron and there's a disagreement, and Ron ends up dead," announced Carmichael. "What was that all about, Wade? Did you ask for more cash to keep quiet and he refused?"

"This is all rubbish," barked Wade, his deadpan expression having suddenly deserted him.

"Then there's the hit and run on Tom," Carmichael added. "Did Tom see you at Ron's house on Thursday? We know he was there shortly before Ron was killed. Did he tell you he'd seen you?"

"I've had enough of this nonsense," Wade hollered, "I want to talk with Mr Fairfax alone. I'm not answering anything more until I've spoken with Mr Fairfax."

Carmichael nodded. "That's perfectly fine, Wade," he replied, calmly. "I'm happy to pause here and talk with you when you're ready to tell us more."

From the much-changed expression on Wade's face, Carmichael felt confident that at their next meeting, Wade would be more forthcoming. Perhaps not to the extent of giving him the whole truth, but maybe enough to allow the investigation to move a few steps forward.

Chapter 61

Ellis stretched out on the bed and gazed keenly at a zigzag crack that stretched across half the width of Verity's bedroom ceiling.
"Do you know," he remarked dreamily, "with all this nonsense going on, I'd just like to pack up the car and drive off somewhere for a few days."
Verity, who was cuddled up tightly next to him, her head resting on his chest, just sniggered.
"What do you think?" Ellis said, his voice now sounding as though he liked the sound of what he'd just said.
"And where would we go?" replied Verity. "And we're both skint, so how are we going to pay for it?"
"I may be a bit short of cash at the moment," Ellis conceded, "but I'm going to be stinking rich any day now, so let's just put a little bit on the tab, so to speak."
Verity eased herself up so she could see Ellis's face.
"In that case you're on," she said excitedly. "Let's just head off for a few days. How about North Wales?"
Ellis sat up. "Gretna Green sounds a better idea," he replied, a broad mischievous smile spread right across his face.

"I'm not sure they do quickie weddings up there anymore," Verity added, in her best sensible voice. "And even if they did, Mum would kill me if we denied her the chance to wear that massive hat, she's bought herself."

Ellis laughed. "And before you suggest it, I don't fancy a night in a tent in the Delph Tea Gardens," he remarked; a dig at his girlfriend who, since childhood, had visited the abandoned local quarry that had become a beauty spot years ago, with its old, abandoned tea-room now barely recognisable in its grounds.

"I can go there anytime," replied Verity, who, as she spoke, gave her boyfriend a massive jab in his side with her elbow.

"Well how about the Lakes then?" suggested Ellis, grabbing Verity's arm to prevent a second painful blow.

"Sounds good to me," shrieked Verity enthusiastically. "Let's do it."

*   *   *   *

"What's the plan now?" DS Watson enquired as he and Carmichael sat together in the incident room.

Carmichael considered DS Watson's question for a few seconds.

"Obviously we need to see what Wade Freeman has to say for himself when he's through with his brief," Carmichael replied. "But while we're waiting, we need to consider who else on our radar is over six feet tall?"

DS Watson looked surprised. "Are you having doubts about Wade being our killer?" he asked.

Carmichael shook his head and smiled. "He's got the motive; his alibis aren't strong for any of the three incidents and his behaviour is very suspicious…"

"And he's well over six foot tall," added DS Watson.
"Yes, that's true, too," conceded Carmichael, "but we don't have any strong evidence linking him with any of

the crimes. No weapon found on him and no forensics at any of the crime scenes that link him with the events, so we need to think about who else it could be."

Although he was certain that Wade Freeman was either wholly or partially involved, Watson found himself nodding as his boss finished talking.

"Well, looking at the eleven names on our suspects list," DS Watson remarked, his eyes now focused on the list they'd written down the day before, "we can scrub off all the women up there. Suzi's probably the tallest and she can't be much above five seven. And as well as Martin Wood being physically unlikely to have been able to murder Doug Pritchard, he's no more than five six or five seven either, as is Spencer. So, they're out."

"Which basically just leaves us with Tom and Ellis," announced Carmichael.

DS Watson nodded. "Tom's certainly over six foot," he said. "But I'm not sure about Ellis. We'd have to ask Rachel about him."

"Let's do that," Carmichael suggested. "I'd also like to find out how Rachel got on talking with Suzi. So, while I do that why don't you call Donna and see how she got on with Coral Freeman.

"Will do," replied DS Watson, extracting his mobile from of his jacket pocket as he spoke.

Chapter 62

DS Dalton had just passed through the automatic doors at the entrance of Southport hospital, when Carmichael's call came through.

"Hi, sir," she said as her eyes quickly scoured around the foyer looking for somewhere quieter where she could talk.

"Rachel, how tall is Ellis Hutton?" Carmichael impatiently enquired, without providing any rationale for his question.

"I'd say about six foot two or maybe six foot three," replied DS Dalton. "Why do you ask?"

"Because Stock's fairly sure our killer, or at least one of the people who attacked Pritchard, was probably over six foot," Carmichael explained. "Freeman is still our prime suspect, but Marc and I are trying to identify any others on our suspects list, who are over six feet."

"Well Ellis definitely is," confirmed DS Dalton.

Carmichael paused for a few seconds before continuing. "Have you any updates for me?" he asked.

"I've not been able to reach Suzi on the phone and she wasn't at home," replied DS Dalton. "So, I've headed over to the hospital. I've just this minute arrived."

"Makes sense," remarked Carmichael. "I'm still a bit confused as to why Suzi would leave the hospital just after Tom started to gain consciousness."

"My only explanation would be that he told her something and she's gone off to confront someone," replied DS Dalton.

"I hope not," continued Carmichael. "We've got enough on our plate without another attempted murder."

DS Dalton laughed. "I'll see if I can talk with Tom," she added. "Maybe he can shed some light on who tried to kill him and where Suzi is."

"Ok," replied Carmichael. "But keep me informed if you do find anything out."

DS Dalton didn't even bother to confirm she would as, just as she'd expected, the line suddenly went dead. Gently shaking her head with frustration, DS Dalton placed her phone in her back pocket and strode purposefully down the hospital corridor.

* * * *

DC Twamley was less than ten miles from Kirkwood police station when the call came in from DS Watson.

"The boss would like to know how you got on with Coral?" DS Watson told her. "Any progress?"

"I think so," she replied, positively. "But I'm almost back at the station, so, if you can wait fifteen minutes, I can fill you both in together."

"Sounds fine to me," replied Watson, "Will give me time to get a coffee from the machine in the canteen."

"Mine's white with no sugar," remarked DC Twamley, more in hope than expectation.

"I see you've settled in ok," responded DS Watson. "Didn't take you long."

* * * *

Carmichael took out his list of questions and after going over them twice, he took out a pen and started to make additional modifications.

- *Why did Mason want to see Suzi and Pam on the afternoon he died?*
- *Why did Mason change his will?*
- *Why was Pritchard killed? <u>He knew something about Chrissy's disappearance.</u>*
- *What weapon was used to kill Pritchard?*
- *What happened to Chrissy? <u>She didn't die on the boat.</u>*
- *Why did Mason lend 3 people so much money for no financial return (not in keeping with his character)?*
- *Why was Mason killed? <u>Most likely linked to Chrissy's disappearance.</u>*
- *Is there one killer or are more than one person involved? ~~Yes~~ <u>unclear.</u>*
- *If more than one did different people murder Pritchard and Mason? ~~No~~ <u>unclear.</u>*

DS Watson had just appeared at the door of the incident room, carrying three cups of coffee on a flimsy cardboard tray he'd found, abandoned behind the canteen counter, when Carmichael's desk phone rang. "Carmichael," the boss announced, the phone at his ear. "That's excellent," he then said. "We'll come down right away."
Once the call was over and the receiver returned to its normal resting place, Carmichael looked over in DS Watson's direction. "Wade Freeman and Mr Fairfax are ready for us, Marc," he proclaimed. "Bring the drinks with you, we can have them when we get in there."

DS Watson rested the tray on the desk then handed one of the cups to Carmichael. "White with one," he said as he passed it over.

"Thank you, Marc," replied Carmichael as he took the hot cup from his sergeant.

Watson then took one of the drinks himself, leaving the last one resting on the tray.

"I assume that's mine," announced DC Twamley, who'd appeared at the door a few seconds before.

* * * *

Pam was already having a bad day. So, the last thing she wanted to see was Suzi's battered van turn into her driveway. Although she'd already had at least three largish liveners to help her cope, she immediately felt the need for another.

"Where is he?" demanded Suzi before she'd even fully emerged from her van.

"Ellis is out with Verity," Pam replied sharply. "He had nothing to do with Tom's accident, so don't start trying to pin that one on him."

"That's not what Tom says," Suzi angrily snapped back. "Why would he say it was Ellis if it wasn't?"

Pam rolled her eyes. "Verity Brook bloody Smith, that's why," she replied. "Tom's clearly not over her yet and blames Ellis. God knows why. In my opinion he had a lucky escape there. She's not the sweet little thing she'd like us all to think she is."

"Rubbish," barked Suzi. "It's got nothing to do with Verity."

By the time she'd finished speaking, Suzi had made it to where Pam was standing. "I see you've been on the bottle again," she announced disdainfully. "You need to talk to someone about that."

Pam shook her head, turned slowly on her heels, and headed back towards her house. "Tell Tom I hope he gets better soon," she shouted, not bothering to look back.

Still furious, but perplexed, too, Suzi watched as Pam disappeared inside her house, slamming shut the front door behind her.

Without any idea of what she was going to do next, Suzi marched back to her van and within a minute, turned it around and was speeding away; fumes spewing out from the rusted, vibrating exhaust pipe, that, by the sound of it, had precious little keeping it attached.

Chapter 63

Flanked by DS Watson and DC Twamley, Carmichael stared directly at Wade Freeman, who looked a worried man.
On their walk down to interview room one, DC Twamley had fully updated her colleagues on her conversation with Coral Freeman, which Carmichael decided to use in his opening.
"Good afternoon again, gentlemen," he said calmly. "For the tape, I'd just like to confirm that Coral has verified she was in Southport on Friday afternoon, with Lydia Brook-Smith, and that they drove there in your car."
A slight smile appeared on Wade Freeman's face, but it didn't stay there for very long.
"We've also now had corroboration from another party that Leah was in a relationship with Ron at the time of the boat tragedy, which may explain why she'd have misled the inquest into Chrissy's death."
Wade Freeman looked nervous but said nothing.
Mr Fairfax, who was sitting to Wade's left, suddenly cleared his throat and pushed his glasses back a few millimetres on his nose. "If I may interject," he announced, "I think it would help all concerned if I was allowed to read out a prepared statement from Mr Freeman."

Carmichael glanced firstly at DS Watson, then at DC Twamley, before fixing his stare on Wade Freeman's brief and nodding. "That would be very welcome, Mr Fairfax," he remarked.

Mr Fairfax turned his notebook to the next page and started to read the statement he and Wade had been preparing for the last hour. "My client wishes it to be acknowledged that he has cooperated fully with the police regarding their investigations into the deaths of Doug Pritchard and Ron Mason; and with the incident yesterday evening involving his nephew, Tom Ashcroft. He not only denies having any involvement in these incidents, but he also wants it put on record that he has no knowledge of who the perpetrator or perpetrators are for any of these three awful events.

With regards to the investigation into the tragic sinking of the Workington Jenny, my client would like to again make it clear that he was not involved or had any knowledge of any events, at that time, that either took place in Lancashire or in Cumbria, that he should have made known to the police or to the court."

For the first time since he'd started to speak, Mr Fairfax took his eyes off his notes and looked briefly at Carmichael, before returning to his prepared speech. "However, my client would also like to make you aware that he had been put under great pressure to state that he'd driven Chrissy Cream from Lancashire to Cumbria on the day the Workington Jenny sailed; a claim that was untrue and one that he deeply regrets. My client will continue to assist the police with their ongoing investigations and sincerely apologises for his actions twenty years ago."

Mr Fairfax exchanged a quick glance with his client before closing his notebook and putting it down on the desk in front of him.

* * * *

The sister in charge of Derby Ward was very specific when she told DS Dalton, she was allowed exactly two minutes with Tom Ashcroft; not a second more, as he was about to be taken up for surgery on his leg.

"Can you tell me what happened last night?" DS Dalton enquired.

"It was Ellis," replied Tom in a weak, barely audible voice.

"Ellis Hutton?" DS Dalton responded, to be sure what Tom was suggesting.

Tom nodded gently.

"Did you see him? Was it his car?" DS Dalton added.

"He was at Ron's, too," Tom muttered.

"On the day Ron died?" DS Dalton asked, keen to get as much clarity she could from, a still very groggy, Tom.

Tom nodded again. "His car was parked in a side street, just off the main road near Ron's drive."

"Are you sure it was Ellis's car?" continued DS Dalton. "Was Ellis in it?"

"Didn't see him, but it was his car," Tom replied.

"Did you tell Ellis you'd seen him?" queried DS Dalton.

"He said it wasn't his car and that he wasn't there," Tom replied. "But I know that's a lie."

At that moment the ward sister entered the room with two short, rotund porters. "You're up to theatre now, Tom," she said kindly, her attention focused entirely on the patient and her facial expression warm and comforting. "And you need to go," she then told DS Dalton, in a much less friendly tone.

DS Dalton watched as the two porters rapidly, and with remarkable dexterity, wheeled Tom out of the room and away down the corridor.

* * * *

"I assume you'll be giving us a copy of that statement?" Carmichael announced, his blue eyes fixed on Mr Fairfax.

Fairfax nodded. "Of course," he replied. "You're welcome to take a photocopy after the interview is over if you'd like, but I'll type it up and email it over to you, too."

Carmichael smiled. "That's very accommodating of you," he remarked, with a smile. "Actually," he continued, "Wade, would you mind signing at the foot of Mr Fairfax's note?"

"That's highly irregular," remarked the brief. "I'd prefer to wait until a proper statement has been prepared and typed up."

Wade shrugged his shoulders. "I'm fine with it," he said. "Give me a pen and I'll sign and date it."

Although it was clear that Mr Fairfax wasn't totally happy with this development, he never-the-less opened his notebook to the pages where he'd written down Wade's statement.

Carmichael passed over his pen to Wade who, grabbing it with his left hand, scribbled an unintelligible looking signature at the foot of the handwritten statement.

"I see you're a leftie," remarked Carmichael, while also shooting first DS Watson then DC Twamley a quick glance.

"In my politics and my writing," Wade replied, with a slight hint of a smile, clearly proud and amused by his own witty remark.

Carmichael didn't return the smile. "Why did you lie to the coroner about taking Chrissy Cream up to Whitehaven?" he enquired sternly.

"I was stupid, I know," replied Wade apologetically. "She said it was to help Chrissy start afresh, away from the whole pop star madness."

"She?" enquired Carmichael. "So, who asked you to lie?"

Wade's brow furrowed, as if he was surprised Carmichael didn't know. "Leah of course," he replied.

"Leah," exclaimed Carmichael. "Not Ron Mason."

Wade shook his head. "Ron could have known from the outset, but it was Leah who spoke with me, and I've always thought it was Leah and Chrissy's plan, so that Chrissy could disappear. There's no way Ron would have been in favour of Chrissy leaving the band, as she was the driving force. The band could have carried on with just her, Suzi and Pam, no problem; but not without Chrissy."

"Are you sure?" DS Watson asked.

Wade shrugged his shoulders. "At the time Leah said it was Chrissy's decision and I just assumed that Ron either didn't know or had reluctantly agreed."

Carmichael considered what Wade had just told them for a few seconds before resuming his questions. "And you just said yes when Leah asked you to perjure yourself?" he continued.

"Absolutely not," Wade replied. "At first, I said no, but Leah said that they'd help me out financially if I told the court about driving Chrissy to the boat and, if Chrissy ever came back or her new life was discovered, Chrissy would swear that I had driven her up there and that she'd just not got on the boat."

"So, why admit it now?" enquired DS Watson. "Why aren't you still sticking to that story?"

Wade shook his head. "Because people are dying all over the place," he replied, his angry eyes glaring in DS Watson's direction. "And …" Wade paused for a few

seconds. "I'm now not totally sure Chrissy did escape to find a new life. I think they may have killed her."
"Who?" Carmichael asked, pointedly.
Wade shrugged his shoulders. "Ron, Leah or whoever it is that killed Pritchard and Ron," he replied animatedly. "I agreed to lie, but I never agreed to cover up for a murder."
"What about Martin Wood and Lydia Brook-Smith?" Carmichael asked. "What part did they all play in this lie?"
Wade Freeman's furrowed brow suggested he was puzzled at the question. "I've no idea," he replied. "Martin may have some idea about what went on, but if so it's news to me. And as for Lydia, she was a young kid back then; maybe fourteen or fifteen. She won't have been involved. Why do you think she would be?"
Having never met Lydia, Carmichael had assumed that she was of a similar age to Coral and Leah, so Wade's reply came as a major shock to him.
"And what about Suzi Ashcroft, Pam Hutton and your wife?" Carmichael enquired. "Did they know you'd lied?"
Wade Freeman shook his head. "I'm certain none of them knew," he replied. "If they did, they'd have come forward by now. No, I'm convinced they all think Chrissy died on that boat."
"Let's leave it there for today," Carmichael suddenly announced, abruptly getting to his feet as he was talking. "We can pick up our discussions in the morning."
Wade Freeman exchanged a panic-stricken look with his brief.
"Aren't you releasing my client?" Mr Fairfax enquired.
Carmichael picked up all the papers he'd had in front of him and shook his head. "We've still got plenty more time on the clock," he replied. "No, Mr Freeman will be

here for at least tonight. I'll review what we do with him overnight and let you both know in the morning."

Chapter 64

Carmichael, DS Watson, and DC Twamley had just made themselves comfortable when Carmichael's mobile rang.

"Perfect timing as always, Rachel," Carmichael cheerily announced, before switching the mobile to speaker and placing it on the table so all of them could hear.

"Hi Rachel," he continued, "I'm with Marc and Donna, and you're on speaker phone. What's the latest from the hospital?"

"Tom's been taken up to theatre for some surgery on his leg," replied DS Dalton. "It's a real mess."

"But were you able to talk to him before he went up?" Carmichael enquired.

"Yes, briefly," confirmed DS Dalton. "He was still very groggy, but he says it was Ellis that tried to run him down and he reckons he saw Ellis, well his car, to be exact, close to Mason's house when he was leaving on Thursday."

"Really," remarked Carmichael, "did he elaborate more on what he saw or why he is sure it was Ellis who was behind the wheel?"

"Sadly, not," replied DS Dalton apologetically. "I only had about two minutes with him before they whisked him away. And to be totally honest, he's still very confused, so I'd not like to make any hasty decisions until we can talk with him properly, but he clearly thinks

Ellis had something to do with Ron's death and he genuinely believes it was Ellis behind the wheel when he was hit last night."

"It's more than enough to bring Ellis in," declared Carmichael, his eyes now focussed on Watson and DC Twamley. "That's a job for you two immediately after this call."

"Will do," replied DS Watson, nodding vigorously as he spoke.

"How are you getting on with Wade Freeman?" DS Dalton enquired.

"We've just this minute come out from interviewing him," replied Carmichael. "We've not even had a chance to compare notes, but what he's now saying is interesting."

"Sounds intriguing," announced DS Dalton. "What did he say?"

"He's admitted that he lied to the coroner about taking Chrissy Cream to Whitehaven on the day the boat sailed," interjected Watson. "But says he had nothing to do with either Pritchard's or Mason's death."

"Or the hit and run on Tom," added DC Twamley.

"He also told us that it was Leah rather than Ron Mason who asked him to lie," added Watson, "and said it was so Chrissy Cream could disappear off somewhere and start a new life for herself."

"And do you believe him?" DS Dalton asked.

There was a slight pause before Carmichael responded. "In the main I think I do," he remarked. "Even though he's still not willing to admit, not even to himself, the importance of the vast amount of money Ron Mason practically gave him, my gut feeling is that Wade isn't our killer. Of course, I may be wrong, and he may be involved in some way. Let's face it, his track record isn't that good given he lied twenty years ago about driving Chrissy to the boat and as recently as last Wednesday when he told us Ron was in the pub for far longer than he was. But in short, Rachel, I think I do believe him when he says he didn't kill either Mason or Pritchard."

"And we now know he's left-handed, too," interjected DS Watson.

"Which means he couldn't have killed Ron Mason," added DC Twamley. "Or struck the second blow to Pritchard."

Carmichael nodded. "That's perfectly correct. He couldn't have done either."

"So, will you be letting Wade go?" DS Dalton enquired.

"Not this evening," replied Carmichael. "Perjury is a serious crime, so I'm going to keep him in for the evening. We'll formally charge him with that in the morning and check with CPS, but I'm pretty sure we'll have to let him go tomorrow."

"Can we do that, without getting approval?" DS Dalton asked.

"I'm doing it," snapped back Carmichael. "And I don't think he's in any position to object. Coming clean about his lie after twenty years may help him at his trial, but it curries no favours with me in the here and now."

"Understood," replied DS Dalton, feeling she'd been more than gently admonished for asking.

"Anyway, have you spoken with Suzi yet?" continued Carmichael abruptly.

"Not yet," admitted DS Dalton.

"Well, with Tom being ruled out of action for a while, that's got to be your priority," instructed Carmichael.

"Yes, sir," replied DS Dalton.

"And you two get on your way to find and bring in Ellis," continued Carmichael. "Actually, if she's with him, bring in Verity, too. It's probably about time I had a word with that young lady."

DS Watson and DC Twamley didn't need to be told for a third time. As soon as Carmichael had finished talking, they hastily headed off.

With the call now ended and all his team having departed, Carmichael picked up the file containing the statements they'd taken for Wednesday evening and started to read through them once more, to see if there'd been anything they'd not followed up fully or if there were any little clues that they'd maybe overlooked.

Chapter 65

Once the call had ended, DS Dalton retreated to the hospital coffee bar by the main entrance. She'd only just sat down when she spotted Suzi Ashcroft striding purposefully toward the hospital's large revolving entrance doors.

"Excellent," DS Dalton muttered under her breath as she leapt up from her chair and walked equally as swiftly to ensure she accosted Tom's mum before she disappeared down the corridor.

"Hello, Ms Ashcroft," DS Dalton said with a warm smile on her face. "Can I have a word with you please?"

It was evident by the exasperated expression on Suzi's face that she wasn't keen to talk. "I've got to get back up and see Tom," she replied, still moving.

DS Dalton stepped sideways into Suzi's path and rested a gentle hand on her forearm.

"Tom is in theatre having surgery on his fractures," DS Dalton explained. "He'll be quite some time. So, why don't you join me in the coffee bar for a few moments and I can ask you those questions?"

With no obvious excuse to avoid talking to DS Dalton, Suzi rolled her eyes skyward, took a deep breath, then did as she was being asked and followed the police officer to a small table; plonking herself in the seat that DS Dalton had occupied just a minute or so earlier. With her arms folded and the air of someone who wasn't about to remain where she was for a second longer than necessary, Suzi fixed a hostile stare on DS Dalton.

"So, what is it you want to ask me?" she said aggressively.

* * * *

Carmichael had spent almost thirty minutes reading over the numerous statements the team had compiled since Wednesday evening. And, when he'd finished, was extremely pleased and relieved that he'd taken the time to review them once more.

Although, in the main, they told him nothing new, there were two interesting things he'd picked up on. One was from Miles Goodwyn's statement. He remembered reading it the first time but realised he hadn't had it followed up. The second was a comment made by only one of the people who'd overheard the argument between Ron Mason and Doug Pritchard. Of course, it may have been nothing, but Carmichael thought there could well be some significance in what that person had said.

Having photocopied both sections from the two statements, Carmichael folded them up and put them in his jacket pocket, before heading out to talk to someone he thought might be able to shed light on why Leah contacted Doug Pritchard and, if he was very lucky, what they'd talked about.

* * * *

In an attempt to get Suzi on side, DS Dalton decided to buy them both a coffee. Upon her return from the queue, she placed the two steaming cups on the table and sat herself down facing Suzi.

"Yours is the one nearest you," DS Dalton advised her. "I didn't sugar it but there's plenty here if you take sugar.

As she spoke, DS Dalton placed six sachets of sugar on the table: two white, two brown and two sweeteners.

"All options covered then," remarked Suzi, before grabbing one of the sweeteners, ripping off the top and pouring half into her disposable coffee cup.

DS Dalton waited until Suzi had stirred her cappuccino before asking her first question.

"I'd like to know a little more about Leah," she said. "What sort of person was she?"

Suzi took a sip from her cup, then answered.

"Leah was a smart lady," Suzi replied. "She was a strong woman too. Wasted being just a PA to Ron, I always thought."

"And how long was she Ron's PA?" DS Dalton asked.

"From almost the day she came back from Asia," replied Suzi. "I'd guess it must have been about seventeen or eighteen years in total."

"But after the Vixens stopped recording, surely there wasn't much going on for Ron to need a PA?" continued DS Dalton.

Suzi smiled and nodded gently. "My thoughts entirely," she replied. "Heaven only knows what she actually did, but he employed her, and I think she was paid pretty well."

DS Dalton smiled. "I hear that before she went to Asia, Leah was quite timid," she remarked. "But on her return, she was much more assertive."

Suzi nodded vigorously. "Very true," she replied, before taking another small sip of her coffee. "She was the same girl but different too," announced Suzi. "Confident, assertive, covered in tattoos and, when she had to be, quite ruthless in an argument, to the point of being a fearsome person when the mood took her."

"And how was she with Ron?" DS Dalton enquired.

Suzi laughed. "He was terrified of her, I think," she replied with a glint of pleasure in her voice. "She was in charge in that partnership that's for sure."

DS Dalton paused for a second. "And this partnership," she said, trying to pick her words carefully. "Was it deeper than just employer and employee?"

Suzi laughed again, but even louder than before. "You're wasted in the police," she remarked.

DS Dalton smiled. "Well, were they having a romantic relationship?" she asked.

Suzi shook her head. "They may have been before Leah went to Asia," she conceded. "Afterall, Ron was after any woman who entered his orbit in those days, and he had the power of being such a big shot to help him get what he wanted. But not after she returned. I'm pretty sure Leah would have had none of that from him after she came home. I think Ron's power pretty much went down with Jo, Chrissy, and that boat."

DS Dalton nodded. "And what about you?" she enquired. "Did you have a relationship with Ron?"

Suzi replied immediately. "Twenty years ago, I had many, many lovers," she conceded, with no hint of remorse. "Including Ron once or twice. Actually, maybe a few more times. But that was two decades ago. My wild party lifestyle dried up within a few years of the band breaking up. And to be honest, I never missed all that. And it's not who I am now."

"Becoming a mum to Tom no doubt had a lot to do with that, I'd assume," remarked DS Dalton.

Suzi smiled. "It certainly did," she replied honestly.

DS Dalton paused for a few seconds before continuing. "So, who do you feel is responsible for Ron's death and for Tom's hit and run?"

Suzi glared deep into DS Daltons eyes. "Tom is sure it's Ellis," she replied. "And if he says it was Ellis, then I believe him."

"But they are cousins," remarked DS Dalton. "Are they not close?"

Suzi rolled her eyes. "They were very close," she conceded. "But that all went sour when Ellis took Verity from him. Or rather when she changed her affections from Tom to Ellis."

"I see," replied DS Dalton, keen to hear more.

"Don't get me wrong," Suzi added, "Tom's over her now, but it's really damaged his relationship with Ellis."

"Understandable, I suppose," remarked DS Dalton.

Suzi drained her coffee cup and stood up. "Are we done?" she asked, in a manner that suggested she was finished even if the detective sergeant wasn't.

"Yes, I think we are," DS Dalton replied, realising that she'd probably got as much as she was going to get. "You've been very helpful."

As DS Dalton watched Suzi Ashcroft march away, she couldn't help feeling a degree of empathy and warmth towards Tom's adopted mum.

There was no doubt that Suzi was a strong character and at times could be prickly and rude, but she was clearly suffering as a result of her sister's death and Tom's horrendous accident, so her behaviour was totally understandable in DS Dalton's mind.

Chapter 66

It was early evening, when Carmichael finally headed down the staircase towards the exit at Kirkwood police station. With his head swirling with information and several questions still to be answered, he didn't notice Coral Freeman standing at the front desk.
"Sir," shouted over the desk sergeant, who's name Carmichael remembered was Hunt. "Are you able to help this lady, please?"
Carmichael, one hand already on the exit door, half turned and looked over in their direction. "Mrs Freeman," he said, the surprise undisguised in his voice.
"When will Wade be coming home?" Coral enquired, anxiously.
"Not tonight, I'm afraid," replied Carmichael. "But he'll probably be released in the morning."
Coral couldn't disguise the shock of what she was hearing.
"Wade wouldn't have killed Pritchard or Ron," she remarked loudly. "And even though they aren't on the best of terms, he wouldn't hurt Tom. He's his nephew for Christ's sake."
Although there were only the three of them in the reception area, Carmichael had no desire to discuss the

case or the charges, in detail, in such a public space, but he also had no intention of being waylaid.

"Mrs Freeman," he announced firmly, "if we were going to charge Wade for the murders and Tom's hit and run, there is no way he'd be released at all. He is being charged in the morning for other offenses, which I'm not at liberty to discuss with you now, and that is why he's staying here overnight."

Satisfyingly, his words seemed to do the trick, as Coral merely nodded and walked towards the exit, without uttering another word.

Carmichael opened the door wide so that she could pass through, a gesture which prompted a small smile from Coral and an almost inaudible, "Thank you."

Coral was a few paces ahead of Carmichael, as they both headed out towards their respective cars, when he spoke.

"Tell me why Wade and Tom aren't on good terms?" he enquired.

Coral stopped and turned to face Carmichael.

"Because Wade had a go at him and Ellis in the pub a few weeks ago," replied Coral. "They had a row and Wade threw them both out. Ellis has pretty much forgotten about it, but Tom's still sulking and says he doesn't want anything to do with Wade. It's a real shame as they've always got on. But Tom's a bit of a misery at the moment. He thinks the whole world is against him."

A small weary smile appeared on her face as she finished talking.

"Mind you, after that horrible accident, maybe he's right," she added.

*   *   *   *

"They're not here," remarked Lydia Brook-Smith, who'd opened the door to DS Watson and DC Twamley. "They've decided to go away for a few days."
"Where to?" DS Watson asked.
Lydia shrugged her shoulders. "You know how young people are," she announced. "It was a last-minute thing and when they headed off, they thought they'd go to the Lake District but knowing them they could have changed their minds on the way."
DS Watson glanced across at his colleague for a few seconds, before turning back. "What time did they set off?" he asked.
"About three hours ago," replied Lydia, "so I'd imagine they've arrived wherever they are. Unless they've carried on towards Scotland."
"Do you think that's likely?" DC Twamley enquired.
Lydia laughed and shook her head. "I doubt it," she replied. "They'll have gone to the Lakes, I'm sure. And if not there, it will have been Blackpool."
"Do you have either of their mobile numbers?" Watson asked.
Lydia frowned. "I've Verity's, obviously," she replied. "I've not got Ellis's. Why do you want to talk with them?"
"We've a few questions we want to ask Ellis," responded DC Twamley, trying hard not to alarm Verity's mum. "Just routine stuff, but we'd like to speak to them as soon as possible."
Lydia scrolled through her phone before showing the two officers the screen containing Verity's number.

"Thanks," replied DC Twamley, who'd input all eleven digits into her mobile in a matter of seconds.
"I told Verity to message me with the details of the place they were staying when they arrived," continued Lydia.

"Do you want me to tell her to contact you when she does?"

"We'll obviously try and call her," replied Watson, "but in case we aren't able to get through, if you can send me over those details when you have them and ask her to call either DC Twamley or I, that would be great."

After finishing his sentence DS Watson handed Lydia a card with his contact details on, which was almost immediately followed by DC Twamley handing Lydia her card, also.

"Will do," said Lydia before closing the door on the two officers.

*   *   *   *

Carmichael was only a few paces away from the entrance to St Jude's when he received the call from DS Dalton.

"Hi Rachel," he remarked. "What have you got for me?"

"I've managed to speak with Suzi," DS Dalton replied. "She said that Tom also told her it was Ellis who tried to kill him."

"So, probably not just the ramblings of a dazed and tired young man," suggested Carmichael.

"No," remarked DS Dalton. "Suzi's sure about what Tom told her and she believes him. She also told me that they'd fallen out over Verity. It appears Verity was with Tom initially then dumped him for Ellis."

Carmichael paused for a few seconds before responding. "Her name's starting to crop up too many times for my liking," he announced. "I'm looking forward to talking to her when Marc and Donna bring her in."

"Suzi couldn't be sure if Leah was in a relationship with Ron Mason before she went travelling in Asia," continued DS Dalton, "but she thinks she may have been. Though she's sure they weren't after she came back."

"Did she tell you anything more about Leah?" Carmichael enquired.

"Only what we've been told already," replied DS Dalton. "That Leah was bright with a strong personality and that when she came back, she'd changed from a quiet person to someone who was much more confident and assertive. She said Leah could be quite ruthless in an argument, to the point of being, in her words, fearsome."

"Having met her, I'd agree," remarked Carmichael.

"Also, in Suzi's view, Leah dominated Ron at work, too," continued DS Dalton. "Suzi reckons Ron was terrified of her and that Leah was wasted being his PA for eighteen years. Which begs the question why she'd want to be his PA for so long."

"Maybe so she could control him," suggested Carmichael.

"You could be right, sir," DS Dalton concurred.

"And what about Suzi?" Carmichael enquired. "Did she have a relationship with Ron?"

"She admitted that without any qualms," replied DS Dalton. "But she played it down. Again, in her words, it was over twenty years ago at a time when she had many, many lovers. Ron was just one of them."

"Sex, drugs and rock and roll," muttered Carmichael.

"Yes, she did make it sound like it was something like that back then," DS Dalton agreed, with a faint smile on her face.

Carmichael thought for a few seconds before continuing. "Why don't you get yourself back to the station," he instructed her. "Hopefully, Marc and Donna will be back there soon with Ellis and Verity. I'd like to get them both interviewed tonight, which will take all four of us. I've just got to see someone first. I'll be along in about an hour."

"Will do," replied DS Dalton, who, despite being intrigued as to who her boss was going to meet, asked him no questions on the matter.

Chapter 67

Ellis parked the car on the wide gravel drive at the front of Scale Force Bed and Breakfast, the secluded guest house Verity had hastily found online and booked as they drove up the M6.

The pretty whitewashed-walled building, just yards away from Crummock Water, Ellis's favourite spot in the Lakes, was perfect. And at just under a hundred pounds a night, they felt they'd found a bargain, especially as their trip was so last-minute.

The couple clambered out of the car then, hand in hand, walked slowly towards the low stone wall that separated the quiet, narrow road and the pebbly shoreline of the serene jet-black lake.

"Isn't this just the best place in the world!" announced Ellis as he eagerly leapt over the wall and landed on the small stones about foot lower down on the other side.

"You'll have to give me a hand," remarked Verity. "I'm not sure junior will be too chuffed if I jump us both like that.

Ellis smiled and held Verity's hand as she sat on the wall and swung her legs over, so she was facing Crummock Water.

Then, as gently as anything, Ellis scooped Verity up in his arms and brought her over to join him; slowly lowering her down until she could feel her feet touch the soft, gritty ground.

"Two days here will be fantastic," Verity said, her cheeks blushed red by the cool air, and her smile as wide as the river Cocker, which started its meandering journey a matter of yards from where they stood.

"Absolutely," replied Ellis, his arm now around Verity's shoulder. "But there's something really important I need to discuss with you," he remarked in earnest.

By the seriousness in his voice Verity realised immediately that something was wrong.

"What is it?" she enquired, her head tilted sideways and her adoring but worried eyes looking up into his.

* * * *

In her expensive-looking, floral blouse and meticulously coiffured hair, Mrs Wright looked a picture of serene efficiency as she offered Carmichael a seat in her large, comfortably furnished, office.

"Would you like some tea?" she enquired.

Carmichael smiled but shook his head. "Thank you, but no," he replied.

"Well, what is it I can do for you?" Mrs Wright asked, her elbows resting firmly on the desk in front of her and her piercing dark eyes transfixed on Carmichael.

"I was hoping you could help me," began Carmichael. "I was wondering if you had any inkling of what Ron Mason and Leah Barnes discussed, during his last visits here?"

Mrs Wright gently cleared her throat before answering. "I wasn't present at their last couple of meetings, but I can give you a sense of what was said," she replied, helpfully, "as I did loiter outside Leah's room on both occasions. Mr Mason was in a foul mood each time and I was concerned for Leah."

"Really," remarked Carmichael. "And when were these visits?"

"The first was almost two weeks ago," announced Mrs Wright, without the need to refer to the visitor book. "On the Sunday."

"That would be Sunday the tenth?" suggested Carmichael.

"Yes," confirmed Mrs Wright. "That's when it was. At about four in the afternoon. Neither that visit nor his last visit the following Friday were particularly long, but sadly both were what I'd call unfriendly encounters."

"So, they argued?" Carmichael suggested.

Mrs Wright nodded vigorously. "They did indeed," she responded.

"And what were they bickering about?" Carmichael asked.

"That's the thing," replied Mrs Wright. "It seemed so trivial, but arguments often are about things that don't appear to be that important, aren't they?"

Carmichael smiled and nodded. "Sadly, they are," he concurred. "So, what sparked the row?"

"A hairdo," replied Mrs Wright.

Carmichael frowned. "You'll have to elaborate on that for me," he remarked, his words delivered with a distinct air of incredulity.

Mrs Wright smiled. "We offer three care packages here at St Jude's," she began. "Silver, gold, or platinum. Leah was on platinum when she arrived, but once she started to get more poorly, Mr Mason decided to move her down to gold."

"The difference being?" enquired Carmichael.

"Oh, the care is exactly the same," Mrs Wright assured him. "It's just we charge extra for a few of the luxury frills which are included in platinum."

"Such as?" Carmichael asked.

"Sessions such as painting and art, and for head massages and beauty treatments."

"So, those are all included in the platinum package but not in the gold package," Carmichael said, in his attempt to ensure he understood.

"Exactly," replied Mrs Wright. "And to be fair to Mr Mason, who was so generously paying for all of Leah's care, it's quite common for people to move down the packages as the resident, sadly, becomes less able."

"I see," said Carmichael. "And Leah took offense at not being able to have her hair done due to the change?"

Mrs Wright looked a little embarrassed. "It's common for family and friends not to mention these changes," she admitted. "Afterall it's a difficult discussion to have. So, when the scenario happens, like it did with Leah, I'd normally quickly call the person paying the bill just to get approval. Then the resident doesn't need to know. However, this happened on my day off when the place was really busy and, unfortunately, the person who was with Leah is quite new and …"

Carmichael nodded. "I take it she didn't manage it as tactfully as you'd have wished."

"Exactly," replied Mrs Wright, relieved that Carmichael had himself been quite considerate with his wording. "Leah, was very upset and summoned Mr Mason."

"The visit on Sunday the tenth of March?" remarked Carmichael.

"Exactly," replied Mrs Wright again.

"And what did you hear?" Carmichael asked.

"Well," began Mrs Wright. "It was a very short meeting, maybe no more than ten minutes, during which Leah said he'd regret crossing her and that he'd pay for being such a skinflint. To be fair to him, he did try and reason with her but …"

Carmichael nodded. "And at the second meeting?"

"As I said, it was on the following Friday," said Mrs Wright. "At this one I didn't hear much of what Leah said. She seemed very calm, but Mr Mason was very angry and told her she'd broken her promise and that she was a nasty piece of work."

Carmichael frowned. "And did you hear what it was that Leah had done, specifically?" he enquired.

"Not as such," replied Mrs Wright. "But I did hear Mr Mason ask if she'd said anything about Chrissy. I think that was the name he mentioned. To which Leah said something along the lines of 'of course not, I'm not stupid. I just told him about the boys.'"

"She definitely said, him and the boys?" repeated Carmichael. "Are you sure she said the boys?"

Mrs Wright nodded vigorously. "I'm absolutely sure about that," she confirmed.

"Did you hear them talk about anything else?" Carmichael enquired.

"Not really," replied Mrs Wright. "However, Leah did say something else after she'd mentioned the boys that got Mr Mason really angry."

"What was that?" Carmichael enquired.

Mrs Wright shook her head slightly. "Leah must have been whispering because I didn't hear what she said," she replied, "but he started swearing at her and I did think I might have to go in as I was concerned for Leah."

"But you didn't" Carmichael said.

"I didn't have to," continued Mrs Wright. "Mr Mason stormed out and that was the last time I saw him."

Carmichael thought for a few seconds. "And how was Leah after their heated exchange?" he asked.

Mrs Wright shrugged her shoulders.

"That's the thing," she said with a hint of surprise in her voice, "Leah seemed very pleased with herself when I went in. Not concerned at all. In fact, I'd say she looked quite triumphant."

"Did she, indeed," muttered Carmichael.

"Has what I've told you been helpful?" enquired Mrs Wright.

"Yes," replied Carmichael. "You've been very helpful."

As Carmichael went to leave, he suddenly turned.

"As a matter of interest," he asked, "roughly how much is a hairdo here?"

Mrs Wright looked astound at the question but answered immediately.

"Our prices are very reasonable," she announced. "They range from a cut and blow dry at forty pounds to around a hundred pounds for styling and colouring."

"And that's reasonable?" Carmichael enquired, his tone indicating he was finding that level of prices hard to digest.

Mrs Wright smiled. "Very reasonable," she assured him. Carmichael nodded gently before turning back and departing, his mind struggling hard to comprehend the amount of money being spent in the alien world of ladies' hairdressing. A topic that, up until very recently, he'd never given a second's thought to.

Chapter 68

It was almost seven o'clock when Carmichael entered the incident room, where he found DS Watson, DS Dalton, and DC Twamley all hard at work at their desks.
"Well done, team," he announced with a smile, before looking across at DS Watson. "Are Ellis and Verity downstairs?"
DS Watson, uneasily, looked up from his computer screen. "Sadly not," he replied. "It would appear that they've decided to, unexpectedly, go on a short break."
Carmichael frowned. "Where to?"
"Verity's mum wasn't that clear," answered DC Twamley, "but we've managed to find Ellis's car on CCTV at about four thirty, on the A66 just outside Keswick, heading west towards Bassenthwaite Lake."
"But nothing after that," added Watson.
"Have you contacted Cumbria Police?" Carmichael enquired.
"We did that as soon as we spotted them on the CCTV," acknowledged DC Twamley.
"The problem is in that area they could have gone anywhere," added DS Dalton. "Cockermouth, Derwent Water, up towards Carlisle, Silloth or Buttermere. They're all accessible in that general direction."
"Or even Whitehaven or Workington," added DS Watson. "Although they're not so touristy."

Realising that there wasn't much more the team could do to find the two young travellers, Carmichael looked over at DS Dalton. "Rachel, have you updated these two on your conversation with Suzi?" he asked.

"I have," replied DS Dalton.

"In that case, let me share with you all what I found out from my visit to St Jude's and my little chat with Mrs Wright," continued Carmichael.

* * * *

Even though it was after eight thirty by the time Carmichael arrived home, Penny was pleasantly surprised to see him at what she considered to be early, given her husband was just three days into the murder case.

"Hello, stranger," she said, plonking a huge kiss on his lips. "Have you answered all those questions you were struggling with this morning?"

Carmichael smiled and took hold of his glass of wine, which Penny had already poured for him even before he'd entered their kitchen.

Carmichael enjoyed mulling over his cases with his wife for several reasons. Firstly, Penny was sharp and would often ask questions or challenge his logic much more readily than his team at Kirkwood, which probably stemmed from the fact that Carmichael wasn't always the best at taking criticism from his subordinates, and they knew it.

Secondly, by sharing his thinking with Penny, Carmichael allowed himself to be far more open and considerably more honest than he ever felt he could be with the team at the station.

However, the main thing he got from talking cases through with his wife was the opportunity to structure his thinking; something that he always found to be beneficial.

"Not all of them," Carmichael conceded. "Having said that, I'm confident we're making good progress and we're narrowing down the field."

By the expression on her face Penny didn't seem particularly impressed. "You'll have to enlighten me a bit more than that," she announced, taking a small sip of her glass of Pinotage.

"Well," continued Carmichael, "it would appear that the root cause of Doug Pritchard and Ron Mason's murders and the attempted murder of Tom Ashcroft, seems to have been down to a very minor issue at St Jude's between Ron and Leah Barnes on Sunday the tenth of March."

Penny looked over at Carmichael, eyes wide open, clearly keen to learn more.

"The disagreement isn't important," continued Carmichael, "however Leah's reaction seems to have started a chain of events that has led not only to two murders, but the attempted murder of a third man and the revelation that a twenty-year-old inquest was misled, and, in the worst scenario, another person was killed back then rather than die in an accident, as had been thought."

"Tell me more," said Penny, who was now very keen to get the finer details.

Carmichael took a huge swig of Pinotage. "That's where it gets a bit complicated," he declared.

"You mean, that's as far as you've got," she announced, slightly scathingly. "What about suspects for the murders?"

Carmichael nodded gently. "For Doug Pritchard's murder we know it was either one tall, right-handed person or maybe two people. But if two, one of them must be right-handed and tall."

"Tall?" enquired Penny, looking for some clarification.

"Well over six foot," Carmichael replied.

"So, who's in the frame?" Penny asked.

"It could have been Ron and Wade Freeman, or it may have been Tom Ashcroft or Ellis Hutton either on their own or with someone else."

"And Ron Mason's death?" Penny enquired.

"The current thinking is that it might have been Ellis Hutton," Carmichael replied. "At least that's what his cousin, Tom Ashcroft, is saying."

"Anyone else potential candidates?" Penny enquired.

"It can't be Wade," replied Carmichael, "as he's a left hander and the murderer was right-handed."

"So, if we are assuming Doug Pritchard's murderer, or at least one of them was the same person who killed Ron Mason, you only have Ellis Hutton and Tom Ashcroft in the frame for the two murders," suggested Penny.

"Yes," concurred Carmichael. "However, if there were two people involved in the first murder it might have been the shorter one who struck the fatal blow to Ron Mason. And being right-handed it could be anyone, even someone that isn't on our suspects list for Doug Pritchard."

"Wow," replied Penny. "If you don't mind me saying, you seem to be miles away from reaching a conclusion."

Carmichael sniggered. "Thanks for the moral support," he remarked, before taking another large swig of Pinotage.

"So, why is Tom Ashcroft saying it was Ellis?" Penny enquired. "And does his suspicion have any substance behind it?"

"He says he saw Ellis near Ron's around the time Ron was murdered and he has told Rachel and his mum that it was Ellis who ran him down," Carmichael replied.

"And what does Ellis have to say for himself?" asked Penny.

"That's the issue," replied Carmichael, despondently. "We tried to bring him and his girlfriend in for questioning, but they've taken an impromptu break, up in the Lakes, and we haven't managed to track them down yet."

Penny thought for a few seconds. "What about motives for these murders and the attempted murder of Tom Ashcroft?" she asked.

Carmichael smiled. "Well, we've been fairly sure for some time that the motive is linked with something that Leah told Doug Pritchard," replied Carmichael. "And we can only think that it was something to do with Chrissy Cream. However, after speaking with Mrs Wright, the owner of Leah Barnes's care home, she's adamant that, in a conversation she overheard between Leah and Ron, Leah denied mentioning Chrissy Cream, but she did say that she'd said something about the boys, and he apparently went ballistic."

"The boys," remarked Penny. "Does that mean Tom and Ellis or are there two other people they'd refer to as the boys?"

Carmichael hadn't even considered it would be anyone other than Tom and Ellis, but an element of doubt suddenly darkened his mind. "I think Tom and Ellis," he replied, somewhat stiltedly, "but of course it may not be them."

"Well," said Penny, as she planted a warm loving kiss on her husband's forehead. "As I said before, you seem to have a way to go, Sherlock, but I've every faith in you."

With his bubble well and truly pierced, Carmichael reflected on what Penny had suggested.

"Shall I order us an Indian?" asked Penny, her focus now far removed from her husband's case.

Chapter 69

Sunday 24th March

As he had been instructed, DS Watson brought Martin Wood into Kirkwood police station bright and early. By eight forty-five, in stark contrast to the symphony of colours, sounds and scents of the beautiful spring morning outside, the distressed and angry ex-lighting and logistics manager for the band Chrissy Cream and the Vixens sat with the duty solicitor in interview room one, his arms folded and an irritated expression on his face.

* * * *

Ellis Hutton pulled Verity close to his bare chest and kissed the top of her head. "So, what do you want to do this morning?" he asked. "Go for a nice long walk around the lake or just stay in bed?"
Verity looked up into his smiling face, her eyes red having spent most of the night crying.
"Let's just stay here," she replied, before kissing him passionately on the lips.

* * * *

Suzi had spent all night at Tom's bedside as he slept. She beamed broadly as, at last, his eyes blinked open, and he looked over at her.
"Good morning, Mr Sleepy," she remarked, as if she was addressing a child of six rather than a young man in his early twenties.
Tom didn't mind. "Morning, Mum," he replied with a faint flash of a smile. "I'm starving, any chance of a coffee and a bacon sandwich?"

*   *   *   *

"Morning, Mr Wood," began Carmichael, who was accompanied by DS Watson and DS Dalton in the interview room. "I think it's about time you told us the truth about what happened to Chrissy Cream twenty years ago, don't you?"
For a split-second Carmichael thought that Wood senior was about to adopt the '*no comment*' line of answering, but he didn't.
"You make it sound like you know the answers already," Wood replied.
Carmichael smiled. "Let's just say we feel we know enough."
"Then tell me, what do you know?" responded Wood, as if he was almost relieved to be able to finally talk about what had taken place.
Carmichael maintained his stare on the decidedly gaunt-looking figure in front of him but smiled briefly before doing as Wood had asked.

"We know that Chrissy Cream didn't board the Workington Jenny on that fateful voyage," Carmichael announced. "Wade Freeman has admitted that. He's admitted he didn't drive her up there as he'd told the inquest. And we know that Ron invested large sums of cash in Wade's pub and in your scaffolding business at around that time, too. Investments which were incredibly generous, with seemingly no requirements for him to be paid dividends or interest on his money." Carmichael stopped talking but retained his glare on Martin Wood.

After a few seconds pause, Martin Wood's head bowed a little and his eyes focussed on the desk between him and Carmichael. "It was an accident," he muttered, his voice trembling as he spoke. "And it happened so quickly."

"What happened, Martin?" asked DS Dalton calmly.

"Chrissy just went for her and the next minute she'd overbalanced and was crashing down the steps," continued Wood, who was clearly reliving the event in his mind. "It happened so fast, but I'm sure Leah never meant to harm her, she just moved quicker than Chrissy had expected. It was Chrissy that was the one who was hell bent on harming Leah, not the other way around."

As he was speaking, tears welled up in Martin Woods eyes.

"Take it slowly," Carmichael said. "Start at the beginning and tell us exactly what occurred."

As he spoke DS Dalton pushed over a box of tissues towards Wood, who grabbed a couple and started to dab his eyes.

"If Ron hadn't been up to his usual tricks, none of this would have happened," Wood proclaimed. "But, as always, mister big shot couldn't resist another pretty thing."

"You mean Leah?" DS Dalton remarked, just to be certain who Wood was talking about.

Wood nodded. "Yes, on this occasion it was Leah," he confirmed. "But she was just the latest in a long line of young women he'd had a good time with."

"And Chrissy didn't approve?" remarked DS Watson.

Wood gazed back at Watson with an air of incredulity. "Well, they were supposed to be a couple back then," he replied. "So, you can understand why Chrissy was so angry and upset. Afterall, she already knew that Ron had had affairs with dozens of women while they were together. And I know for a fact that those women he'd been with included, Suzi and Jo."

"Really," remarked Carmichael. "Are you sure?"

Wood nodded. "I was with him a lot of the time back then," he said. "I know."

"But what about Chrissy," interjected Carmichael. "Did she know about Ron and Suzi and Ron and Jo?"

"I'm not sure," replied Wood. "But Chrissy wasn't stupid, and Ron wasn't anywhere near as discrete as you'd expect him to be, so I wouldn't be surprised if she had known."

"So, what happened on the day Chrissy died?" Carmichael asked.

"It was a Friday morning," Wood replied. "I'd gone in early to meet with Chrissy and Ron about the arrangements for the American tour. I got there at about nine in the morning, which was a very early start back then."

"When you say you'd gone in," interjected Carmichael, "where do you mean?"

"Ron's place," replied Wood. "We had all our business meetings there. It was open house for the band and the key members of the team. People were going in and out all the time."

Carmichael nodded and gestured to Wood to carry on.

"I arrived, but when I got into Ron's hallway," Wood advised them, "a massive ornate affair with a sweeping marble staircase…"

"We've seen it," remarked Carmichael. "Very grand."

"Well, I heard Chrissy's voice," continued Wood. "She was at the top of the stairs and was yelling at Leah, who was stood up there, too. Leah was wearing what looked like one of Ron's tee shirts, but nothing else, so it didn't take a brain surgeon to work out what had been going on. Ron then appeared from the bedroom wearing just a pair of shorts, and at that point Chrissy stopped yelling at Leah and moved over to vent her spleen at Ron."

"You say Chrissy and Ron were in a relationship at that time," remarked DS Dalton, trying to make sure Wood shared all the facts.

Wood nodded. "Absolutely," he replied.

"So how did this argument culminate in Chrissy being killed?" Carmichael enquired. "Which I think is what you're telling us."

Wood went silent for a few seconds before continuing.

"As I said," continued Wood, his voice becoming more agitated, "Chrissy was really having a go at Ron. Then Leah said something. I don't know what. But whatever it was it enraged Chrissy. She called Leah a slut and made a grab for her."

Wood stopped talking for a few seconds before continuing; his voice now gentler and his words more deliberate.

"Leah moved out of the way and Chrissy just fell," Wood recounted. "She came tumbling down the staircase like a rag doll, bashing her head almost every time she reached a new step. We all knew she was dead as soon as she reached the bottom. Nobody could have survived all those heavy knocks."

After another short pause, Carmichael spoke, his voice calm but firm. "If it was an accident, why didn't you just report it?" he enquired. "Why did you decide to fabricate that story about her being on the boat with Jo?"

Martin Wood shook his head, as if he still couldn't quite believe what they'd done.

"That was all down to Ron," he announced. "Ron didn't want any adverse publicity, and he said he wanted the public to believe that Chrissy was still alive but had just gone away for some rest. He still wanted the US tour to go ahead, and he reckoned that between them Jo, Suzi and Pam could pull off the tour maybe with a guest vocalist to replace Chrissy."

"But that doesn't stack up with you all saying she died when the Workington Jenny went down," pronounced DS Watson.

"You've got to remember that this all happened literally days before the boat sank," Wood replied. "It was only when we knew it had gone down that Ron realised, he couldn't hide Chrissy's death. If she had gone away, she'd have come back once she knew Jo was dead. And there was now no way the US tour could go ahead with just Suzi and Pam."

"You all changed your stories," DS Dalton remarked.

"We hadn't even announced the first one by the time the Workington Jenny sank," Wood replied. "So, we changed our plan but didn't have to change the story as there wasn't one out there to change."

"So, what did you do with Chrissy's body?" Carmichael asked.

Martin Wood hung his head low, unable or unwilling to make eye contact with Carmichael or any of his team.

"I buried her in Ron's rose garden," he replied. "I can show you where she's been lying these past twenty years."

Carmichael looked across at DS Watson. "Get forensics down there right away," he ordered him. "Take Mr Wood and let's get poor Chrissy Cream out of there, so she can be examined and, when the time's right, buried properly."

DS Watson stood up, handcuffed Martin Wood, and led him towards the door. However, before they could make it to the exit, Carmichael spoke once more.

"A couple more questions," he said firmly. "Why did you get Wade Freeman to lie about taking Chrissy up to Whitehaven on the day the boat sailed? Why didn't you or Leah say you took her?"

Wood half turned and sighed. "Because at the time, I was serving a six-month driving ban and Leah hadn't passed her test."

"But what about Ron?" DS Dalton enquired.

Wood laughed sarcastically. "He wasn't going to get his hands dirty, not slippery Ron. No, he left this sort of stuff to us minions."

"But he paid you all well to do it with those interest free loans, and no doubt funding Leah's two-year trip to Asia," observed Carmichael.

"True," conceded Wood. "I've no excuses for what I did."

"And what part did Lydia Brook-Smith play in all this?" Carmichael asked.

"The woman who runs that cake shop?" Wood remarked, a look of puzzlement on his face. "Nothing, as far as I'm aware. She wasn't at the house when Chrissy died, and she wasn't asked to say anything at the coroner's court hearing, as far as I know. She did do some work back then with Leah, now and then, but she was just a kid. She's not to blame for any of this."

"And what about Suzi Ashcroft and Pam Hutton," enquired Carmichael, "do they know Chrissy is buried in Ron's garden?"

Martin Wood shook his head vigorously. "No, they weren't there and I'm sure they don't know. They'd have been horrified had they have known exactly what happened to Chrissy. Those four girls were all so close, back then."

Carmichael nodded slowly before gesturing that DS Watson should take Wood away.

Chapter 70

He was clearly in a great deal of pain and was finding it almost impossible to get comfortable, but even so, Tom Ashcroft was in reasonably good spirits. Having constant attention from very friendly nurses and being pampered rotten by his mum, who didn't seem to have any plans to leave his side soon and was keen to deliver upon any tiny wish he had, were unquestionably the major contributors to his *bonne humeur*.

With his head propped up by two large pillows, and looking as though he was about as comfortable as he was going to get, Suzi decided to broach the subject that still concerned her.

"I need you to tell me the truth, Tom," she said; a phrase that he'd not heard her use for years, but which instantly reminded Tom of conversations they'd had when he was about eight or nine.

"This all sounds ominous," he replied with a faint smile.

"Last Thursday, when I got home," Suzi continued, her face looking serious, almost afraid to be given an answer, "why was Spencer there and what did I see you give him?"

Tom rolled his eyes. "Mum," he exclaimed. "It was nothing. You've absolutely nothing to worry about, and Spencer coming round that evening hasn't anything to do with Ellis running me down or Ron getting killed. I promise."

Tom's response didn't convince Suzi.

"I need to know the truth, Tom," she insisted. "Tell me now."

"I asked him to sort out the arrangements for your fiftieth in May," Tom replied. "You're so nosey, I knew I'd never get away with doing everything myself, but I thought I might keep it quiet from you if I got Spencer to sort out the details for me. So, if you must know, that money you saw me give Spencer was to pay for the venue. Do you want to know any more details about your surprise birthday party?"

Relieved that she knew the truth but now mortified that she'd been so insistent and so distrusting of her son, the only thing Suzi could bring herself to do was squeeze his hand and, with true remorse, say, "I'm so sorry, Tom. You must think I'm a dreadful mother."

"You are and I do," replied Tom with a smug smile etched across his face.

*　　*　　*　　*

"I didn't expect Martin Wood to be so obliging," announced Carmichael, cheerily, as he and DS Dalton entered the incident room, where they joined forces with DC Twamley.

"I take it that all went well?" remarked DC Twamley, who had just finished writing up the timeline Carmichael had asked her to compile.

"It would appear that Chrissy Cream died a few days before the Workington Jenny set sail," DS Dalton informed her, "and she's been buried in Ron Mason's rose bed ever since."

"Really?" replied DC Twamley, who seemed genuinely shocked at the news.

"Yes, Marc's going over there now with Wood and a forensics team to locate the body," interjected Carmichael. "So, the mystery of what really happened to Chrissy Cream may soon be resolved."

"Blimey," remarked DC Twamley, as she put the cap on the blue marker she'd been using.

"Anyway, fast forward twenty-odd years," continued Carmichael, looking up at the whiteboard. "Run through what you've got for us on the timeline for our murders."

DC Twamley was pleased with her handiwork so was delighted to share it with Carmichael and DS Dalton.

"The first significant event was on Sunday the tenth of March," she began. "That's the date Mrs Wright gave you for Mason's first visit to see Leah."

"When she was angry with him for changing her care package and denying her a free haircut," interjected Carmichael.

"That's correct," confirmed DC Twamley, before pointing at her second noted event. "From Doug Pritchard's mobile activity report, the next event was a call from Leah to Doug Pritchard on Thursday the fourteenth March. That lasted twenty-two minutes."

"Enough time for Leah to tell him plenty," observed Carmichael.

DC Twamley nodded and pointed again, this time to the third item on her list. "That's confirmed by the text message that Doug Pritchard sent to the editor, Ted Heslegrave, just ten minutes after he'd finished his call with Leah Barnes."

DS Dalton and Carmichael, looked up at the note that DC Twamley had written next to that item.

'GIVE ME A CALL TED. I'VE GOT THE SCOOP OF THE YEAR'

"Doug Pritchard was clearly excited on the fourteenth," continued DC Twamley, keen to move on, "as he also made two calls to Liam Thomas and one to Ted Heslegrave that day."
"Then another two failed calls to Ted Heslegrave on Friday the fifteenth of March," added DS Dalton.
"Yes," confirmed DC Twamley, "but only one of those calls appears to have been picked up; that was one of the calls he made to Liam Thomas."
"Doug Pritchard certainly was a busy man on those two days," observed Carmichael.
DC Twamley nodded then pointed to the next item she'd noted in her timeline. "It was on Friday the fifteenth that Ron went back to see Leah," she announced.
"Which was when he found out what Leah had done," Carmichael remarked. "Which, according to Mrs Wright, upset him so much."
"So, up until then, Doug hadn't made contact with Ron Mason," remarked DS Dalton. "That's surprising."
DC Twamley nodded. "That's true," she confirmed. "They started exchanging messages on Saturday the sixteenth," she stated, again pointing to the items that came next on her timeline. "Nothing earthshattering in terms of details at first, just suggesting they needed to meet. But then agreeing to have a meeting on Wednesday the twentieth and then, after Doug Pritchard had booked his B&B, agreeing the specifics of when they'd meet up."
Carmichael nodded gently, his eyes intently following along DC Twamley's timeline. "Doug Pritchard finally talks to Ted Heslegrave on Tuesday the nineteenth of March," he muttered. "And then he arrives, on the

twentieth, gets picked up by Ron Mason, they go to the pub, there's a heated exchange and within literally minutes of him leaving the pub, he's murdered."

Both DS Dalton and DC Twamley nodded, but neither said anything.

"Good job, Donna," Carmichael announced. "That's very helpful."

"So, where do we go from here?" DS Dalton asked.

Carmichael turned his head to face his detective sergeant.

"Well, given this latest development about Chrissy Cream, I think you and I need to get over and talk with Pam Hutton and Suzi Ashcroft," he announced. "They need to know before this all becomes public, and the press are swarming all over them."

"What about me?" enquired DC Twamley.

Carmichael smiled and turned his head to face the newest member of the team.

"There's quite a few things you could do for me," he replied, "but some of them will be tricky to do on a Sunday. So, for now I'd like you to focus on just two things. Firstly, talk to Miles Goodwyn. Find out if there was anyone else at the pub on Wednesday evening with a motorbike."

By the expression on both DC Twamley and DS Dalton's faces, it was clear they were totally bemused by this instruction.

"Why?" enquired DS Dalton.

Carmichael pulled out the extract from Miles Goodwyn's statement and passed it over to his DS.

"We didn't follow this up properly," he remarked, pointing at the mention of Miles seeing a taillight in the distance down Jay Bank Lane. "It may be of no consequence at all, but it needs following up."

"And if there was another biker at the pub, do you think he'd remember?" DC Twamley asked.

Carmichael smiled. "I'm not a biker myself," he confessed, "however I do know that one of the things bikers love more than anything else, is talking about their beloved machines and looking at other people's bikes. I'd bet a week's wages that if there was another motorbike there, Miles will remember. He'll probably know the make, year and any modifications that have been made to it, too. They are a bit anal like that."

DC Twamley laughed and nodded. "Will do, sir," she replied dutifully.

"The main thing I'd like you to do though," continued Carmichael, "is track down Ellis Hutton. We need to talk with him urgently, so use all available CCTV and see if you can track his and Verity's mobiles to locate them. Ellis has a lot of questions to answer."

Chapter 71

DS Dalton and Carmichael looked on as the duty sergeant discharged Wade Freeman from custody. Having received back possession of all the items they'd taken from him, Wade, looking decidedly tired and nervous, signed the necessary paperwork and quietly walked over to the exit, where Coral was waiting for him.

As he reached the doorway, he turned to face Carmichael. "So, what happens now?" he asked uneasily, as if he was not expecting to be told any good news.

Carmichael retained a blank look on his face. "You'll be hearing from us," he replied. "There will be a date communicated to you to appear in court and the judicial system will take its course."

Wade nodded slowly then turned to walk away.

"There is one thing you could help me with though," Carmichael announced, before Wade had managed to take another step. "On Wednesday evening, when you went out for that smoke, did you notice any other motorbikes outside the pub, other than Miles Goodwyn's?"

Wade Freeman half turned and made eye contact with Carmichael. "Not that I can recall," he replied, his expression signifying he found the question somewhat bizarre.

Carmichael nodded. "Thanks," he said.
DS Dalton and Carmichael watched as Wade exited the building and, with her arm linked with his, headed off with Coral to their parked car.
"You didn't mention to him about us being at Ron's looking for Chrissy Cream's body," remarked DS Dalton.
"That's correct," Carmichael replied. "He's not related to her, and he and his wife have done little else than lie to us since we met them. He doesn't deserve any advanced warning about what Marc and the forensics team may well find."
DS Dalton nodded. "I suppose not," she said quietly.
"Anyway, Rachel," continued Carmichael, "I think Wade has other things he needs to talk to his wife about on their way home, other than whether or not Chrissy Cream is buried in Ron's garden."
DS Dalton nodded. "Yes, I suspect the journey back to The Three Bells will be quite a tricky one for him."
Carmichael smirked at DS Dalton's choice of words. "Tricky indeed," he concurred.

* * * *

In spite of it being Sunday, the forensics team having only been there for thirty minutes, and there being only a handful of people aware of what the police were doing in Ron Mason's garden, DS Watson was staggered when the first thing he saw as he looked up from the area they were digging, was Norfolk George.
Standing just behind the yellow and black police cordon, the owner and chief reporter of the local newspaper seemed to be grilling the officers on duty about what was going on.

After emitting a massive sigh of exasperation, DS Watson strode over to where the local hack was standing. "What the hell are you doing here, George?" he asked, with no attempt to hide his irritation.

"Sources tell me that you're looking for a body," remarked Norfolk George, already in journalistic mode.

"No comment," replied Watson. "And I don't need to tell you that we don't want any of this to be reported or shared with any of your chums on the nationals. Carmichael will eat you alive if you start any stupid rumours."

DS Watson's words only strengthened Norfolk George's desire to unearth what was going on; but he knew the drill. "If I cooperate," he continued, "I want to be the first to get the full story. Is that a deal?"

DS Watson smiled. "No deals," he replied, "but I'll mention to Carmichael that you're here."

Norfolk George remained focused on the team of white clad forensics. "Four of Stock's team on a Sunday," he remarked. "Must be important."

"Like I said already, George," DS Watson responded, "no comment."

After giving Norfolk George a threatening scowl, DS Watson turned and started to walk back towards the dig. "PC Richardson," he remarked without breaking stride, "make sure nobody crosses that cordon. If they do, arrest them. And no small talk with anyone about anything."

"Right you are," replied PC Richardson, who at the same time gave Norfolk George his best disapproving stare.

*   *   *   *

Pam Hutton was already waiting on the doorstep when Carmichael and DS Dalton walked up her drive.

"I saw you through the window," she explained. "I assume you want to talk with Ellis. Well, if you do, you've wasted your journey as he's away with that girl somewhere."

From those few words, Carmichael deduced two things. Firstly, Pam didn't care much for Verity and secondly, by the slight slurring in her delivery, she'd probably had a drink or two.

"Actually, it's you we've come to see," Carmichael explained, as the two officers arrived at the door. "May we come in?"

"Be my guest," replied Pam, as she theatrically threw open the front door to allow them to enter.

Carmichael smiled and stepped inside, quickly followed by DS Dalton, who had to take a quick sidestep to avoid standing on a rapidly exiting, handsome Bengal cat.

"Be a little careful of Benji," remarked Pam. "He's a gorgeous looking chap, but he's not the friendliest of my animals."

Fortunately for DS Dalton, Benji didn't seem interested in anything other than scarpering as quickly as he could.

"So, what can I do for you today?" enquired Pam once they'd all sat themselves down in her living room.

Carmichael forced one of his best reassuring smiles.

"We'd like to talk to you about Chrissy Cream," he said calmly. "We'd like to know whether you'd ever had any doubts about her dying when the Workington Jenny sank?"

Pam looked back firstly at Carmichael then DS Dalton, her expression one of suspicious bewilderment. "Why do you ask?" she replied.

Carmichael briefly glanced across at DS Dalton, who was sat next to him on the decidedly soft sofa.

"We have reason to believe that she may not have died as the inquest concluded, back then," he replied, choosing his words carefully.

Pam nodded. "That wouldn't totally surprise me," she replied. "At the time it did seem odd to me, but why do you now doubt what the coroner said back then?"

"When you say it seemed odd, what do you mean?" Carmichael enquired.

Pam tilted her head back and looked up at the ceiling. "Well, two things always struck me as being weird," she replied. "Firstly, I know for a fact that when the tragedy happened Chrissy and Jo weren't on great terms," Pam announced. "So, it did seem strange for them to go off together on a boat."

"Do you know why they'd fallen out?" DS Dalton asked.

Pam shook her head. "Not totally," she admitted. "It wasn't unusual. A sibling thing I guess, but I think it was something to do with their tangled love lives. As I say, it wasn't unusual, and they always did make up."

"What do you mean about their tangled love lives?" Carmichael enquired.

"Those three were forever in love then out of love," remarked Pam, a hint of exasperation in her voice. "One minute, Chrissy was dating someone, then it would be Suzi, then it would be Jo. They must have shared countless lovers over the years."

"I see," remarked Carmichael, with a raise of his eyebrow. "Including Ron, I assume."

"Oh, I'm sure it would have included Ron," replied Pam, cynically. "Ron was even more promiscuous than them! Mind you, men can be, can't they? It's much more acceptable for men to play the field, not so much for women. Especially back then. Even stars like

Chrissy, Jo and Suzi would get judged far differently than male musicians."

DS Dalton smiled. "I take it you weren't as …."

"As morally uninhibited, I think you're trying to say," interjected Pam bluntly, sensing DS Dalton was struggling to find the right words.

"Yes," replied DS Dalton, pleased for the assistance.

"God, no" announced Pam firmly. "I wasn't totally celibate, but leaping from one bed to another was never my style."

Carmichael smiled. "You said there were a couple of things that seemed strange about the coroner's conclusion," he said. "What else gave you doubts?"

Pam smiled broadly. "Chrissy hated boats," she replied matter-of-factly. "I know for a fact that she got terribly seasick, even when the water was as calm as a mill pond. For her to decide to go out on a boat into the North Sea, at that time of the year, never made any sense to me."

"But why didn't you mention your concerns at the time?" DS Dalton asked.

Pam shrugged her shoulders. "If it had been just Ron that had testified, I probably would have," she replied. "But Leah and Wade both swore that she got on that boat. Wade even said he drove her there. I've never trusted Ron, but Wade and Leah wouldn't have lied about something like that. Or are you saying they did?"

Carmichael again looked across at DS Dalton, but this time it was a longer more telling look.

Chapter 72

After having explained to Pam Hutton in some detail what they were doing at Ron Mason's house, Carmichael was just about to bring the conversation to an end when the call came through from DS Watson. By the way her boss was listening to every word and the lack of anything significant coming from his lips, DS Dalton knew it was DS Watson on the other end of the line and was fairly confident she knew what Carmichael was being told.

"Keep me updated and say nothing to Norfolk George at this stage," was all Carmichael said before ending the call.

After a quick exchanged glance with DS Dalton, Carmichael turned to face Pam Hutton, his expression circumspect and serious.

"That was DS Watson on the phone," he remarked. "Sadly, he informs me that they've just found a body buried in Ron's garden. Clearly, at this stage, we have no way of knowing who it is, but we have to consider the strong possibility that it's Chrissy Cream."

Pam stared directly ahead in silence, as she digested Carmichael's words. "It will be her, won't it," she eventually remarked. "There's no doubt, it will be Chrissy."

"I'm afraid that is the most likely answer," Carmichael concurred. "But at this stage we really don't know."

"Poor Tom," Pam muttered. "What a horrible shock this will be for him."

Carmichael looked across at DS Dalton for a second. "Yes, we're going to head over to see him now," he said, "Will you be ok on your own?"

Pam looked back at Carmichael, giving him a forced smile. "I'll be fine," she replied. "But I do feel for Tom. This is such awful news."

Carmichael and DS Dalton rose from their chairs and headed towards the door.

Before they'd gone no more than two or three paces, Carmichael turned around to face Pam. "Actually," he said earnestly, "there are some more things I'd like to ask you."

"Fire away," replied Pam, who had not risen out of her chair and her dazed disposition suggesting her thoughts were elsewhere.

"You referred to Verity as 'that girl'," he reminded her. "From that can we take it that you don't like her much?"

Pam turned her head to face DS Dalton and Carmichael. "It's not that I don't like her," she replied bluntly. "I just think she's too young to be having a child. She's no more than a child herself and she behaves like one too. Mind you, it's a family trait. Her mum was no better. She was even younger when she had Verity, so what sort of example she's been, God only knows."

After a brief pause, Pam continued. "But she's Ellis's choice and she's having his baby, so what option do I have other than to accept her?"

Having met both Lydia and Verity, DS Dalton felt Pam Hutton was being unduly critical but decided to say nothing.

"I see," remarked Carmichael.

"And the other thing?" enquired Pam, getting gingerly to her feet as she spoke. "You said there were things you wanted to ask."

"Yes," replied Carmichael. "Does Ellis have a motorbike?"

Pam shook her head. "No," she said firmly. "Tom's the motorbike nut. Ellis has never wanted one, I'm pleased to say. Why do you ask?"

Carmichael shrugged his shoulders. "It's not important, just something that came up during our enquiries."

By the look on her face, Pam didn't buy Carmichael's offhanded reply, but she, too, said nothing and allowed the two officers to say their goodbyes and depart.

Chapter 73

For over an hour, DC Twamley had struggled to contact Miles Goodwyn, and none of the cameras in Cumbria that she and the two uniformed colleagues, she'd managed to enlist to help her, had sighted Ellis Hutton's car.
Then, as if it had been choreographed by an invisible positive force, her mobile rang and Miles's number appeared on the small screen, and just a split second after, PC Horrabin, one of the seconded PCs, shouted excitedly, "He's on the A66 heading east towards Penrith."
DC Twamley smiled and gave her colleague a thumbs up before taking the incoming call.

* * * *

"So, Martin Wood was telling the truth about Chrissy being buried in the rose garden," announced DS Dalton, as she and Carmichael sat in his stationary car.
"Yes, it looks like it, doesn't it," Carmichael concurred.
"I couldn't work out if Pam Hutton was shocked or not when you told her," DS Dalton continued.
"Nor I," replied Carmichael, who thought for a few seconds before continuing. "On balance I'd say she was surprised but not totally. But what is absolutely clear, is that she didn't much care for Ron Mason."

DS Dalton raised her eyebrows. "Or for either Lydia or Verity," she remarked. "I didn't speak a lot with Verity, but I did talk with Lydia for a fair time, and I found her to be very pleasant. I thought Pam's characterisation of them as, well, being practically the village tarts, was a bit unfair."

Carmichael, laughed. "I'm not sure it was as bad as that, but you are right. However, you've got to look at it from Pam's perspective. The bottom line here is that she was talking about a young woman who's leapfrogged over her and is now her son's number one love," he replied. "Maybe, Pam's spite was really more about her demotion in the pecking order of Ellis's affection rather than her real feelings towards the Brook-Smiths."

DS Dalton nodded. "Maybe," she said, "but I got the impression she still didn't really like either of them."

Carmichael started the engine. "There was one other thing Marc told me," he said, as his black BMW started to pull away, "Norfolk George was at the house when they were digging."

"How did he get wind of them going there?" DS Dalton asked, her voice indicating her surprise. "With it being a Sunday, too."

Carmichael turned to face his sergeant and shrugged his shoulders. "My thoughts entirely," he replied. "He's obviously got a source, either at the station or in Stock's forensic team."

* * * *

"Where are they now?" DC Twamley enquired as soon as she put the phone down on Miles Goodwyn.

"They've just turned onto the M6, at junction forty," replied PC Horrabin. "Heading south back in our direction."

"Really," DC Twamley proclaimed excitedly. "Do we have good cameras along that stretch of the M6?"
The PC pulled a face which provided DC Twamley with her answer before she'd even moved her lips. "It's patchy," she replied.
DC Twamley looked up at one of the screens in front of them, which showed there to be about an hour's drive and a dozen junctions before Ellis's car arrived at the nearest junction to Kirkwood police station.
"Keep your eye on them and I'll organise for a patrol car to follow them as soon as they get into Lancashire."
PC Horrabin nodded. "I'll do my best," she replied.

* * * *

Tom was propped up in bed, with his mother sitting on a chair, pushed forward as close as she could locate it to her son, when Carmichael and DS Dalton entered the room.
Despite knowing there was soon to be a very difficult conversation taking place, Carmichael instinctively found himself smiling at the pair. However, by the confused look on their faces, it instantly became clear to Carmichael that what he thought was a friendly expression was probably little more than a signal that something unpleasant was coming, which of course it was.

"I was hoping to catch you both together," Carmichael announced. "I need to bring you both up to speed on some developments."
"What developments?" enquired Suzi, directly, her face now looking very uneasy.

Chapter 74

"Did you know about this?" Tom demanded; his angry eyes fixed intently on Suzi.
"No," implored Suzi, her voice croaking as she spoke. "I promise you, Tom, I didn't."
"As Inspector Carmichael said," interjected DS Dalton, "we've not yet confirmed the body is Chrissy's, so it may not be her …"
"It will be," interrupted Tom. "You know it, as you wouldn't have told us unless you were a hundred percent sure in your minds. It is my mum."
Carmichael glanced across at Suzi's expression on hearing Tom call Chrissy his mum. The words seemed to make her look even more crestfallen and anxious.
"So, who did know?" Tom enquired; his gaze now firmly aimed at Carmichael. "And more importantly, who put her there?"
Carmichael paused for a few seconds before answering. "DS Dalton is right," he began, choosing his words carefully. "We don't know for sure it's Chrissy that's been found, but we have a strong reason to believe it is. I took the decision to tell you now as I'm sure there will be a press frenzy about this, should the person we've found, be your birth mother. I'm sorry, we can't tell you anything more at this stage, but we do believe we know who buried her in Ron's garden."

Tom now stared at the wall in front of him, as he absorbed the dreadful information he'd just been told. "So, Uncle Wade, Ron and Leah must have all lied about Mum being on that boat," he remarked. "I'd expect it of Ron, but Wade and Leah?"

"And Coral, too," added Suzi. "Did she know?"

Carmichael shook his head. "I can't tell you much, but we've no evidence that Coral knew anything about this."

"But Leah and Uncle Wade did," Tom said for a second time.

Carmichael cleared his throat before continuing.

"It would help us enormously if we could have a sample of your DNA," he told Tom. "It should speed up the process of identifying the body we've found. Would you be prepared to do that for us, Tom?"

The dazed young man nodded. "Yes, of course," he replied.

Under normal circumstances, Carmichael would have left Tom and Suzi there and then, but he needed to know more about Tom's accusations against Ellis, so he remained.

"Can I just clarify why you think it was Ellis who killed Ron and why you believe he also tried to run you down?" Carmichael asked.

Tom looked again at Carmichael, his eyes now watery and red. "I saw him parked close to Ron's house when I went to see him on Thursday," replied Tom. "I asked Ellis about it, and he denied it, but I know it was him."

"Is that what the fight was about?" DS Dalton enquired.

"In fairness to him I threw the first punch," Tom conceded, "but, yes, it was."

"And the hit and run?" added Carmichael. "Did you see Ellis at the wheel? Was it his car?"

Tom shrugged his shoulders. "To be honest I wasn't watching the road. I had my music on and was looking at my feet when the vehicle hit me. I only saw it for a split second before it crashed into me. Just enough time to move a little out of the way; but not enough."

"So, you couldn't be totally sure Ellis was driving," DS Dalton remarked.

"I know it was him," replied Tom.

Carmichael nodded gently and smiled. "That will be all for now, Tom," he said calmly. "We'll let you know if we get any more news as soon as we are able."

The two officers were making their way towards the exit when Carmichael suddenly stopped and turned back to face Tom and Suzi. "I hear you're into motorbikes, Tom," he remarked.

Tom frowned, Carmichael's comment seeming quite random, given the discussions that had preceded it.

"I suppose I am," he replied, "but I won't be doing much for the foreseeable future, even if I still had a bike."

"So, you don't own a bike at the moment?" Carmichael announced.

Tom shook his head. "No, I sold mine about three months ago to a mate."

"Anyone we'd know?" enquired Carmichael.

"Spencer Wood, as it happens," responded Tom. "Now he is a real bike nut case. He's been riding for years, and he must have four or five bikes."

"Really," replied Carmichael. "That's interesting to know."

Unsure what Carmichael's reasons might be for asking about motorbikes, Tom and Suzi watched in silence as Carmichael and DS Dalton departed.

"Do you think Ron, Leah and Wade murdered Chrissy?" Tom asked his mother.

"I don't know what to believe anymore," Suzi replied. "I really don't."

*   *   *   *

Between Tebay Services and Junction 32 of the M6, there are few CCTV cameras on the south bound carriageway; a fact which made PC Horrabin and DC Twamley very uncomfortable as they scoured the screens for a sighting of Ellis Hutton's car.
"I hope he hasn't turned off," DC Twamley mumbled out loud, after twenty minutes had elapsed since their last sighting of his red car.
"No, there he is," exclaimed PC Horrabin, pointing vigorously at one of her screens. "He's just gone past junction thirty-two."
"Excellent," remarked DC Twamley, as she made a grab for the phone on her desk. "I'll get a patrol car to try and follow him, now they're back in Lancashire."

Chapter 75

"What now?" enquired DS Dalton as she and Carmichael sat together in Carmichael's black BMW in the hospital car park.
"Let's just take a minute to try and make sense of what's going on here," he said, his tone suggesting to DS Dalton that he may well have, or be close to, a plausible theory.
"Ok," replied DS Dalton. "Where do you want to start?"
"Let's start with a motive," suggested Carmichael. "Why would someone have wanted to kill Doug Pritchard?"
DS Dalton shrugged her shoulders. "To silence him," she replied. "I can't think of any other reason."
Carmichael nodded gently. "I agree, but hardly anyone knew he was coming to the area," he remarked. "So, his killer or killers were either someone in the pub that night or someone who he'd told he was coming."
"Or was tipped off by someone in the pub," DS Dalton added.
"Yes," agreed Carmichael. "That's plausible."

After a short pause DS Dalton tilted her head to one side and looked intently at her boss. "Do you think there were two people involved?"
Carmichael slowly shook his head. "Well, if Stock's right and if there was just one person, they are right-

handed and tall," he replied. "But I have to admit that I am starting to think there may have been two people involved in that murder."

"Then what about Ron Mason?" DS Dalton asked. "Why was he killed?"

Carmichael thought for a few seconds. "Could be for the same reason," he replied. "To keep him silent. But that doesn't make too much sense as by the sound of things whatever Doug Pritchard knew was going to be damaging to Ron, so he probably wasn't going to say anything."

"Maybe he was killed by someone different," suggested DS Dalton. "Or maybe he and someone else killed Doug Pritchard then that other person killed Ron, to make sure there were no living witnesses to the first death."

Carmichael nodded. "That works, too, I suppose," he concurred.

"And as for the hit and run on Tom," continued DS Dalton, "that's probably the same person who killed Ron trying to silence Tom, who presumably knew something they didn't want to come out."

Carmichael nodded. "It sounds like we're suggesting that Ron and Ellis killed Doug," he announced, "Ellis then killed Ron, and having been seen by Tom outside Ron's house, Ellis then tried to kill Tom."

DS Dalton shrugged her shoulders. "That fits," she said. "Not sure what it was that Doug Pritchard knew that would be so damaging to Ellis, given that he was about two when his mother died, but it does fit."

"If I'm being honest, I'm not totally convinced," responded Carmichael reflectively, "but it would also tie in with what Mrs Wright told me yesterday, that, in the heat of their argument, Leah told Ron that she'd just told Doug about the boys. What exactly that was she told him isn't clear, but it does potentially implicate Ellis in some way."

When DS Dalton didn't speak. Carmichael started the engine. "Anyway," he said as they pulled away from the parking space, "the sooner we talk with Ellis Hutton the better. Whether this theory is right or wrong, I think Ellis is involved in some way; so, let's hope Donna has located him. Actually, why don't you call her and see how she's getting on? It would be good to get an update before we get back to the station, even if the news isn't what we'd like."

DS Dalton nodded and dialled DC Twamley's mobile number.

* * * *

"Fantastic news," DC Twamley squealed, upon hearing from the patrol car tailing Ellis and Verity, that they were within two minutes of Kirkwood police station. "I reckon he's turning himself in. Carmichael will be well chuffed when he hears that."

Indeed, Carmichael was well chuffed when DS Dalton gave him the good news and even more delighted at the prospect of Ellis being in interview room 1 waiting for him when they arrived back at the station.

Chapter 76

"Did Donna mention whether she'd spoken with Miles about him possibly seeing a motorbike outside The Three Bells?" Carmichael asked.

DS Dalton shrugged her shoulders. "She didn't say anything about it. But in fairness, I didn't exactly ask her."

Carmichael eyes remained fixed on the road ahead. "I'm sure she'll tell us when we get there," he remarked.

"That's Lydia and Verity," announced DS Dalton as the brightly painted van sped past them on the opposite side of the road.

Carmichael checked his rear-view mirror and caught a glimpse of The Muffin Maid van turning right at the junction they'd just come out of, red brake light bright on the left-hand side of the car and the amber indicator flashing brightly on the right.

"Why the hell didn't they keep her at the station too," exclaimed Carmichael in frustration. "I wanted to talk with both of them not just Ellis."

DS Dalton shrugged her shoulders. Given that he'd not mentioned this up until then, she had great sympathy for the officer who had let Verity leave but felt glad it hadn't been her.

For the next five minutes as they completed the last half mile of their journey, neither Carmichael nor DS Dalton spoke. Carmichael still looked irritated, and DS Dalton didn't want to feel the brunt of his anger; not if she could avoid it.

* * * *

As instructed, Tom Ashcroft provided the ward sister with a saliva sample for the DNA test, which the officer on duty had been instructed to take immediately, and in person, hand it to Dr Stock at the lab.
"It's going to be Chrissy, isn't it?" Tom said to Suzi as soon as the PC disappeared from the room.
"I think it will be," concurred Suzi who squeezed her son's hand even tighter. "I'm sorry to say."

* * * *

Upon his arrival at the station, Carmichael spared no time in heading over to interview room 1. With DS Dalton and DC Twamley in tow, he strode purposefully down the corridor and after entering the room, quickly made himself comfortable sitting directly opposite Ellis Hutton. DS Dalton and DC Twamley silently slipped in next to him, one on either side.
"Afternoon, Ellis," Carmichael said firmly and confidently, "I'm pleased you've presented yourself here today as I wanted to talk with you. But before we start, I need to confirm to you that you are not under arrest. However, you need to know that based upon what you tell us we may decide to hold you here and subsequently arrest you. Is that understood?"
"Perfectly clear," Ellis replied confidently.
"Then why don't you tell us why you've come to Kirkwood police station this afternoon?" Carmichael suggested.

Ellis looked first at DC Twamley, then at DS Dalton before concentrating his attention on Carmichael.

"Firstly," he said firmly, "I haven't killed anyone, not that journalist and not Ron. I'll admit it was me with Tom the other night, but I've had nothing to do with those murders."

Carmichael nodded calmly. "So, Ellis, you admit that you were behind the wheel of the vehicle that collided with your cousin, Tom Ashcroft, on Friday the twenty-second of March?"

"Yes, that was me," confirmed Ellis. "But I didn't intend to kill him. In fact, I only wanted to scare him, but I misjudged things and accidentally knocked him into the ditch."

"If it was an accident, Ellis," interjected DS Dalton, "why didn't you stop?"

Ellis shrugged his shoulders. "I panicked," he replied. "I only just clipped him, so I knew he'd be alright."

"He's got very serious injuries," DS Dalton said firmly. "He's very lucky to be alive."

Ellis shrugged his shoulders. "Well, it's obviously more serious than I thought at the time, but I swear I only just made contact with him."

"Ellis," remarked Carmichael, "you were on the wrong side of the road doing at least thirty miles an hour when you hit him. From what our forensic team have discovered, it's a miracle Tom wasn't killed."

"Obviously, I'm sorry," Ellis added. "But I can assure you all that I didn't go out with the intention of doing Tom any harm," he implored. "It just sort of happened."

Carmichael paused for a few seconds, before continuing. "How did you know Tom would be out running down that particular road?" he enquired.

Ellis smiled. "Tom is the most predictable person in the world when it comes to running," he replied casually.

"He always leaves home at the same sort of time in the evening and always follows the same route."

Carmichael nodded. "I see," he acknowledged, before pausing again for a few more seconds. "You say you just wanted to scare him," Carmichael continued. "Why?"

Ellis shuffled in his seat. "Tom and I had an argument earlier that day," he began, "he accused me of killing Ron, which made me really angry given that I think it was him who you should be talking to about Ron's death."

"And why should we do that?" DS Dalton asked.

"Because he was at Ron's that afternoon, too. He went to talk with Ron after I'd finished my meeting," Ellis explained. "So, it's got to be him, hasn't it?"

"You're saying you had a meeting with Ron at his house on the day he was killed?" reiterated Carmichael.

"Yes, I did," replied Ellis. "And I was just about to drive off when I saw Tom arrive."

"And at what time was that?" Carmichael asked.

Initially, Ellis looked unsure and took his time before responding; but when he did, he sounded confident that he was being accurate.

"My meeting was organised to start at one fifteen," he announced. "So, I'd say I saw Tom at about one twenty-five at the latest."

"And the meeting," continued Carmichael. "I take it this wasn't an ad hoc thing; you had an appointment?"

"I did," replied Ellis. "It had been organised by Doug Pritchard for the three of us."

Carmichael and his two officers exchanged furtive, astonished looks upon hearing Ellis's claim.

"And what was the meeting about?" Carmichael asked.

Ellis shrugged his shoulders. "I've no idea," he replied nonchalantly. "He never told me."

"Who never told you?" probed DS Dalton, a slight sign of unmistakable irritation noticeable in her voice.

"Doug Pritchard," replied Ellis, as if her question was a dumb one.

"So, it was Doug Pritchard who set up the meeting?" Carmichael asked.

"Yes," replied Ellis, firmly.

"So, did Doug Pritchard call you about the meeting?" DC Twamley asked, knowing full well that there wasn't a record of the two having talked on the mobile activity report from Doug Pritchard's phone, which she'd meticulously gone over a matter of hours earlier.

Again, Ellis took his time before replying.

"No, he sent me a letter," Ellis replied. "I got it on Tuesday. First proper letter I've had in ages."

"And do you still have the letter?" DS Dalton quickly interjected.

"Not sure," replied Ellis, vaguely. "It may still be hanging around at home, but I may have just thrown it away. It was very short and to the point, so I probably binned it."

"And what did the letter say?" Carmichael asked.

Ellis shrugged his shoulders again. "As I said, it was very short and to the point," replied Ellis. "He basically asked me to attend a meeting with him and Ron at Ron's house, Thursday at one fifteen, when he'd tell me something that would be to my advantage."

"And that was it?" enquired DS Dalton.

"Yes," replied Ellis. "That was it. Except he also said to tell no one about the meeting."

Carmichael frowned. "Did you not find this all a bit strange?" he enquired.

"Very strange," Ellis remarked. "But with it being at Ron's house I saw no reason to be concerned."

"I take it you did as you were asked and told no one?" added DC Twamley.

"I googled him, of course," responded Ellis. "Just to be sure who he was, but when I saw he was an aging hack, I didn't think there was anything to be worried about other than it being just a ruse to get me to talk about my birth mum and Chrissy Cream."

"Did you not even tell Verity?" DS Dalton asked.

Ellis shook his head. "She's pregnant and she worries, so I made a point of not mentioning it to her. That was, not until after Tom and I had that altercation. I needed to tell her then to help explain why he'd gone off on one at me."

"So, what happened when you arrived at Ron's house?" Carmichael enquired.

"I arrived as I'd been asked, at the correct time," replied Ellis, "but it was just Ron there. I asked him about the meeting, and he said there wasn't going to be a meeting; that it was all a misunderstanding and that he'd sorted it."

"Presumably you asked Ron to elaborate a little more," suggested DS Dalton.

Ellis shook his head and laughed. "No point," he replied curtly. "I knew Ron really well and I can assure you he wouldn't have expanded on what he'd told me, so I didn't waste my breath."

"So, you just left," announced DC Twamley.

"I just left," confirmed Ellis, with a wry almost defiant smile.

Carmichael took a few seconds to think before continuing. "What about the evening of Wednesday the twentieth, between nine and ten?" Carmichael asked. "Where were you then?"

"Last Wednesday," responded Ellis, who put his hand on his chin as if to emphasise that he was giving due thought to the question. "I was at home doing an assignment for college. In fact, at about that time I was probably submitting it online to Mr McCready"

"And you didn't go out at all?" Carmichael enquired.

"Actually, I did go for a drive at about ten," Ellis replied. "Just after I'd sent McCready the assignment. I drove around for about half an hour then came home."

"Do you often do that?" DS Dalton asked.

"Yes," replied Ellis matter-of-factly. "I find it helps me unwind."

"Where did you drive to?" Carmichael asked.

"Just around the lanes," replied Ellis vaguely.

"Anywhere near The Three Bells?" Carmichael continued.

Ellis shook his head. "No, I was only out for half an hour, tops, and I went in the other direction, towards Preston."

"Can anyone vouch for you being at home; and for the short drive you had?" DS Dalton asked.

"Mum, obviously," Ellis replied. "She was at home, although she'd gone to bed when I went for the drive." Ellis then turned his attention on Carmichael before continuing. "But if you check my emails you'll find when I sent the essay. That should prove I was at home around the hour you mentioned, Inspector."

Carmichael nodded. "We'll do that," he said calmly. "If you would be so good as to tell us your password."

Initially, Ellis looked worried about the prospect of sharing such an important piece of information, but after a few seconds of pondering, he relented.

"It's BigBoy21" he replied, much to the amusement of DC Twamley and DS Dalton, who both valiantly managed to stifle their involuntary desire to smile.

Carmichael sensed that now was probably a good time to pause and take stock with his team. "Why don't we have a short break," he said.
Ellis leaned back in his chair. "Any chance of a cup of tea?" he enquired cockily.

Chapter 77

Lydia and Verity drove back to The Muffin Maid in silence; a sure sign that all was not well between them. It was only when the van pulled up outside the shop front that Lydia decided to speak.
"What's going on?" she asked. "Why is Ellis at the police station?"
Verity sighed deeply before replying. "He's decided to tell them some stuff that he feels might help them."
"Regarding Ron's death?" Lydia asked, her voice trembling with anxious anticipation.
"Ellis hasn't killed anyone, Mum," Verity replied, trying her hardest to reassure her mother. "He's not responsible for either that journalist's death or Ron's. You must believe me."
"But did he have anything to do with Tom's hit and run?" Lydia enquired. "Did he have anything to do with that?"
Verity turned her head away from her mother and looked out through the side window; but said nothing.
"Good God!" Lydia shouted. "What sort of person is he? There's no way I'm having you marrying someone that would deliberately try and hurt someone like that. You need to stay well clear of him, Verity."
Angrily, Verity turned her head back and stared at Lydia and put her hand on her tummy. "He's the father of my

baby and I love him," she snapped. "He'd do anything for me, and I don't care what he has or hasn't done, I'm sticking by him."

* * * *

DS Watson was already in the incident room when Carmichael, DS Dalton and DC Twamley arrived. "Did he tell you much?" he asked eagerly.
DS Dalton nodded vigorously. "Big Boy certainly did," she remarked. "But whether we believe him is another question."
Carmichael sniggered and walked over to the window, without looking at DS Watson, who was about to ask what DS Dalton meant when Carmichael started speaking. "Rachel's right," he concurred. "But, in fairness, Ellis did tell us a tale which is, to a degree, plausible, albeit not what I was expecting and certainly not without a few things we will need to check up on." As he spoke Carmichael reached the window which looked down on the staff car park, two floors below.
"I'm intrigued," announced Watson. "So, is someone going to fill me in on precisely what happened down there?"
Carmichael's attention was momentarily distracted by Sergeant Hunt, who he watched below tinkering about with something under the bonnet of his gleaming, but decidedly aging, Volvo.
Carmichael smiled. "I've only ever known one other person who had a Volvo," he mumbled, as he remembered the ancient car that DS Cooper had loved so much. "And that was a wreck, too."
"Sorry," remarked DS Dalton, who assumed the boss was talking to the team.

"Nothing," replied Carmichael, turning his back to the window, and once again giving his team his undivided attention. "Why don't you update Marc about our interview with Big Boy," he instructed DS Dalton. "I need to talk to Stock."

"Will do," DS Dalton replied, with a massive grin on her face, before commencing to recount what had just transpired in interview room 1.

"Donna," Carmichael said, as he reached his office door. "Did Miles Goodwyn shed any light on there being any other motorbikes outside The Three Bells on Wednesday?"

DC Twamley shook her head. "He was adamant his was the only one," she replied.

Carmichael nodded "So, it seems the motorbike line of enquiry may have hit a dead end."

"It does," concurred DC Twamley.

But to her surprise Carmichael didn't seem to mind.

"Well, you know what they say," he remarked jovially, "as one door shuts another ...."

Without finishing the cliché, Carmichael disappeared into his office and closed the door behind him.

* * * *

Stock's mobile rang several times before it was answered.

"Stock, it's Carmichael. Any updates on the body and the DNA analysis?" Carmichael enquired.

Stock sucked in a huge gulp of air; something he often did when he was frustrated. "It will take a little more time for the DNA results," he replied, "remember it's Sunday, so I've not got the resource around me that I have during normal working hours."

Although Carmichael realised that he was pushing his luck, he never-the-less, persisted. "I've got a question for you and there's another thing I'd like you and the team to do for me, please," he continued.

"Fire away," Stock responded, his tone one of exasperation. "But I'm not promising you any miracles. Not today, Carmichael. I've a lot to get through already, so bear that in mind before you start asking me for the impossible."

Chapter 78

By the expression on Ellis Hutton's face, Carmichael could see he was shocked when the interview recommenced with him and DS Watson rather than the two female officers who'd been present earlier.

"Have the others clocked off for the day?" he asked flippantly.

"We never clock off when we're investigating a murder," Carmichael remarked with a stern expression on his face. "DS Dalton and DC Twamley are following up a few things for me. Some of which relate to what you told us earlier."

His comments seemed to have the desired effect on Ellis, who appeared unnerved by Carmichael's words.

"Anyway, did you enjoy your tea?" Carmichael enquired.

Ellis nodded slowly but said nothing.

Carmichael smiled. "I'd like to get a few details correct for the record," he said. "Firstly, can you confirm what vehicle you were driving when you hit Tom the other evening?"

"It was Lydia's van," Ellis replied.

"Are you insured to drive Lydia's van?" Carmichael asked.

Ellis shrugged his shoulders. "I expect my car insurance covers me, but I don't honestly know."

Carmichael nodded gently. "And did Lydia give you permission to drive her van?" he asked.

Ellis shook his head. "Not exactly," he replied. "She was out so she couldn't."

"So, did Verity?" DS Watson enquired.

Again, Ellis shook his head. "No, she was asleep when I went out in it," he explained. "She often has a nap in the afternoon, now she's expecting."

"Why did you not go out in your car?" Carmichael asked.

Ellis shrugged his shoulders again. "That was the plan, but mine was blocked in by the van. I went out with the intention of just moving the van, but once I'd reversed into the road, I decided to go for a drive in that."

"A spur of the moment decision then?" Carmichael suggested.

"Yes," replied Ellis. "That's exactly how I'd describe it."

"And you went out to frighten Tom, who you'd fought with earlier in the day and who you knew would be jogging down that particular road at that time," continued Carmichael.

"Apart from the fact that Tom never jogs, he runs flat out, you're right," replied Ellis.

"Well, I can assure you he won't be jogging for a good few months," interjected DS Watson, who couldn't resist the barbed comment.

Ellis took a deep breath but didn't respond.

"And was Lydia back or Verity awake when you got back to their house?" Carmichael asked.

Ellis shook his head. "No, Lydia was still out shopping, and Verity had hardly moved at all from how she was when I left."

"And what about the van?" Carmichael enquired. "Was that damaged by the impact with Tom?"

Ellis looked puzzled, suggesting he didn't know. "I never thought to check," he confessed. "It was such a glancing blow; I doubt there's any damage to the van."

"We'll check that, don't worry," Carmichael remarked with a wide grin. "But I'd be very surprised if there isn't any damage."

Ellis's demeanour immediately altered, and he started to perspire and shuffle uncomfortably in his chair.

"Let's move on to the meeting you had with Ron Mason on Thursday," Carmichael continued. "You said that was at one fifteen."

"That's correct," responded Ellis.

"And was over by one twenty-five," Carmichael added.

"Correct again," Ellis replied.

"And I assume for that meeting you went in your own car?" continued Carmichael.

"I did," Ellis confirmed.

"And what make of car is that?" DS Watson asked.

"It's a red Ford Focus," confirmed Ellis.

"And where exactly did you park?" Carmichael asked.

Ellis again looked perplexed. "I'm not totally sure I can remember," he replied ambiguously, "but on the road outside the house."

"So that would be Bentley Lane," suggested Carmichael.

"That's right," replied Ellis.

"Why didn't you drive onto Ron's driveway?" Carmichael asked. "High Moor Grange has a very large drive, so it would have easily accommodated your Ford Focus?"

Ellis shrugged his shoulders. "No reason," he replied. "I just decided to park on the road."

"On which side of the road did you park?" Carmichael asked. "Was it on the same side as Ron's house or on the other side of the road?"

"And was it facing towards the village or away out into the countryside?" added DS Watson.

Ellis shrugged his shoulders. "I can't remember exactly," he replied. "But I came from my house, so I'd imagine I was on the same side as Ron's house facing the village."

"It was only four days ago," remarked Carmichael. "I find it hard to believe you don't remember."

"Well, a lot has happened since then," Ellis snapped back. "And I don't."

Again, Carmichael smiled. "Let's now talk about Wednesday evening," he said calmly. "Remind us of where you were and what you were doing between nine and ten on Wednesday evening."

Ellis gave Carmichael a look of exasperation before responding. "I was at home doing an assignment, which I sent to my lecturer at about the time you seem to be interested in," he replied. "I then went for a short drive around the local lanes for about thirty minutes to clear my head, then I came home."

Carmichael smiled before looking momentarily at DS Watson and then picking up the papers in front of him. "I think that's enough for the time being, Ellis," he announced calmly but firmly. "I appreciate you coming in."

"So, can I go?" Ellis enquired, a degree of astonishment at the prospect clear in his voice.

Carmichael frowned. "No, that won't be possible," he replied. "We can keep you for twenty-four hours before charging you, which is what I intend to do. I'm afraid you'll be sleeping in the cells tonight. And, depending upon what the CPS say in the morning, it may well be for longer."

Ellis didn't argue. It was clear he'd fully expected to be detained when he handed himself in.

"One thing I'd like to get from you tonight though, is a DNA sample," Carmichael announced. "It would help speed up the elimination of you from the deaths of Doug Pritchard and Ron Mason. Are you happy to do that for us?"

Ellis shrugged his shoulders. "If it helps prove I didn't kill them then, yes, I'm more than happy to give you some DNA."

"Thank you," replied Carmichael. Then turning to DS Watson, he continued. "Can you take him down to the custody sergeant, please and do the honours?"

DS Watson smiled before escorting Ellis out of interview room 1.

Chapter 79

Having left DS Watson to book Ellis Hutton in and ensure the DNA sample was taken, and with DS Dalton and DC Twamley elsewhere carrying out the instructions he'd given them earlier, Carmichael found himself alone in the incident room.

Typically, Carmichael enjoyed these periods of solitude as he could think with no external interruptions. And this occasion was no exception.

The mist that had shrouded the case was, at last, lifting and although he was waiting for DS Dalton, DC Twamley and Dr Stock to furnish him with more information, this was more to substantiate his deductions and provide evidence that would improve the chances of a conviction rather than to add any additional insight into what had been going on in the sleepy village of High Maudsey.

Carmichael pulled out the list of the nine questions he'd written down two days earlier, and, one by one, wrote answers against all but one of them.

Then, with a smug look of triumph on his face, he screwed the sheet of paper into a small tight ball and threw it towards the paper bin, three metres away. It missed, but he didn't care.

"All sorted," announced DS Watson as he bounded through the door. "Ellis is in his cell next to Martin

Wood and his DNA is being transported, as we speak, over to Stock."

Carmichael looked over at his sergeant. "Don't get comfortable, Marc," he told him, just moments before Watson reached his desk. "We're going out."

"Where to?" DS Watson enquired.

"Somewhere I should have gone days ago," replied Carmichael, obtusely.

* * * *

DC Twamley and the two uniformed officers who had accompanied her to Pam Hutton's house quickly established that Ellis did send his assignment to Mr McCready on Wednesday evening, at almost exactly the time the first murder was committed: 9:40pm. However, that's as far as the positive news went, as they were having no luck finding the letter Ellis maintained he'd received from Doug Pritchard on Tuesday.

Unaware that it had been her son who'd suggested the letter had been sent, Pam Hutton had made DC Twamley aware, on numerous occasions and in no uncertain terms, that they were on a wild goose chase. She insisted that Ellis almost never received any letters and that if he had, she'd have seen them first, being the person who always picked up the mail from their doormat.

DC Twamley was as certain as she could be that what Pam was saying was right, but as the bins had not been taken away since Tuesday and they didn't have a shredder, DC Twamley and her colleagues felt obliged to search everywhere including the recycling bin and the general waste bins; the latter task DC Twamley had, sensibly, delegated to the two uniformed PCs.

With her arms folded tightly against her chest, Pam once again couldn't resist telling DC Twamley, who was riffling through Ellis's college textbooks, that she was wasting her time.

"Ellis didn't know Doug Pritchard," she remarked loudly. "Why on earth would they have been exchanging letters. People use email and WhatsApp now. Letters are from the dark ages to them."

It was on the tip of DC Twamley's tongue to tell Pam exactly what she thought of her continual berating, when a message came through on her mobile. It was from PC Richardson, who she'd asked to look at the last electoral roll for the area; another one of the urgent tasks Carmichael had given her.

"Brilliant," she muttered, before barging past Pam and going outside, where she could call the boss without being heard.

* * * *

"What did you make of the interview with Ellis?" DS Watson enquired as Carmichael's black BMW flew down the narrow Lancashire Lanes.

"It told me something I already knew," Carmichael replied elusively, "namely that even people who are normally very rational, when they're head over heels in love, can be unbelievably foolish."

"So, you didn't believe what he told us?" continued Watson.

Carmichael smiled. "I believe he didn't kill either Doug Pritchard or Ron Mason. I think he's telling us the truth there. But as for the rest of it, I think it was a pack of lies. Verity is our killer. And I think she was the one who tried to kill Tom, too."

As he finished talking, Carmichael's mobile rang. It was DS Dalton.

Carmichael pressed the button on his steering wheel and DS Dalton's voice came through loud and clear over the speaker.

"I've checked with Tom, and he says that Ellis's car was parked on a side road just off Bentley Lane, the afternoon when Ron Mason was killed," she said. "He thinks it's called Mill Street, but he isn't sure. He also says he didn't actually see Ellis, but he is certain it was Ellis's car."

"That fits," replied Carmichael. "Anything else?"

"No, that's about it," replied DS Dalton. "Do you want me to head back to the station?"

"No," replied Carmichael firmly. "We're on our way to Lydia and Verity Brook–Smith's. We may be in need of your help here, Rachel, so why don't you head over, and we'll meet you there."

"Will do," replied DS Dalton, a fraction of a second before Carmichael cut her off."

* * * *

"Damn," exclaimed DS Twamley as she tried for a third time to call Carmichael, only to again find line to be engaged. She decided to text, instead.

* * * *

As Carmichael's car pulled up outside The Muffin Maid, DS Watson suddenly turned to face his boss. "I didn't know we had DNA evidence at the two murder scenes," he remarked.

"We don't," replied Carmichael.

"Then why did you want a DNA sample from Ellis?" DS Watson enquired.

Carmichael smiled. "To confirm something that I think is the root cause of all this," he replied. "If I'm right, and I think I am, all that I need to discover is what Verity used to kill Doug Pritchard. Other than that, I think I know what's been going on here."

As he spoke, DC Twamley's text arrived on Carmichael's mobile.

The broad smile that swept across Carmichael's face indicated to DS Watson that the information she'd sent him was even more evidence to support his theory.

Chapter 80

It was already getting dark, when Verity clambered out of The Muffin Maid van and started to walk up the narrow, half-stone, half-dirt, track towards the small ledge overlooking the Delph Tea Gardens.
When she was a young girl, she'd played in the abandoned huts that served afternoon teas some fifty years before, so she knew the overgrown sandstone quarry intimately, and was familiar with its trails, even when they were thick with vegetation, where nature had reclaimed the land not mined in the last hundred years.
Upon reaching the top of the pathway, Verity paused and took a deep breath before sitting down, cross legged on an overhanging stone slab, some twenty metres above where she'd abandoned the bakery van.
She took out her mobile and, in the failing light, started to construct a text message.

*　　*　　*　　*

"Are we not waiting for Rachel?" enquired DS Watson as he and Carmichael reached the side door of The Muffin Maid, the entrance to Lydia and Verity's accommodation. Carmichael shook his head. "No," he replied bluntly, "it's important we talk with Lydia and Verity, so now's not the time to be hesitant."

* * * *

Satisfied that the short text message had conveyed all she wanted to say but knowing it would not be read for many hours, Verity pressed send and started to type the second message. This one would be longer and need to be more carefully worded than the one she'd just sent Ellis. Coming to terms with her only daughter taking her own life would be difficult enough for her mum to handle, without it being compounded by a final message that didn't reassure her mum just how much she was loved by Verity and just how sorry she was for taking the cowards way out. So, Verity knew it would take her some time to get right.

* * * *

From the look on her face, Lydia Brook–Smith didn't appear to be in the least surprised at seeing two officers on her doorstep, but she did look worried.
"She says Ellis had nothing to do with the murders," Lydia blurted out. "Is she right?"
Carmichael tried to retain a blank expression but didn't answer her question. "Is Verity in?" he asked. "I'd like to talk with you together if I may."
Lydia shook her head. "No, she's gone off in the van," she replied. "We had words then someone called her, which put her in an even fouler mood."
"Who was that?" Carmichael enquired.
"Search me," replied Lydia. With a shrug of her shoulders. "One of her mates, I assume. But whoever it was, she wasn't best pleased when she came off the call. Then a couple of minutes later, she announced that she needed to get her head straight and went off in the van."

"Is that normal behaviour for Verity?" Carmichael asked.

Lydia took a few seconds to respond. "Not normal, no," she replied, defensively. "But she has quite an up and down personality, so it's not completely uncharacteristic for her to get a cob on when the mood suits her. I suspect she'll be back soon."

"These words you had with her," remarked Carmichael. "What were they about?"

"Ellis, of course," responded Lydia, "being arrested by you lot."

"He's not been arrested," DS Watson said. "He came in of his own accord. He's just helping us with our enquiries."

Lydia looked puzzled. "So, you don't think it was him who killed Ron Mason, that journalist, and tried to kill Tom?"

Carmichael shook his head. "He says he didn't commit the murders but has confessed to the hit and run on Tom."

"And you believe him," Lydia remarked, her tone suggesting she was shocked but also relieved.

Carmichael picked his words carefully. "I'm inclined to believe that what he's telling us is largely true, but not totally," he responded. An answer that seemed to confuse rather than enlighten Lydia.

"Can we come in?" Carmichael added.

Lydia, still looking perplexed, nodded and opened the door wide to allow Carmichael and DS Watson to enter her house.

*   *   *   *

With over thirty years in forensic science behind him, the last fifteen of these heading up the team in mid-

Lancashire, there was precious little that took Dr Harry Stock by surprise anymore, well when he was at work anyway. However, the speed at which he got back the results, and the clarity of the findings, certainly made him raise an eyebrow.

He read the report for a second time before picking up his mobile and dialling Carmichael's number.

*   *   *   *

"I don't want to beat about the bush with you, Lydia," announced Carmichael, as soon as the trio were seated in Lydia's tiny lounge. "I need you to tell me when you told Verity who her father was?"

"I've never told her," replied Lydia forcefully. "She doesn't know because I'm not really sure. It was a reckless fling when I was very young and foolish. I never knew the boy's name and never saw him again."

Carmichael shook his head and was about to tell her he didn't believe her when his mobile rang.

Chapter 81

Carmichael listened intently as Stock delivered a detailed summary of the findings from the DNA analysis.

"And those results are a hundred percent accurate?" Carmichael said when Stock had finished talking.

"No," replied Stock firmly and with more than a hint of desperation in his voice. "Nothing is that accurate, Carmichael, but the chance of error is miniscule, so you can take what I've told you as so close to fact as makes no difference."

"That good enough for me," remarked Carmichael before ending the call.

After placing his mobile back in his jacket pocket Carmichael turned his attention, once more, upon Lydia Brook-Smith.

"Lydia," he said calmly, "I don't believe the reckless fling story you've been spinning for the best part of the last twenty years. I know what happened, I know who Verity's father is and I think she does, too."

Lydia's expression changed as she absorbed what she'd just been told; and Carmichael could see in her eyes that she believed him.

"For obvious reasons, I've never told Verity," announced Lydia, her voice quiet but clear. "So, there's no way she knows."

Without a clue what they were referring to, DS Watson interjected. "So, who is Verity's dad?" he enquired.

Carmichael looked over at Lydia, now deep in thought, her gaze having fallen to a point on the floor somewhere between the two officers' feet.

When Lydia didn't answer, Carmichael glanced over at Watson.

"It's Ron Mason," he remarked. "And based upon what Donna has discovered from the electoral roll, he made Lydia pregnant when she was just fifteen."

"It was consensual," announced Lydia indignantly, "but, it's true that Ron was over ten years older than me and, of course, he didn't want anyone to know."

"Hence the loan for the bakery," DS Watson muttered, as he began to piece together what the other two already knew.

"Yes," replied Lydia. "Ron was very generous to me and my mum. He gave her money to buy a small place in Spain, where she saw out the rest of her days. I stayed here, had Verity, and Ron paid for everything."

"Including significant funding for the purchase of the bakery," Carmichael added. "But I take it, the price was your silence."

Lydia nodded. "Yes, I suppose, putting it bluntly, it was," she replied. "I agreed never to tell anyone. The foolish fling story seemed to be accepted without much trouble, so much so that in the end I almost started to believe it myself. Once the loan for the bakery was paid to me, I also agreed with Ron never to make any contact with him again."

"And you kept to that promise?" enquired Carmichael.

Lydia, once again, stared back at Carmichael and DS Watson. "I kept my side of the bargain. I never spoke out or contacted Ron," she replied. "But I did tell one person the truth a few years ago. Something I regretted as soon as I told her, but I swore her to silence, and I don't think she told anyone."

Carmichael nodded gently. "Would that person have been Leah Barnes, by any chance?" he asked.

Lydia looked shocked.

"It was," she replied. "How did you know?"

Carmichael shrugged his shoulders. "Because it would explain a few things."

"Why did you tell Leah?" DS Watson enquired; his brow furrowed reflecting his astonishment.

"We became very good friends, Leah, Coral and I over the years," continued Lydia. "One wine filled evening when Coral had fallen asleep, Leah said she'd tell me about her husband if I told her about Verity's dad. It was one of those senseless conversations that you have when you're drunk. And, well, stupidly I told her that Ron was Verity's dad. She promised she'd not tell a soul, which I think she kept to. But I did regret telling her."

"And her husband?" remarked DS Watson. "Who was he?"

Lydia laughed. "That was it," she replied, "there apparently was no husband. She'd made him up. She had just started to call herself Mrs Barnes when she was in Asia. One of her crazy, impulsive, decisions. But something she kept alive when she came home."

"Just as you had with your foolish fling story," remarked DS Watson.

As he finished talking, Lydia's mobile made the noise that indicated she'd received a message. She glanced down at the screen.

"It's from Verity," Lydia announced, as she started to scroll through her daughter's carefully crafted message.

Chapter 82

"There's been a change of plan, Rachel," Carmichael anxiously announced into his mobile. "Do you know where the Delph Tea Gardens are?"
"Yes," replied DS Dalton. "I used to play there when I was a girl. As it happens, I'm about two minutes from there now."
"Good," remarked Carmichael. "Get over there straight away. We think Verity's there and might be going to take her own life. Marc's calling for back-up and then we'll be on our way over, too."
"I'm on my way," replied DS Dalton, before the line went dead, cutting off her boss. DS Dalton wasn't surprised, as her car had just gone through a small, wooded area, which she knew from experience had bad signal.
"Damn," muttered Carmichael angrily, who had wanted to give DS Dalton the heads up on why they were worried about Verity's safety.
He tried her line again, but it was unobtainable.
"Blast it," he remarked before putting his mobile in his pocket.
"I'm coming with you," announced Lydia.
For a split-second Carmichael considered saying no. However, he wasn't about to leave her at the bakery on

her own and he didn't want DS Watson to remain with her either, so he reluctantly agreed.
"Ok," he replied before making a dash for the door.

* * * *

Verity stood close to the edge of the overhang, her heart racing as she tried to imagine what it would feel like to hit the ground from such a height. She wasn't good with pain at the best of times, but she kept telling herself that it would all happen so quickly that she'd hardly feel a thing.
Her mouth now dry, and her hands clammy, Verity counted to ten then went to jump, but her legs wouldn't let her; they fixed themselves firm to the ledge like limpets in the rock pools in Porthdinllaen where she and her Mum had played during their summer holidays in Wales, when she was small. Nothing could shift them. It was almost as if her head and her legs were ganging-up on her and denying her the chance to end it all.
She took a deep breath and tried again.

* * * *

DS Rachel Dalton's car skidded to a swift halt right next to The Muffin Maid van; and she quickly jumped out. Although it was becoming more night than day, and the tall trees that had grown up around the old, abandoned quarry made the visibility even worse, DS Dalton amazingly managed to spot Verity high up on the ledge within a few seconds.

"Verity," she yelled up at the young woman. "It's Rachel Dalton. Just stay where you are. I'm coming up."

Frozen with fear, but still determined to end it all, Verity remained rooted to the spot and didn't answer.

Chapter 83

It took just five minutes for Carmichael, DS Watson, and Lydia to arrive at the quarry; by which time two patrol cars were already at the scene and DS Dalton was on the ledge a couple of metres from Verity.
"Oh god, no," muttered Lydia, as she spied her daughter so close to the edge.
"Try and stay quiet," Carmichael replied, putting a comforting hand on her shoulder as he spoke. "DS Dalton is up there with Verity. We just need to try and remain calm while Rachel talks to your daughter."

* * * *

"Why don't you come away from the edge, Verity?" DS Dalton suggested.
The blank expression on Verity's face and the fact she neither responded nor moved a muscle, worried Rachel.
"Why don't we just talk about this?" she then suggested.
Verity shook her head. "Talk about what?" she remarked.
"Why you're here?" replied DS Dalton in a friendly, reassuring tone of voice.
"Isn't it obvious," replied Verity, abruptly.
"It's really not," remarked DS Dalton honestly.

"How many proper boyfriends have you had, Rachel?" Verity asked.

"Not that many," replied DS Dalton, somewhat perplexed at the question.

"More than me though, I'd imagine," continued Verity. "More than two."

"Not many more, than that" DS Dalton added, trying to reassure the young woman standing just centimetres away from a twenty-metre drop.

"What about brothers and sisters," continued Verity. "How many have you got?"

"I've two older brothers," replied DS Dalton.

"Snap," replied Verity in a loud voice.

DS Dalton wasn't aware that Verity had brothers, something that became abundantly clear to Verity from the expression on her face.

"Up until last Wednesday I thought I was an only child," continued Verity, "but it turns out I'm not. I only found out when I was serving that Doug Pritchard in The Three Bells. Yes, I've got two older brothers, too. The problem I have is that they're not only my brothers but also my only two lovers. And one of them is the father of my unborn child."

DS Dalton hadn't been expecting that piece of information, something once more her expression failed to conceal.

Verity clutched her belly tightly. "So, this little one's mummy and daddy are brother and sister," she added angrily, ensuring that DS Dalton was under no illusions about the predicament Verity had found herself in.

"That's even worse than being born to a mother who was underage and a father, who was much older than her at the time I was conceived, being, technically, what I guess you'd call a paedophile."

For the first time since she'd arrived at the ledge, DS Dalton started to doubt her chances of successfully talking Verity down.

* * * *

"Lydia," Carmichael whispered. "I'd like you to stay with these officers while DS Watson and I go up to join DS Dalton."
"No," replied Lydia firmly. "I'm going with you."
Carmichael looked sternly in Lydia's direction. "I'm sorry," he replied, "I must insist you stay here. Please trust me when I say it will be easier to bring Verity down safely if you leave it to us."
In truth, he wasn't totally sure what was the right thing to do, but he couldn't risk Verity doing something stupid if she saw her mum.
Lydia didn't like it but remained rooted to the spot as Carmichael and DS Watson disappeared into the undergrowth.

* * * *

"I know you're upset and confused, Verity," DS Dalton said in as calm a voice as she could, "but maybe Doug Pritchard had it wrong. Surely you shouldn't just take his word for it."
Verity shook her head. "It's true," she replied. "I've known for a few months now that Ron Mason was my father. I did a DNA test then got onto one of those ancestry websites. It didn't take long for them to say they had a second cousin match; a bloke called Michael Commerford in North America who'd put up a very detailed family tree. And there he was, Ron Mason his

mother's cousin. So, I didn't need to be Einstein to work out that he was my dad."

"And did you talk with your mum about it?" DS Dalton asked.

Verity shook her head. "No," she replied with a look of incredulity. "How do you bring up something like that with your mum? She's obviously so ashamed that she doesn't want anyone to know, so why I should rake over those painful old coals with her?"

DS Dalton tried to think what she'd have done in Verity's position, and although she couldn't be sure, she was certain she'd have talked with Lydia. Not that that was of any consequence.

"And what about Ron Mason," DS Dalton continued. "Did you approach him about it?"

"I thought about it," Verity replied, "but I was too scared to."

"And anyway, even if you are Ron's daughter, what proof did Doug Pritchard have about Ron Mason being Ellis or Tom's father?" DS Dalton enquired.

"Or?" exclaimed Verity angrily. "Doug Pritchard said, very clearly, when I was a matter of a foot away, that he had it on very good authority that Chrissy and Jo Cream's boys were Ron's. And despite him going ballistic, you could tell by the look on Ron's face that it was true."

"Even if you are right, you've done nothing wrong, Verity," DS Dalton said in an assured friendly voice. "And neither has your unborn child. You're both innocent parties in all this."

"Not quite," responded Verity. "Not anymore."

DS Dalton wasn't sure what to say next, so was relieved when Carmichael quietly joined her, his arms held up in the air in an attempt to allay any fears Verity might have had.

"DS Dalton's right, Verity" he said slowly and calmly. "Your mum's down there and she's worried sick. Please come away from the edge, even if just one or two steps."
Verity remained fixed to the spot.
"What did Ellis tell you?" she asked.
"Ellis told us he'd run into Tom in your mum's van," Carmichael replied. "But he claims that he had nothing to do with the two murders."
"And do you believe him?" Verity asked.
"I'm certain Ellis isn't the person who killed Doug Pritchard and Ron Mason," replied Carmichael.
"But you know who did, don't you?" Verity declared.
"Yes, Verity," replied Carmichael, "I think I do."
DS Dalton looked over at Carmichael for a split second, as it dawned on her what they were talking about.
"Case closed for you then," remarked Verity, her voice now sounding more relaxed, as if she'd suddenly had the stress lifted from her.
"Please come down, Verity," DS Dalton said in as composed a manner as she could. "Let's go and see your mum, she'll be worried sick down there."
Verity didn't reply and for a few seconds nobody spoke. Then slowly Verity took two steps in the direction of the two officers.
"Can you guarantee that Ellis won't be sent to prison?" Verity enquired as she made a third step towards safety.
Carmichael nodded. "I've no plans to even charge him," he replied, reassuringly.
On hearing this Verity stopped in her tracks, looked over at Carmichael and DS Dalton, smiled, then turning quickly, her back now all they could see, Verity started to run towards the cliff edge.
"No!" shouted DS Dalton, as Verity leapt towards the twenty-metre drop and certain death.

Chapter 84

It was almost midnight when Carmichael eventually arrived home, there having been so much he'd had to do following Verity's suicidal leap.
He'd debriefed his team, so they all knew the full facts and, where some information was yet to be ascertained, shared his working hypothesis on what was still unproven. And then, of course, there was the long conversation with Chief Inspector Hewitt; never something Carmichael enjoyed.
With it being so late, Carmichael hadn't expected Penny to be still awake, so he was surprised when she greeted him as he came through the front door and into the hallway.
"From what they've reported on the news, it sounds like you've had a hectic day," Penny remarked, before planting a massive kiss on her husband's lips.
"You could say that" he replied, pulling her close and hugging her tightly.
"They said an officer prevented someone jumping off a ledge at the old Delph Tea Gardens quarry. Is that true?" Penny enquired.
Carmichael looked deep into his wife's eyes, a resigned but sceptical look on his face. "You're going to tell me you used to play there as a child, aren't you?" he remarked, dolefully.

"Well, as it happens, I did," replied Penny with enthusiasm. "It was a place lots of us used to go to."
Carmichael, in exasperation, shook his head slowly. "If you know it so well, can you tell me, why is it called the Delph Tea Gardens?" he enquired.
Penny shrugged her shoulders. "I'm not totally sure," she replied, "but my Granny reckoned that after the second world war a few old dears had a café built in there and they used to serve tea to people on the grass near a lake that had emerged from one of the old quarry pits. Apparently, it was quite a sophisticated place for people to take afternoon tea in the nineteen fifties."
Carmichael nodded gently. "Well, all that decadence has either been removed or is now buried deep below the overgrowth," he remarked. "All that's left as far as I could see, are steep slopes, cliff edges and lots and lots of trees, weeds, brambles and thick grass."
"Enough of all that," continued Penny impatiently. "Who stopped someone jumping over the edge?"
Carmichael laughed. "If I asked you to guess, you'd never get it," he replied. "I swear, it was the fastest I've ever seen this person move. Leapt like a salmon and literally caught the would-be jumper in mid-air, a matter of inches away from the cliff edge."
Penny took a few seconds to think about it.
"It was Marc, wasn't it," she said with conviction.
"How did you know?" enquired Carmichael, a genuine look of astonishment on his face.
"Well, you'd never dare be so disparaging about Rachel or the new girl, Donna, so that just leaves Marc," Penny replied.
Carmichael nodded sagely. "I did sort of give that away, I guess," he conceded. "But fair play to him, he came up trumps when we needed him and there's no doubt he saved her life, and that of the child she's carrying."

"Sounds like there may be some sort of award coming his way," Penny remarked.

Carmichael nodded. "That's what Hewitt's now talking about. Although, being Hewitt, you can bet his motivation is more self-serving than benevolent."

"What do you mean?" Penny enquired.

"Well, he'll get to polish his buttons and shine his shoes and he'll no doubt make sure he's central in any publicity that comes out of all this," explained Carmichael. "Normally, Hewitt hasn't a kind word to say about Marc, but if it gets him a bit of kudos, he'll park that for a month or two."

"That's a very cynical view," remarked Penny.

"But true," Carmichael replied.

Penny sniggered. "Why don't you go through and sit yourself down in the lounge," she said, with her customary broad smile. "I'll get us a drink and you can fill me in on what's been happening."

"In that case I'll need a large red wine," Carmichael responded. "There's a lot we've uncovered today, so it may take some time."

* * * *

Verity Brook-Smith sat alone in her cell, clad in the all-in-one white prison outfit that she'd been given when all her clothes and possessions had been taken away.

With just a blanket and a pillow for company, she wept uncontrollably knowing her life would now be changed forever.

The desk sergeant had been given strict instructions to make sure someone checked on Verity every fifteen minutes; a directive he was observing tenaciously, even though Verity remonstrated in the strongest of terms every time the spy hole was opened; protests that went unheeded by the officer on the other side of the door.

Chapter 85

Carmichael was on his second glass of Pinotage by the time he'd finished recounting what he and the team had uncovered.

"So, Chrissy Cream never went on that boat, she was dead and buried in Ron Mason's garden all along," she remarked.

Carmichael nodded. "Yes, but we're fairly sure only three people knew, Ron Mason, Leah Barnes and Martin Wood."

"And you don't think either of the Vixens or Wade Freeman knew she'd been killed even before the boat had set sail?"

"The Vixens didn't know. I'm certain of that," Carmichael replied. "As for Wade Freeman, I'm not as sure. However, on balance I think he just lied about taking her up to Cumbria, as he thought Chrissy genuinely wanted to get away. I'd imagine over the years, when nothing was seen or heard of her, he may have questioned whether he was told the truth by Leah and Ron. But if he did, he seems to have been happy not to challenge them and to remain silent."

"What do you think will happen to him?" Penny asked.
Carmichael took a swig from his wine glass. "A good question," he replied. "I'm not sure, but there's got to be

a real chance of a custodial sentence for the way he deliberately misled the investigation back then and also for lying to the coroner at the inquest."

"And Martin Wood?" enquired Penny. "What will happen to him?"

"If convicted, he's certainly looking at being put away," replied Carmichael. "He may not have been responsible for her death, but he deliberately and knowingly aided the other two in covering it up. No, he faces a good stretch in prison, in my view."

Penny nodded gently as she digested what her husband had said." And what about Lydia?" she asked.

Carmichael shrugged his shoulders. "She's one of the victims in all this," he replied forthrightly. "She may well have been a willing lover back then, and she was clearly happy to take Ron Mason's money to stay silent once she got pregnant, but at the time she was a child. It's as simple and clear cut as that."

"And what about the boyfriend, Ellis?" Penny then asked. "Is he just going to be released without charge?"

Carmichael smiled. "We could charge him with wasting police time," he replied, "but unless the CPS insist that we charge him, which I'm certain they won't, then we'll release him in the morning."

"Which just leaves poor Verity," remarked Penny with a sorrowful sigh.

"Two cold blooded murders and an attempted murder will see her behind bars for decades," announced Carmichael.

Draining the last dregs of Pinotage from his glass, Carmichael rose to his feet. "And as I've an appointment to interview Ms Brook-Smith in the morning, I guess I should try and get some shut eye,"

Penny didn't make any attempt to join him, remaining put on the sofa. "How did you work out it was Verity?"

she enquired. "This morning you didn't even hint that it was her."

Carmichael turned back to face his wife.

"We'd always kept an open mind on whether there were one or two people involved in Doug Pritchard's murder," he replied. "When Stock suggested that one of them was probably over six foot tall then she didn't figure in our thinking at all. Even though she was in the pub, heard them arguing close-up and, we knew, drove off from the pub soon after Pritchard left, the idea that Verity, who is a tiny young woman, and pregnant too, could have singlehandedly overpowered him down that badly lit lane didn't seem likely. And there was no obvious motive either, as far as we could see. Verity didn't know Pritchard and until very recently, we didn't think she knew Mason either. So why would she want to kill them?"

"So, what made you change your mind?" Penny enquired.

Carmichael smiled. "A few things," he replied. "I went back over the statements of the people we'd interviewed, and I found two things that struck me as potentially important. Firstly, Miles Goodwyn, the young man who found the body, had mentioned seeing a taillight far down Jay Bank Lane. Being a solitary light, I thought that was a motorbike, but when I saw The Muffin Maid van braking at a junction earlier today, I realised that what he saw was Verity's van, as only one of its brake lights is working."

Penny nodded. "I see," she remarked. "And the other thing you found from the statements. What was that?"

Carmichael pulled out the copy of Verity's statement he'd taken earlier in the day and passed it over to Penny.

"Ron said she's dead you pillock," Penny said, reading aloud what was written on the paper in her hands. "She died in that bloody accident years ago".

With a perplexed look on her face, Penny shrugged her shoulders. "What's so telling about that?" she enquired.

Carmichael smiled. "Of all the people we interviewed who were at the pub on Wednesday evening, Verity was the only one who said she heard the two men talking about Chrissy Cream." announced Carmichael. "Nobody else mentioned hearing her name. And when I spoke with Mrs Wright, at the hospice, she told me that she'd overheard Leah tell Mason that she hadn't mentioned anything about Chrissy's death to Pritchard. Why would she, given she was so directly involved. So, whatever they argued about wasn't to do with Chrissy Cream's death."

"So, you knew Verity was lying" said Penny, impressed at her husband's powers of deduction.

Carmichael smiled and nodded. "Any more questions before I go to bed?" he enquired.

Penny laughed. "Just one," she responded. "How did Verity, if she's as small as you say, manage to make Stock think she was taller?"

Carmichael smiled again. "I have to thank Sergeant Hunt for helping me with that," he replied. "And, of course, his clapped-out car. And, in fairness to Stock, he only said that the probable first blow to Pritchard was horizontal and on the back of his head. It was our assumption that the person who inflicted it was either standing on something to raise them up or they were over six foot tall."

"So, was Verity standing on something?" Penny enquired.

Carmichael shook his head. "It's something I'll be asking her in the morning," he replied, "but I think he was bending over when that first blow was struck. I think she most likely got him to look at her engine. Then hit him when he was leaning over."

"Killed while aiding a damsel in distress," remarked Penny.

Carmichael nodded. "That's my assumption and there was a bruise on his forehead, too, which could well have been caused by his head being pushed down forcefully onto the engine when he was struck."

"This Verity sounds like quite a violent young lady," Penny added.

Carmichael nodded. "She certainly is," he replied, before turning away, and heading off to his bed.

Chapter 86

Monday 25th March

It was ten o'clock exactly when Carmichael commenced his interview with Verity Brook-Smith. He'd decided to just bring DS Dalton into the interview room with him, leaving DS Watson, DC Twamley and Chief Inspector Hewitt watching and listening to proceedings from behind the two-way mirror.
Verity, pale faced and still clad in an all-in-one white custody outfit, sat opposite Carmichael with her legal counsel, a serious looking Mr Fairfax, to her right. Although, from the look of her, Carmichael doubted that Verity had slept very much, she was surprisingly relaxed, almost as if she'd resigned herself to what lay in front of her in the hours, days, months, and years ahead.
"Verity, for the purpose of the recording we'd like to confirm that you have been charged with the murder of Doug Pritchard on Wednesday the twentieth of March, the murder of Ron Mason on Thursday the twenty-first of March and the attempted murder of Tom Ashcroft on Friday the twenty-second of March," Carmichael said. "Would you like to make any comment about those charges?"
Verity shook her head.
Carmichael took a deep breath before continuing.

"Do you admit that it was you who killed Doug Pritchard and Ron Mason?" he asked.

Without any hesitation Verity nodded. "Yes, it was me," she replied, but made no attempt to elaborate any further.

Carmichael looked briefly over at DS Dalton, who remained silent, her eyes focused on Verity.

"Let's talk about Doug Pritchard first," Carmichael continued. "Why did you murder him?"

With a bemused expression on her face, Verity looked astonished as if the question was the most ridiculous thing she'd ever heard. "Because he was basically going to tell everyone that I was having my brother's baby," she responded.

Carmichael nodded. "So, for clarity, am I correct that you didn't hear Doug Pritchard talking about Chrissy Cream's death, as you previously told DS Dalton, but that he was talking about Ron being the father of Ellis and Tom?"

"Correct," replied Verity, with a disdainful grin. "It's clear how you came to be an Inspector."

"And how exactly did you manage to kill Doug Pritchard?" Carmichael continued, ignoring Verity's mocking tone.

Verity sat back and folded her arms across her chest. "I passed by him down the lane and pulled over just around the corner in one of the passing places," she said, her voice steady and assured. "I lifted the bonnet and when he arrived, asked him if he could help me. He said he wasn't an expert on cars, but he still walked over and leant over the bonnet to take a look."

"And what did you do then?" Carmichael asked.

"I hit him as hard as I could with one of Mum's rolling pins," replied Verity, who seemed to be enjoying

recounting her actions. "She keeps a few in the van, for when she's doing demonstrations,"
"And did you hit him just once?" Carmichael enquired.
"Twice," replied Verity. "Once when he was bending over, then again on his forehead when he staggered back. The second one knocked him backwards into the ditch. I knew he was dead. I then simply climbed back into the van and headed off."
"And did anyone see you?" Carmichael asked.
Verity shook her head. "No," she replied, "it was over in about two minutes, and nobody drove past us."
"What about Ron Mason?" Carmichael asked. "Why did you kill him?"
Verity took a deep breath, leaned back in her chair and gazed up at the ceiling.
"I hadn't planned on hurting him," she stated. "I just went round to his house to find out whether he was going to say anything about Tom and Ellis being his sons. I'd hoped he wasn't and that the secret could stay hidden from everyone."
"And what did he say?" Carmichael asked.
"It was a massive mistake," Verity announced. "As soon as I started talking to him it dawned on me that he didn't even know who I was. I'd lived locally all my life. I'd served him in the pub the evening before and he only twigged I was the child he'd created with Mum when I started talking to him. He said that he was just about to go over and talk with Pam and Suzi and tell them that their adopted boys were his. He said he didn't want to, but after the argument he'd had with Pritchard the night before, he had no choice. He said it was better they heard from him rather than from a random stranger who may have heard Pritchard spouting his mouth off in The Three Bells."

"And when did he realise that he was your father, too?" DS Dalton asked.

"He asked why I was so interested," replied Verity. "Then he saw my bump and it was almost as if it came to him all at once."

Carmichael and DS Dalton remained silent waiting for Verity to continue.

"He suddenly said ...you're Lydia's daughter, aren't you?" continued Verity. "And I take it that's either Tom or Ellis's child you're carrying?"

"And what did you say?" DS Dalton asked.

Verity thought for a few seconds before responding. "I implored him not to tell Suzi and Pam that he was the father of the boys," she said. "But he refused. He said it didn't matter, as other than him, my mum and I, nobody knew I was his daughter and that he wasn't about to tell anyone."

"So, why did you kill him?" Carmichael asked.

Verity fixed her stare on her interrogator. "I couldn't risk it," she replied emotionlessly. "If Suzi and Pam knew then Tom and Ellis would know. Then my mum would know, and I was worried at how all that would play out. I guess I must have panicked. I remember picking up one of his golf clubs from a bag that was next to us, by his car. Then the next thing I recall was him on the floor blood pouring from his head. I wiped the grip of the golf club on my dress, dropped it and ran."

"And did anyone see you?" Carmichael asked.

"I didn't think so," replied Verity, "but I saw Tom coming from Ron Mason's house just as I arrived and parked. I didn't think he saw me at the time, but he must have spotted the car as he accused Ellis of being there and being involved in Ron's death, the next day."

Carmichael nodded. "He recognised Ellis's car and naturally assumed it was him," he remarked. "Which begs the question why were you in Ellis's car?"

Verity smiled. "Mum had taken the van and Ellis said I could borrow his car."

"Ellis knew you were going to talk with Ron?" Carmichael asked.

Verity shook her head. "No. I told him I'd left my purse at The Three Bells and needed to get it. He semi-offered to drive me, but I told him he could stay in and continue his game of Street Fighter, which I knew he'd prefer to do."

"I see," Carmichael remarked, "but what about the altercation Ellis had with Tom? Surely Ellis must have figured out that it was you outside Ron Mason's when Tom started accusing him?"

Verity smiled. "Ellis trusts me," she replied. "So, when I told him I'd just parked up near Ron's to make a call to my friend Becca, he believed me."

"And did you tell him anything else?" DS Dalton asked.

Verity shrugged her shoulders. "I may have told him that I saw Tom driving away looking very serious," she conceded, "just so he thought it was Tom who was involved rather than me. Ellis said I needed to tell you lot what I'd seen, but I said I didn't want to get involved and that there was enough bad feeling between Tom and Ellis already, what with ..."

"With you moving on from Tom to Ellis," interjected DS Dalton.

"That's right, Rachel," replied Verity, who shot an evil stare in DS Dalton's direction.

"So, you're saying that Ellis never suspected you of either of the murders," reiterated Carmichael out loud.

Verity again shook her head and put her hand on her tummy. "We're a team, and he loves me," she remarked. "Why would he?"

Carmichael took a few seconds to gather his thoughts before proceeding. "What about the hit and run," he stated. "Now surely Ellis must have realised that was you?"

For the first time Verity looked less comfortable, noticeably shuffling about in her chair. "We talked about that when we were up in the lakes," she replied. "I admitted that it was me, but I told Ellis it was a spur of the moment thing when I happened to see Tom running towards me."

"But that isn't true, is it, Verity?" Carmichael proposed, his voice raised slightly from where it was previously.

"Of course, it isn't," sniggered Verity. "I mean I knew he'd probably be there as he's predictable with his running. I did only intend to frighten him, but then something just flipped in my head, and I didn't swerve away as I'd planned."

"So, what was the motive for you wanting to frighten him?" DS Dalton asked. "That doesn't make much sense to me."

Verity shrugged her shoulders. "Does everything you do always have a reason behind it?" she responded contemptuously. "Actually, I bet it does."

DS Dalton remained relaxed and expressionless but said nothing.

"So, the gallant Ellis swallows your lies and even offers to say it was him that ran into Tom," proclaimed Carmichael. "He must really love you."

Verity smiled. "He certainly does," she replied. "And I love him, too."

Carmichael paused for a few moments, and even took a sip of water from the plastic cup in front of him.

"That, then, just begs one more question from me," he announced. "Why did you, last night, decide to end it all? If you'd got Ellis saying he was responsible for the hit and run, what made you send him, and your mother, text messages confessing to the murders and then attempt to end your life and that of your unborn child?"

Verity once more stared up at the ceiling.

"When we were driving back down to Lancashire yesterday, I'd already started to think that you may well find some evidence that may lead you to me," Verity responded. "But then I got a call from Coral."

"That was just before you went to the Delph Tea Gardens, I take it?" Carmichael asked.

Verity nodded. "On the call Coral said just before she died, Leah had mentioned to her that Mum had said who my father was and although Leah had not given Coral a name, Leah had told her it was someone close to home."

"But why would that make you decide to end it all?" DS Dalton enquired.

"Because Coral said she was only telling me as she'd decided it might have a bearing on the murders and was going to tell you."

"I see," Carmichael said. "And what did you say to her?"

"I told her that I knew who my father was and asked her to wait until I could get over and see her before telling you," replied Verity. "It's all I could think of at the time."

"And did she agree?" DS Dalton asked.

Verity nodded. "She did."

"I'm surprised you didn't think of killing her," Carmichael remarked.

Verity's expression remained totally placid.

"I did, as a matter of fact," she replied, "but I like Coral, I couldn't bring myself to do that to her. So, I decided the only other alternative was to end my life."

Carmichael looked over at DS Dalton before returning his attention to Verity. "I pity you, Verity," he remarked, "and I feel for you being in the position you found yourself. But surely, now, you must realise that what you did to Doug Pritchard, Ron Mason and Tom was totally inexcusable?"

Verity shrugged her shoulders and fixed her gaze directly on Carmichael.

"Blood matters, Inspector," she replied. "I've known that all my life, as until recently I only had one living person who I knew had the same blood as me, my mum. You may not realise what that's like, but it's a very lonely place to be at times. Then, suddenly, I find out who my father is and then who my brothers are. Finding all that out should be joyous, shouldn't it? But not for me, as my dad was an unpleasant human being who didn't want to know me and who thought it was ok to sleep with a child. To cap it all off, I find my two half-brothers are also my only lovers. And worse still, my unborn child's father and the man I love more than anything in the world, has the same blood as me flowing through his veins. So, tell me again, why what I did was so wrong."

Carmichael paused for a few seconds before answering. "I have to inform you, Verity, that as part of our investigations we've taken DNA samples from Ron Mason, from Tom and from Ellis," he said, choosing his words as carefully as he could. "The tests we've carried out are very accurate and they confirm that Tom is Ron Mason's son. So, if as you believe, Ron was also your father, then yes, Tom is your half-brother. However, the tests we did using Ellis's DNA show clearly that he is related to Tom, but they are not brothers. We don't know who Ellis's father is, but we are one hundred percent sure it's not Ron Mason."

Verity's eyes opened wide and started to fill with watery tears.

"I'm certain that Ron and Leah believed Ellis was Ron's son, and so did Doug Pritchard when Leah told him," continued Carmichael, "but the truth is that Ellis isn't related to Ron and as a result, isn't a blood relation to you."

For the next thirty seconds all that could be heard in the room was Verity sobbing deeply, her head in her hands.

"Rachel, I suggest you stay with Verity and her solicitor for the time being," Carmichael remarked. "But as far as I'm concerned this interview is now over."

Carmichael stood up, and without looking back made his exit from interview room 1.

Printed in Great Britain
by Amazon